D.A. DIARY

ROBB PETERS

authorHOUSE®

AuthorHouse™ UK Ltd.
1663 Liberty Drive
Bloomington, IN 47403 USA
www.authorhouse.co.uk
Phone: 0800.197.4150

Published by AuthorHouse 02/06/2014

ISBN: 978-1-4918-9389-0 (sc)
ISBN: 978-1-4918-9388-3 (e)

Dedicated to everyone from
Hanwell, Ealing W7
Langley, Slough SL3

Repercussions

Mum If you publish this book it will have repercussions?

Peters Everything we do in life has repercussions.
Sometimes you've just got to take that risk.

Mum But why publish this book?, why not any of the
Other books you've written through the years?

Peters Because this is the beginning!!!!

Introduction

At the stroke of midnight on 1st November 2008 it happened. The date was now the 2nd November which meant I had achieved 10 years of recording a diary of my life. Almost every day since the 2nd November 1998 I had recorded details of my life. I felt a sense of achievement.

But at the DIARY PARTY, there were people who still didn't understand the reason why I had thrown a party, nor understand what the countdown was for. But I felt a sense of achievement. I knew what I had achieved. It wasn't the sense of achievement I've felt before, this was a lot different. When I came home and looked at my life recorded in 10 books, the first word that came to my head was 'wow'. I was asking myself 'did I really write these entire Diaries'?

My next mission was to now get D.A DIARY out there. My original Diary needed to be published and made into a book for all to read. But this book is not like other books. In my experience, diaries were normally written by girls but this is different. It's the diary of a 15 year old teenage boy with all the antics I was getting up to at that age. This book is very unique and rare. I can promise you that you've not read anything like this. I also want this book to be used as a guide book for people. Mostly for young people but I think older people too can benefit from it.

If D.A DIARY offends you in any way please stop reading it and I really do apologise for those I have annoyed in the past. Please remember I was 15.

D.A DIARY'S like marmite, you'll either love it or hate it.

An Autobiography, are you crazy?!!!

This book is not an autobiography. I think it would be crazy for me (currently at 25) to be writing a story of my life. I may do that one day when I'm 77 (that's the life expectancy for men in the UK) but for now just D.A DIARY. I can wait till age 77 because I know I'll be getting in every single detail.

But this book is only part of my life, a year in fact, from 2nd November 1998 to 2nd November 1999. My life at 15 years of age.

Before publishing the book I have had people telling me if they were to write a book it would be more interesting because their life was sad. Well I thought I'm happy my life wasn't sad and I'd rather release a book that will make people happy and put a smile on people's faces. I don't like sad stories; I want mine to be funny.

I've been criticised by many people about releasing this book. People have told me it's wrong to release such a book with so much information about people. But I did ask everyone's permission beforehand and they all saw the good side of it. Also I had to remind people that it's things we did when we were kids, it doesn't actually reflect on us now.

Even my own mother criticised me about my life when I was 15. She said "why don't you publish the Diaries of when you were an adult when you went travelling and became a teacher?". She probably thought that I'd be embarrassed about people finding out about things I did in the past. But I thought, you have nothing to be worried about me telling people about things I did when I was 15. I was just a dirty bastard.

Maybe the other editions of D.A DIARY may come out in the future. But as for now it has to be the book from when I was 15 because people can hopefully forgive me for things I did then, 18 onwards I've got no excuse.

D.A DIARY is everything. It's funny, entertaining, will inspire you and it's boring. Yes I did say boring. The reason it's boring is because I have typed out my entire original diary. So at times it will just talk about me travelling somewhere and will have every single detail. It'll make you think, "did this guy really have to write all this irrelevant and irreverent information?" Some of the stuff I wrote in D.A Diary is quite embarrassing. It makes me cringe. At times I think, "did I really write this?" I'm a much changed person from D.A DIARY. Reading it back I can agree with some aspects of my personality that are still the same.

But ten years on you wouldn't think this is the same person that wrote D.A DIARY. I am arrogant (don't like this word)..... confident enough to believe that everyone will enjoy and laugh at some parts of this book. When you read it you will think to yourself, how the hell did this guy turn out to be a teacher?

Youngsters need guidance

How do we learn things by not having anyone to guide us? Well we do, but sometimes by trial and error. But sometimes the error could leave us in all sorts of trouble. So all young people need someone to guide them and give them advice (teach them right from wrong).

Like all 15 year olds I thought I knew it all. Everything the world had to offer. I had and everything there was to do I had done. But I was so wrong.

I grew up as an only child just me and my mother. Yes I did play by myself (talking about toys). I think for a single parent my mum brought me up well and I always had high respect for her, which all youngsters should have for their parents. Respect was just something my mother taught me to have; not just for her but for everyone. I remember having a friend that used to be so rude to his mother. He would tell her to f**K off and he was allowed to do what he wanted at any time. I used to think if I acted like that I'd be in the hospital the next day.

But I wasn't an angel. At times I would steal, vandalise places and all types of things. But that was my own fault, which was me, showing weakness to the people in this world; the people that try to lead you off the straight path. I call them the snakes in the grass.

But parents aren't always to blame for youngster going astray. Parents tell you what is right but then you have to be careful of the bad influences in life.

It's like we're blind people and if you haven't got the right people to show you the way. You will most likely fall in a hole.

Spelling and Grammar

At 15 my spelling and grammar was terrible. But I never admitted that. As you get older you feel more embarrassed that you can't spell. In D.A DIARY my spelling and grammar was very bad but luckily for you (the reader), the spellings have all been corrected but the grammar has been left in the book. So readers can get a sense of the way I spoke when I was 15. Some.

In general a lot of people from the areas I grew up couldn't speak properly. For example, any word with TH like thought we would pronounce as fort and thirty three would be firty free. If you have a problem pronouncing your Th words best thing to do is say the, then the next part of the word after the TH. For example thought would be

The-ought.

But say it fast!

There are also moments in D.A DIARY where the grammar will not make any sense to some people. So if you're unsure just ask someone who may speak like a 15 year old me.

Some of the words/grammar that has not been changed are words like:-

Cos - which obviously means because, it was quicker to say.

Wanna - which is an alternative to saying want to

Gonna - which I still use today because I feel too posh saying going to.

Gotta - I have to.

Writ – My past tense for when you wrote something

Rid – My past tense for when I rode my bike

I have kept in all these words we used at the time. Without some words the book wouldn't be D.A DIARY.

Stealing and Shoplifting

Stealing and Shoplifting are wrong, wrong and wrong.

You will read in this book about times in school when I would steal from other people. It wasn't publicly robbing people (we called that getting jacked); it was stealing out of bags and coats. We would do this thing we called BARE RAZE. This meant stealing lots of things. I did it in school all the time and thought it was funny.

But there was a day when I stole someone's Walkman and after when I saw how sad that person was, it made me feel regretful for stealing that person's personal belongings.

I was also slightly involved in shoplifting. Before D.A DIARY I was arrested twice for shoplifting. But I never learnt my lesson because in this book you will find times when I'm still stealing small things from shops. I used that as my excuse for thinking it was ok; that it was only small things. But small things lead to big things. Before D.A DIARY I would go out with a friend and we'd both have back packs and try and see who could get the biggest thing. And sometimes it would just be something stupid like garden tools or other things we didn't need.

There is another incident in D.A DIARY where I was on my school work experience in HMV. And the amount of stuff I stole was unbelievable. And doing things like this is really stupid because in any situation where someone puts trust in you to do a job and then you steal, that shows you can't be trusted; it really shows that you're not a nice person.

Also I remember (at HMV) they said to me I can have 20% discount on any item I want to buy but I remember thinking "forget that I want 100% discount."

Now robbery was something I could never do. I had friends that would get on the train and try to find a group of teenagers they could rob. We would call this jacking people and if it happened to you. You would have been jacked.

There are a few incidents in D.A DIARY when people did try to jack us. The way people would do it was by firstly approaching you like a friend then they would try and get you to give them £1, but after they would use all types of intimidation to get things from you. But I was lucky enough to not have anything taken from me.

The main message is nobody ever likes getting things stolen off them so don't do it to others. Get a job and earn money to pay for things yourself, you'll feel a lot better.

Sex and Relationships

As a teenager, things like girls and sex were normally on my mind 24/7. But if you would have said relationships to me, I probably would have asked "what's that?" even though in DA DIARY you will read about my girlfriend I was with for just over 6 months. But I wasn't very good at the whole relationship thing. Actually I didn't care for her feelings and just did what I pleased without consulting her. I was not a good boyfriend at 15.

I had my first sexual experiences at an early age. At 12 I remember sucking a girl's tits in a graveyard. A week before DA DIARY I lost my virginity, well at least I think I did. I was at Paul Simmons' party with a girl from Reading (who I only met the day before) and I was so drunk I tried to put it in but it was soft and I think I did something. But being honest that didn't count. So being truthful to everyone I lost my virginity to Rachel Levi, who you will read about in this book.

My first relationship is written about in this book and like I've mentioned, I was not a good boyfriend. But relationships are things I always advise people of 15 not to get involved in.

Relationships can be a big distraction. So if you're too young don't get involved in a relationship. Please just enjoy your life. There was a newspaper article saying that people do not have proper relationships until they're 17. This, even for me, is young. But I remember being under 17 years old and relationships meant nothing. I had no feelings for the person; I could be going out with a girl one minute then be with her friend the next day.

If you've got a boyfriend or girlfriend when you're a kid it's no stress whatsoever, it's easy going. I wish sometimes relationships were as easy going when you become older.

In 2006 I fell into depression for the first time in my life and that was because of incidents in a relationship. This messed up my head for a long time and it changed me a lot.

Sometimes you need to establish with someone if you want just sex or a relationship. Because a lot of the time as young people we just want to have fun with nothing serious (no strings attached). So my advice to people (if you're going to have sex with someone) let that person know what you want first. And if it is just sex let them know. If it's only a fling and you're both happy with that, that's what it is. But for guys that's easier said than done.

Good

Relationship

Trust

And

Understanding

The topic of sex and relationships is a very strange topic to discuss with young people. Some youngsters are very open with their parents about these things, others are not. I think my mum always knew I was sexually active but we hardly spoke about things like that. However, Mum was always open, honest and approachable. But I do remember my mother giving me a talk about condoms.

But condoms were things I hated. I grow up with the myth that condoms take away all the feeling and sex isn't as good with them. But guys, those bad boys will save your life. 'SERIOUSLY'!!!

As a teenager I would try hard not to use a condom. I would make excuses to not use them, even saying I'm allergic to rubber. But as I said before, they'll save your life. But luckily I never caught any STI's (sexually transmitted infections) or get anyone pregnant. People at school said I would be one of the first people to have a kid. And luckily I still have no kids, thank God. If I did have, it would have been hard to do all the things I've done in life. Which brings me to another debate, WHAT IS A GOOD AGE TO HAVE KIDS? Well, I've had this discussion with so many people. And some people want kids as soon as they leave school, some say 18, 25 or over 30. I always think its better to have kids in your 30's because your 20's are for having fun. I know a lot of my friends disagree because they say, have your kids young then you're still young while they're growing up and thereafter you have more time to yourself when you're older. People also tell me, that if you have children older you won't be as fit as you used to be and won't be able to play with your children much which is crazy because 40 years old is not exactly ancient? But there's no right or wrong answer to the having kids question. The only right answer is making sure you're stable. And that you can provide a happy life and environment for your child. Because you're bringing a life into the world, which is a job you have all your life.

I think it's a good thing for teenage boys to practice putting condoms on because that was one of my problems. I'd be rushing trying to get the thing on before I go soft, I'd put the condom out of use. But young people, you do need to practice your putting on a condom skill or you'll face the same problems as I did - even if you need to have a posh wank. This is when you masturbate with a condom on. But this can still cause problems if you don't hold the tip to make sure there's no air inside. I put one on and had a PW (posh wank) but I never pinched the top and when I was ejaculating it felt like my helmet (the top of your penis) was going to explode. Not a nice experience.

Bullying

I was never much of a bully when I was younger. I say "never much of" because I think everybody in their life has contributed to some sort of bullying at some stage in their life. This can also be things like just laughing at the expense of someone being insulted. From teaching, my view of bullying is anytime you are making a person feel uncomfortable.

In D.A DIARY the only person I could say I bullied was my friend JD. Yes he was my friend but because I thought I knew more things than him I would constantly be making fun of him. So, I'm sorry JD. Are we cool?

In and out of school I saw a lot of bullying going on. I was the type of person no one bullied but I still didn't think I was one of the tough ones at school.

But being the person I was. I could have stuck up for the little people instead of watching these things go on. If you do have the power to be a voice, please be a voice instead of letting these things go on. Letting bullying go on when you have the power to maybe stop the bully means you are also a bully.

In school, I was never really bullied. I'm still not sure why because I was a pussy. But I did kickboxing so I think people just assumed I was a dangerous dude. I did have people trying to fight me and test me in my first few school years. But young boys do this to see where you stand in the pecking order of tough people. But I was so placid I would laugh it off. I would say to some people if they wanted to fight me they could come down to my boxing gym and we could have an organised fight where, after we're friends. Because that's a problem with people in England; they hold on to things and drag other people into feuds. But even though I do kickboxing I still believe fighting is wrong. So I do contradict myself in this area. Like the old saying said it takes a bigger man to walk away.

With fighting and feuds there are always Don Kings, the Promoter people. These are the people that don't actually fight themselves just stir up a fight. These are the people that are always telling others to hit another person. How about next time saying to them how about someone hit you then see how you like it. Because it's all good watching someone take a punch but receiving one, is a different story.

Since working in a School and throughout life I've seen all types of bullying. And all types of people being bullied or bullying people. The worst cases are there are people who are really not strong enough; people who become really cracked by being bullied in school. Every so often you read a paper and someone has committed suicide from being bullied at school. This makes me angry and upset. Some children do not realise how cruel they can be.

If I was to say a positive thing that bullying has done for people, is that it makes some people stronger. You could be a person that been through a period of being bullied then after you come out a lot stronger (emotionally stronger). But that can have a negative effect, where I've seen children who have been bullied now found someone who they think they can take advantage of and became a bully themselves. If you've been bullied, you know how it feels so you shouldn't be cruel and do it to others if in the past you were in their shoes.

And their shoes are painful!

People will normally push the limits with a person because they think they are stronger then that person (either physically or mentally). That's not always the case; sometimes people just want a reaction from you. Bullies know what buttons to push, what can trigger any sort of emotion from you? When I first started teaching (2005) I had a class where the students would do things just to make me shout. Once I got more experienced with teaching I learnt different ways of handling things.

You don't always need to shout to be heard!

I learnt a lot of things from a lady called Janine. We both started teaching at the school the same time. I was working at the school two years before

I started teaching, but I worked in an office (counselling kids) which was a lot different from being in the classroom.

Janine told me the students knew I was a nice person and they would try to take advantage of that. So Janine taught me how to be strict with the kids. She told me with teaching you need a balance. If you're a teacher you have to be in control. And students should know not to push limits. But you still need respect from children.

The main thing with bullying is that in life, you need to make sure people aren't walking all over you. But this does not necessarily need to be violence. We just all need to know when we are taking advantage of a person because we think they're weaker than us. Some people often mistake niceness with weakness. So it seems in life we can't always be too nice to people. We need a balance. But please do not mistake the not being nice balance for something that hurts people. It just means you have the right to say no if people are putting you under pressure.

Intelligence and ignorance

With young people in England, they make fun of people that are clever. But being confronted about not knowing something they feel embarrassed. In school it was not nice to be put in what was known as the dumb classes. These were the classes where there were people who couldn't do their 5 times table and couldn't "read to save their lives". Poor guys; hard to live up or down to such a label.

At school I was put in most of the low ability classes and I wasn't happy about it. This was due not to my lack of knowledge but, I feel, my bad spelling skills. However, my reading was way above average. I always felt I had some sort of knowledge.

One of my teachers once said that you learn something new every day. So in D.A DIARY after every day I would write a fact. These were called DID U KNOWS.

To be honest some of the DID U KNOW facts might not be completely accurate. But I decided not to change any information. There's one DID

U KNOW about a black Beethoven. I know that's going to P a few people off.

Being ignorant only occurs a few times with me in D.A DIARY. There are occasions when I'm insulting people from Northern England or if they live in the countryside. But I never remember there being any seriousness in saying it. It was just young people stupid jokes.

Some of the words I have used in D.A DIARY make me sound very unintelligent. Words like "half caste" for example, which I know people still use today to describe a person of mixed race. But I would never use that word today. I think mixed race sounds a lot nicer. Half caste sounds like you're half of something and half of the other. Even though my mum is black and my father is white I've always referred to myself as black. People have said to me that if I say that, I'm forgetting the white side. But for me that's not the case because I'm happy I have mixed origins(I think it's a beautiful thing). The reason I refer myself as a black person is that fact that people will not look at me and say I'm a white person. In the 1940's I wouldn't have been able to say to Hitler don't kill me because my dad's white. He'd just see another Black person.

But I think it's good for everyone to know their background. A lot of people are very ignorant and do not look at history to see where their families actually originated from. A thing to remember - The United Kingdom is an Island nobody was just grown here. We all came from somewhere else.

My next topic brings me to stereotypes; the belief that because you look a certain way or are from a certain place you that should behave in a certain way. For example I have a friend that is half Native American but this person knows nothing about Native Americans or their culture. Also they've never been to the USA. So my belief is-Culture is just whatever you grow up around.

Example if you're a white man who grew up in Jamaica. You will be acting like a Jamaican. Not trying to be black

In May 2003 I started working in a School in Slough as a Youth Project Worker. This was a big change in my life because I was only 19 and working in a school forced me to grow up and be responsible quick. I used to work in an office and opposite the office was a classroom called the EAL room. This was a class for people who had English as a second language. I was amazed by the places some of these kids had come from; places like Africa, Asia and Eastern Europe. I made good friends with the EAL teacher (Sam).I first got talking to Sam because I had borrowed a book from his room called World Encyclopaedia (a book about every country in the world) , I was reading about my Mum's country, Saint Vincent and the Grenadines. I was speaking to him about Saint Vincent and the Grenadines and I was surprised he knew about it and he was one of the only white English people I knew (at the time) that had been there. Through life I was used to people thinking Saint Vincent and the Grenadines was in Jamaica and not realising it's actually a separate country in the Caribbean. He also fascinated me because he had travelled to almost every country in the world. Sam not only gave me a drive to travel but a passion to read. I would spend my lunch times at work just reading the encyclopaedia because I was fascinated in learning new things.

But a lot of the things I was reading at the time were children's books, just because of the pictures. People like me will understand; I get bored quickly. If a book's not gripping me, my mind wanders. That's why I decided to make this book colourful. That's the way I learn and how I teach.

In about 2 years of working at the school, I felt I had l had learnt so much, not only through reading but through the whole experience. When I was 21 I felt more intelligent than people that were 41. I loved having intelligent debates with people. But I was sounding more intelligent than people that were 41 and had 20 years on me. I'm thinking they should have more knowledge than me.

I am also learning that some people are so stubborn once they reach a certain age. There's a saying "you can't teach an old dog new tricks". This is not true. We can all learn new things at any age. Just have to be patient and willing to learn.

Lots of people like living in a box and not thinking about there's more to life. When you don't question things you will stay without questions.

Something to do

Like I always say, "young people are bored and need something to do". I used to have friends that would just go around smashing up the phone box. I would think why are you doing that? It is winter and I'm going to be cold. Another time I remember going to use a phone box and someone had put dog's poo all over the mouth piece. You just think to yourself "what is wrong with these people?" There's never an excuse for doing things like that. But young people are a lot of the time bored. But every generation of kids seem to get more then the last. A lot of kids these days are ungrateful for all the things they get. I think nowadays there's too much choice.

When I was younger I would love going out. I was playing out from young age because our estate was safe. But I especially liked going to new places where I could see new things and meet new people. The excitement when you're young and you go to your friends' area and playing out; places like Copley Close.

I did a lot of clubs and things while I was young. My mum used to get me involved in all types of clubs. In Langley we had Horsemoor green youth club. But when I was 14 I stopped going because I started getting changing and getting interested in other things. Girls.

Me at 14/15 (School year 10)

D.A DIARY starts 6 days before my 15th birthday. Back then I was a Drifter, which is like a Nerd and a popular person. Most people knew me (I was known) but I could hang around with the Nerds. But I never got into any fights or had any major problems with anyone. People knew I did kickboxing so they just presumed I was a tough guy.

In school I could be friends with anyone; the geeks and the popular people. But I never really enjoyed hanging around with the so called popular people because they just annoyed me and usually they were bullies. I didn't want to be with the in crowd. I was happy being the out crowd. But I like people knowing who I was. So I suppose I didn't want to be a complete outcast.

A lot of boys in my school were interested in cars and bikes. I never got in to those things. I didn't care about what bike I rode to school. At one point I was riding an old granny bike; sorry I do not know the correct term for an old granny bike. I've just typed *old granny bike* into Google and it's just showed me the bike I rode to school. Mine looked a lot worse. Even today with my cars, I'm not fussed on the make as long as it gets me from one place to another. If you ask me about my car I would tell you its silver and it works.

But I was really interested in girls. I do look back sometimes and think that's the only reason some people were my friend. They'd only hang out with me because I knew a lot of girls. I first got a reputation of being a ladies' man when I was in year 9. I went on a date with a Langley Grammar 6th form girl. Everyone thought she was the fittest girl in Langley Grammar and all my friends were jealous.

I wasn't afraid to chat up girls. I remember I would go up to large group of girls and try to chat up all up them while my friends would stand there watching. Even today I see a few of my friends using my old techniques.

Besides girls I was into my kickboxing (as already mentioned) and I was a storyteller. People knew Robert Peters as the person who makes up stories. In school I would have groups of people surrounding me just listening to one of my stories. People told me my stories were like watching a movie. Because I would get so into explaining the story, I would be doing all the actions and the sound FX's. When I was younger I promised all my friends when I grow up I will publish one of my stories. I never realised it would be my own diary.

Life before D.A DIARY

So now I'm going to talk about my life before I was 14. Well I enjoyed playing with my He-men, THUNDERCATS, GHOSTBUSTERS, and NINJA TURTLE toys and on Super Mario on the NES (the consoles where you have to blow inside the games to get them to work). Ok being serious now.

I was born in Hammersmith Hospital on the 7th November at the start of the 80's.I spent my early childhood in Hanwell, Ealing. My favourite memories of Hanwell are from the Bunny Park. It's an amazing place they've got monkeys. Unless they've got rid of the monkeys now. This information was correct at time of print.

Bunny park is my favourite place on earth. My joint 2^{nds} are Machu Picchu in Peru, India, Iceland and Thailand.

Growing up I never really knew my dad that much. He and my mum weren't together as I was growing up. And my mum disliked him. I remember him coming to our house when I was about 7 and I said mum there's a man at the door. And my mum replied that's your dad. I was like ok then. Sometimes people ask, didn't you miss not having your dad around? The answer's easy. No. If you haven't got a person there, it doesn't affect you. Growing up with just one parent doesn't mess up your life. I'm currently writing this book sitting enjoying 'Chaka Khan I FEEL FOR YOU' on a hot sunny beach in Asia. Life is what you make it. YOU can't always blame other people.

The schools I went to in Hanwel, Hobbayne Primary School and Drayton Manor High. Then in 1996 (a few years before D.A Diary started) I and my mother moved to Langley, Slough. Langley was a place where my mother had grown up and where we had lots of family. SO I see myself as a Hanwell/Langely person. Ealing and Slough are my home towns.

Ok yes that's really about it for life before D.A Diary. Only one more section to read then the moment you've been waiting for ....

Decoding D.A DIARY

Word's that not everybody may understand explained

BARE

Now, the word "bare" just means a lot. So for example there could be bare girls, bare boys, bare food etc. It's still used today and its one word that I always say. The word has Caribbean origins. It's funny because the word bare normally means naked. I remember the first time I went to the USA and I was at the mall with my cousin and I said 'wow there is bare girls here'. He got excited because he thought I meant naked girls.

SKEET /YATTS

In Slough in 1998 "skeet" was the main word for girls. This word you will hear a lot in D.A DIARY. I never heard this word until I came to Slough but we used it all the time.

Also people used to say Yatts or Yattys.

Brare

This is one of the strangest ways to describe a man. But that's the word we used. Possible origin for this is Brer Rabbit – meaning "brother" but hey, I was not that cultured.

FLEX/FLEXED

Now words like "flex" I feel embarrassed that I ever said. Flex means a few things for example to go somewhere you flex there. Or flex could be something you're doing. For example the man was doing something crazy was "this brare was on a crazy flex".

FUNNIEST THING ALL DAY

After writing every day I would try and remember the things that made me laugh throughout the day. This was known as funniest thing all day. In this book I wouldn't expect people to understand what some of them are about but I still wanted every part of the book included.

OTT

OTT just was short for On the Train. We used the trains quite a lot so we came up with shorter terms for things like TM means ticket man(we didn't like those guys that much).

WID

This meant to write in my diary. I'd write this because it was a lot shorter. So some days will say things like after "I just WIDed".

CHERPES

The word cherpes (pronounced chirps) is classic. It just basically means to chat up a girl/girls. So if you were talking to a girl and you were trying to make things happen you would be cherpsing.

I'm not sure on the correct spelling for this word so sorry if you do not understand.

BRASSED
Now in D.A DIARY this word meant to steal something. But it normally means when you haven't got any money. If I didn't have any money I would say I'm brass.

RAGS / RAGO
For this word I had to think about for a long time of words to explain the meaning. My conclusion is that it means – "DEFIANTLY"

DARK
This word has two meanings in D.A DIARY. I used it for when something was really good or for when someone did something bad that would be dark.

BOOM
How old skool is this word, but you've still got to love it. Boom just means when something is good. It also used for someone you think is really sexy. For example the girls from Vanilla are boom. Vanilla were some rubbish girl group that came out in 1998 they were terrible.

BO
Bo was used a long time before the programme Bo Selecta on Channel 4. It was the 1998 word that you would just shout out when you were in a club and a good song came on (for example).

HuHH
This word was just made up by my Hanwell boys. So it's unique to this book. It just means when something's not good. The spelling is big H small u and two capital H's. There's actually a shop in St Albans, Hertfordshire called HuHH. It's a hairdresser's. If you go there they can give you a HuHH (heads up hair home) haircut.

Press
This word just meant sex; to have sex with someone.

3

RN

RN is an abbreviation of Rhythm Nation. Which was an under 18's disco we went to all the time.

Jaze

Jaze means being alone. On your own = On your jaze.

OFFKEY

Offkey was normally said for when a girl was ugly or someone was doing something that was a bit weird - like farting in someone's face while they're asleep for example

TICK

Like the word "boom", this just means something is really good.

LIPS/ Lipsed

The word lips means to kiss someone. But a tongue kiss not just lips (even though it's called lips). Lipsed is the past tense.

Biff

A Biff was another word for an afro or big hair. But in Southend it meant a women's private part.

Cotched to cotch

Cotch means to relax. So for example you may be cotching reading this book.

Raze

This was the word we used if you were to steal something. A stolen item would be something you razed. Remember guys I don't agree with stealing so don't judge me for things I razed when I was 15. Also I couldn't even spell the word I've written "raised".

Batty

Batty just means your bum bum. There's a lot of talk in this book about girls battys.

Jokes
When something funny happened, we would say it was jokes.

Shiners
Shiners just meant oral sex, but only for a woman giving to a man.

Slosher
Slosher is a girl who is very easy to get it on with.

McyD's
Even McDonald's restaurant had its own slang name. Yes, McyD's simply means McDonalds.

Breeze
Instead of saying the boring word, go. We would say breeze.

Butterz
This is said when someone is ugly.

Buff
Buff again was another word that meant good. But in later years it became a word that girls would say for a guy they thought was attractive. So we stopped saying it.

Sick
Another word that means something is good. But in some areas it we say things like sick brare. This just means a guy was doing something crazy or said something sick.

MC
In D.A Diary (1998 -1999) UK garage was the music of the time. So there are a lot of areas where I'm talking about me getting on the mic and rapping (or MC-ing as it's known).

Shibbz
Shibbz a.k.a Shibby is my cat. People who know me well know I love my pussy.

Draw , zoot and spliff

These are all to do with drugs which are very naughty children, that's why I never used them.

Arms / arms house

Both words mean to fight.

Now I hope that's all the slang covered. The words I've missed are the hopefully obvious words.

Hope you enjoy D.A Diary.

The first 2 months didn't really take off with my writing. So if you get bored straight away skip through. I won't be offended.

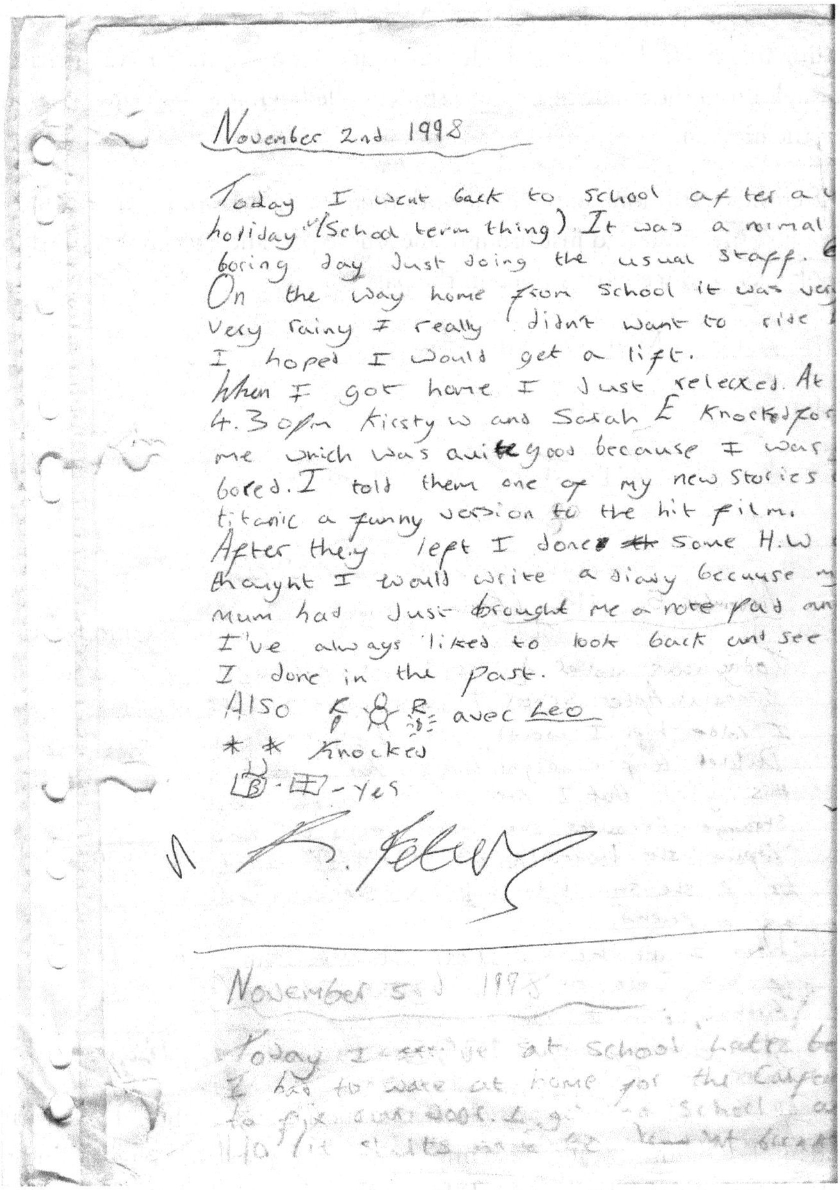

November 2nd 1998

Today I went back to school after a
holiday w/(School term thing) It was a normal
boring day Just doing the usual stuff.
On the way home from School it was very
very rainy I really didn't want to ride
I hoped I would get a lift.
When I got home I Just relaxed. At
4.30pm Kirsty W and Sarah E knocked for
me which was quite good because I was
bored. I told them one of my new stories
titanic a funny version to the hit film.
After they left I done some H.W
thought I would write a diary because my
mum had Just brought me a note pad an
I've always liked to look back and see
I done in the past.
Also avec Leo
** knocked
\- Yes

November 2nd 1998

Today I went back to school after a week's holiday (school term thing). It was a normal boring day just doing the usual stuff. On the way home from school it was very rainy, I really didn't want to ride home. I hoped I would get a lift.

When I got home I just relaxed. At 4.30pm, Kirsty Wood and Sarah Elliman knocked for me which was quite good because I was getting bored. I told them one of my new stories called 'Titanic' a Funny Version to the hit film.

After they left I done some homework then thought I would write a diary because my mum had just brought me a note pad and I've always liked to look back and see what I done in the past.

Also, Rang Fat Man avec Leo

Chris Harvey knocked

Found my birthday presents in the cupboard. Yes!

November 3rd 1998

Today I arrived at school late because I had to wait at home for the Carpenter to fix our door. I got to school at 11.10am (it started at 8.40am). At break time I rode home with JD and then I saw Nicholas and he came in for a while. Just doing what he usually does making me laugh.

At 6.30pm I went Kickboxing it was an alright lesson and I did quite well. I was preparing for my fight on 19th November a title fight.

There was a boom skeet at kickboxing she was about 19.

November 5th 1998 (Bonfire Night)

Today was another day at school nothing special. After school I was with Adam. I told him I would meet him at the Datchet Bonfire Night thingy. Then I saw this girl that I knew (Felicity). It was strange because she looked really tick, and before, she looked a bit HuHH. I asked her if she still liked me and she said "yeh as a friend."

When I got home I rang Katie to see if we were still meeting on Saturday (my birthday) then I rang Lauren to see if I was still meeting her as well. It's all good.

Later on Guv came round and we went to the Bonfire thing in Ryvers School. After the bonfire we went round Simmons and watched a film, Class Act.

On the way home we saw Chris and Nathan just chilling then went home.

November 7ᵗʰ 1998 (Birthday) 15

Today when I woke up I got a big Happy Birthday welcome from my Mum.

Went to meet Lauren and Fish but we arrived late and had missed her. The next plan was to meet all the Hanwell lot. I went with Fish, Simmons and Ben.

When we arrived at Ealing they all gave me a present - 2 Mugs, Titty Mug and Sex Position one. Kieron had got me an organiser (for skeet), and Jason got me a lighter with a finger saying F**k U on it.

We hung about at Ealing because at 4.00pm we were meeting Katie. We had some fireworks and we were lighting them in the park.

Around 4.00pm we waited but they didn't come. After that we saw a gang of boys. They came up to us and asked for our money. I didn't give them any money, but them lot did (£36) they nicked. I didn't know they had taken so much money until they told me. Leo told the Police and the Police questioned us.

We got back to my house and got pissed then went over to Upton Fireworks Display. I didn't really want to go there as it was my birthday, but nobody could be arsed to go to London OTT (on the train).

After the fair about 20 people came to my house because Nicholas told everyone I was having a party. All night I kept telling people to be quiet because my Mum was only upstairs.

1. Later on in the night I threw a few people out.

2. Leo was sick and beaten.

3. Liam put D's hand on Hayley's tit when they both were asleep.

November 8th 1998

Today I didn't play football because Ben didn't pick me up. (He thought I had a hangover.

I saw the film The Exorcist with my Mum and Guv. It wasn't as scary as I expected it to be. (Minor film) it was just creepy.

That's all I did today. Oh yeah I also went to the shop.

Wow

November 12th 1998

Today was a normal boring Thursday at school – Double Drama - double Tech and History.

After school I got home had a game of the Tekken 3 then went downstairs to watch TV (television). Today they had the MTV Music Awards which they have been going on for 4 days, and guess what, it was proper shit.

After MTV I chatted to my Mum about old times. (Bare memories). It was really funny some of the things I remembered.

P.S: Yesterday was Remembrance Day - show some respect you bitch.

Friday 13th November 1998

Today was Friday 13th but who gives a f**king shit, because nothing has ever happened to me anyway. School was shit. Everything was muffed up:-

1. We were supposed to learn about sex, but we had a stupid video on smoking.

2. My house was supposed to play Inter-house football but we only had three players.

3. It was gay altogether.

When I got home from school I went Kickboxing avec Terry Loveridge (Terry Beverage). Finished kickboxing early because we were going out.

When I got home I got ready to go out. When we arrived where we were going it was very dry (Pulse in Slough). There was hardly anyone there and the girls were HuHH. There was only about 4 boom girls. And the boomest girl had no batty.

We got the taxi home with Lindsey G to the train station then got a train to Langley then bopped home.

See, Friday 13th is not unlucky you stupid Dicks.

Saturday 14th November 1998
and
Sunday 15th November 1998

On Saturday me and Simmons looked for jobs. We got applications for Cookie Jar and JJB.

After Slough went home had dinner and got ready to go to a party in Colnbrook. This party was some girl from Langley Grammar who was 16, the bad thing at this party was her parents were there and they wouldn't let us in.

About 20 minutes later Simrit let me in through the window. The party was proper shit (basically the music). After there was a fight and this brare was pulling the other brares hair and screaming like a girl. It was a little bit funny.

On Sunday I woke up early for Kickboxing (8.00am). When I arrived at Sensei's house he was still in bed. At 9.45 we met everyone down the Gym. Then we left, we got to Hounslow about 10.30am.

I was supposed to fight for a title but I didn't. But what happened was, the person I was fighting for the title, I fought anyway. Kicked his Mother F**king Bitch Ass. So basically, in my view I am the Champion.

Singing Ooh Baby!

17ᵗʰ November 1998

School was not too bad today. We had those people; come in from err err, anyway who gives a f**k. This was a laugh and also because it took up 2 hours of shit lessons. (The discussion was on drugs).

After school I went to Slough and got my biff cut off. When I got home I got ready to go Kickboxing. I really didn't feel like going but Dave said the papers were coming in to take photos of the club. Obviously that was bullshit. It was probably just a scam to get people to come.

When I finished kickboxing I went over to Simmons house for a bit. I then went home and me and my Mum looked out for those shooting stars that were supposed to appear. But unfortunately we didn't see them.

Also when I got home my new phone arrived but it wasn't a Panasonic. I decided to keep it, it was also good because I got all the numbers in the phone which I needed - Aliza, Amanda and Helen.

Saturday 21ˢᵗ November 1998

Today I was supposed to meet Katie. I rang her in the morning and she said she had to go shopping with her mum. So I rang Lauren (well Michael did) and she was already out.

In the early evening Maurice came round he was going to the cinema with my Mum. At the time when Maurice was round I was with Michael which had been his birthday the day before and he had been grounded (what a f**king bitch). So we said we'll pretend it's your birthday today (we gave him, bare beats). I was also with Simmons and Beverage.

We all went into Slough and met Ben. We hung about in Slough for a bit. We lost Beverage and Simmons so we went Ben's house.

When we got back to my house I got ready for Rhythm Nation. We were meeting everyone at 6.30pm at Langley Station. Beverage and Fish were both not supposed to be with us because they both had to go home. We met Darren R and Sati at the Station.

When we got Ben, there was still a long Q. At RN I met Aliza and everyone wanted her. I can't believe it! They were shocked when I said I knew her.

I gave out a few cards in RN. I gave one to a fit skeet but her f**king nose was 10 x 10. Also gave one to Aliza and I slipped one in this girl's bag.

After RN there was a fight between a Bouncer and some Geezer. Michael was getting on our nerves because he couldn't find this girl that said she would meet him after.

When we got home on the train me and Nicholas kept running to each end of the train when it stopped and we almost got stuck because the train was very packed.

When I got home I just relaxed and watched Ben's film but it was boring and I switched it off for Con Air.

(Terry's sister picked him up)

- Stevie Girl 2
- Nicholas doing Usher dance at Train Station

Sunday 22nd November 1998

Today when I woke up I was very happy because nobody had stayed at my house and sometimes it gets on my nerves. I laid in bed relaxing watching the morning shows on BBC.

At 1.00pm I got ready to go to football. Ben picked me up at 1.30pm with his mad brothers. We played in Taplow against the best team in the League. They beat us 7-1.

When I got home my Mum told me that a girl called Charlotte rang. I thought to myself who the f**k is Charlotte? Was it that girl with the big f**k up nose, I thought. But my Mum said she'll be ringing back soon (but she never). Later on I got a call from Kirsty the girl I slipped my card into her bag (just talking shit). This proved to me that the cards were working.

Kirsty O'Connor 2.

Friday 27th November 1998

Today we had a day off school. Ben came round, he bunked school. At lunchtime we went down the shops and we met Terry.

Later on in the day, everyone was round my house and we were deciding where to go. I was Fuel or Pulse. I promised Adam I would go to Fuel so we went there and Terry and Ben went to Pulse. We went to Fuel with Nicholas and Simmons as well.

We got to Fuel 0we took one look at it and thought allow that. But because Adam kept saying we've come all this way might as well go in. So I took a look and it was so dry. There was hardly any one there and it was in a church.

We got really bored so we went in and only paid 25p.

On the decks were no MCs so we asked them if we could MC and they let us. As soon as the garage came on we started MCing and we smashed it (basically we rocked the party).

When it finished one of the Geezers took my number down and said we could MC there all the time.

Afterwards we met up with Guv and we went to the hotel for a raze. We stayed in the hotel for a bit. Adam was complaining so much about how he wanted to go home. We ran around the hotel brassed bare cookies and we brassed a cash box. We got about £14 each, Me, Simmons, Guv and Nicholas.

When we got in Adam was so amazed. He couldn't believe he got in at 3.45am (that's dark).

Bare Dollars.

28ᵗʰ November 1998

Today I was supposed to meet Vicky (the major fit one) but we got to Ealing too late because Adam's dad took long to pick him up.

Me and Simmons hung about in Ealing, but got bored so went back Slough. In Slough there was a fair in the High Street and lots of Christmas decorations;

When I got home I had dinner then me, Simmons, Nicholas, Hanghei and Clint Eastwood went to Rhythm Nation (RN). I really couldn't be bothered to go but went anyway.

When we got there, there was a massive rumble and I got in free. But guess f**king what? The man caught me and I had to pay. I met Jo there and she seemed happy to see me. And so was I (get my tings init). Kirsty O'Connor 2 was also there and her friend said she likes you. Then I saw this proper fit skeet and Hanghei said "she was at Pulse yesterday." So I said to her, "you were at Pulse yesterday weren't you?" "Yeah" she replied, "Are you from Slough? I asked. Then I said, "No I'm from George Green", the skeet replied. (Duh that the same thing).

"So would you like to dance" asked the One and Only

"Yes" said the skeet. They begin to grind hard.

"Can I have a kiss?" asked the One and Only.

"Yes" said the skeet.

"Slurp" both of them said (That's dark).

I was quite shocked because I thought she would blast me. When I was kissing her someone was punching my back. Afterwards I gave her one of my cards. (I hope she rings). I asked Kirsty's friend, who it was that kept punching me, and it was Kirsty.

After RN me, Nicholas and Simmons went on the train to Piccadilly Circus. When we got there we had to get past the machines. Simmons and Nicholas barged through them and I done a dark little slide under the barriers. We hung about in Trocadero and Leicester Square. At 1.00am it was getting boring, so we got a bus to Paddington. We jumped it, pushed the button on the other doors.

When we got to the station we found out there were no more trains until 6.45 am this morning and the time was 2.00am. We walked around for 30 mins then got on a wrong bus that took us into North London, and Nicholas wouldn't let us get off. Then I got off and I was on my jaze then I saw them and we walked to a hotel and stayed inside there for an hour and a half just relaxing and using the phone to phone bare people (it was free). The dumb security brare caught us on the phone and Nicholas told him we were in the hotel because we were the sons of an African Chief. It was jokes.

We got chucked out then we walked around Paddington trying to find another hotel to chill in. At 3.40 am or 4.00am (can't remember) we went to the station and met two of Nicholas' mates. We walked about and jumped on any bus. Then we went in St Mary's Hospital and Nicholas was going around in a wheelchair. We all fell asleep in these chairs whilst Nicholas gave Simmons a joyride in the wheelchair and smashed it. There was an empty chair so I went to sleep on it and Nicholas ran over to it and slept on it. All the chairs were taken so I slept on a mashed up wheelchair. At 6.10am everyone woke up and we bopped back to the station. When I got back to the station I was so f**king happy I could shit.

We had to walk from Slough. We got home about 8.00am. The first thing I did was went to bed. It was so good it was like having a multiple orgasm.

PS: Big f**k off nose girl is called Lizzi.

So who the f**k is Charlotte ??? Unsolved Mysteries.

Sunday 29th November 1998

Today I was supposed to play football (f**ked from last night). I had a boring day, woke up, did f**k all.

Oh yeah I did some HomeWork that's all.

30th November 1998

Today I got up early for school because I couldn't get to sleep in the night (had bare sleep that morning). After school I gave Terry a lift to Slough Grammar because he was meeting Chantelle. When we got there, there was bare Police. Shelly told me that there was a bomb in the park (roads were blocked). I walked back to my house with Chantelle, Terry, Hanghei and Clint. Chantelle and Terry came to my yard. I left them in the room then listened at the door but could only hear kissing. When my Mum got home they both left and I was on my Jaze. I got so bored I did some HOMEWORK. Then I thought I'd ring Jo. Jo seemed really happy to hear from me and desperately wanted to meet me (gagging for it) so I said yeah. As I was speaking I had Stevie and Chanel on the other line. Stevie wanted me to take her out but I told her I couldn't because I was going out with my Mum. That was the truth.

At night I watched TV.

South Park, Singled Out, Celebrity Death Match. The programmes all finished at 12.00am then I thought f**k it's 1st of December isn't this year going fast. HuHH.

3rd December 1998

Today was Terry's birthday. After school we met Kelly, and then met up with Ben. We hung about in Slough for a bit and I got my Mum a birthday present. When I got home Fish came round and we played on Tekken 3. Terry rang me afterwards and said "I know I've had a shit birthday, but we are going to have a boom weekend" (whatever). Simmons rang after and was telling me that we were playing each other on Sunday (The Big Match). Langley Lions vs Colnbrook.

Science Exam (easy).

Friday 4th December 1998

Today there were two funny things at school.

1. My friends said these two little year 7 were gonna have sex (just imagine that).
2. Adam Irwin didn't know the date of Xmas and he is 15. He didn't know it was on the 25th (how thick)!

After school I met Terry. Then we went to Slough to meet Kelly. In Slough I got my mum a present (chocolates) and forgot the damn card. When we got home everyone rang and asked if I was going E&D. But I said Nah, because I was going with my Mum to a restaurant. Terry wasn't going to come until Kelly said she was staying in. The restaurant we went to was called Mister Lai. It was very nice and the dinner was tick.

We got back about 12 and just watched some telly and went to sleep.

Skeet at party

5th December 1998

Today was my Mum's actual birthday. I gave her a card and made her laugh (a big happy birthday welcome). That day I did f**k all until about 6.00. We decided to go to Rhythm Nation. I went with Chris, Simmons, Guv, Terry and Nathan. And Nicholas met us down there. When we got there Nicholas, Chris and Guv went off to smoke a zoot. They said they would meet us inside.

About half an hour later when we were inside. Guv said that Chris had been chucked out because he was stoned (so what). I met Jo and that fit girl from last week (the one from Langley). Penny gave me a big sloppy kiss (the one from Langley) and it was boom. I only took three cards and used them. I gave one to Penny because she said she had lost it. The other two were to these girls (I can't remember names).

About 10.50pm everyone started leaving then my eyes started getting watery and I couldn't breathe. I walked out and everybody was coughing and choking. The Bouncer told us someone had had let off CS gas. One man was almost dead from it. There was a fight after as well. Some boy was getting kicked by bare brares.

When I got home we watched some porno because it was on. It was shit though.

Nicholas was taking the piss out of Nathan because he brought a ticket.

On the way home the train had another train attached, but with no one in it so we went in the driver's room and beeped the horn and made announcements.

Terry was arguing with a man about football.

6th December 1998

Today, played football against Simmons' team. We lost 5-0 and I almost scored. When I got home, Me, Terry and Daniel Mountain went to meet Danielle and some Slough Grammar crew (It was HuHH). That's all I did today.

9th December 1998

Today, there was hardly anyone at school because most people had gone to the Clothes Show. It was a normal school day nothing special.

After school I stayed in and watched TV, then I rang Gemma (Jo's friend) and just chatted to her and asked if she had Penny's number. She said that Jo had it. So I rang Jo and because I knew that Jo didn't like Penny I said that Penny had been saying bad things about me and I needed her number to speak to her (lies). I also didn't want Jo to feel jealous (I'm not vain). I rang Penny and she said the reason she didn't ring me was because she was waiting for me to ring her. I said how the f**k am I supposed to ring if I haven't got your number.

That night also called Simmons and Jason rang on his mobile phone. After I finished talking to everyone on the phone I watched a programme about teenagers who had problems.

At 10.30pm I watched Evil Dead 2. It made me laugh so much just by the cheap effects etc and the bits that are supposed to be scary but are not. Then I went to bed and thought of bare skeet (it's all good).

Friday 11th December 1998

Today I never went to school because I didn't feel too good. I just stayed at home relaxing and watching telly. Later on in the day about 7pm, me and Simmons went to meet Nicholas at the Foyer. Nicholas was drunk because he had drunk a bottle of champagne. We got on the train (OTT) to go to Northolt. We were supposed to have a massive event called Naughty but Nice. When we got there it was a small pub and no women. There was also nowhere to move. This was so shit we only stayed for an hour (£5 to go in). Afterwards we went to KFC then went to Slough to see if anyone was outside Pulse. But we got there too late and everyone was gone.

We bopped around and then met up with Dot and then this man called Lee. Lee had a car and he took us for a little joyride. It was dark. After that I went home and munched on some cereal that Nicholas gave me. Them lot went on to London.

- (Ring Penny Wednesday 6 o'clock)
- Girl from Drayton Manor on the train, tipsy.

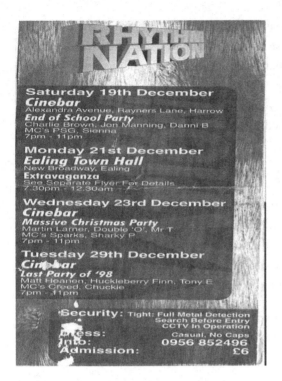

Saturday 12th December 1998

Today, I couldn't be bothered to go out so I slept in until about 2.30pm. At 3.00pm Fish came around and we played Tekken. After about 7ish Simmons came round. We were all gonna go Rhythm Nation but we were waiting for Chris and he took too long so we were at Langley Station and we saw a helicopter flying about looking for someone. We went to the Village and there had been a massive car crash with a few of our mates and a taxi. There were bare Police and Ambulances.

Later on we met Gemma P and Lisa W and they were going to a party at Stacey G's house. Me, Simmons and Ryan went there whilst Chris, Guv and Fish went to get a draw. When we got to the party there were bare people from Churchmead and the girls were all drunk (take one back to my yard). The bad thing was the parents were in the next room having a separate party. Later on we met Hanghei, Clint and Andrew and we went with them to get some drink. I didn't drink none just thought I'd save some until 18th December (last day of school).

About 11.00pm everyone was standing outside drinking. Then, me and Simmons went in the house and guess what I saw Gemma P (fitness) dealing with Scott Ford (that's sick). I thought if she was that drunk I could have taken back to my yard but I got there too late. Suddenly Stacey went on sick and chucked us out. I bopped home and relaxed, also gave my Mum a beer that I brassed.

Wednesday 16th December 1998

Today I met Penny with Guv after school. We met Penny and her friend in George Green. We just chilled out. George Green was proper dry. Later on we were in this park and Guv was saying "I think I've got a chance with Penny." He kept asking me to go the shops because he wanted her but he went to the shops; and I lipsed her.

On the way home I kept getting weird calls from Jason. He kept saying shit like "Robert you're gay" then hanging up. Got home, ate dinner.

Spanish Fly in drink.

Jokes - (Slang Our Language).

17th December 1998

Today school was jokes, can't remember why, but it was jokes!

Today I found out that Gemma P was now going out with Scott Ford. She must be desperate. So at the party she wasn't that drunk.

After school Nicholas knocked with Fish and we went out. On Trelawney Avenue there was a coach and on the coach there was bare (lots of) fit girls. We opened the back doors and the girls let me in. The problem was they were French. They were all holding me down and telling me to shush. I thought to myself these girls are boom, but I am not staying on this coach and ending up in Dover or some shit. So I stood up and suddenly this crazy W**ker shithead man grabbed me and started yelling at me. The only thing I could understand was I'm going to call the Police do you understand!? I just said oui (yes in French innit) to everything he said. Then he raised his fist and I thought he was going to punch me and I thought that if he does I am just going to go psycho and bust his monkey ass. He threw me off the bus and I started shouting at him, calling him names in French. The man was a nuttah.

Later on Guv came round and we were practising our MCing doing a line each.

Hope I meet those girls.

• Ring skeet.

18th December 1998

Today was the last day of school. I had some drink but didn't get pissed. Today we finished at 1.30pm.

After school I went for a job at Christmas in Hollywood. I had to come back at 3.00pm said the man. So at 3.00pm I came back with Simmons and Nicholas. We managed to get a job. The bad thing was it was at 8.00am in the morning, tomorrow. I went home and told my Mum.

About 7ish we went to E&D in Greenford. I met Kieron and Jason etc down there. I got 2 numbers, they were alright girls. Names, Rachael and Selina.

On the way home we were gonna go in the drivers room to do the announcement and do the horn but there was a man on the train and he was a British Transport Policeman. When we got to Slough, Simmons, Guv and Nicholas went to meet Dot, but I couldn't be f**ked so I bopped home with Grant.

- Fish lipsing girl first time.
- Gripping up Selina's batty while I was lipsing.
- I had blue hair.

19th December 1998

Today was our first day at our new job. Because we got there early we had to do bare washing up, lifting shit and cleaning. About 1.00ish bare skeet came in everyone was from Wales. I thought what's the f**king point about coming all this way.

At 7.00 bare customers arrived and Me, Fish Guv and Simmons were waiters. I must say I think I did good for someone who has never waitered before. I was funny and served well. I got a lot of help from this woman from Newport. Without her I would have been proper f**ked. We also had lots of staff meetings, which led to bare fights and arguments, this was mainly the customers' fault. At 12 we found out we found out that we couldn't get paid until Monday. So they also asked us to work on Sunday (made £80). So we didn't get paid today but met lots of new people and cherpsed lots of skeet.

I got home and gave my Mum some Bailey's Irish Cream that I brassed from behind the bar. We also got Malibu which we were saving for Monday.

- Guv got a skeet.
- Got Southampton girl's number.
- Mopped floor.
- Girl angry because I couldn't silver serve.

Sunday 20th December 1998

Today I was supposed to be at work at 9.00am but checked in at 10.00am. We washed bare dishes. At 1.25 Simmons had to go football. So at this time, Me and Fish had a lunch break. On our break we met Guv and he came back to work. When Simmons got back at 4pm he told us about his 4-0 win. When we got back to work Fish and Guv just went without permission to Harvester for a munch. When we told the man he said that he was taking 2 hours off their pay and putting it on ours. They got back about 7pm and had to scrub the big f**k off dirty dishes. Me and Simmons worked on the glasses. It was proper jokes but took 3 hours. I got a call from one of the girls at E&D (Selina). Selina said that one of her friends liked Fish. We were all shocked. Selina spoke to me on the mobile for 24 minutes and 20 seconds (long ting). After we finished all the dishes we checked out and brassed bare drinks like Champs, Wine, Beer, Spirits etc. Sometimes we were smashing glasses instead of washing them. It got a bit long,

When I got home I relaxed and watched Scrooged. Tomorrow working 8am till 5pm.

- Five days to Christmas.

Monday 21st December 1998

Today I felt pissed off again because I started early and they wouldn't pay us. The job is cash in hand. You're supposed to get paid the same f**king day. Nicholas worked with us today as well. It was a bit better with him there.

About 11am Fish got fired because he was so tired he started stretching in front of our boss so the man just said go home. I was tired too because we had been working 30 hours (that is illegal) in three days.

At 5pm we waited to get paid but they said the boss was out and we had to come back about 1.00am or 2.00am. As we had planned to go to Extravaganza we went there. We were queuing up for some time and by the time we got in it was 10.00pm leaving 2 hours. Extravaganza was quite shit but we met bare girls that I knew including Claire Lassiter. There were 2 rooms there a drum and bass room and a house and garage room. Me, Guv and Fish left about 12.20am. We bopped down to Burger King and then breezed on a train to Langley.

We went back to work about 1.30am and they said we can't pay you because Patrick (the boss) ain't here, come back tomorrow. After that I was getting so pissed off I felt like smashing their f**king piece of shit up (the tent).

- Mad Chef singing "suck on my balls".

Tuesday 22nd December 1998

Today I had the best lie in ever. No work, that's dark.

At 3.20pm Me and Fish met Selina and her butterz mate. Speaking off butterz Selina looked a bit baff today as well. Today we were gonna go Harrow on the HuHH (Hill) but we ended up going to central London.

In London we went down to MTV and got on tele, only for 5 minutes though. The place where they shot it was so small and they make it look so tonk (big) on tele.

Me and Fish also went on a few rides in Leicester square. Then a strange thing happened, I looked and I saw Laura from East London talking to Selina. I thought how the f**k do they know each other. I asked Laura how she knew her and she said she doesn't she was just asking for a fag, then spotted me. I asked Laura where Carly was and she said she was really sick and didn't come.

On the way home we sent the girls on the wrong train. Didn't even get a lips so they deserved it. Also Simmons rang and said he was meeting us at work to collect our wages (bare dollars).

On the train back to Langley, Simmons rang and said we're getting our money tomorrow in the morning. This really began to piss me off. So my mum rang then up and told them if they don't pay us she's reporting them.

They said come late about 2.30am on Wednesday. So this means I'm going shopping on Christmas Eve.

3 days till Christmas

Wednesday 23rd December 1998

Today I had a f**king dark sleep. Apart from the phone kept ringing and Fish knocked really early. I woke up about 1.30pm. At 3.00pm, Me, Fish and Nicholas went on a raze in our work. We never got nothing so we decided to see if we could get our dollars. The man gave us a timesheet and we got it signed. The bad thing was he was saying to come back at 1.30am to collect our money.

At 7.30pm we breezed down to RN (Rhythm Nation). We met up with crazy Liam OTT. It was a special Xmas ting. Guess what, there was hardly anyone there. Later on Liam got off with this fat offkey HuHH girl. This girl had a friend, she was quite butterz but I still chatted to her. Her friend was coming on to me but I thought she was weird because she had three tattoos, her tongue pierced and said she had a boyfriend. Suddenly she started kissing me so I though f**k it, give it to her!

A bit later Liam was saying she wanted to give me a shiner (BJ). So Me and Liam took them in the toilets outside. Liam got a shiner. I thought I would end up sh**gging this girl by the way she was carrying on, but she said she didn't. I took her in the toilet and sucked her boobies and fingered her. While I was dealing with this skeet I was thinking shit I don't even know this girl. She is a slosher. I also got some other information about this girl. That she raves, she takes drugs such as Speed, Weed and Tablets.

After we had finished, we met up with Fish, Simmons, Nicholas and Guv. Liam wants to meet the girls tomorrow but I don't know because tomorrow is Christmas Eve. I have tomorrow planned anyway.

- 10.00am Granny B (talking shit).
- 11.00am - Get Mum present.

- 12.00 noon – Just either stay at home or get a sh*g. Must think about this one.

About 1.30 we went back to work to get paid. Guess f**king what, we got paid, but it was only £140. So we are coming back on New Year's Eve to get more (greed). Afterwards we went to Slough and did f**k all and then we came home.

- Skeet at work
- MC at Rhythm Nation
- Chat, Do You Really Like It?

Christmas Eve 1998

Today I done my Christmas shopping in Slough. I got my Mum, chocolate, Soaps and Titanic. When I got home I wrapped them then put them under the tree for tomorrow.

Liam rang me and he was asking if I wanted to meet Zara and Betty, the girls from Rhythm Nation on Wednesday. Later on he rang me and he asked me if I wanted to come out and have a piss up. I was feeling sick so I didn't go. Plus that brares a bit too crazy for me. That night I basically did f**k all, watched TV and played computer.

Granny B came round (talking shit). I forgot!

Christmas Day 1998

Today is Christmas day, I was supposed to go church today but I felt sick, my mum still went though.

When she got back we opened our presents, my mum got me loads of small things this was mainly cos I've got everything and she didn't know what to get me. It was quite a nice day apart from I was feeling very sick, it was just me and my mum, we watched films played games and had jokes.

During the day I kept getting phone calls from Ben in Wales. I also got a call from Betty and she was asking if I wanted to go Club Coliseum but there was two problems, one there was no transport and two I was sick, well that's my Christmas.

Boxing Day 1998

Today was another day indoors. Still sick, it's beginning to get on my f**king nerves.

Today I rang Julie and I asked her if she wanted to go out sometime, she said yes but I have to ring her back tomorrow. That reminds me I rang Penny on Christmas Eve and she wants to go out as well. So I have to arrange the dates.

I also rang this girl called Rachael and I'm meeting her on Monday.

27th December 1998

Today me and Liam went to Kingston to meet Betty and Zara, when we got there it was just Zara there, and we had to meet Betty at the home.

When we arrived Betty was asleep so we went back to Zara's yard. At Zara's yard it was sick because they were just doing tings on the bed while I was facing the other way. They were doing shit like shiners, wanks, fanny sucking and other forms of oral sex. I was just facing the wall and listening to her garage tapes.

Later on Betty rang and said she couldn't come out today. After we went to Shepherds Bush to meet Liam's cousin at this bar place. It was quite a good bar, Liam's cousin got us some beers. We got a lift all the way back to Slough from Liam's cousin. As soon as I got in my mum was moaning because I hadn't told her where I was. At 10pm Simmons and Guv came round and we just chilled at my yard, we watched bare pornos.

Monday 28th December 1998

Today I was supposed to meet Rachael from Hounslow but didn't because we couldn't get any trains because it was Bank Holiday Monday. So I just hung about in Slough, I was gonna go cinema with my Mum but changed my mind because there was bare (lots of) people in Slough. In Slough Michael nicked some hair dye (blond).

When we got back to my yard me, Simmons and Fish all dyed our hair blond, my mum didn't really mind but from now on I'm a blondie.

29th December 1998

Today Jason knocked for me really early. We played some MK (Mortal Kombat) then went to Central London. In London we went down to MTV and we actually managed to get on TV. We talked to Donna and Richard Blackwood and we also chose and dedicated a video. I choose the video Chocolate Salty Balls and dedicated it to anyone who knows Robert the one and only Peters (Me).I know for a fact my mum didn't see it. But Lauren did cos Lauren rang me on the mobile.

At 8.30 I went RN with the crew. It was quite packed I saw a few people like Amanda, Aliza and Katie's mate, can't remember her name. Later on some girl came up to me and said I saw you on TV but she was butterz. I was hoping more skeet (girls) saw on me on TV but fitter ones.

After RN when we were in Langley, me and Liam were in the phonebox talking to this girl and he was pretending to cry, it was so funny. Everyone else was outside and they were smashing the phonebox and they were throwing bottles out of the recycling bin.

When we got out the phonebox they were gone so I went home, later on Simmons rang me and said he got arrested. So it was quite lucky we were in the phonebox because they wouldn't have believed me if I said I didn't do it. I have the perfect crime features, black, tall and blond hair.

30th December 1998

Today went on MTV again but this time with Simmons. We didn't get to speak but managed to get on TV but this time my Mum taped it. Can't remember what I did after. Just watch me on TV kept rewinding it to my part. You see my face 4 times.

New Years Eve 1998

Today is the biggest day with parties, but guess what we're not going to any, what we did was go London. On the train to London there were bare Slough people going to London. When we got to London Paddington everyone got through the ticket machines easily and I did my boom little slide under the barriers.

We got off the train at Oxford Circus then bopped to Piccadilly Circus. At Piccadilly we met my ex-girlfriend Charly from Chingford, everyone thought she looked butterz and I thought she looked butterz as well. We all went back to Trafalgar Square where we went into the New Year, F**k it's now 1999 I thought.

The streets were packed; we walked all around Piccadilly and Leicester Square. There were street parties, everything like people just shacking out to the beats in this guy's car. I met lots of people I knew, I also got people coming up to me saying you were on MTV init. I think the only way these people recognise me is cos my hair is bright blond. There's these other boys I know and no one recognises them and they go there everyday. On the way home we tried to stay in this posh hotel but the Police threw us out, so we stayed in St Marys hospital for about 2 hours, we just f**ked about.

About 6.30am we got a train back home. When I got home it was 7.10 and I just went bed and slept it was like having a multiple orgasm.

- Note. Kissing skeet, Happy New Year.
- Nicholas in London dancing.

1st January 1999 New Years Day

Well it's 1999 and guess what it's the f**king same. What I mean is this year's supposed to be futuristic or maybe the world will end, some says Jesus will come back this year, but who knows you'll just have to find out, stay tuned for part 2.

Well do you want to know how I spent this day? I just slept now f**k off.

Saturday 2nd January 1999

Today I got my hair cut with Michael (Fish) we were trying to get the blond out. But it never came out so I guess I'm going school with blond hair.

After we decided we were gonna go Reading. We had some trouble getting there cos this ticket man kept getting on our train, I dunno how the f**k we did it but he was a professional, he never caught us though.

At one point we ended up in Twyford, Twyford was so shit and I mean proper shit. We did manage to get in Reading, and when we did we looked for Skeet (Fit girls). Simmons met us in Reading about half an hour after and I think this was good luck cos when we met him we met some skeet. These girls were boom and I was thinking 'shit were some lucky niggas'. Guess what we even went MacDonalds with them, and shit they asked us to come.

After that we went back to Slough to meet Liam, yes I did get them Skeets numbers.

We got on another train, then we went to Tolworth to meet Zara, we messed about in her yard and brassed (nicked) bare shit. Simmons was jokes he feed her fish two whole pots of fish food. That night I ended up getting home at 1am, but it was alright cos my Mum had gone to her friend's party.

I relaxed and watched some television, I also thought if I needed to do New Year's Resolutions, but I don't.

Sunday 3rd January 1999

Today I'm writing in my diary neat and carefully, because I was just reading through it and I could barely understand a ting.

In the morning I got a phone call from Zara. She wanted Simmons number, cos it turns out Simmons accidently killed her fish yesterday. He put too much food in the tank, I never gave her his number, I said I didn't have it. I said I don't really know him he ain't even my friend, he's Liam's bredwin.

Today I did fuck all just relaxed. I rang Katrina and I'm meeting her tomorrow. I tried to call Julia but she wasn't in so I guess our date is cancelled. But that doesn't really bother me cos I'm meeting Katrina at 1.30pm and Kirsty at 4pm. The good thing is Kirsty is coming back to my Yard (Home) so I don't really need to go out with Julia tomorrow.

After a while Simmons rang me and I told him Zara's mum wants him to pay £200 because those fish were expensive.

- Did some homework.

4ᵗʰ January 1999

Today when I woke up I was in a hyper mood. I don't know why, I just was.

I got ready to go Hanwell to meet that girl, I lost track of time of time and the time I left my yard was the time I was meeting Katrina, 1.30pm.

When I was on the train it was weird cos I met Katrina, I said why are you so late and she just said why are you so late, she was HuHH.

At Hanwell, me, Katrina, Jason, Kieron and her friend Janisha. Janisha didn't like Kieron and J, so they didn't come with us. We ended up in Ealing Broadway, this was a bitch cos we went to the train station at 4pm, I was supposed to meet Kirsty at this time. I thought shit, what will I do, shall I tell Katrina I have to go, or just f**k Kirsty and go with Katrina.

Guess what option I chose, yes stay with Katrina and f**k Kirsty. We ended up going Acton Town cos there was supposed to be a massive fight, there wasn't a fight.

Around 5ish I got OTB (On the Bus) with Katrina and Janisha, they got off at Northolt cos Janisha had to go to the doctors, I didn't even kiss (get off with) her. That's HuHH.

After that I went to Kieron's yard. I got a call from Kirsty and she was proper pissed off. I told her I was there, but I must have missed her, that's the truth if you think about it.

When I got home I relaxed and watched White Men Can't Jump on BBC4.

- Notes. Thames trains are the best, 20.50, 21.08

Friday 8ᵗʰ January 1999

Thank God it's Friday, I had a gay week. Tuesday was HuHH, Wednesday didn't go school, Thursday my Head of Year was saying I had to get the dye out my hair and today, well actually today was jokes. Adam Irwin made me laugh, and I was in Isolation because of my hair. At night I didn't do nothing, just spent my Friday night indoors. I also read my diary to my Mum, she thought it was boom; I missed out the rude bits.

New thing for 99:- Funniest Thing All Day

- Adam Irwin's kick and Keith falling over

This was a waste of a day; some days are not important but still have to live them.

Saturday 9ᵗʰ January 1999

Today I went to Slough with Simmons and Nicholas. We just hung in the High Street and we stayed in the Foyer (Nico's Yard). About 6.30pm we met Darren at his work, Sport Soccer, then me, Simmons, Nicholas and Darren went Rhythm Nation. At RN it was Ladies Night and all the girls got in for £3 and the boys got in for the normal price of £6. I didn't get any skeet but I didn't mind, just thought I'd mention that. After RN Nicholas was getting on my nerves, he was just being gay. I had a play fight with him in Ealing Broadway for time but I didn't want too.

OTT we went in the driver's bit, I said 'Attention this is your driver speaking', and then started MCing. We all split up cos the Transport Police came and stopped the train. I was sitting on my own and the man was asking if anyone saw anything, luckily everyone said nah.

I hung about in Slough in the kebab shop with Guv, Simmons and Nico but they were all getting on my nerves so I bopped home. When I got in I watched TV then went to bed.

Funniest thing all day:-

- Dick with a nose, cussing Nicolas

11ᵗʰ January 1999

Today I had a really weird breakfast, I had noodles, then I rode to school. It was just a normal day at school, I didn't get into trouble today for my hair. When I got home I washed all the dishes cos there were bare dishes, I just relaxed after and watched TV.

Funniest thing all day:-

- Programme Kenan and Kel

Friday 15ᵗʰ January 1999

Well Thank God it's Friday, I had a normal boring week at school, now it's time for some hard clubbing.

After school I got a call from Terry, which was really weird cos I hadn't seen him in time. He told me he had now left school at 15 and is a bricklayer, he's also getting £1,200 for just 1 month, we all met Terry at Slough to go E&D in Greenford, it was me, Terry, Ben, Guv and Nico. We got off at Southall when we were OTT and got a bus to Greenford.

E&D was quite good, it was joke. I saw Leo down there, he was jokes. Also Katrina and Selina, my bredwins kept slapping her batty and she thought it was me a few times (Selina). When we were on the train home Terry nicked a train map for me but I needed the other one that was South East England.

Terry and Ben both stayed round my house and we watched some shitty film called George of the Jungle. And I put my train map up on my wall.

Funniest thing of the day:-

- Adam Irwin – Jokes at school
- Mel K and Tina Allen pretending to lips

Saturday 16th January 1999

Today me, Terry and Ben were all going to go into Slough, but didn't go cos we started playing Worms, that's a computer game so don't get the wrong idea. We played it till about 4.30pm, then Simmons rang and said he was going RN, but he wanted to leave early cos it was a foam party and they're usually packed. I told him I wasn't coming cos I had no money, Terry rang his dad for dollars and his dad said we could get in for free because he knew one of the bouncers. I rang Simmons back and told him to meet us down there.

When we got to the train station we had to dus (run) for the train. We got on the train then we saw a ticket man and got straight off, the next train was in half an hour so we bopped to the shops. Down the shops we saw some churchmead boys, like Chris P, Alex and Dean M, they were just smoking, nothing that good. As we bopped back to the station Hanghei, Clint Eastwood and Guv. They were going RN as well. When we got to the station and he had his bike, so he locked it up to these gates in the station.

When we got RN, we met Simmons and Nico. The queue was really long, but guess what we skipped it and got in free, because of Terry's dad's mate. That was lucky cos that guy is not always there and we would have been f**ked if he wasn't there.

There was lots of skeet today and it was good. When the foam came on we had our little rumbles, also a strange thing happened, I started grinding with this girl and I said 'so what's your name'. 'Keighley' she said. Then she said, 'don't you remember me', she kept saying she met me in Brentford on a bus. Then I remembered, I got her number but hadn't rung cos I thought she wouldn't remember me. I'm gonna give her a ring now. That club seemed like it was going on for years. (Gas Threat).

This was because we got there really early and usually got there really late. Near the end I got this fit girls number, her name was Claire, I hope it's the right number. When we got back to Langley, we looked at Chris' bike and it was gone. That doesn't make any sense, we rang Chris but he didn't seem to care, when I got home I watched the boxing on Front HuHH (Row)

P.s Got the train map I needed.

Funniest thing of the day:-

- Nick pulled Chris' trousers down and bike gone.

Sunday 17th January 1998

Today was a f**king weird day-

In the morning me and Terry were ringing girls because Terry was in the mood for meeting girls. We arrange to meet Selina from Hillingdon. When we got to the train station we just missed a train and the next one was in an hour (it was a Sunday). We were already late so me and terry got on the train to Reading, we thought f**k it's too late to go now.

In Reading Terry kept saying let's get a train to Southampton. I couldn't be f**ked. Then I got a call from Selina and she was asking where I was. I said Ealing Broadway. Then Terry said the stupidest thing "let's go Ealing" and we were in Reading. But I changed my mind and we went Ealing, it was long. So we went Reading for no reason and now were going Ealing.

When we got Ealing we meet up with Simmons. Then I called Selina to see if she was still waiting but she wasn't. So we went back to Slough. We track back and forth for no reason.

We just bopped through Slough then went back to my yard (home). I had my dinner then went to the station with Terry. I waited at the train station until his train came.

Well don't you think that was a weird day?

Funniest thing all day:-

- MY BIG BLACK BATTY

Monday 18th January 1998

Today I went back to school after another one of my weird weekends. At school these people came in and they did this thing on sex and it was jokes

it also took up 2 hours of HuHH (any word that means shit) lessons. These people done a play and I think it was the rudest thing they've ever showed us at school. It was different from those boring films that just talk bullshit.

At break Adam Irwin told me he was moving to shepperton, it's near Staines. I was quite shocked because I thought he'd always be in Datchet. I'll suppose I'll miss him because he was jokes and there'll be nobody to crack hard jokes.

Anyway I'll see him when we go Fuel again to m.c.

After school Nicholas and Chris Harvey came round and they were acting gay. Nicholas lit a zoot (spliff) in my yard. I said to Chris he could build it but not smoke it. He also dirtied my bed sheets. He can be a bit stupid at times and he thinks everything's funny. Most of the time he's jokes but sometimes he acts so stupid and immature and he's coming up 17.

After they left Fish came round and like we always do we played computer. Did some homework after then went bed," Rags"

Funniest thing all day:-

- Shibbz –just standing here for my health

Tuesday 19th January 1999

Today I didn't go to school because I woke up at 9.30am and I didn't want to get in trouble. I think I should have gone. Later in the day I rang Clare the girl I met at RN. She seemed really nice. We were just chatting about which school she went to, how old she was and shit like what she does and where she lives.

After, I went to Kickboxing it was an alright lesson. I've got a competition in Windsor which I might do but I have to train.

After Kickboxing I went to Simmons' yard and just listened to tunes etc.

When I got home I ate my dinner and watched House Sitter and Best of the Best 2, the reason I write those kinds of things is because in the future, you'll think 'shit, I can't believe I remember that.'

Funniest thing all day:-

- Shibbz - open your eyes.

Friday 22nd January 1999

Today I had a funny day at school it was just so funny. Daniel Sturgess was giving me bare jokes, just talking his sick shit. Cell bock 17.

After school I went to Kickboxing. I met Guv and he borrowed my bike to go to Simmons' yard (home). Kickboxing was alright today, I've got a competition on 14th February, which is Valentine's Day.

After Kickboxing I went to collect my bike from Simmons' yard. I got my bike from his flat but he was out when I knocked for him. So I went home and did f**k all. I made a few phone calls. I called Keighley , Julia, Maria and some other girls.

Later on I got a call from Rachel Levi. That night I watched Star Ship Troopers. The only reason I am writing this is because I would like to remember these things in the future. Starship Troopers is a bit shit though. They didn't even kill all the aliens what the fuck!

Funniest things all day:-

- School was bare jokes - Daniel S messed up talk (Cell Block 17)
- Adam Irwin watched this thing

Saturday 23rd January 1999

Today I was supposed to meet Amanda, but didn't because she was supposed to meet a friend or some shit like that. At 12.45 pm I bopped to Slough. I got some money then went to get my hair cut (trim). I got my hair cut at 1.30pm. I managed to get all the blond out and I got my hair back to its normal black hair.

After, I got my hair cut I got a militant little kebab. At 6.00pm I went to the Station to meet Terry, I was with Fish. When we got to the Station we met Sarah Elliman and Tracey. We also met Javan and Russell. Russell had a knife and we were pretending to cut each other up.

When the train arrived we saw Terry. We were about to get on the train then suddenly we got grabbed by Police, we missed our train. The Police were questioning us. They said we were fighting with dangerous weapons, which we weren't, but someone witnessed us messing about and thought we were fighting.

We met Terry at Ealing about 7.30pm. He was with three girls. There was only one nice one and she was still about HuHHed up. On the train there, it was dark because at one point I saw her fanny flaps in full view. I swear she wasn't wearing no knickers.

When we got there me and Terry went to see if we could get in free again, but that guy wasn't there today so we queued up. A bit later in the queue we met up with Dot, Nathan, Chris Harvey and this other boy, who looks like Ren from Ren and stimpy.

The queue was taking the piss. When we got to the front it was 10.10pm leaving us 50 minutes so we thought f**k it, and just went to get some munch. We went to Pizza Hut and I think it was better than RN because they were playing a Garage Nation tape and we had sick munch.

About 11.00pm we waited for everyone to come out. We met up with Terry's girls and they were really excited and they really enjoyed it. I met Clare, Amanda and Katrina. I just chatted to them.

On the tube home Chris Harvey and Guv got taxed. Chris Harvey got his mobile nicked and Guv got his ring nicked. They also took money off the rest. The funny thing is they didn't even say nothing to me. On the train to Ealing bare people gassed the train. It really made my nose f**ked. On the way home we were gonna go to a party in Wexham but we thought f**k it, so we went back to my yard, Me and Terry.

Funniest things all day:-

- My weird dream about floating cows.

- Nathan - Those are Terry's girls behind you.
- Little Dread Brare - North London - East London - South London - Bang Bang

Monday 25th January 1999

Today, I went to school with black hair. I know that sounds gay but I haven't done that in ages. Everyone kept saying; where's your blond gone? Or, why did you take it out? Thick people.

When I got in from school I just did a number of things like, watch TV, wash up and play computer. When my mum got in she was telling me that we were going to New York this year, which is dark. Me and my Mum watched this film on BBC5 called Face, and it was really good. I also was feeling hungry at one point so I decided to bake a cake, but it didn't come out right so I threw it away.

Ingredients:

1. Flour - Fuck Knows?
2. Eggs - 1
3. Sugar - Forgot to put it in
4. Butter - 2 Spoonfuls
5. Ice Cream - Bare
6. Chocolate - F**k Lost Count

I also got a call from Amanda and I am definitely meeting her this Saturday with fit sexy Vickii, I hope!

Funniest Thing All Day:-

- Breaking Samina's Knife

Did u Know?

There are 8760 hours in a year.

Friday 29th January 1999

Yes, it's Friday! I've had an alright week though, it's been jokes. There has been about four fire alarms set off this week, false alarms. Lots of fights, this guy called Tit fights and always gets beaten up. Daniel Mountain beat him up one day and some traveller guy beat him up the next day.

In the morning, we had RE, which was shit, then we had PSE. We did Sex Education. After, we had double Tech which really f**king pisses me off. But today, it was safe. Me and Christian Bolton just made whatever the f**k we wanted to. The fire alarm just went off just when we were doing Tech. Our last lesson was Maths, which was alright because Miss Netherwood wasn't there but we had thick Mr Carter. I just told a story to Bredwins, 'Master of the Ticks'.

After school I went to Slough with my Mum to get a coat. We breezed down to Burger King where they were giving out free chips, f**k knows why! When we got home Hanghei came round and we went to Kickboxing. We did it in a Drama room.

After Kickboxing I went round Hanghei's yard and we chilled. There's a boom tune that's been going through my head all day, it's called Chocolate Boy. When I got in I played Fifa World Cup 98. I was my favourite team Cook Islands. I never win it because that team are the shittest team in the game. But today I won and I was so f**king happy I cried. My little team won! I am probably the only person in the country that plays with that team. Just because they're dark. While I was playing I was listening to Chocolate Boy and it gave me the power, er No Robert!

Well I think I had a militant day. It may not seem exciting to you but it is to me. Also, got a called from Rachel Levi, party cancelled but going out with her Saturday, next Saturday.

Funniest Thing All Day:-

* Set me a small piece - gives him a small piece.

Saturday 30ᵗʰ January 1999

This morning Fish and Ben Smith came round. Then we all went to meet Amanda and her friends. We were supposed to meet Amanda at 2.00pm at Ealing Broadway but we got there at 2.24pm. Amanda was there though. There were only two problems:-

1. She had no friends because they were all at work.
2. She had to look after her Godson and she brought him with her.
3. Oh yeah, she also has a boyfriend and is very faithful, that's my day ruined.

We all went to Park Royal and just chilled in Superbowl. Later on I went to the Trains Station with Amanda while Ben Smith and Fish waited at Superbowl. I didn't get anything off Amanda but I didn't really mind. After, I went back to Superbowl and then we all just went back to my yard. Later we all knocked for Hanghei then we all went to meet Craig etc.

We all chilled out in Upton Park just drinking and them lot were smoking. After the park we went to Slough to meet Darren and Fish. There was about ten of us, there was Me, Fish, Ben Smith, Hanghei, Clint Eastwood, Grant, Darren, Daniel, Craig, Sati and some boy that was just following us. We went to the Ice Arena; it was just the usual people down there. After, we bopped through Slough and just got some munch. When I got home I watched Big Trouble in Little China, but I didn't watch it all because I fell asleep.

Funniest Thing All Day:-

- Mark in the Park on ride

Sunday 31ˢᵗ January 1999

About 1.00pm today I went to the cinema with my Mum. It's a Sunday no one will see me. We saw this film called Practical Magic. It was alright but a bit slow. When we got home we watched two videos we got from Blockbusters, after the cinema. We got Jerry Springer, Too Hot for TV, which wasn't that good. We also got Wish Master which was tick and had some militant scenes. I'm definitely buying it when it's out to buy.

Funniest Thing All Day:-

- This one says Ert

1st February 1999

Well it's February and boy am I gonna be busy, it's Valentine's Day in 13 days. This month I already have planned.

Next week- Saturday –Either taking Rachael out or raving.

Week after –Friday – Fuel then cousin's birthday party in Acton.

Saturday-Party in Datchet-probably link girls in day.

Valentines Sunday – Kickboxing competition then either staying in Southampton and getting s.e.x or going extravaganza.

After- just girls... hope .

Well anyway today school was jokes. I always say that I must think of something else to say. It's getting old, this is 1999. After school I watched Wish Master again. I also tried to do tape to tape but it didn't work.

Later on, Fish came round and like f**king always and always we played computer. But this time he brought some cheats with him for mk4 which he got off the internet, useful things.

After that I watched this film with my mother but it was HuHH (if you still don't know what that word means you're gay). So I went to bed.

Funniest thing all day:-

- Mrs Tucker chasing us at school
- Biffmans shoe

Thursday 4th February 1999

I'm writing this and thinking shit isn't this week going fast, its Friday tomorrow. Also this year is going fast, its February already.

School wasn't too bad today. After school I just relaxed. A bit later Guv came round and we went to Simmons house.

We bopped down to Horsemoor Green, a youth centre which I haven't been to in about three years. It was quite boom we just played basket ball and chilled.

After, I just went home and relaxed.

Funniest thing all day:-

- Give me my pencil case back, foul

Friday 5th February 1999

Today I didn't go school because I woke up late and didn't wanna get in trouble. During the day I just played computer, listen to tunes and just watched TV.

About 4.50pm I went to meet my mum in Slough to get some shopping. On the way I met Fish and he came with me. When we got Slough we just quickly did the shopping then breezed home, o yeah also got a burger.

I helped my mum unpack and wash up then went to kickboxing. Kickboxing was quite tiring today. After kickboxing, me and Hanghei went to Crystal's yard because she was supposed to be having a party. But it was just a little get together. It was quite shit so, me Hanghei, Grant and Sati stayed in the kitchen and made some dark toasted sandwiches. Cheese, ham, baked beans and cheese on top. Wow.

A bit later all the crew came round and we had to leave. We all bopped (walked) round Slough. After we met these F**ked up girls and just went to the station with them and chatted. Nicholas was jokes he farted on the girl.

After we finished chatting to them we went to the Foyer. Outside the Foyer were all these druggy people talking about drugs and sex, it was like a soap opera.

After me, Nicholas, Simmons, fish and some other guy tried to get Simmons car starting. It didn't start so me and Fish bopped home (the rest stayed there). Me and Fish went to Slough train station and Fish rang a taxi. When the taxi came we got in it, obviously. The taxi man said the taxi would be about £5.50 but we only had £2.10 between us. I got off at Spencer Rd and ran home. I was thinking I hope Michael gets away, kind of. Michael came round a bit later and said he was locked out. So he stayed. Guess what I'm looking at him now (asleep) and he's f**king ugly.

Funniest things all day:-

- Licking pussy in club story
- Nicholas running that girl.

Ps: meeting Rachael tomorrow 8pm

Sunday meeting Kirsty O'Connor 2

Saturday 6th February 1999

During the day I did f**k all. It was just me, Fish, Ben chilling at my yard. About 6pn everyone was ringing me to see if I was going E&D Brentford, but as you know today was my date with Rachael.

At 6.45pm I left to go and meet Rachael. I got OTT to Ealing Broadway then to ActonTown then one more train that took me there, think that's worth it when I could of got one bus, but I didn't know.

When I got to Hounslow East it was ten to 8 and I was meeting her at 8pm. so I bopped to the shop to waste time. Do you wanna know how much time I wasted, about one minute? When I got back to the station I got a call from Rachael and she was on her way.

When Rachael got to the station she was looking really sexy, it was turning me on. We got on the bus to Feltham to go cinema.

When we got in the cinema we couldn't decide which movie to see. We decided to see this film called "Opposites of Sex" which we didn't even know what it was.

The film was an 18 and the woman at the box office asked me for my date of birth, but as I'm always lying about my age I said a date of birth straight away.

The film was really weird it was about a bunch of gay men and a little girl who was a slut that shagged anyone. Me and Rachael thought it was quite shit but were making each other laugh.

After the movie we were gonna go in Superbowl but we didn't get in because after 6pm you have to be accompanied by an adult. So Rachael said to me do you want to stay and what do you think I said, yes of course I said yes I'm not turning down sex, "rags"

On the way back to Rachael's yard, Rachael brought me a McDonalds because I paid for her to get in the cinema. When we got back to her yard I met her parents and they were safe (ok). When they went to bed me and Rachael watched a film. We watched Nowhere to Run.

It was a bit weird because I hadn't even lipsed her. So I lipsed her and started rubbing her up I wanted her to get horny and just give it to me, I was up for sex. I didn't get nothing though.

We still were up about 2-3 in the morning. She started falling asleep and this was getting on my nerves because I was really horny. But Guess what she f**king fell asleep, so what was the point of asking me to stay.

Later on I started getting tired so I started cuddling up to her and I was getting a major boner. I don't know why but she made me hard straight away. This was really turning me on and I wanted to f**k her before it was too late.

About 4ish she woke up and kept saying she couldn't get back to sleep. So I started lipsing her and she started getting horny. We didn't have sex but we did everything else apart from shiners (bj) and licking out. I didn't really mind after that because it was alright. And I didn't really care if we didn't have sex, seriously. After Rachael's mum came down and she told

Rachael to go bed because she wasn't supposed to be sleeping in the same room as me. Then I fell asleep.

Funniest thing all day:-

- Film with crazy man
- Can I borrow your toilet?

Sunday 7ᵗʰ February 1999

Today Rachael's little brother woke me up about 8am and I was so f**king tired. So her mum let me sleep in Rachael's room because everyone was coming in the living room. They had an extra bed and they let me sleep in that. I woke up about 11am and Rachael's little brother came in and she was getting on my nerves.

After, we went downstairs and had breakfast and I got ready to go home. But first we watched a bit of TV. At 1.30pm Rachael went with me to the bus station and saw me off, of course I lipsed it you prick. I was gonna get the bus home from Hounslow but I missed it and the next one was in an hour. So I thought f**k it and got the train home.

When I got to Slough I got a chase from the TM because I jumped over the fence to get out the station, they have bare TM's there now. When I got in, Simmons came round and I told him about my date. After that relaxed and wrote in this Diary.

Funniest thing all day:-

- Shibbz – Bloody me bum smell

Did u know?

King Hussain of Jordan died today.

Friday 12ᵗʰ February 1999

In the morning JD came round and we got a lift of his dad because both of us had punctured tyres.

After school JD and Christian came round and we played a bit of computer. Then after I went kickboxing but finished early (about 7.50pm) to go to Fuel, to M.C remember. When I came out of kickboxing I met Christian and he said he was coming to Fuel.

On the way there we met Nicholas, Darren, Hanghei and Clint. When we got to Fuel they let us in free because we were M.C's. Simmons and Guv were there when we got there. It was alright apart from they kept playing some shitty tunes which I couldn't M.C to properly.

After Fuel I left to go to my cousin's yard but I got there about 2am because all my bredwins were holding me up me. Nicholas made us walk across all this mud and said it was a short cut to the station but it was just a dead end.

At my cousin's yard all I did was watch Pet Semetry 2 then went to bed.

Saturday 13th February 1999

In the morning me and my mum left my cousins quite early. We got to Slough about 12.50 and I was getting my hair cut at 2pm. So I breezed home. When I got home I couldn't find my key so I bopped to Simmons work. I chilled there till about 1.45 then went slough to get my hair cut.

After my hair cut I met fish and Nicholas, we breezed round Slough for a bit then I went yard.

There was a party on today which we won't going to but Hanghei didn't want Nicholas to come because he could only get about 9 people in, Simmons got rid of him somehow. There was about ten of us. it was me, Hanghei, Clint, Sati, Simmons, Denzil,Fish, Grant, Andrew, Matthew, Craig and Guv, but he met us down there. He got a lift of his brother.

The party was in Datchet Cricket Club and all the girls were from St Bernard's School. The party was alright apart from the music and when the garage came on we tried to use the mic but it didn't come on properly, it kept f**king going silent.

After the party there was a massive fight between Denzil's massive and some boys from St Bernard's. The St Bernard's boys got f**ked up.

When I got home Terry was with me and he had to stay but it's gonna be a bit f**ked because I'm leaving at 8.30am tomorrow morning for kickboxing.

Also got girls number- quite boom AMY.

Funniest thing all day:-

- Denzel shouting-"your mamma pussy stink"

Valentine's Day Sunday 14th February 1999

Today I woke up about 7.50am to get ready for kickboxing. I left my yard at 8.30am then went to meet Hanghei. We got the train to Windsor and got to the place about 9.42am, exactly, not. The competition hadn't even started as a matter of fact we the first people there, got there too early.

About 10.30am everyone came. The competition started about 11.45am. I was in 2 categories today.

1. Light continuous fighting
2. Kick fighting (kicks only no punching)

I had my first fight against this Asian boy. I killed him; his nose was bleeding proper because I kept upper cutting him and giving him bare roundhouses to the face. My next fight was against Darren. I lost but I think I could of won, I didn't fight my best. Maybe because I know him and he's from the same club.

After the guy said I had 3rd place because the next person who I was gonna fight dropped out, scared innit.

During today I chatted to bare girls. I even got off with this girl and I only just met her. All I said was "its Valentine's day might as well set me a kiss innit". This girls name's Lauren and she's from Watford. I lipsed her on the stairs just before my fight.

Later on I did the kick fighting and came first. So had two nice trophy's.

About 6.10pm we left, it would have been earlier but I couldn't find my bag for about 20 minutes.

When I got in I showed my mum the trophy, had dinner washed and then left for Extravaganza.

When we got to Extravaganza there was still a massive queue and Simmons was right at the front and wanted us to cut in but we couldn't. So we queued up while Nicholas went round the back and tried to find another way in. And guess what the mother f**Ker found another way in. We climbed through this smashed window and went through a door and just started blending in with everyone.

It was really packed today, Valentines special. I meet all the usual girls and I met Rachael and she was asking if I still was staying over her house.

After Extravaganza me, Rachael and two ugly girls got in a taxi to Rachael's house. When I got there, there was two other boys which I didn't know but slept in the same room as them. But they were safe and jokes at times. As all the girls were going to bed Rachael gave me a Valentines card which said:-

"I know I should ask you to your face but will you go out with me?"

I thought, shall I go out with her? Then she called me in the kitchen and said "yeah so what you saying then Robert". I started messing about and said "saying about what" she kept saying you know you know that you know. Then I just said "alright then" and lipsed her. I'm going out with her now but don't think that stops me seeing other girls, ha ha think again.

At night me and them other two boys watched, Don't be a Menace to south Central While Drinking Your Juice in the Hood, but I feel asleep.

Funniest things all day:-

- Dogs are craving these days
- You might as well set me a kiss
- Card, shame – throwing it

15th February 1999

In the morning everyone came downstairs and we watched two movies, (remember I'm still at Rachael's yard). While we were watching the films Rachael kept rubbing up my leg and she kept getting higher and I know she wanted to rub up my ding a ling but she never. I was thinking if you wanna touch it just f**king touch it you HuHH. .Her mum was in the room that was the only problem.

Later on Rachael walked me with me to the OTB station and she kept saying that she wanted me to stay but I had to leave because her mum was in a HuHH mood.

I got the bus home today and it was pretty tick because it stops right by me.

When I got in JD came round then a bit later Ben came round. When JD left Simmons came round then we got a taxi to go Pulse (Ben didn't come).

When we got Pulse it seemed a bit weird because we hadn't been there in time (ages). It was alright (I suppose) but wasn't all that.

After Pulse I started walking home then I saw Denzel and mans. They offered to give me a lift on some old man scrambler. But it didn't even work so I bopped (well ran) home.

At this moment I'm just eating some skittles, shit sorry they're M&M'S.

16th February 1999

Well today nothing happened apart from I got a call from Kirsty O'Connor 2 and I'm meeting her at 2pm tomorrow then Rachael (my girlfriends) rang and I'm meeting her after. But Rachel (my girlfriend) wanted to talk on the phone for time.

I also rang Julie and she wants me to meet her in Park Royal at some party on Friday.

What I did today was just play computer with JD and rested, just letting you know.

Funniest thing all day:-

- There wasn't one because I had a shitty day

17ᵗʰ February 1999

In the morning I got ready to go meet Kirsty O'Connor 2. I left my yard about 1.25pm to get the 1.31pm to Ealing.

When I got to the station the train was there and I had to duss. I got to the doors and they just closed in my face, shame. I got the next train at 2.01pm. I got Ealing about 2.30pm and luckily she was still waiting. Kirsty looked f**ked up, this was the first time I saw her in light because I always saw her in clubs. She had bare spots, trust.

We went down to Central London. We breezed round Marble Arch and Oxford Street and went Trafalgar square. When we were at Trafalgar Square I tried to lips her but she said no, I got rejected.

About 6pm I got a call from Rachael (my girlfriend) and I told her I'd come over her yard. But I told her I was with mates.

As I went to leave, Kirsty O'Conner 2 kept rubbing up against me but still wouldn't kiss me, she kept saying I'll kiss you tomorrow when I come round. I never even said I wanted her to come round tomorrow. I told her I might be busy and she then said;

"Well you can be busy with me"

I did manage to get rid of her then I went to Rachael's (my girlfriends) yard. I got there about 7.15pm. Me and Rachael (my girlfriend) watch the film Forest Gump. As we were watching it Rachael's brother had a mate and he was really stupid, he kept getting on my nerves, just being childish. These bastard year 7s.

After the film I left and told Rachael (my girlfriend) that I was still staying tomorrow. That night I got in at midnight. Shit I left home at 1.25pm and got home at midnight.

18th February 1999

In the morning JD came round and we just played some FIFA 99. JD left about 1pm then Kirsty O'Connor 2 rang and said she was coming round. I met Kirsty O'Connor 2 and she was with her friend Na-cheek-ka. We bopped to my house from the train station.

When we got to my yard Kirsty and me were downstairs and she horribly left her friend upstairs in my room. Kirsty kept saying "Na-cheek-ka likes you. But I don't like her. Kirsty then started kissing me on my cheek and rubbing up to me, but she still wouldn't lips me. She kept saying "it's because Na-cheek-ka likes you". All I could say was "SO".

Kirsty was really dirty she kept saying "I'm coming round tomorrow and we're gonna f** k hard". But there's only one problem I'm staying at Rachael's (my girlfriend) yard tonight and probably be back late tomorrow. Didn't tell her that though.

There's also another thing Kirsty said to me which made me laugh.

KIRSTY- You're a dog

THE1ANDONLY- What do you mean?

KIRSTY – Well what do dogs do?

THE1ANDONLY- They lick people's faces and annoy you

KIRSTY- Well how do they make babies?

THE1ANDONLY- They f**k

KIRSTY- Exactly

(That just made me laugh and if you're not laughing you're a boring old fart.)

About 7pm I walked with them to the station. Kirsty kept saying see you tomorrow" and also saying "I want you". Shut up you stupid hoe, I thought.

When I got back I had some munch then got on the bus to Hounslow to go Rachael's (my girlfriends) yard.

I got to Rachael's (my girlfriends) house about 10pm. We watched two films then just messed about. She went to bed about 4am, I was sleeping downstairs.

19th February 1999

In the morning 3 things woke me up. Rachael's brother, her mate and the f**king stupid ugly dog. It kept biting me, it was playing but it was pissing me off. So I went upstairs to sleep in Rachael's (I can't be f**ked to write my girlfriend anymore so just f**k it yeah, alright cool) room.

I woke up later about 12pm then went downstairs with Rachael and had some breakfast. Later on I went to the shop to get some chips, that's all. When I got back we watched Sister Act 2.

After the film Rachel said to me if I ask you to have sex with me what would you say?

I said yeah she then said she'd do it then and there but her parents were in.

So we just started kissing then she took off her bra, I mean I took it off.

I had a nice little play with her tits after I had a little suck on um.

I was making her laugh a lot while I was doing this because you know me crack joke any time I feel, even when sucking boobies.

After I said can you suck mine she started sucking and licking my nipples and f**k it felt really tick. It was giving me a orgasm. I didn't know that shit was so good. Oh yeah another reason I didn't do anything else with her was because she was on her period. But the nipple licking was dangerous.

I left Rachael's at about 7-8 pm. When I got home John (mums ex) and Michael was round. Me and Michael left to go Park Royal, there's a party remember.

When we got to Park Royal we couldn't find shit. After Simmons, Nicholas and Guv met up with us.

We all got the train to Central London. We went down to Westminster. When we were in Westminster we saw this drunk guy and Michael did the lamest thing. He nicked the guy's bag. We checked the bag and there was shit in it. After that we bopped through Leicester square and Piccadilly Circus me Guv and Michael jumped on a bus because we couldn't be bothered to hang about any more (it was 2am). The bus driver drove about 20 yards then stopped and chucked us off because we never paid.

On the way to Paddington Station it was weird because we met up with Nicolas and Simmons them lot all nicked a bike, not one each just one. Simmons was getting a lift on the handle bars.

When we got to the station about 3:08am. When the train came Simmons noticed that behind this shop (in the station) were bare cakes. We got everybody and we just nicked them all. We kept running back to get more. We put them on a seat and I tell you we had about 30 cakes.

When we got Slough we bopped home. Simmons had a massive bag of cakes, he's probably munching them now, the fat HuHH. I couldn't be bothered to take none.

Funniest thing all day:-

- Nicking cake crate

Saturday 20th February 1999

In the morning I got a call from Kirsty O'Connor 2 and she said she was sorry for not coming round the other day. But this didn't matter because I wasn't in anyway.

Around 3ish Nicholas came round. We went to Simmons work and on the way we met up with Fish. After that we got the 81 bus to meet Rachael.

When we got to Hounslow. Rachael was in a bad mood because Nicholas and Fish were with me and they were pissing her off.

We all got on a bus to Rachael's yard, well all the way to Brentford because Nicholas kept us on the bus with his fat self. When we got to Rachael's drum (house), Rachael was saying that I was the only person allowed in. Them lot were all going "if you go in your lame". So I said to Rachael I'd go with them then ditch them.

Simmons rang a bit later and we waited for him at the shops. When he came we got the bus to Brentford to go E&D (Education and Dance).

When we got there it was proper poop (shit). So I stay till about 9.15pm the left to go Rachael's, like I promised. I got to Rachael's and she was saying she defiantly wants to shag me but her parents were in. We had joke though, when I'm with her we're always messing about. If we were having sex we wouldn't be able to stop laughing.

I left Rachael's about 11pm and she wanted me to stay but I couldn't because of her parents. I walked down to Hounslow bus station and met up with the crew. They said that E&D was shitter after I left. They kept saying to me what did you do with Rachael, but I didn't really want to tell them because Rachael said don't tell anyone what we do. I already had told them about the nipple thing and Rachael didn't even like that. So shit imagine if I told them about some other stuff, she'd get really pissed off. So what I did was just nod my head. They think I shagged her but I will tell them I didn't.

Anyway we missed the bus to Slough so we had to get the train. OTT Nicholas took out the fire extinguisher and he was spraying it so I just grabbed it off him and sprayed him a bit then just pretended to spray him so he would f**k off.

The train stop at Northfields and this was the last stop so we got the bus to Ealing Broadway station. We luckily got the train because it was late we would have had to wait an hour.

When we got to Slough, me and Michael breezed home while Simmons and Nicholas went to chill in a car that don't even work.

When I got in I had my dinner then watched Dr Dolittle but I didn't watch it all because it was about 2.45pm and I was quite tired. So I went bed.

Funniest thing all day:-

- Michael pissing on car
- Putting bag over Rachael's head

Sunday 21st February 1999

Well tomorrow I'm going back to school and I had a good little week off. I went to fuel to M.C, stayed round Chantelles(cousins), went to a party in Datchet, kickboxed, went raving, had jokes in London, rang/met bare girls and the best thing was going around Rachael's yard.

Well anyway today all I did was cut the grass in the morning then later on me and Fish went to Blockbuster video, rented Bloodsport 3.

Funniest thing all day:-

- SHAME
- Nipple licking good

R.I.P

STEVEN LAWRENCE 1974-1993

Monday 22nd February 1999

I really don't know why I'm writing in my diary today because f**k all happened. All I did was go school and come home. Well school was jokes today that's probably why I'm writing in it, just to remember these things in the future. Like the massive Royal Rumble we had in English when the teacher walked out.

When I got home I rang Rachael I told her that I wouldn't cheat on her and I think I might not, but its f**king hard not to. But I want to be faithful for once (can't believe I said that). Also I told her I'll come round on Sunday so we can do some homework together, if you know what I mean.

Funniest thing all day:-

- THE STORY IN CLASS – in another country in a school beating everyone up getting chase from old granny, escape by smashing through the window

Friday 26ᵗʰ February 1999

Today I never went to school because I had a really bad foot from playing football at school. I just relaxed and rested my foot.

Later on in the day I got lots of calls from Simmons etc and they were just asking if I was going E&D but I never went because of my foot.

About 8.30pm I got a call from Terry. He came over then we just breezed to the shops (first time I went out). When we got in we just watched some T.V and just stayed in.

Saturday 27ᵗʰ February 1999

In the morning Fish rang me and he was telling about E&D. He even got off with a girl and this was shocking because we've never seen him with any girls before.

At 1.30pm Guv, Fish, Wayne Flex and Sean came round my house then we left to go to London. On the way to the station we went in this shop for a raze and got bare chocolates. When we got to the train station we met up with Nicholas.

On the train we met up with two of Nicholas's friend from the Foyer and they came with us. When we got to Paddington I had some trouble getting through the machines. So I had to pay. We got off at Oxford Circus then bopped through Carnaby Street and Soho to go through Piccadilly Circus. On the way I met these fit girls and I got one of their numbers. There was only one problem these girls live all the way in Bath (80 miles away). But rags I'd breeze there for them. I'm on this Bath Shower whatever ting.

After we bopped in Trocadero and I met some more girls. These girls were from Hammersmith and I got their numbers as well.

We bopped through London and we were just looking for skeet. We also went on MTV for a bit but not for long. When we were in Leicester square I met this nice girl from East London, I got her number as well.

Later on we breezed through China Town and I lost the crew because they nicked some drinks from a truck and we had to duss. So I just got the train to go Rachael's yard.

When I got to Rachael's she kept saying that I should have come earlier because all her family were out. But I got there when they just got back.

At Rachael's we watched a few films like always. At 10.30pm my mum rang me and she was in a mood and wanted me to come home. Terry was round my yard as well.

As I was leaving I said "see you tomorrow". Then gave her a little kiss then if just couldn't stop we just kept kissing for ages. I also fingered her a bit but not properly because she was wearing tight trousers and I was just putting my hands down. It was like when you're trying to get the screwball out of the ice cream, shit's difficult. I was doing all this for about 30 minutes before I left.

I got the bus about 11.25pm to go home. On the bus I met this guy from Slough who used to live in Hounslow and he was safe, just thought i'd mention that.

When I got home it was midnight. I ate some Indian that my mum got for dinner (that sounds sick). Terry was round as well. We watched the film Good Burger then went bed and just chat about the day. We got bare skeet, trust.

Sunday 28th February 1999 (the homework day remember)

Well as we all know today is the last day of February and it's been quite an alright month.

Today around 2pm me and Terry left my house. I left to go to Rachael's and Terry left to go home. We breezed down to the London Road bus stop and I was just checking what time the bus was coming. The bus was arriving at 2.34pm so I bopped with Terry to the train station.

When we got to the station I decided to get the train. My train came and Terry still had to wait 20 minutes. I got off at Ealing Broadway then went to Acton Town then Hounslow East. On the train I got a call from Simmons and he was telling me about last night. They all went down to London and it was supposed to be proper jokes, Fish got off with some drunk girl, Liam fingered a girl from Norway and they got bare booze off some van. But last night I was with Rachael, they still could have rang me though.

Anyway I got to Rachael's about 4pm which was the time I told my mum I was coming back. So I rang her and said I'd be home later.

At Rachael's we watched The Craft and later had dinner. We had some nasty roast dinner. But as I was being polite I said "thank you for the lovely dinner it was delicious", not.

My mum rang me about 7pm and she wanted me to come back. I gave Rachael a goodbye kiss then shit I couldn't let go of her. I said I'll stay another ten minutes.

We got into it so much we both started playing with each other – fingering, wanking, nipple sucking (both of us) and just doing dirtiness (if that's a word).

As I left I strangely remembered something. Someone once said to me after you finger a girl smell your fingers. So I smelt my fingers and "phew" they stank. It was a fishy smell (if you know what I mean).

When I got to the bus station I found out the next bus was in 45 minutes so I thought f**k it and I got the train from Hounslow East.

When I got to Ealing I breezed past the TM to get on the British Rail. Suddenly I heard "oi you", it was a f**king TM. He asked me for a ticket and where I got on from. I told him I got on from Ealing Common, the f**king c*nt made me pay 90p. After this I had only 58p which was not enough for anything. I just needed to get past the TM'S but didn't have enough.

I got the bus to Southall train station and on the bus was a fit skeet but I didn't cherpes her because she was with a boy, doh.

When I got to the station it was about 9pm, shit I wish I waited for that f**king bus in Hounslow now.

When I got home I had dinner then went bed. I also had a sexy dream of Rachael that night but I can't exactly remember it too well. You were hoping I was gonna write something really dirty innit you dirty bastards. I got loads of that shit already for your dirty pleasure.

Funniest thing all day:-

- Why do your pants smell of perfume?
- Tyson Mike – do you know Robert Peters, he's a militant brare
- In your dream I was in the corner.
- Go heaven God shows you how many times you w*nked.
- The germs still remain.

Did u know?

Karoke means "empty orchestra" in Japanese.

1st March 1999

The first of March is here, so who gives a f**k. But from now on I have decided every first of each month I am gonna write in my Diary, even if I have a shitty day.

Well today Terry was back at school. The last time he was in school was in November. But he still just only going to school because of the Court Welfare. After a month he is leaving again and going back to work.

After school I watched Deep Impact. At 7.00pm I got a call from Fish and he was telling me about Saturday and he was saying it was tick as well (damn I wish I was there, there would have been something for the Diary).

After that I breezed to Blockbusters to take the videos back. When I got in I did some homework and rang Rachel because she left some dirty messages on my phone. I also rang that girl from East London who I met on Saturday. I might be meeting her on Saturday. In the night I am going out with Rachel.

Funniest thing all day:-

- How much will the Diary be worth in the future? - Nothing, it's priceless.

Thursday 4th March 1999

Today I arrived at school late because someone had nicked Nicholas' bike and I used it for school. So I had to get a taxi to school.

School was alright today, Adam Irwin was making me laugh throughout today. I can't remember what he said, but remember today being jokes. After school I sneaked on the Colnbrook coach to get home. When I got to Colnbrook I got to the shops then waited for a bus to Langley. When the bus came and I got on the bus I only had 40p. But the man was safe and let me on free because I told him I was only going one stop, I lied it's about 8 maybe 9.

When I got in Fish came around and was telling me about his first day at Slough Grammar (he's moved school). Later on my Mum sent me round Brian G's house to get my bike because he had borrowed it. When I got there he wasn't there but I met Michael on the way and he was going to meet him. So I just told him to tell Brian to bring my bike back. Later Brian knocked and he gave my bike back.

Funniest thing all day:-

- Here's your wheels man!

Friday 5th March 1999

Today I got to school late f**k knows why, I mean I woke up at 7.30am. My first lesson was RE and that was shit. After, I had PSE and we did this thing about alcohol. We watched a film and it was quite good. The last three lessons were double Tech and Maths and they were all shit!

After school I rid home with JD. On the way home I met Fish and he was there for a while. When we left I had my dinner then got ready to go ice skating. Ben knocked for me so he came with me as well. When we got to Langley Train Station we met with Simmons and Fish. There were also lots of other people going ice skating and everyone was also talking about a massive fight that was supposed to be going on down there. When we got there Fish got us in free because he had tickets. Ice skating was really really shit, all we did was just walk around and chat to people we knew. Plus i kept falling over and that's not enjoyable. We met up with Hanghei and Clint but they got thrown out straight away because they never paid to get in.

After ice skating there wasn't any fight, but who really cares. So we breezed down to McDonalds. Simmons was asking me and Fish if we wanted to go to London to link Nicholas, Guv and Wayne Flex (the time was 11.30pm). We went to the station with him and got the train back to Langley but Simmons stayed on to go to London.

When I got in I relaxed and thought shame to Simmons, Guv and Wayne because they are outside in the cold doing f**k all.

Funniest thing all day:-

- BIG – You make me sick - Porno Wanking
- Terry Loveridge started longest shurrrrrrrrrrrrrrrrt up (volume control)

6ᵗʰ March 1999

Today when I awoke I felt really good for some reason. I had quite a nice sleep. I had a nice dream about Rachel again. Around 11.00am Fish rang and said he'd meet me outside New Directions (the place where I get my haircut) after I get my haircut.

At 1.00pm I left to get my haircut. I got there about 1.20pm, Justin was there and he just finished getting a trim and he said he'd wait for me.

Whilst I was getting my haircut, the hairdresser crew were jokes. They were cussing me about my shoe size, but they were only messing about. It was still funny. After, me and Justin went into the Kebab shop and waited for Michael. I had a militant little kebab with bare chilli sauce, it was dark! When Fish came we bopped to Slough Young People's Centre. Only because Justin asked us to come. Me and Fish chilled in there for about half an hour and thought, "this is shit let us go"!

We were gonna go Reading but then we couldn't be f**ked so we got the bus back to my yard. We met some of Lauren's friends on the way and I asked them if they wanted to come round my yard for a bit. They said no though, shame.

When I got in Simmons rang and said yesterday he went to Paddington and them lot weren't there. So he went straight back to Langley.

After I rang Rachael, if you don't know we're not going on a date but I'm going round her house and we're just gonna watch a film and have a little sex, I hope.

I got Rachael's yard about 8.15pm. When I got there we watched "Dusk till Dawn". Rachael wanted to watch it because she said the last time she was watching it she was having sex and couldn't watch it properly.

After we watched Candyman. After Candyman we put on Money Train but didn't really watch it we were just kissing and ting. After Money Train we put on The Rock. While we were watching it Rachael started getting really horny and got on top of me and started wobbling her sexy tits in my face.

We were gonna have sex today but she didn't have any condoms, neither did I. It did feel like we had sex though. I fingered her for about an hour and she was really enjoying it because she started squeezing me really tight. She also gave me a lovely little wank.

At one point we were masturbating each other really fast and I had about 4 fingers up her. This was also nice because we were both naked and were all sweating and hot. We were licking each other all other, it's the 90's man kids are dirtier.

The time was about 4am when we stopped messing about. I was lying in the bed with her and started falling asleep so I slept in the spare bed, like I was supposed to be.

Funniest thing all day:-

- No more crunchie explosions- don't f**king lie
- Err no – kebab man
- That brare still saying than after all this time

Did u know?

Yesterday was first OTT of this month

Sunday 7th March 1999

Today I woke up at 12pm and Rachael's mum came in the room and was asking if I'd like a cup of tea (typical English people). But it was too early. I breezed downstairs and had some crusty egg sandwich which Rachael made for breakfast.

After breakfast me and Rachael went back upstairs and watched the film Demolition Man. After we watched Speed and during this we started messing about. I started kissing her and "shit" my tongue was killing me and I couldn't really kiss her, too much kissing last night.

About 6.50pm I left Rachel's. Rachael walked me to the bus station and saw me off.

When I got in I did some homework and got a call from Simmons and he was asking if I shagged Rachael but I never, who cares anyway.

Funniest thing all day:-

- In your face mate

300 days left, to the millennium you dick.

Did u know?

The first mobile phone arrived in Britain on Jan 1st 1985

Tuesday 9th March 1999

In the morning I got to school a little bit late because I was relaxing in bed and was tired. When I got to school my maths teacher came running up to me and said "hurry you're supposed to be in an exam". I f**king forgot all about the Maths exam I was doing today. It didn't really matter though because I missed ten minutes, which I had at the end.

When I got in from school I listened to this tape what Latoya lent me with the new mix of Shine On (spirit of the sun), I needed this tune.

After, I watched Wrestlemania 8 because JD lent me it yesterday and I really wanted to see it, I haven't seen it in time.

My mum came home about 5.15pm then I got ready to go Kickboxing. But I never went because I started eating, but I really must go if I want to fight this month, and also to keep practice.

Later on Fish (Fish is Michael P from now on I am just going to write MJP because Fish is out of order). As I was saying MJP came round and we just listened to a few tunes and played a bit of Tekken 3. MJP left about 9.00pm and then I just went downstairs to watch TV. I am writing my diary at this very moment and the times is 9.20pm and in a minute I am gonna watch True Lies. I might ring my darling Rachel as well.

Funniest thing all day:-

• Crunchie explosion not over yet - one more left (fainted)

Also - can't be fucked to ring Rachel might ring her tomorrow - oh shit I forgot I can't ring anyway she has changed her number and it comes on tomorrow.

Also - cast your mind back to February 27th, I still need to ring the girl I met in Trocadero, I've rang the girl from Bath and the East London girl.

Did u know?

That Russia used to be part of USA until the Ice Age split up and then hundreds of years to float to the other side.

That Britain used to be a part of Europe but the same thing happened (it split up).

Friday 12th March 1999 (Comic Relief - Red Nose Day)

In the morning JD came round to ride to school with me. Today was Red Nose Day and we also had a non uniform day, but the thing is you have to pay £1. So we thought f**k it and got to school late so we wouldn't have to pay. At school today it was just a normal day, I thought it would be a fun day so I didn't bring any equipment (I was f**ked).

At break today there was a doughnut sale and I did the lamest thing. I just grabbed the box of doughnuts and just legged it. I got caught though so I gave them about a £1 (I got 10 doughnut though).

After school I was chilling with Adam because today was his last day at Churchmead and in Datchet. When he left I chilled for a bit with Lisa Barney, Najwa, Yvonne and Moppy.

As soon as I got in Simmons rang and said that everyone was meeting at 5.30pm to go to Extravaganza, but this was a bit gay because I had only just got in and the time was about 4.30pm. So we decided to leave about 6.00pm. Me and Simmons breezed round Sean's yard. We waited for Nicholas and Wayne and when they came we left. We went to this shop down Parlaunt Road (one stop) and we razed so much booze it was unbelievable. The people in the shop were so thick all we were doing were walking in the shop and blatantly putting it under our coats.

Here's a list of what we got:-

1. 2 x Old English - Lager (3 litres each)
2. Some other lager
3. 8 small bottles of Beer (can't remember label)
4. Woodpecker - Cider
5. Scrumpy Jack - Cider

We also got an Easter egg and a few other sweets. After, we carried all our booze to the train station. Down the station we met Guv and he was coming as well. I didn't want to drink too much drink in case I got f**ked, and also today they were talking about the way drink affects you and it goes straight to your heart. So that's why I didn't drink that much.

OTT I did drink a bit more and this got me tipsy, but that's all I drank after that. When we got to Ealing we got the bus to Acton (it's in Acton not Ealing this time) we got there about 9.00pm. This left us about 3 hours.

When I was inside the club I felt f**ked from the drink so I just chilled. I also chatted to any girl that was going past.

I did get this girl's number but she was a bit fat but I can get away with that because I was a bit drunk. But what was the lamest thing is that I got off with this girl. Well not exactly I thought it was lame on my girlfriend so it was only for a few seconds.

Later on we were all chilling in this rest bit when this light skinned girl with some f**king beautiful tits called me. This girl was really hyper and always laughing, well she called me and said "oh bredwin come and sit on my knee." I thought, later, and sat on her knee. She just chatted bare shit, her and her friends. I went to get the girl's number when this bad tune came on and she got up and said "this is a tune" and just bopped off and I lost her. (Life's a bitch).

Later around 11.15pm Simmons, Guv, Wayne and Sean left. Well Sean got thrown out earlier for fighting. It was me and Nicholas, I cherped some girl but she said she doesn't give her number out and she didn't take mine because she didn't have a pen.

After cherpsing that skeet me and Nicholas left. I wanted to stay longer but Nicholas was leaving so I left. I also wanted to find that girl with the titties.

We met up with the crew but we got the train to Ealing and they waited for a bus. When we got to Ealing we got on a train and the time was about 12.10am.

OTT - Sean gave some 19 year old girl his number and he thinks he used a good chat up line by saying "I beg you, give me your number." Anyways them lot stayed on the train to Slough whilst I got off at Langley.

I breezed down to the kebab shop, I only had £2 and the man let me off. But let me tell you something the kebab I got was so f**king lovely it was the best kebab I have ever had in my life. It was just tick, boom, brilliant, excellent, militant, yaze, beautiful, sexy, delicious, fantastic and it just basically tasted dark.

When I got in I was so hyper I wished I was still out. I really wanted that big titty girl, I better see her again. I was even gonna go into London again, but them lot didn't want to (that makes a change).

There was some free pornos on so I watched them. I also played this bad tune that was going through my head all day, then after, I went and watched this film Face Off.

Also - meeting Rachel tomorrow to make her feel better. She's sick.

Also - rang that girl from Trocadero and the funny thing is she lives right by Rachel, but her friend lives in Hammersmith.

Funniest thing all day:-

• Nicking drink. in and out of shop.

Did u know?

The hippo's name is from the Greek word potumus meaning river and hippo meaning horse- river horse

Saturday 13th March 1999

In the morning I got a call from Jason and Rachael. They both wanted me to bop down their areas. So I said to Jason I'll come down and told Rachael I'll come down after.

I left my yard at 1.20pm to get the 1.30pm train to Hanwell. When I got to the station the train was right there and I just breezed on. OTT I met MJP and he came with me. Also saw Adrian at the village shops, ain't seen that brare in time.

Anyways we got off at Hanwell station then bopped to the shop. We went in the shop and there was no one in the shop. Me and MJP just looked at each other then started loading our pockets with bare sweets, drinks and chocolates. We almost got caught though because the man was only behind the counter knelling down.

When we got out the shop we just started benning up (laughing out loud) and eating our bare munch.

On the way I met Cass and he was really safe, he gave me £10. Then we knocked for Jason. We gave him some chocolates because we were feeling proper sick.

We decided to breeze down to central London (like always). We went to Paddington then got the tube to Piccadilly. O yeah shit also on the way to Paddington I cherpes this woman and got her number. She was 22 and believed I was 18 she also was Swedish and very very sexy.

Anyway, when we got to Piccadilly we chilled round Troc. After we breezed down Leicester square to go on MTV. We did kind of get on TV but not exactly (you could just see our fat heads).next to the place where they have MTV is a cafe and we went in there because there were bare skeet in there and there was a very sexy waitress.

As we were leaving we started chatting up these 3 girls from some place near Enfield. They were quite nice but I think they gave us the wrong numbers.

After that we left. I got on a different train because I was going to visit Rachel, she's sick; I'll make her feel better.

When I got there I just watched a bit of TV and we messed about. Today I was really focusing on her tits. I was f**king going mad on um. I couldn't be bothered to finger her so it was just titties today (o well).

About 9.30pm Jason and MJP rang me and were asking me to come back because they were staying round my yard. I left at 10pm and got home about 11pm (I got the bus).

Them lot came round and were moaning at me because I always come back late when I go round Rachel's, well what do you expect.

Today the boxing was on it was the big fight between Lewis and Holyfield.

Later on Simmons, Guv and Sean knocked, they had come from a party just down the road. They said they didn't ring me because they thought I was staying round sexy Rachel's house.

They all came round and we waited for the boxing to come on. While we waited we just watched a few pornos and TVX. The fight came on about 4am and most of us were half asleep. But we did watch it. It was a good fight but ended up as a draw and Lewis clearly won it. It was so f**ked up, I feel sorry for Lennox Lewis, man.

After we all tried to get to sleep. WHY WAS 6 SCARED OF 7 BECAUSE 7 89

Funniest things all day:

- "BARE RAZE"
- I GOT SCHOOL IN THE MORNING (TIME 10AM)

DID U KNOW?

SOME FRENCH WORDS ACTUALLY ORIGINATE FROM ARAB COUNTRIES.

Sunday 14th March 1999

When everyone left in the morning, me and Jason just had some massive breakfast. We didn't wanna eat in front of them or they would have wanted some (couldn't be f**ked to make loads). My toasties are too boom, mans go nuts for um.

Later on me and Jason decided we were gonna go into London, but then we couldn't because we didn't have any money. Jason still needed to get back to Hanwell though, so we thought we'd go Ealing then from Ealing to Boston Manor (then just bop from there).

When we got to the station the next train to London was in 45 minutes. So we got the train to Slough and waited for the fast train straight to Ealing. But this train was in about 30 minutes and there was a train going Paddington so we thought we'd get on that train then get one from Ealing Broadway. When we got to Paddington Jason wanted to walk to Piccadilly Circus but I told him how far it was and he just thought f**k it (about 3-4 miles). So we just breezed round Paddington. We had no money at all and just bopped the streets hungry and tired. So we thought f**k lets go.

When we got on the train I stayed on the train to Langley because I wanted to get home and I had no money. But Jason got off at Ealing to go Boston Manor and then bop home (all the way to Hanwell).

When I got home I slept for a bit because I hardly got any sleep last night. JD rang a bit later and was asking if I could bring his bag round because I left it on Friday. After I finished chatting to JD I rang a few girls just to catch up on some (they forget after a while). I rang Hannah from Newbury Park in East London and I'm meeting her on Saturday during the day. I also rang sexy Claire and guess what she wants to go out with me on Saturday night. The only problem is Rachel wants to stay on Saturday. After all she is my girlfriend. But I might choose Claire.

Around 8pm I breezed round JD'S. I played some computer and borrowed 2 wrestling videos then left.

On the way home I met Simmons and Guv and they were just going Chris's yard. When I got in I wrote in my diary good bye

Funniest thing all day:-

- Man on train- smiling reading newspaper.

DID U KNOW?

THE WORD MONTH COMES FROM THE MOON

Wednesday 17th March ST Patrick's Day

This morning I woke up about 7am for school. But then thought F**k it it's too early I'll go sleep for about 20 minutes, then opened my eyes and it was 8am.

JD knocked so I rushed to get to school. I didn't even have any breakfast. But when I got in to Datchet I bought some breakfast (an iced bun and a sprite).

School was so much jokes today. Matthew Kenworthy was just taking the piss out of Jonny about his wrestling and it was so funny. Jonny said him and his brothers have fights against business men, Asians and a group called the Adams Family (he's f**ked up). But it's all shit, seriously if you heard him say it you'd know. He even looks so serious when he says it.

Later on MJP knocked and we went round this girl, Jodie's yard. We only stayed for about ½ an hour then breezed.

On the way home I was telling him my story ToySstack 2. We were just creasing up and we also chatted about Jonny and the way he wrestles business men. We've got some mental people at our school.

When I got in I watched this thing called Foul Play which was about people fighting in sport.

F**k I'm tired good night.

Funniest thing all day:-

- The business men- JD- power slam MJP running him
- JD brother 23 scimby shorts
- Toy Stack 2- man with two sides

DID U KNOW?

IT TAKES 8 MINUTES FOR LIGHT TO TRAVEL FROM THE SUN TO EARTH.

Friday 19th March 1999

Today was the most f**ked up day ever. I'll tell you all about it now.

In the morning I rid to school with JD .School was alright today but was just a normal day, if you know what I mean. After school everyone was ringing me to see if I was coming E&D, and I was. Around 6.50pm every one came to my yard (well not everyone Michael, Liam, Simmons and Nicholas). We left about 7.30pm to get to the train station.

We got on the train to Slough then we were gonna go back (it's the same train). On the train we did our little M.Cing thing in the driver's bit. When the train arrived at Slough there was bare TM's getting on the train looking for us because we went in the driver's bit.

As we got off there was a train to Southall and we got on it, but got thrown off straight away. So we just got a ticket to Langley just to get on the train. But it left and we went to get on the first train we were going on. But the driver didn't let us on because he said we were messing about (which we were, but still).

They kept throwing us off the trains so in the end we all chipped in for a taxi to get on a train at Langley.

When we got Langley there were 3 girls who Liam knew. He started messing about with this girl and took a tenner off her, he then passed it to me but I gave it straight back. These girls then left to go Slough.

We got the train and the time was about 9pm.when the train arrived at Hayes there was barP police and we were thinking what the f**k is going on? Suddenly we had to get off the train and the Police arrested us for suspicion of robbery. We didn't really care that much because we knew we had done no robbery and were innocent.

We had to go to Uxbridge Police Station. We went there in a police van. When we got to the station I was in the van for about half an hour on my jaze hand cuffed. When I got in the station I had all my stuff taken and had to answer a few questions like age, name address etc. I did ring my mum when I was in the van and told her I didn't do nothing.

After, the man put me in a cell. The cell was f**ked up. The bed was just a bit of wood the toilet was really low down and it was HuHH. When I was in the cell I didn't know what to do, so I did a bit of kickboxing for about half an hour.

After I was just walking up and down and just doing F**k all.

The time was about 11pm when I went in the cell. This man kept checking on me throughout the night. I left the cell about 3.10am; Simmons's mum's boyfriend took us home. I still have to go back tomorrow at 6pm for an interview.

When I got in I chatted to my mum about the incident then had something to eat. Then went to bed. See wasn't that a f**ked up day. It's probably gonna ruin my life (goes on record).

There's also another thing, the person who got robbed was that girl at Langley station who we took the tenner off. She lied and said we robbed her (the f**king bitch).

Funniest thing all day:-

- (STILL LAUGHING WHEN BEING CHARGED FOR ROBBERY AND CRIMINAL DAMAGE)
- 54544HuHH

Saturday 20 March 1999

Today my mum has grounded me for being innocent. She said because I'm in trouble with Police (yeah but I'm still innocent).

In the morning I watched another one of JD's wrestling videos then cut the grass and did bare housework. My mum made me do bare shit.

About 5pm me and my mum left my house to go to the interview. We stopped at Simmons shop for a bit and chatted a bit about last night. I also tried to get some condoms but Simmons manager was watching me. It's because Rachel's hopefully staying round tonight but I'm not sure because my mum's pissed off.

We got to Slough police station about 5.15pm and waited for the P.C to come. The P.C came about 6.15pm and he interviewed me. In the interview he mentioned the thing on the train (MCing in the driver's bit) but I just denied it and said it must have looked like I was doing it because I was walking up and down OTT. He also talked about the robbery thing and I just told him the truth. But what the girls said is that I handed them a bit of rubbish and nicked the £10.

When we got in, Rachel rang from home and was asking if she was still staying. My mum said she couldn't but I said she was already on the bus and on her way, so my mum said "she has to stay then" (militant liar).

Rachel got to Langley about 9.30pm then I went to the bus stop to meet her. She came to my yard and met my mum and my mum really liked her. We chilled in my room then around 12am went downstairs. We watched a bit of TV and just messed about. I still haven't had sex with her and everyone's getting on my nerves about it. But I'm quite sensible and won't get pressured in doing it or feeling embarrassed just because I've been with her for a month and a week and still haven't done it. It doesn't really matter that much to me anyway.

There were 2 reasons we didn't have sex:-

1. She was on her period
2. No Johnnies

I fell asleep about 3am and I think she stayed up.

DID U KNOW?

Approximately 70% of children with migraines have a close relative who has it

Sunday 21st March 1999

In the morning my mum went to a car boot sale with Yongy (Alex). Me and Rachel just went upstairs she went to sleep and I watched some kiddies morning shows.

Later on me and Rachel watched 2 films then she got ready to leave. As she was leaving I gave her a nice little back message, she was lying on her belly and I was just rubbing her up and down. It was nice.

At 4.15pm I walked her to the bus stop and the bus got there early and we just missed it (well she did) and because it was Sunday we had to wait an hour. As I was waiting I rang JD to breeze round and get his films.

When the bus came I gave Rachel a kiss goodbye and then she gave me a card and said don't open it until you get home. On the way home I met JD and he breezed to my yard and we watched a bit of this video. O shit yeah I also opened that card and it was just a card saying I really like you I hope feel the same way to. It was quite nice of her to do that. Anyway JD left about 7.45pm then I went to the kebab shop and got some dinner.

At this moment I'm watching the Shawshank Redemption on BBC 4. I'm gonna go upstairs now and watch it in bed.

Funniest thing all day:-

- Power Rangers VS Teenage Mutant Ninja Turtles on tv
- JD – Royal Rumble (Drawn 17)

Did u know?

In 1449 James 2nd begins to rule Scotland

Monday 22nd March 1999

Today I woke up about 7am for school. I had breakfast then like always JD knocked. We got school quite early today but not that early.

Loads of people were talking to me about me getting arrested (information travels fast). I thought how the f**k do these people know.

Today school was not too bad there was a fight today with two girls, Vicky and some Somalian girl. It was also jokes because Jonny was talking to me about he had a fight with business men on the weekend. He won the fight with a powerdriver he said. If you powerdrivered someone in a real fight they'd be dead.

I rid home with JD today, yeah that's all I wanted to say you prick.

When I got in I watched another wrestling video. F**k I've been watching so many wrestling videos lately. I'm worried. But I aint watched it since Wrestlemania 10 I wanna catch up. There's new people like Stone Cold Geza. What happened to the Nasty Boys and the Ultimate Warrior. The Bush Whackers used to bite peoples battys as their finishing move.

When my mum got in I just stayed in my room watching a few videos (I think you know which ones) and did a little homework.

Later on I got a call from Danielle and she was just chatting some fartness.

After I got a call from Jo and she asking if I wanted to probably go out on Saturday, but I said maybe. The thing is there's Rachel and also I think there's a party in Harrow on Saturday. I also badly wanna go out with that girl Claire. But I might be grounded, damn. But there's one thing I know for sure I'm getting a trim, grounded or not grounded I'm not meeting girls looking like someone from Jackson 5. I'm going to sleep now so have a nice day.

Funniest thing all day:-

- DANIEL MOUTAIN-School with Mr. Booth- I'm going to see your wife- I've got English
- Shout out to Robert Peters, he just so sexy- at ice-skating.

Robb Peters

Jokes

There were two flies on a woman's pussy which one was on drugs?

THE ONE ON THE CRACK

Why do cannibals not eat clowns?

BECAUSE THEY TASTE FUNNY

DID U KNOW?

FERTILLIZERS ARE SUBSTANCES THAT HELP PLANTS GROWTH BY PROVIDING THE SOIL WITH VITAL ELEMENTS.

Wednesday 24th March 1999

Nothing much happened today I was just in the mood for W.I.D (writing in Diary). All I did today was go school and then later MJP came round.

Well tomorrow I'm getting £30, do you wanna know why. Ok here's the story.

It was a nice Tuesday evening and I was just on my bike riding home. When I noticed a phone on the ground slightly broken. It was working though. So I took it home and made bare calls (spoke to Rachel for an hour). There was also a game on it (SNAKE), this phone was bad. Anyway I took it to school and showed Kenworthy and he's willing to pay me thirty quid for it, with no cover and can't even see the buttons.

Well that's my story.

Funniest thing all day:-

- Throwing penny

DID U KNOW?

THE MOVIE DANGEROUS MINDS WAS WRITTEN BY STEVIE WONDER (THE BLIND MAN)

Thursday 25th March

Well today didn't go as well as I planned. I never got that £30 because the phone had a special security lock thing. We found this out because Kenwothy had his chip and we tried it. All through today we were trying to get through the lock but couldn't.

Didn't do anything else after so bye you can go now.

Also – gave the phone to friend that is trying to get through the lock

Funniest thing all day:-

- Girl tripped

DID U KNOW?

IN 1932 AMERICAN PRESIDENT ROSEVELT WAS ELECTED.

Friday 26th March 1999

Today I really couldn't be bothered to go school because it's last day, half a day and not exactly gonna learn anything (Easter holiday).

Today I just slept and watched some TV. About 1.30pm Rachel rang and asked if I still wanted her to come round, of course I said yes. I met Rachel at 2pm at the dirty Hounslow bus station. She just left straight from school and was in her uniform.

When we got to my house we watched a film then went to my room to mess about. There's also another thing, she's scared to have sex in case she gets pregnant or gets a disease, has done it before but is trying to be careful. I do understand what she means and I think she's right, I'd use protection anyway.

At 5pm my mum came home which was a bit f**ked up cos at this time I had my fingers half way up Rachel's "BLEEP".

Around 6.30pm I walked Rachel to the bus stop and waited with her for the bus. When it came I lipsed her then went home to get ready to go kickboxing.

But I never ended up going kickboxing cos I got home at 7pm then ate some dinner and the time was 7.30pm (kickboxing starts at 6pm).

Tonight I never went out, just stayed in. My mum did though; she went to some Salsa night thing. But me, I stayed in and watched some TV. My mum got home about 12am and she was all excited she was telling all about her night out. I wasn't really listening because I was half asleep on the sofa.

Also- saw Rachel's school book and all over them say ;

Rachel and Robert 4ever

Rachel and Robert 100%

To be honest with you I never known a girl that likes me so much.

Saturday 27th March 1999

Today I woke up about 8.00am because my body is so used to getting up early for school it came naturally. So as I was up I watched some Kenan and Kel, it was jokes.

Around 12.50pm I left my drum to go and get my haircut. On the way I stopped off at Simmons' shop and got a few things like some glasses, sweets and some condoms. I waited in Simmons' shop for the bus and guess what the f**king bus came at 1.30pm which was the time I had my appointment.

When I got there I met MJP and he was saying he missed his appointment too. So I went to see if I could still get my haircut but I never so I got an appointment for Tuesday at 3.00pm.

Me and MJP got a little kebab then decided to, like always breeze into London. But first MJP wanted to go to Simmons' work and get more stuff because I showed him what I got and he wanted to get some stuff as well.

We didn't get any stuff because the manager was watching us so we just went to the station and got OTT to London. OTT I got a call from Rachel and she was asking me if I wanted to stay tonight, but I'm going to some party down the road.

When we got to London we breezed around looking for girls but couldn't find none. So we went (stayed for about an hour). MJP wanted to go Reading instead so we got OTT to go there. The train stopped at Slough so we thought f**k reading and got off at Slough. We then got the train to Langley.

MJP came to my yard and I had some dinner then my mum let me go out (was grounded remember). We bopped to this party which was held at Horsemoor Green youth centre. It was £5 to get in but we didn't go in because there were only three girls and everyone was saying it was shit. So we chilled outside for a while.

A bit later on, around 10pm loads of people came and we just breezed in for free. We M.Ced there and everyone thought we were bad. After the party Clint Eastwood almost had a fight with G because G nicked his bike. Clint sparked him round the face then G suddenly out of nowhere pulled out a baseball bat and was trying to hit him. Nothing really happened after that they both just walked off, but everyone was saying G should have fought him without the weapon. I just think its all stupidness to tell you the truth. Well I left and I don't know if anything happened after but I doubt it because they both walked different ways, if you know what I'm chatting about. When I got in I just relaxed and wrote in my fabulous diary.

Funniest thing all day:-

- APS- Super goal (jumping)
- Illegal to take a piss – cops pull up and check your dick
- MJP chatting at party- I want to know

DID U KNOW?

IF A CATS EARS ARE FLATTENED CLOSED TO THE HEAD THIS INDICATES A CAT IS IN A BAD MOOD.

83

Sunday 28th March 1999

Today around 1ish JD came round. We just played a bit of computer and shit. Later on my mum asked me if I would go to blockbusters and get her a film. So me and JD left, I didn't have my bike so I gave JD lift.

When I got blockbuster videos I rented the film kiss the girls then I went to JD's for a bit and played a little football but didn't stay long because I wanted to go home and get some dinner.

Around 6ish I was ringing bare local friends because I wanted Sarah Elliman's number. This was because today we were supposed to be going to a club in Staines with her. But no one had her number. But we still decided to go.

Later on, Ben Smith and MJP came round and we got ready to go to this place in Staines. But we didn't end up going because the time was 8.45pm and by the time we would get there it would be finishing. So them two stayed for a bit and watched a bit of Gremlins 2 but left and I just watched TV on my jaze.

Well anyway now I'm going bed because tomorrow I've got to be up early. I'm going to see a solicitor at my mum's work place. This is because of the incident last week.

Funniest thing all day:-

- Gas fire – cook brother
- South park-alien one

DID U KNOW?

THERE HAVE BEEN MAMMALS LIVING ON THE EARTH FOR OVER 200 MILLION YEARS- LONGER THE US OBVIOUSLY.

Monday 29th March 1999

Today I woke up at 7am to get ready to go with my mum to her work. We left about 7.30ish then got the bus to Slough.

When we got to Slough we then had to get a train to Windsor which was gay because I had to buy a ticket (they have machines).

The place where my mum works is quite small I was expecting some big f**k off solicitors office place, if you get what I'm chatting about. It was an old Windsor house but actually when I got inside it was quite big.

My mum's office is some small piece of shit but she likes it. I helped my mum a bit with her work until the geza came to see me.

When I met the guy he just chatting about last week and what happened. I told him it all and now he's coming with me on April 8th (this solicitor was free by the way).

I left my mum's work about 10am and on the way home, and don't know why I'm writing this (just thought i'd mention it). Well saw these two fit girls and they were blatantly looking at me and I didn't even cherpes them.

I got the train back to slough then bopped through Slough because I needed to go Blockbusters and take some videos back. After I took it back, I got the bus home.

When I got in I rang JD and told him I was coming over to give his bike back. I then rang Rachel to tell her I was coming over early (remember this is still morning).

When I got JD's I watched a bit of Wrestlemania 15 and played some computer. I left his house about 2pm then JD waited with me until the bus arrived. So "shur tup".

When I got to Rachel's the time was about 3.30pm and Rachel's mum was saying some shit about they made a bet to see what time I would arrive (and she won).

In the night I slept in Rachel's room again but her little sister was there today sleeping in the top bunk. I was sleeping in the bed with Rachel just messing about.

Today when I was fingering her I was using a special technique which I saw off a movie. But f**k you I'm not explaining it, so "shur tup".

85

Later on it was so f**ked up, we started to have sex but guess f**king what her fanny was sore from where I had been playing. She kept going "ouch" and "go slow because it hurts". This was so funny. Also her little sister woke up and Rachel was trying to get her back to sleep. But she wouldn't sleep (the bitch) so we didn't have proper sex.

Funniest thing all day:-

- Kenan and Kel- monkey head
- Dog fight

DID U KNOW?

YOU CAN GET TO SOUTHEND BY GETTING A TRAIN FROM LIVERPOOL STREET STATION.

Tuesday 30th March 1999

Today I woke up at 12pm Rachel was going out with her Dad.

Anyway I stayed at Rachel's and just chatted to her mum. She just chatted about her wedding and shit. And showed me Rachael's baby photos. I got jealous there was a picture with Rachael naked in the bath with some brare. She was only 2 but still that's rude. I used to piss in the bath when I was `little. The water would go yellow. The coco pops effect.

ANYWAY around 1.30pm Rachel came back and at this time I had to leave so Rachel walked me to the Bus Station and saw me off. I got the bus all the way to Slough and the time was 3.00pm. The reason I left so early was because I was getting my haircut.

When I arrived there, MJP was there. He got his haircut after me. After, we didn't know what to do so we went to JD's house. It was jokes, MJP was was jokes. Later on at home, little Ryan and Terrie knocked for me then we went over to Simmons' drum to see what he was up to. Simmons was going to London with Wayne Flex and he was asking if I wanted to come. All three of us went to London and got the train from Slough. When we arrived at London we had to go to Edgware Road Station because we couldn't get through at Paddington. We got the train to Piccadilly Circus, we just chilled round Troc and then Leicester Square. We didn't get any girls today but it was alright.

We left about 12.00am to get the last tube. When we got to the station I got caught trying to get through the machines so I thought I'd walk to Paddington (them lot got on the tube). I started walking and when I was about Regent Street this woman (about 49) came up to me and asked me if I had 50p. I just said "sorry I don't have any money." Then the woman started saying "I've just been thrown out of this club by my husband, I have nowhere to go, what I shall do?" I just said "f**k knows."

I was with this woman for over half an hour and every time I tried to leave she kept saying "Robert, don't leave me, everyone always walks away from me." I felt a bit sorry so I rang her husband for her and let her speak to him. He was telling her to just go home but she didn't have any money or anything.

I did manage to lose this woman, and when I did I was at Oxford Circus, I ran hard, and it was about 2 miles. When I got to the station I luckily got the train and met Simmons and Wayne. And because I was so hot, I just stripped on the train (I was proper tired from bare running).

When we got back to Slough we went in Tesco and Wayne nicked bare shit like drinks and crisps. When we got back to my drum I and Simmons watched a few pornos and then Simmons left about 3.30am. I then went to bed.

Funniest things all day:-

- Get out of here (the tune)
- Wayne's stories £4.99
- Off key Business Man
- Come I sit down

Wednesday 31st March 1999

Today I had a nice little lay in. I woke up about 2.00pm. I got a call from Rachel, JD and some other people, but I said I could not be f**ked to go anywhere today. I was actually gonna go to Rachael's today but I told her that it probably wasn't worth it. Because I'm probably going Pulse today. Rachel seemed pissed off when I told her but I thought, why is she pissed off when she can see me any other day.

Later on Rachel rang back and was saying she was sorry for being so rude on the phone. I just said it's alright and than forgetting I was going out, I asked her to stay. She said yes, of course. (Getting lift in car).

When she arrived we went to Langley Village because I had to get out some money from the cashpoint. We were gonna get a video but we couldn't be bothered to go to Blockbusters in Slough.

Well today I can't be bothered to write what me and Rachel did so all I am going to write is then we watched a film and then messed about. Plus I think that bitch might be reading the diary. Just joking babes you're not a bitch. Kiss kiss

DID U KNOW?

1996 was supposed to be the Millennium because the years began when Jesus was 4 years old

April Fool's Day – 1st April 1999

Like I said every first of the month I'm gonna WID even if I have a shitty day. But today was alright a bit tiring but OK. Well in the morning Rachel got ready to leave. I also got a call from Adam Irwin and he was asking if I was still coming around, and I was.

Well I tidied up, then walked Rachel to the bus stop and walked with her until the bus came. When I left Rachel I knocked for MJP then we got on the train to go to Shepperton to go to Adam's. We got the train to Slough, then Windsor, then Staines, and then at Staines we got a bus that took us to Shepperton Train Station. Shepperton was some crusty countryside area.

At the station I rang Adam and he told us how to get to his drum, so we bopped there. When we got there Adam came out with us and we knocked for this girl called Coco. She was alright, the only thing was she was young but looked older.

We breezed down to this park and on the way we met two ugly girls that came with us. In the park we just chilled and chatted to these girls.

The time was about 7.30pm when we left and I thought I'd get that Coco's number, so I did. We decided to get the train home and we knew it would take long but didn't really care. The bus also took the piss (coming like some every hour). The only bus I saw was the bus we got on. These areas are dry.

The train took so f**king long it was so offkey. We went to Teddington, then Twickenham, then one more to Windsor. At Teddington I got this girl's number, she is not too bad.

When we got to Windsor we got some McyD's then got the train home.

When I got in it was 11.00pm and Simmons came round to get his tape. I also relaxed because I was so tired (out all day).

At this moment I am watching Sphere and just hoping this month will be a good one. Well tomorrow is Good Friday, I think I'm going to church in the morning, not sure if I can wake up.

Funniest Things All Day:-

- Sick Brare - Bus Driver - Where you going?
- Head Butt - Adam Irwin
- Train - Wrong Way - MJP Scream
- Laughing at Woman trip – chase (through water)
- Tell the guy at Slough
- Beaten up Adam's bro - Sick Dog
- Bus to Slough
- Wanking over Dog
- Willy Out
- Chase OTT

Robb Peters

DID U KNOW?

SHARON STONE WAS BORN IN 1959, SHIT OLDER THEN MY MUM

Friday 2ⁿᵈ April 1999

Today is Good Friday. My mum went to church today but I stayed in bed because I was proper tired. Well I celebrated my Good Friday shaking out with some garage tunes, fool.

Later in the day I got a call from Rachel and she was asking if I wanted to go cinema with her. I said alright then. So Rachel said I'm leaving then, the time was about 12pm.

Rachel arrived about 1.30pm and today I didn't have to meet her at the bus stop because she remembered where I lived and knocked.

As we were gonna go to Slough Cinema, Rachel said "Robert I've gotta go home first" I thought what the f**k is the point of coming all the way to Slough then going home. But we went to Feltham Cinema anyway. On the way to the bus station I had to go to the cashpoint to get out some money.

When we got to Rachel's yard she got ready and ting (she got undressed in front of me). The time was about 7.30pm and we got the 235 bus from Hounslow to Feltham. We got to the cinema at 8.00pm which was f**ked up because all the good films started about 9 ish. The film we wanted to see was Urban Legends but it started at midnight. Allow that we thought.

We saw the film Blast from the Past. It was alright I suppose but not that good. It was quite funny at times. Today was different, the cinema, from when we went the first time, maybe because last time we didn't know each other and basically weren't all over each other (we were sitting at the back). And catching jokes. I threw a popcorn at this man's head, 4 pieces.

After the movie I rang my Mum (the time was 11.00pm) and said I was staying at Rachel's because it was too late to come home. We got to Rachel's about midnight I didn't do nothing with Rachel today because tomorrow she has work in the morning.

FIVE MONTHS OF DIARY, YEAH MAN!

Funniest Things all Day:-

- Trying to bop - Asian Guy
- Fat Girl Dancing - Cinema
- Rachel running

Also, my Mum found Johnnies in my pocket and now she is acting gay, if you know what I mean. But how can you blame her she's a Mum.

DID U KNOW?

WEARING SUN GLASSES WHILST WATCHING TV CAN F**K UP YOUR EYES.

Saturday 3rd April 1999

Today I woke up at 12.00pm and Rachel had already left for work. Rachel's little brother was annoying me this morning because he kept dancing.

Most of the evening Rachel's parents were out and I was on my own but this didn't matter because I was just drinking away on the Bailey's Cream. It doesn't really matter though because it has been there for ages and I have never seen anyone drink it.

Also, all day Rachel's little brother has been asking me to take him to the cinema, but I've just been saying Nah Man. But could you imagine that, me with a year 7, shut up. So I said no.

Later on about 3.00pm I went with Rachel's little brother to the pub to meet his dad. It was some dirty pub with bare old people and typical dirty smelly beer breath mans. Rachel finished work early today and I waited. I was gonna meet my Mum in Hanwell to see Maurice and co. But I stayed with Rachel, she finished at 3.00pm. At this time I was feeling a bit sick and a little bit drunk, had an Easter Egg also.

We went upstairs when her parents came back but because I was a bit drunk I was all horny and was messing about with her. Around 7.00pm me and Rachel went to the Hounslow kebab shop and got a few kebabs for dinner. They weren't as nice as the ones down in the shop in Langley Village.

At 9.00pm I got a call from my Mum and she wanted me to come straight home. So I gave Rachel a goodbye kiss and played with her. She played with me then I left. O shit yeah there's a thing that Rachel did that felt nice, I took my trousers down and she was biting my dick while it was in my pants. She doesn't do shiners (bj's) but this wasn't really a shiner, just a bite thing innit.

She walked me to the bus station then I got the 81 bus back to Langley. I got home about 10pm and just relaxed.

At this moment I'm watching T.V.

Funniest things all day:-

- Kissing bum- Rachel's hand
- MJP funny message- it's only me

DID U KNOW?

JACKIE CHAN IS 45 ON THE 7TH APRIL (THIS WEDNESDAY)

DID U KNOW?

1 IN 650 CHILDREN UNDER 15 DEVELOPE CANCER IN THE UK

Easter Sunday 4th April 1999

Today has been a bit boring. This morning I was thinking to myself shall I tell Rachel my real age? It's because she's a year older than me and I've been lying about my age. But now I fell a bit lame and think I should tell her. She said she has been out with my age before so I suppose she won't mind that much, but will be pissed off with me for lying.

Well anyway today I just stayed in. My mum went to the Cinema at 6pm and its 10pm and still hasn't come back. Maybe she got run over, joke.

MJP also came round and we were doing kickboxing.

Also hopefully meeting Katherine from Teddington with MJP.

Funniest thing all day:-

- Same pants
- Hot dog advert
- Have you <u>HAD HAD</u> you've been hadded

DID U KNOW? ONION IS GOOD FOR GETTING RID OF RUST

Bank holiday Monday 5ᵗʰ April 1999

Today I woke up about 10am. I was gonna go with my mum to her friend's house but like always I couldn't be f**ked. When my mum left I had a bath then rang up MJP to see if he was still meeting that girl Catherine, but he wasn't so he said he'd just come round then we'd breeze down to London or something.

When he came round we just played a bit of the old Tekhen 2. The time we finished playing it was about 7.30pm. At this time I had to have my dinner so MJP breezed home. It was an Indian and it was tick.

Around 9.10pm Hanghei and Clint came round. So I went out with them. We all went down to Glen Close to knock for Grant. We were all on our bikes. But my bikes f**ked up because the back wheel is buckled, this makes it f**king hard to ride.

We all breezed to Slough and met up with Liam and Craig at McyD's (MacDonald's). We chilled there for a while then around 10pm we bopped to the ice arena. On the way we met up with Nathan and his trampy friend. When we got to the ice arena we just chatted to the usual people that go down there.

Later this man was trying to beat everyone up because they were all crowding round his car and he was getting pissed off. When he came out he raised his fist and was shouting "come on then which one of ya wants it". Everyone just started crowding round him and I thought he would get jumped but he just went back into his car and drove off.

There was also almost another fight. It was Adam from my school and two other boys trying to beat up these two boys just for no reason. After we all breezed down to MacDonald's at this time we were also with Kelly, Shelly and two other girls. Liam left with Kelly because she was supposed to be giving him a shiner.

We left Slough about 12am but on the way home we stopped off at favourite chicken. The people were safe and gave me some shit for free. My bike was also f**ked up, so what I did was ride Grants while pushing my bike along at the same time. Clint got a lift.

When I got in I had something to drink and at this moment I'm watching and taping kiss the girls on Front Row.

Have a nice day.

Also – yesterday rang Shelly and probably going out with her on Wednesday. Going to club Options tomorrow and gonna tell Rachel my real age. AND – meeting girl from Bath on Saturday but in London.

Funniest things all day:-

- Shiners – phone down pants
- Tekhen 2- mans can't even buss a side step
- Did you have a nice Easter, err no
- Nathan gunning girl- you wore them trousers yesterday.

DID U KNOW?

THE BRA ARRIVED IN BRITAIN IN 1914; I WISH I LIVED BEFORE THEN. BRA LESS WOMEN.

DID U KNOW?

NOSTRADAMUS'S FULL NAME WAS MICHEAL DE NOSTRADAME

Tuesday 6th April 1999

In the morning I bopped to the shops to get DA Shibbz some cat food because he was annoying me. On the way back I met up with Sean and he told me the plans for today, going Options in Kingston.

About 1.30pm I went to MJP'S drum then we got a train to go to Slough. OTT we met Michael Jo and bopped into Slough with us.

In Slough we met up with Hanghei and the crew. Tonight they're all going down to Winkers in Chalfont. They asked us if we wanted to come but I promised Rachel I was going to options. MJP wanted to go though.

We left Slough about 5pm then went down to Simmons house to see if he wanted to come with us. But he didn't have any money (weird for Simmons). So me and MJP went back to my yard and got ready. Sean rang and he's meeting us down at the station to come Options.

We got to the station about 6.20pm and Sean wasn't sure if he wanted to come because it was just the three of us. He was also telling us that Liam got a shiner off this girl and Sod shagged her up the arse in KiddyPark (this girl was drunk). This seemed quite funny at the time but isn't really that funny, oi stop laughing. Sean didn't end up coming so it was just me and MJP. We kept saying "this is gonna be offkey, just the two of us".

Anyway we got off the train at Ealing Broadway then waited for the 65 bus to Kingston. When we got on the bus we only paid 60p, the man asked us where we were going and we just South Ealing. The driver was f**king gay though when we got to South Ealing he stopped the bus and walked up the bus and said "this is where your fare ends". What a sick brare. This is the second time this has happened. But he's a dick there were bare people on the bus as well.

The next bus came 5 minutes after anyway. When the bus was coming up to Kingston we met these girls and we just chatted to them. We weren't really cherpsing them just chatting, they weren't all that you see. But they gave us a flyer and we got in for a fiver (£5).

When we got in the club we didn't even get searched. This club was a proper club but some of the music was frath (not good). It was supposed to be a special house and garage night but they didn't play that much.

I did meet Rachel down there but it was offkey because there was so many girls. I told MJP to cherpes but he was only really talking to them girls that we came in with, butters.

Me and MJP kept leaving Rachel and her friends and going for walks. I did want to cherpes a few girls but I couldn't really. There was a time when I bopped round with Rachel but it was HuHH.

After there was a fight between one of Rachel's friends and some girl. Boy, it was rough the other girl was giving her bare head butts.

After, MJP got on the bus to Ealing while I bopped with Rachel to the bus stop to go round her house. At the bus stop Rachel kept asking me what it was that was so important that I had to tell her (you know the age thing). I did manage to tell her but it wasn't easy I said I was sorry for lying but she didn't mind, but you could tell she was pissed off. When we were on the bus home she didn't speak to me at all.

We got back to her house about 12am. When we got home Rachel was all moody.

In the night me and Rachel watched a film but I fell asleep. We didn't do nothing, she was just pissed off today, but I just lipsed her and was saying are you alright and sorry and shit like that.

Funniest things all day:-

1. Bus driver – sick brare 2
2. MJP – do I look like someone who would suck your nipples and bite your dick?
3. Mans can't even bus a side step out the way
4. Future man – ww5

DID U KNOW?

POORING COLD WATER OVER SOMEONE WHILE THERE
ASLEEP COULD KILL THEM- SO DONT TRY IT

Wednesday 7ᵗʰ April 1999

Today I woke up around 11am but I couldn't be f**ked to get out of
bed, so I just slept longer (at Rachel's remember). Rachel was alright this
morning, she wasn't all pissed off. She was like how she usually is and
this was safe.

At 5pm I went with Rachel and her brother to Brentford Leisure Centre.
Rachel just had to drop him off, so I just came along as well. After we
dropped him off I was gonna go home but I thought I'd go back to Rachel's
drum to get some tings.

When I got back to Rachel's I got bare calls from Simmons, Nicholas,
MJP and Sean. Tonight there's some club in Holborn. But I don't think
I'm going (no money). Anyway I messed about with Rachel (she's alright
now) the I left about 6pm she came to the bus station with me because she
had to get a bus as well to go and pick up her sister.

Today the bus home was a double Decker and I've never been on a 81
double Decker bus (it just seemed strange).

At this moment just watching TV. Just been watching Miami Uncovered
and Blind Fury.

Mardi Ggras Bombing –Chiswick man

DID U KNOW?

BEETHOVEN WAS A BLACK MAN, WELL HALF CASTE WHAT
EVER YOU WANT TO CALL IT, I'M NOT JUST SAYING THAT
BECAUSE I'M BLACK.

Thursday 8th April 1999

At 2.15pm me and my mum left to go to our 3pm appointment at the Police station. We got there about 2.45pm and we met my solicitor down there (you know the one from mum's work).

The man we were waiting for (the interview man brare) came a bit late, about 15 minutes. When we met him he told us that I was being charged for robbery and have to go to Court on May 10th. It's Liam as well but not Simmons and MJP or Nicholas because we were the only people that touched the money. My mum was pissed off, but I'm not as worried as I was this morning. It's because I'm not getting charged for the train (pay fine innit), but I'm getting charged for something I didn't do.

Today I also had to get my fingerprints done and a photo taken.

After, we bopped down to SFC (Southern Fried Chicken, a cheap imitation of KFC). Then me and my mum met up with one of my cousins which I haven't seen in years. We bopped through Slough then after I got a train to go to Hanwell and meet Kieron.

When I got to Hanwell I met up with Kieron, Stevie and Leo. I played a bit of football. Later on Jason and Colin breezed down and we just played some more football and basketball. There's nothing better to do in Hanwell.

I decided to stay round Kieron's because I couldn't be f**ked to go home, so I rang my mum and told her.

At night I watched Marked For Death then went to sleep because I couldn't be f**ked to stay up. Also Kieron was asleep because tomorrow he's going to some diet thing at Ealing hospital.

Funniest things all day:-

- Jonny – flakiness snap crackle and Jonny
- Raisins- what do you call an old black man? Raisin

DID U KNOW?

THERE WERE 2O MILLION SLAVES KIDNAPPED FROM AFRICA
TO GO TO THE USA

Friday 9th April 1999

Today I woke up about 8am to go with Kieron to his diet thing at the hospital. In the end we didn't end up going so I went back to sleep.

I woke up later about 11am and at this time Jason and Leo knocked. We decided to go to London. So I quickly had a bath then about 11.30am we left. I never usually go this early.

We got to Central London about 12.15pm. Like always we breezed down to Oxford Street, Piccadilly and Leicester square. Down the square we went in Capital Cafe (95.8), we stayed in there for about half an hour mainly because Jason was taking long playing the Rugrats game on Playstation.

Around 2pm we went down to the MTV cafe and there were bare girls waiting for select MTV to start at 4pm (stupid arses). Jason was also saying let's wait but I thought f**k that. Anyway in the cafe the waiter was getting pissed off with us because we were taking too long to order. I kept saying I want to be served by the sexy waitress, he kept saying "alright man calm down she's not here today" (he must of known who I was chatting about). "GET ME THAT F**KING SEXY WAITRESS".

Around 2-3pm we went just chilling round the Square. At 3.15pm we went round Troc for a bit then went back to MTV around 3.45pm.

Now when we were there, there were bare people. But I just told them lot when it starts we'll just barged to the front. At this time the waiter from the cafe came out and he told only us that they weren't shooting today. We didn't go because we thought he was trying to get rid of us (only told us innit).

At 4pm it didn't start, so I guess that brare was telling the truth. But I did get a girl's number, Kate from Kingston. I know it's the right number because I rang it and her mum said "sorry she's gone London".

At 4.15pm we met MJP and at this time we decided to breeze home, shame. We did go through Piccadilly with him but that was it.

When we got to Paddington everyone just wanted to go Reading. So we got the fast train from Paddington to Reading.

When the train approached Slough MJP said he was getting off to go home. But the train didn't stop it just breezed past. We were creasing. But it did stop at Maidenhead and MJP got off there.

When we got to Reading it was about 5.50pm. In the station we went in this shop and I done some tick little bit of razing (some crisps). I took off my cap then put the crisps in my hat, walked past, put crisps in my pocket, put hat back on then walked off.

After that we bopped through Reading High Street. In the High Street there were 4 girls looking at us but the bad thing was they were not in the same group. We didn't know who to cherpes they were both on each side of us. We did get both numbers because the first girls came to us and I gave her my number while Jason chatted to the other girl, so they wouldn't go anywhere. Then after I came and got the digits.

OTT back them lot stayed on to go Ealing while I got off at Slough to catch the train to Langley.

When I got home I waited for Rachel to come round (tonight not going out, having sex instead). Rachel came round about 9pm and at this time my mum went out (singles night). We watched Good Burger. Then about 11pm my mum came home with her friend from the pub and he stayed on the sofa, but don't get the wrong idea he's just a friend.

At night me and Rachel did bare did bare dirtiness. We were rubbing up each other naked. I was on top of her then she was riding me.

I had my dick up her a few times, but I was being careful because I didn't have any condoms.

Funniest things all day:-

- Cream egg- under hat

- You don't know where that's been – it's been there. (Leo just drinking some opened can off the train)
- Grannies and granddads don't like the way that I chat.
- Mans smile orange Jaffa cake man

Saturday 10th April 1999

In the morning MJP and the Hanwell crew rang me to see if we were still meeting those girls from Bath. "Yeah" I said. But first I had to get rid of Levi (you know Rachel).

At 1pm I walked Rachel to the bus stop and also got some cat food from the shop. Then when I got back in I fed Shibbz then got my phone and bopped.

When I was on the way to MJP's yard I rang Sarah (from Bath) to see if she was in London. But guess what she said she's not going because her friends couldn't be f**ked to go. That's just f**ked up.

When I got to MJP's I told him we weren't meeting them girls and he was screwing, trust they're boom. We got OTT about 3pm to meet Jason, Kieron and Leo. We thought we'd still go to meet Jason etc and also cherpes some NEW skeet.

We got to London about 3.45pm. We bopped through Troc to see if we could find the massive (the Hanwell mans). After, we bopped down to the MTV cafe and at MTV met them lot. After that we breezed through Leicester square and just chilled. Down Leicester Square there was almost a fight between this black brare from Brixton and some proper NF man who thought he was militant. But we left and I think the man must of brocked him up.

As we were leaving London Jason and MJP started setting me up with this girl. At this time I was munching some chicken from KFC. I chatted to this girl and she's from Hackney and her name's Gemma. She was alright but not all that, nice batty. I've seen her before but never cherps her.

At Piccadilly station we got through the machines because we went through with some man in a wheelchair, he was safe. We had trouble getting back because the tubes were f**ked up.

We got Hanwell about 7pm and then me, Jason, MJP and Kieron left to go to my drum. The Boxing's on tonight (Prince Naseem). Leo was gonna stay as well but no one wanted him to stay.

When we got to Langley we breezed to the fair for a bit but because it was frath we bopped to my house.

When I got in I met one of my mum's school friends which she hasn't seen in about 17 years. She was from Nottingham and was offkey.

When the boxing was on round my drum was me, Kieron, Jason, Simmons, Guv, Daniel and Sod. It was a good fight and in the end Naseem won. During the fight I kept getting calls from Rachel's mum and she wanted to know what was going on in the fight.

Later on around 1.20am some man rang and was asking for me. I started messing about and doing my Tony and Shibby voice and going yeah this is Robert who the f**k is this. The man then said he was Hannah's (from East London) dad and she's been missing for over 24 hours. At this time everyone was laughing so I told them all to shut up because it was serious. The man was getting really pissed off. But I told him I hardly know Hannah, met her once rang her a few times that's all. The man had a Northern accent and he was offkey. he asked for my address and I gave him a false one and he also asked for the name of my friend which was speaking on the phone (it was me). I just said Shibby, after everyone was creasing up because Shibby's the cat. But shibbz does have a voice if you must know.

After I finished chatting that man we just had jokes, it's not funny that Hannah's missing but the shit the Northern man was saying was jokes.

Around 4am I went sleep. Staying round was Jason, Kieron and MJP but everyone left after the fight.

Funniest thing all day:-

1. Daniel F MCing -Move to the beat to the beats let's move gggggettt up inside the place better get up and jump

2. Northern man – "you can tell Shibby he's a focking wanker. Give Shibbay a good kick op the ass for me"

DID U KNOW?

THE CABLE CHANNEL SKY MOVIES GOLD (SKY CINEMA) MADE ITS DEBUT ON OCTOBER 1ST 1992

DID U KNOW?

THE FILM TAKING CARE OF BUSINESS USED TOO BE CALLED FILOFAX

Sunday 11th April 1999

In the morning me, Jason and Kieron done bare housework for my mum (MJP was gone). Them lot washed up and hoovered and cut the grass. Later on I rang Hannah's dad to see if Hannah had come home. He was being f**king gay he kept saying "I'm f**king pissed off with your mate Shibby, he's a focking wanker"

He also kept saying "you lot all acting like dicks stoned out of your brains, you weren't helping". This pissed me off so I told him straight. I said sorry about your daughter but there's nothing I can do because I hardly knew her". He carried on swearing and pissing me off so I just said "f**k you" and hung up on his Northern ass.

About 3pm Kieron and Jason left and they wanted me to come but I couldn't be f**ked. Rachel rang me after and was asking if I wanted to come over but I told her I had no money and it's Sunday.

At 5pm Jonny came round and we played some computer and he told me about his holiday. He went to South Africa. When he left I watched a WWF video then after I rang Kieron Cremin because tomorrow is his birthday (breezing down there). After I rang Rachel and just chatted for a while because I was bored.

At night I just stayed in and watched some T.V. also I'm going back school this Tuesday.

DID U KNOW?

80% OF PEOPLE IN UK ARE RIGHT HANDED

Monday 12th April 1999

Well today is my last day of my two weeks off. It's been alright just breezing down to London and meeting girls, also Rachel. But the thing that pisses me off is the Ealing schools all have another week till they go back.

Well today I left my yard about 1.00pm to go out. I got the bus to Slough to go the Magistrates Court and get a Legal Aid form (for when I get to Court). About 1.30pm I went to Slough to get the train to go to Kieron C house. I got to Ealing about 2.00pm and just missed the 2.01 to go to Castlebar Park (Copley Close). The next train came at 2.31pm so I just waited till it came. I got to Kieron's about 2.40pm then we breezed out because today was his birthday. I asked him if he wanted to go London but he didn't so we went out and knocked for an old friend, Meresankh. But she wasn't in so we knocked for another old friend, Riga. We chatted to him but he didn't want to come out because it was raining hard and he also had his girlfriend round.

After we breezed down to my old primary school in Hanwell and it brought back bare memories. But we got thrown out by the Caretaker geezer. After that we were down the shops and we met up with Claire L and another old friend. When they left we decided to breeze down Ealing Broadway because we didn't know what to do, got a bus.

When we got to Ealing we only stayed for a while then breezed on a bus to go to West Ealing. We stayed at West Ealing for a bit then thought we'd bop to Hanwell to knock for Jason. When we got to Jason's he came out with us, we all breezed to Adam Murray's house, another old bredwin we chatted about primary school. Some of the shit I could remember was weird.

After we went down near White flats and tried to find Jonathan's house but couldn't find it so we went to knock for Riga again, but now with Jason. We chatted to Riga for about five minutes then down his road we met these girls. This girl took down my number but I doubt she'll ring me. She was 18, not bad, her name was Sophia or Sarah or something like that.

After, we just hung about round the Greenford Avenue shops, then we decided to see what was going on but no one was there so we all went home. Kieron bopped on his own. I got the train about 7.54 pm and got home about 8.20pm. I rang that girl Nicole from Hounslow and I am meeting her on Friday after Kickboxing.

DID U KNOW?

A THOUSAND YEARS AGO HINDU LEGEND SAID THAT THE EARTH STOOD ON A GOLDEN PLATE SUPPORTED ON BACKS OF ELEPHANTS WHOSE MOVEMENTS CAUSED EARTHQUAKES. THE ELEPHANTS STOOD ON A TURTLE REPRESENTING THE WATER GOD VISHU

Funniest Thing All Day:-

- Jonathan - Disabled
- "Allow dis brare"

Tuesday 13th April 1999

Today when I was back at school I found myself writing like the way I W.I.D, like scribbling and writing whatever the f**k I want. But I will write neatly. Today I was once again late and I'm gonna get in trouble if I'm late again (my bike is f**ked up).

After school I got a lift from Johnny G's brother. He thought he was militant bussing out all the garage tunes. The tunes I heard last year.

When I got in Nadia (Alien) and Catherine came round. They stayed till about 6pm, they were being stupid like usual.

At 6.30pm I went to kickboxing, it was alright and felt good because when you stop for a while you're not as flexible and get f**ked up.

When I got in Guv and Wayne came round and they just played computer while I chatted to my girl on the phone. Rachel told me what she wanted to tell me and do you know what she said, "Robert I think I love you". I didn't know what to say, "Are you sure"? I replied. She just then said, "I've never felt like this before for anyone, I know we're young and everything and it sounds stupid". She said something like that. So I just said thank you and yeah it's alright. I didn't take the piss but its giving me second thoughts about meeting Nicole on Friday.

I also rang Simmons and MJP to see if they were still coming with me tomorrow to see my solicitor.

Ok so that was my day and I'm thinking this month is going fast but it's been jokes. I just read from April 1st and this month's going alright, apart from the Court case thing. There's also 263 days left till 2000 AD.

DID U KNOW?

A U.F.O CRASHED IN ROSWELL NEW MEXICO 1947.

Wednesday 14th April 1999

Today me and JD were late again and if I'm late tomorrow I get in trouble. I gave JD a lift on his velo (that's French for bike). Terry was at school today for the first time in ages but he's only staying for like 2 weeks or something. School was alright today

After school I got a lift from Richard then walked down London Road and met up with Simmons. He had just finished school and was coming Windsor with me to see my solicitor. We went to Simmons house then he got dressed them we quickly went to my house. Down my house we met MJP then we breezed down to Langley train station.

We just about got the train when we got to the station (had to jump over the tracks). When we got to Slough we then got the train to Windsor. OTT to Windsor we got caught with no ticket but the man let us off and said we need a ticket on the way back.

When I got to my mum's work them two chatted to my solicitor. They just told him what happened. We were only there for about 20 minutes. When we left, Simmons went to Windsor Riverside Station because he was getting picked up to go football. Me and MJP got some McyD's then got the train. My mum was also on this train but she's HuHH. We had tickets and we met the same T.M and he thought he was bad.

When we got to Slough we were gonna get the train to Langley but that was long so we went to the bus station.

Down the bus station I chatted to bare people we knew. I even met Bushwall and chatted to her for a while.

When I got in I rang Lauren from Burnham (LFB) and chatted to her because I haven't spoke to her in time. Well that's not the real reason, I just wanted to get her friends number off her because she's boom (she didn't have it).

After I rang Kate then after rang Rachel and chatted to her (remember she loves me). She wanted to know how I feel about her. I didn't know what to say. But I do like her a lot but I just like other girls as well, I'm only human.

At this moment I'm watching Under Siege 2. It's just started.

Funniest thing all day:-

- Shut up – throws ice
- Terry – don't check me if your hair ain't combed
- Shibbz story – wrestling, racist fight after school beats up 20 bouncers

DID U KNOW?

CHILDREN OFTEN HAVE SIX TO EIGHT COLDS PER YEAR, CAUSED BY MANY DIFFERENT VIRUSES.

Robb Peters

DID U KNOW?

THE HORNET IS ONE OF THE LARGEST MEMEBERS OF THE WASP FAMILY, TONK BRARE.

Thursday 15th April 1999

Today I went to school. On the way found a video card, gonna get bare videos and just keep them.

I was late again. At break I razed a phone out of someone's bag . Kenworthy took it home.

After school MJP and Ami came round. Ami brought Tekhen 3 over because mine is buss up. When he was living we swap his one for my brock one, shame. But we did it slyly when he went to the toilet.

When my mum got home Kenworthy rang and he said the boy was ringing the phone (some dick from year 11) and saying were gonna kill him and shit. So he said he smashed the phone (stupid dick).

Well that's all I did but last night about 12am Sarah (the boom one from Bath) rang me and my mum was screwing. She hung up on her because my mum was sleeping. But I rang Sarah today and she's breezing down to London and I'm meeting up with her. Also not meeting Nicole tomorrow.

Funniest things all day:-

- JD middle finger up
- Switching Ami's game in the toilet. MJP saying go get the game I already had it.

DID U KNOW?

DRINKING LOTS OF ALCOHOL CAN DECREASE YOUR DICK SIZE AND LOWER YOUR SPERM COUNT.

Friday 16th April 1999

After school today JD came round and we played some of his new games-
Rugrats and Boxing 99 mess. But when I came straight back from school I
had a massive shit and it was lovely (I was dying to go).Like the old saying
said "there's nothing like shitting in your own toilet".

Anyway, after JD left, these little year 9 girls from my school knocked and
a few fancy me. But I never let them in because they're some offkey Asian
girls, not that I have anything against Asians it's just these girls are butterz.
Actually Samira at school is boom.

At night I never went out just stayed in and watched Summer Slam 98
and some pornos. I think Simmons, MJP, Nicholas and Guv breezed to
E&D but I'm not sure.

At 1.30am Sarah rang me. I was a bit shocked because she's boom
remember. She's still going London and I'm meeting her after I get a trim.
She rang on her mobile and it kept cutting out every 5 minutes, she didn't
care about the bill. Sarah was talking for about an hour and telling me she
wants to shag me and how she likes it(I never told her I have a girlfriend
who's madly in love with me). Sarah was quite dirty but feel bad because
I really want to meet her but know I'll be doing tings and the way Rachel
feels about me makes me feel bad. But I'm staying round hers tomorrow
that should keep her happy.

At 2.30am I went to bed.

DID U KNOW?

MARS HAS THE BIGGEST VOLCANOE IN OUR SOLAR SYSTEM,
1000 TIMES BIGGER THEN EVEREST

Saturday 17th April 1999

Today was just offkey. I don't like this day at all, everything was just not
how I planned, if you know what I mean.

At 12pm today I left my drum to get my hair cut at 12.30pm. On the way I stopped off at Simmons work to get some supplies, but I couldn't because the boss was watching me.

I got the bus to Slough at 12.20pm and when I got to the hairdressers it was exactly 12.30pm. After getting my trim I started bopping to the train station, I was gonna go with MJP but instead rang Kieron to meet me at Hanwell then breeze to London. Remember today I'm meeting Sarah from Bath (the horny one).

Anyway I got the train about 1.27pm and met Kieron about 1.50pm (he got on my train). We got to London Paddington about 2pm. MJP rang and wanted to meet us in Paddington but we thought f**k that and got on the tube to Piccadilly Circus, he can meet us there innit.

When we got to London we just chilled for half an hour in the middle of Piccadilly. Kieron was just smoking and looking around for girls. After me and Kieron bopped through Leicester Square and got one of those £1.00 slices of pizza. At 2.30pm I rang Sarah's mobile to see where she was, cos rang before and it was engaged.

When I rang Sarah's mobile it wasn't Sarah it was a friend of Sarah's with her phone, hope you're following this. I said "where's Sarah?" and she said "she's in London but left her F**KING mobile at home". This was offkey because she kept ringing up and telling us to meet her in different places. Her friend was in Bath by the way.

At 3pm we met MJP, he was chatting to these two girls we know from that place near Enfield. We chilled round by MTV and just chatted to them girls. Me and Kieron had some Bacardi and drunk that (Kieron got it).

At 4pm select MTV started and we just chilled outside the window. At 4.30pm they came outside and they chatted to one of the girls with us (Lee). This got us on TV as well, mainly because we kept getting in front of the camera.

At 5pm we went to Troc because we were supposed to be meeting Sarah and co at Sega World, we never met them though. But we did meet two girls but they ran away from us because of MJP. It's because they said do you have girlfriends and we said no. They said "how come?", then MJP as a joke said "because we're players". This girl looked at me and said "he's just ruined your chance with us". Then she went. It doesn't really matter, they weren't all that.

After London I went back home to get some dinner (time was 8pm). I'm staying round Rachel's today but Terry rang earlier and told me about some party but I never rang back. I also kept getting calls from this girl from Brixton and she likes me, but she's butterz.

I left my house about 8.15pm. On the way I went to Blockbusters. As I was walking to Blockbusters I met Hanghei and Clint. Tonight they were going to some place in Watford.

When I got to Blockbusters I tried to use the card (which I found the other day) but it didn't work so I had to use my own. I was just gonna keep the films.

After, I bopped the bus station (Slough). The bus was coming in 40 minutes so I thought allow that it'll get the train. I got the train at 9.30pm and I met Javan he was going round his girl's house in West Drayton.

I got off the train at Hanwell to bus it to Hounslow (instead of bare trains). when I was in Hanwell the bus was taking long so I bopped all the way to Boston Manor. At Boston Manor I got a train to Hounslow East station. The time was about 10.30.

I got to Rachel's about 11pm. I was quite tired. Me and Rachel didn't do much. Just messed about, couldn't really do a lot she was on her period. Actually you can do a lot if you use your imagination.

See that day was f**king offkey

1. No boom Sarah
2. Blockbuster card not working
3. Long arse journey to Rachel's yard

Funniest thing all day:

• Stick um in your mouth

Robb Peters

DID U KNOW?

A CAMEL USES ITS HUMP AS A PORTABLE STOREHOUSE OF FAT FROM WHICH TO DRAW NOURISHMENT WHEN FOOD IS SCARCE.

Sunday 18th April 1999

Well today was much better then yesterday. Yesterday was just proper f**ked, didn't meet girls, that Blockbuster card didn't work and I had to trek to Rachel's.

Well today I woke up about 12pm and was relaxing in bed (Rachel's bed). Then I went downstairs and had some coco pops, o shit I mean Chocó crispys. Those bastard bitches have changed the name.

At 1pm me and Rachel watched Species 2 downstairs and messed about. Whilst we were watching the film Rachel got a call from someone, I didn't know who it was but Rachel was speaking to them and getting excited. After she finished speaking to this person, Rachel said it was her auntie, and she said she could get us into the Another Level tour thing for free (she works at the place). I rang my Mum and told her I was going to this place (Shepherds Bush Empire). Me and Rachel left her house about 5.30pm to meet her auntie in Shepherds Bush.

When we got to Rachel's auntie me and Rachel went into the kitchen and had bare munch. Rachel's auntie was offkey she was short with purple hair and was bunning bare weed. In her kitchen I had these German chocolates called Reho Meight Regel, some shit like that. It's because her boyfriend is some offkey German brare with funky trousers.

We left her auntie's about 6.50 pm and got there for 7.00pm. At the Shepherds Bush Empire there were bare girls but I couldn't cherpes. Also, did I mention The Click and a group called Fierce are also performing.

When we got in the Empire Rachel's auntie got me a pint (it was free). At 7.30pm The Click came on everyone was going mad (the girls). There was bare screaming, trust. Da Click were alright but I wasn't excited to see them but I've seen them all before at all the raves we go to. All dem mans like PSG, Creed, MC Unknown, Piper and that HuHH woman who sings the chorus. They were only on for 20 minutes singing Good Rhymes and We are The Click.

At 8.00pm the other group came on called Fierce or something like that. They were alright and there was one boom one wearing pink. I was just watching her. Rachel was getting jealous. They finished about 8.20pm and then all the girls were just waiting for Another Level to come on.

At 9.00pm Another Level came on and everyone was going mad. There was bare girls screams. Another Level lasted for about one and a half hours. They sang all their tunes and it was quite good. During this, Rachel's auntie gave us some vodka and coke and Rachel was a bit drunk. Me and Rachel were watching it on the first floor and right above their heads.

When it finished the time was about 10.20pm we met up with Rachel's aunt and then she bopped us to the bus stop. I got the same bus as Rachel but should have got the bus to Ealing then the train. I got home at midnight and told my Mother about my day. I have also got school tomorrow but don't think I will wake up. I WID after then went to bed.

DID U KNOW?

THE FILM LEON IS CALEED THE PROFESSIONAL IN THE USA

Monday 19th April 1999

Well today I woke up for school but went straight back to sleep. I didnt go school just stayed in and watched TV.

At this moment I'm watching TV and WID but in a minute I'm going to take videos back. The time is 4.30 so I'm gonna have some munch but I'm not finishing my day because something might happen (life's so unexpected).

Well after I breezed to Jim's house to get my bike back. But he wasn't in, he was already round my house. After I went to Blockbusters and took the videos back, then bopped to JD's and chilled for about an hour.

As I was leaving I showed him a porno I taped for him and you should have seen the little man's face, he was so happy. They weren't even all that, they're hardcore but don't show everything properly. I left JD's about 9pm and he was rushing me to leave, I wonder why, f**king dirty bastard. Wants to play with his winkle probably.

I bopped all the way home but I didn't mind that much like I usually do.

Funniest things all day:-

- JD – nice set of tits
- Daily sport
- Da game finals- sky box office

DID U KNOW?

THE MALE BEE DIES WHEN THERE IS NO MORE NECTAR AVAILABLE FROM THE FIELDS

Tuesday 20th April 1999

Today JD never knocked for me so I got to school by getting a bus to Slough. I then waited for a Datchet bus but it was taking the piss so I got the train to Windsor then to Datchet. I got to school at 10.30am. Missed first lesson and second lesson was finishing.

Well school was alright today. After school I was supposed to have a detention but I forgot. I got a lift from JD on his bike to get home.

After school Jim came round and he gave me my bike back. So now I'm not gonna be late for school (I think). After I rang a few girls like Lee from that place near Enfield (yes Lee's a girl) and Kate from Kingston.

I also rang Rachel and we were messing about having phone sex. She was creasing up. I was just explaining what was happening.

Funniest thing all day:-

- Mr Colborn trip – don't laugh Ha Ha

- Rachel's phone sex – swatting

HISTORY FILE

BRIXTON BOMBING- NAIL BOMB KID WITH NAIL THROUGH HEAD

DID U KNOW?

THERE ARE 12 TUBES LINES IN LONDON

HOW MUCH WOOD WOULD A WOOD CHUCK CHUCK IF A WOOD CHUCK WOULD CHUCK WOOD

Friday 23ʳᵈ April 1999

Well today I arrived at school early for once. In the morning I broke a bit of the ceiling in my form room, I upper cutted it. The walls are made of some cardboard mess.

Well school was alright I had Business Studies, PSE, double Tech and Maths. Those are all shit lessons but today was jokes.

Well when I got home it was 3.30pm and Rachel came round. She got to my house about 4pm and 10 minutes after my mum came back.

Today me and Rachel were rubbing up to each other but my mum kept coming upstairs so we quickly had had to keep pulling up our trousers. Rachel usually doesn't like doing tings in the day; she doesn't like exposing her bits. But we were under covers.

Rachel left about 7.30pm and I walked to the bus stop with her. When I got back Terry Loveridge came round. Me and Terry breezed to MJP's house because his parents weren't in and there were a few people round.

We stayed at MJP for about 30 minutes. Them lot were just boning and shit. We were supposed to go to this party in Burnham but we never went in the end. We just chilled round the kebab shop with Danni, Paddy, Ryan and these two offkey girls.

Me and Terry just got a kebab then breezed to my drum. Simmons came round and just chilled. After we watched a few films then breezed to bed.

Funniest thing all day:-

- Bum flapps/fanny cheeks
- Willies and Fannies
- Yeah man, err
- Aliens- red and green
- Willy Wonka

Saturday 24th April 1999

Today I woke up about 10.30am. At 12pm I started to get ready to go London, like always. At 12.30pm Ben came round and was coming as well.

When we left we bopped to Simmons' work to get a few things. I got bare shit today, I was razing hard. I got:-

1. X2 sunglasses
2. Harley Davison aftershave
3. Hair gel
4. Bon Bons (diabetic ones)
5. Slim fast drinks
6. Lolly pops
7. And some ribbed condoms (Rachel likes em)

We started bopping to the train station about 1pm and the next train was at 1.20pm. We got that train Paddington.

At Paddington we met MJP then we all got OTT to Piccadilly Circus. The time was around 2pm – 2.30pm. We just chilled, then at 2.45pm I rang Sarah to see where she was, but she was still on the coach. So I told her to meet us at 3.30pm at Troc. At this time I cherpes this girl with some nice tiities, I took down her friend's number as well but she was butterz. The friend was so f**king dodgy, trust bredwin.

Around 4pm we breezed down to MTV. I rang Rachel to tell her to watch it, but she missed me because at 4.30pm they came outside.

After we went back to Troc and I got this girl's number, Laura from Tottenham. At 5pm we waited for Sarah in Troc. At this time we were with those first girls we cherpes (titty one) and Terry lipsed the one with the titties. The butterz one wanted to lips me so i just lipsed her for jokes anyway.

At 5.30pm we met up with Sarah and she looked boom, needed some titties but looked boom. I started chatting to Sarah then she said we have to meet up later because her friends wanted to go round London. So us lot just breezed round Leicester Square and Trafalgar Square to waste time. Terry and Ben kept moaning because they wanted to go home. But I wanted to stay because I've been wanting to meet this girl for ages.

After we breezed through Leicester Square and we saw the girls. I told Sarah we might as well stay together and bop round London together. Her friends didn't like this, and trust her friends were rude. They kept saying shit like "we don't even like you f**k off". They were f**ked up Bath girls. But Sarah was safe and sexy. The only problem was her friends kept walking off and saying we don't want to go round London with them (in there funky Bath accents).

At one point when we were with them we almost got robbed but we didn't, but that's minor man.

Anyway as I was saying Sarah's friends were being offkey. Sarah just said we'll have to meet another time, just the two of us. This pissed me off and I thought I must at least get a kiss before she leaves. So I said can I at least get a goodbye kiss then she said "no I can't in the middle of London". I thought "what a dick".

After that I was really pissed off. So I thought I'd cherpes these girls I saw, quite boom. I cherpes these girls from Reading and got their numbers.

After that Simmons met us but we couldn't be f**ked to stay in London any longer, so we breezed.

We got back to Langley about 8.30pm. I had some munch and after I rang Rachel to tell her I wasn't staying tonight.

At 10pm we all breezed to the ice arena to see who was down there and hardly anyone was. We just chilled down there for a while then after got the train home.

On the way home me, Terry and Simmons stopped off to buss a few kebabs innit. After we breezed home and at this moment Terry is being HuHH and I'm still f**king pissed off with them f**king dumb stupid Bath girls.

Good night, time is 2am.

Funniest things all day:-

- The game – Header
- So far away in time

DID U KNOW? TODAY IS SHAKESPEARE'S BIRTHDAY

DID U KNOW?

THE RHINO IS PART OF THE HORSE FAMILY

Sunday 25ᵗʰ April 1999

Today I woke up at 8.30am and Shibby was really getting on my nerves. He kept meowing outside my room. So I threw him out then cotched.

Today my mum went to the car boot sale and when she got back she had a NES which I haven't played in about 7 years. So we played some Duck Hunt and Mario 1. It was really weird. You still have to blow in the games to make them work.

At 1pm me and Terry breezed to the shops for some munch. We chilled round there for a piece then got back about 1.20pm. Today I was going to

Rachel's but I missed the bus at 1.25pm and they're every hour. But I still need to give Terry a lift to Datchet (on my bike). We got to Datchet around 2pm and I just thought I'd get a train to Hounslow as I was in Datchet. So me and Terry breezed round Datchet and we met up with Anthony and his crew, so we just played a bit of football until our train came (about half hour). They were all shit, trust.

We got our train around 2.50pm – 3.00pm. Terry got off at Wraysbury (where he lives) and I had to get off at Feltham. I asked the man what time was the next train to Hounslow. Bastard said 50 minutes. I thought allow that. So I rid all the way from Feltham to Hounslow. I remembered the route from when me and Rachel do cinema, well not exactly I got lost at one point.

When I got to Rachel's it was about 4pm. Me and Rachel just messed about. We were doing what we doing the other day. Bare sex, trust.

I left hers about 7.30pm and she kept saying can't I at least stay till 8, she's HuHH. I thought nah allow dat, it's all good getting tings but Sunday service is f**ked, so I breezed.

I rid to Hounslow East station. Then got the tube to South Ealing then because Ealing Broadway's only round the corner, I rid there.

When I got to the station I bought a ticket to Southall just to get through the machines. I got to Slough about 8.40pm. When I got to Slough I asked this brare when the next train was that stops at all the stops eg: Langley. He said where you going and because I had some Southall ticket I said Southall. There was a train at 21.17 and he kept saying it goes to Southall but the thing is it didn't stop at Langley. He was quite safe. I was trying to go by saying can you just let me get out of the station to get some munch because I've got about 15 minutes. I only wanted to get out of Slough train station then duss on my bike. But the man kept saying I can't let you go out because if I get caught letting you out with that ticket then back in, I'll get in trouble.

Well the train came and the man saw me on. I got off at West Drayton then checked when the next Langley one was. It was in about an hour but there was one in ten minutes to Slough. I was just gonna buy a ticket then breeze from Slough but I thought that man might see me. So I done the stupidest thing, yeah that's right I rid from West Drayton to Langley. But it was only 10 minutes to get there because I was dussing.

In Langley I stopped off at the fish and chip shop and the girl was safe. She gave me 2 large portions of chips for 90p, yes 90p, yeah 90p. All I can say is I got hooked up.

When I got in I ate then watched South Park then breezed to bed. What a stupid day.

Funniest thing all day:-

- Sick brare – the game
- Green alien – thinking you're green and ting

Thou shall not steal

DID U KNOW?

THE CAPITAL OF INDONESIA IS JAKATA AND THEY WIPE THEIR BUMS WITH THEIR LONG FINGER NAILS.

Wednesday 28ᵗʰ April 1999

Today was proper jokes at school. Terry was giving me jokes with JD in English. There was also a little fight between JD and Christian, a fake one of course.

Today me and Kenworthy were doing bare razes through people's bags, it was jokes. Yesterday I got the CD "NO SCRUBS" and a proper disc man (I'm cold). Well today I got the pen which I'm writing with now, some more pens and Kenworthy got a rape alarm. I'm just gonna give that to Rachel. I swear me and Kenworthy are getting addicted to this shit but have to be careful.

Well after school Rachel rang and in a few weeks it's her brother's birthday and he's getting a Playstation. I'm gonna go round and play bare games allow Rachel. I might be going Riches this Friday but I'm not sure because E&D's on.

After chatting to Rachel I watched "Scream" then the Simpsons, a bit of Mortal Kombat and then "Big Trouble in Little China". While I was watching all these things I also rang Kate and the place where she lives is Chisant, it's kinda near Enfield. I might be meeting her Saturday.

Well at this moment I'm watching "Problem Child 2" and now I'm breezing, later fellow Robert the1andonly fans.

Funniest things all day:-

- That brare still wearing that t-shirt
- Terry- JD can't speak volume control
- Christian vs. JD slap takes him down, push

History file

Jill Dando killed on Monday 26th April 1999

Also – Slough's gonna get nail bombed by C18, it's on the list, Brixton was bombed.

DID U KNOW?

THE WORLDS HIGHEST WATERFALL IS IN VENEZUELA, SOUTH AMERICA

Friday 30ᵗʰ April 1999

Yes it's Friday but shit this week has gone fast. Yesterday didn't go school but did today, it was jokes.

Today was really hot and when I got in from school I had bare drinks and a nice cold bath and blared the tunes. After I got a call from Rachel and she was asking if I wanted her to stay but I told her I'm going E&D. She was pissed off she kept saying please come round, what a desperate bbbbb......., person.

At 6pm I had some Indian for dinner then around 7ish Simmons came round to go E&D. We left at 7.30pm. We breezed to Darvils (the shop where 12 year olds can buy beer) to meet some people from Simmons' school. But they weren't there, so we breezed to the station and met MJP.

We got the train about 8pm and it was just us three, Michael Jo was gonna come but he didn't in the end.

When we got to Ealing we then got the bus to Greenford. Today E&D wasn't that packed but it was alright because the last time I went raving was at Options. I didn't meet any girls I knew but I lipsed this nice girl called Vicki, she's from Twickenham or Ickenham, I couldn't hear her properly. After I finished getting off with this girl I realised I just cheated on Rachel. But I didn't really care. It feels good to kiss some next girl.

At 10.40pm we left E&D. Outside this guy gave us this flyer for this rave next week and V.I.P passes. So we're probably going there.

Anyway we got the bus to Ealing Broadway and I got a Burger King £1.99 ting. About 23.21 we got the train back to Langley.

At Langley we met Chris, Guv, Brian, kieron and Kalvin. But I couldn't be f**ked to hang around so I breezed home.

When I got home I just relaxed and watched Karate Kid 3. I'm also thinking of that girl I lipsed, she was boom, o yeah I'm thinking of Rachel a bit as well.

Funniest thing all day:-

- Johnny g – oo I love her
- Crazy man- you wanna buy some sun glass
- School- royal rumble

DID U KNOW?

WRESTLING IS FAKE KIDS

Saturday 1st May 1999

Today I had to do bare gardening. I had to cut the grass, do all the weeds and water the plants. I just wanted to lay in bed but my mum was being a batty hole. At 1pm JD came round but by this time I had finished all the gardening. We just played some FIFA 99 and WWF.

Around 2pm MJP came round and we were playing WWF as the jumpers (a tag team we made up). During today I kept getting calls from Rachel and she wanted me to come round and stay. But I did piss her about because I kept saying I was coming over but I wasn't really because there's a party in Uxbridge tonight.

We went to Langley train station and met Sean, Wayne, Brian, Sod, Daniel F, Lee B, Guv and Chris. Chris was supposed to have tickets for us but he said we have to get them at the door.

We all got the train to West Drayton apart from Wayne and Brian, they were waiting for Hanghei and Clint and all them lot.

When we got to West Drayton we then got the U1 bus to Uxbridge. I got on free because when they were paying I just jumped on. We got off the bus at Uxbridge High Street outside McyD's. We bopped from there to the party and it was long. The party was at the ski slopes in a sort of like pub cabin place thing. It was only £3 to get in and the party was boom, trust it smashed it.

I was M.Cing at this party and there were bare people. There were other MC's as well like Guv, Brian, Chris and there were some proper M.C's from Rhythm Nation. I met a few girls down there like Penny, Amy and there were these nice girls from Windsor Girl's School. I lipsed one of them called Holly, she was alright. All the girls were letting off hard; they were just walking up to us and kissing us. Everybody was drunk. I wasn't though, didn't have no money. I nicked a few drinks of the table. Also met Hanghei and the crew.

Around 11.30pm everybody was just chilling outside because one of the amps had blown and there was no music. Everyone was throwing bottles onto the fake ski slope ting. At this point Simmons, Lee and the rest were all trying to get this girl from Windsor Girls' School.

When the tunes came back on everybody was raving again. I wanted this girl from High Wycombe but because I lipsed her friend she didn't kiss me. But there was one girl who was so boom. Her name was Stacey. I tried to lipsed her. But she had a boyfriend, I still tried to get her number but she wouldn't give it to me. All through the night I was trying to get her number but she never gave it to me. This girl was from Ruislip and had some alright friends as well but they all had mans and one was engaged (she was boom).

The party finished at 1.30am and we lost Sean and Wayne because they got beaten up by the bouncers. They ran off. We also lost Guv, Lee and Daniel and some other people. Well it was me, Simmons, Hanghei, Brian, Chris and Lamar.

We didn't know how to get home, so we just started walking. We decided to walk all the way home. It's 6 miles and they were no trains or buses and we had no money. When we got to Cowley, Chris, Brian and Lamar ditched us to get a taxi. But we carried on walking the 4 more miles.

I got home about 4.30am and Hanghei stayed as well. But when I got in I had bare drink and just relaxed because my body was killing me all over.

After that I just breezed to bed the time was about 5 am.

Funniest thing all day:-

- Come come, bang
- Me, oh
- You don't know the trek
- Brian-laughing –long ain't the word

AND NOW I'VE DECIDED TO DO FUNNIEST THING ALL MONTH. THE TOP 5 THINGS

FUNNIEST THING ALL MONTH (APRIL)

5. JD RAISIN

4. STICK EM IN YOUR MOUTH

3. MOVE TO THE BEATS

2. ER, YOU WORE THOSE TROUSERS YESTERDAY

1. MANS CAN'T EVEN BUSS A SIDE STEP

DID U KNOW?

THE PLAYSTAION CAME INTO BRITAIN IN 1996

Sunday 2nd May 1999

Today I woke up about 12pm (me and Hanghei). At 1pm I rang that girl from Friday (Vicki) and I'm meeting her next week. After I rang this girl called Natalie and just chatted to her, she was in London and I told her to go down to MTV at 4pm and I could see her. But cos my cable was fucked up I never saw her.

Well anyway today I am staying round Rachel's. So I left my drum at 6.20pm and got the bus at 6.38pm.

At Rachels I was just playing her Super Nintendo and messing about with her. At one point I feel asleep on top of her naked, it was jokes.

DID U KNOW?

THIS IS HALF A YEAR OF DIARY AND I'VE DONE SO MUCH SHIT IT'S AMAZING. WELL THAT'S ONLY A MINOR BIT OF MY LIFE THIS IS THE NEXT CHAPTER.

Bank Holiday Monday 3rd May 1999

New chapter

Today when I woke up I was lying naked in Rachel's bed with a massive boner, I swear she must have been playing with me when I was asleep. So I quickly got my shorts off the floor and jumped into my bed with my dick pointing up.

At 11pm Rachel was awake so I went back in the bed. I kept rubbing up her leg and she was saying "I fell quite dirty". She started riding me and it was really nice. But I thought this is f**ked up, you know having sex in the morning.

I left Rachel's about 5pm and got the bus home. While I was waiting for the bus this brare was chatting to me, he was offkey.

When I got home my uncle from Florida was round and he's staying tonight. He also brought me some trainers and clothes from America. So he's well safe. My new best uncle.

After I had my dinner the watched the film "Lock Stock and Two Smoking Barrels". After I just went to Blockbuster's to take the videos back. When I got home I rang that girl from the party, Holly.

Funniest thing all day:-

• Deaf – yaaaaaaaaaaaa

DID U KNOW?

THAT SATURDAY WAS THE 1ST SATURDAY IN A MONTH THAT I DIDN'T BREEZE TO LONDON

Friday 7th May 1999

This morning Christian came and knocked for me. He gave me a lift to school on his bike. I still didn't get to school on time.

School was not too bad today. We didn't raze today at lunch because it was raining and there were bare people in the building.

Yesterday all the year 11's left so I'm on top of the school because our school doesn't have a sixth form.

After school I rang Holly to see if she was still meeting up with me. But I couldn't get through to her. So tonight I didn't know what to do.

Later on I got a call from Liam, which was weird because I hadn't seen him in time. He just wanted me to come out with him. But I didn't go because my mum doesn't like Liam and wanted me to stay in.

Later on Rachel rang and she asked if she could stay tonight. So as I wasn't doing nothing I said she could stay.

Rachel got to my house around 10.30ish just after my uncle from Florida went to bed.

Me and Rachel just did the usual stuff tonight, just this and that, willies and fannies.

She slept downstairs and I slept upstairs, but went up about 4.30am.

Funniest thing all day:-

• David Goodes' birthday- they found him

DID U KNOW?

THE FILM BLADE WAS DIRECTED BY STEPHEN NORRINGTON

Saturday 8th May 1999

At 11.30am Jason knocked to go out, then we both walked Rachel to the bus stop and saw her off. On the way back we stopped off at Simmons' shop for a while, but couldn't get nothing because the boss was there.

When we got back to my yard Ben knocked then around 1pm we left to go out. The plans for today were meet these girls in Richmond. But 1st I had to get a trim. So we went to Slough, we stopped off at WH Smiths because I had to take some books back.

At 1.30pm I got my haircut then after we breezed to the train station. We got the train to Windsor. We bopped through Windsor and met them girls from the party last week, just chatted for a while.

After we went Riverside station to get the train to Riverside station to get the train to Richmond

We were on a late flex because we were meeting the girls at 3pm and we got on the train at 2.55pm. OTT we met some of the Datchet crew and we were chatting to them for a while.

When the train was coming up near Staines the train stopped for about half an hour and it was making us even more late. When the train got to Staines it now was only stopping at Clapham, Vauxhall and waterloo. So we got off at Staines and we got the next train 10 minutes later.

OTT we got caught by TM's and had to get off at Feltham. The time was coming up 4pm so we thought f**k going to meet them and go somewhere else. So we breezed to Feltham Superbowl but it was shit so we got a bus to Hounslow. It was weird because I never thought I'd be down those sides today. In Hounslow we just hung about near the bus station. Around 5.30pm we got the bus home. OTB there was some weird Romanian guy who was speaking to himself through the whole journey to Slough, offkey.

On the way back to my house we knocked for Simmons. Guv, Wayne and Sean were round there as well. We only stayed for a little while because Simmons' mum came back and we had to breeze.

We chilled down Trelawney Avenue for a while but then me and J went back to my drum. We didn't know what to do tonight so we just breezed to Langley Village.

Down the village we met Kenworthy and he was drunk. We were outside the fish and chip shop. So I went in there and got 2 large portion of chips, 2 saveloys and a sausage for only 10p, yes that's right 10p. I knew the girl from school.

A while later we met up with bare people like Hanghei, Ben, Brian and more. We were all just chilled round Langley Village. Simmons, Michael, Brian and Hanghei went to some pub in Slough but everyone else stayed in Langley.

Me and J left about 9.50pm and just chilled round Trelawney with Guv and Sean for a while.

On the way home we heard some tunes coming from someone's house. We thought there was a party but it was just some brare playing his tunes loud. But we knock at the door and he said we could only come in if we had weed or skeet. We didn't have none.

We got in about 11pm and I was in a mood with my mum because I wanted her to tape this film and she forgot. Alright good night. Also I slept upstairs Jason stayed downstairs.

Funniest thing all day:-

- Baby on the bus - it was him
- Ben - Kieron's beating

DID U KNOW?

30 FRANC IS THE SAME AS £3

Sunday 9th May 1999

Today me and J woke up quite early and my mum made us mow the lawn at the back. Jason helped as well.

At 1pm MJP came over then around 1.30ish we left to go out. We breezed down to Langley fish and chips to see if we could get hooked up with some 10p munch but there was some fat girl which I didn't know.

We breezed to Langley train station after, then got a train to Ealing. The plans for today were to go Gurnell swimming pool and watch Vicky swim (basically perving) or go to this thing in Greenford (some dry club in the day ting).

We didn't have tickets to get through Ealing so we got on the Central Line to either go Gurnell or Greenford. We got off the train at North Acton and we were gonna get another train but then Jason saw some boys that wanted to fight him in the past, so we breezed back on the train. There was about 15 of them. We got off at the next stop which was East Acton. We bopped round East Acton for a while because we were gonna get a bus to Gurnell. But we just went back to the station because the buses were dodgy.

We got another train and them two decided to go to that place in Greenford.

At Greenford there were some ticket machines, but they were a minor to get through.

We started bopping to the place then them two changed their minds because they couldn't be bothered to go. They wanted to go to Gurnell instead. So we took a long bop to the nearest station which was Northolt. We got the train to Perivale which is where Gurnell is. We had to bop there but wasn't really that far.

When we got to Gurnell I just sat down because my legs were killing me from bopping around, then I looked for Vicki but I never saw her. But we sneeked in an swam in our boxer shorts.

Later on we got chucked out because we weren't with a club or anything. After we didn't know what to do so we got a bus to Ealing. But had trouble getting on because we hardly had any money. But we got help from this bald headed rough looking man who was on the way to church, he lent us money, well not lent, gave.

When we got Ealing we couldn't get pass the men and didn't have no money. We only had about 20 minutes till out train and couldn't think of what to do. Jason didn't care cos he only lives down the road from there.

We were gonna go Ealing Common and get a tube but that was stupid. But I remembered the other way of getting into the station. We had to climb over this fence and under the bridge then onto the tracks to the platform. It was boom how we done it. Some mission impossible shit.

We got our train about 6.53pm. When we got to Langley I borrowed MJP's bike to get home and school tomorrow, I have an exam in the morning so I must get there early.

Well when I got in I had some dinner then rang Rachel and JD rang after. My mum was having a go at me because them lot told JD to come over and we breezed out. She was also moaning because I told Rachel I MIGHT come over but never.

The End

Funniest thing all day:-

- Let's go rhythm nation for cats
- White armpits (MJP)
- Train mission – over the fence
- Err, I beg you

ALSO –MY UNCLE LEFT TODAY. RACHEL FROM HIGH WYCOMBE RANG, LEFT PHONE MESSAGE.

DID U KNOW?

ALL THE SIDES OF A DICE ADD UP TO 7

Monday 10th May 1999

Today I had an English Exam which was easy. It was some mess about homeless people and like one question that lasted an hour or so.

When I got home I tried to fix my bike but its f**ked, I need a new inner tube. After I just done some revision for my History and Business Studies exams that I have tomorrow.

Later in the day MJP came round and we played some Tekhen 2. We had some little tournament. During this Vicki rang me, she said she saw me yesterday at swimming but I was just leaving. She also wants to go out this Friday, but with friends, like to cinema or something, but in the night.

At 10pm I watched South Park and at this moment Candyman is on and I'm watching it. I'm a piece scared, it's up to the bit when he's calling Helen;s name in the car park. Big scary black man with a hook for a hand.

Funniest thing all day:-

- Why beg- Katie saying - I beg you set me some coke
- Michelle - bussing out Wang's toe kick

DID U KNOW?

100 MILLION YEARS AGO ANTARCTICA DIDN'T HAVE NO ICE IT WAS NORMAL LAND

Tuesday 11th May 1999

In the morning I had an option 3 History exam at school. Which was really easy, it was about WW1 and the Fepression. Trust me I know I'm getting good marks on that, I read everything the night before.

After lunch we had an Option 1 Business Studies exam. This was hard but jokes because Kenworthy was sitting right in front of me and we were just quietly chatting to each other about the questions, we were sitting right at the back. Also next to me sat Sheppard and he had done lots of work, so I quickly grabbed his work and copied a few answers (it was milli how I done it). Trust I done it so fast, but if I get catched I would of been fucked.

Well after the exam I left to go home. When I got home I was gonna go to Halfords then I just remembered it was closed down. I still didn't fix my bike.

Around 5ish MJP came round, we just played Tekhen. At 6pm JD came round just to lend MJP WWF Warzone then left straight away.

MJP left about 7pm then I left to go kickboxing. I got there about 7.15pm, it starts at 6.30pm. I done a quick warm up then some sparring etc because there's a competition on May 23rd all the way in Birmingham, actually it ain't that far.

After kickboxing I was hanging down Trelawney Avenue with bare Trelawney crew. Can't be f**ked to write names. Kieron, Kalvin, Kemar etc.

After they all came back to my yard for a while it was Craig Al, Kelly B and some other two girls. When we were in my room we heard some glass smashing and something smashing. We looked out my window and there was some man trying to break into this house and get someone. Then bare cop cars came down and ambulances. This was the most exciting thing I've ever seen on my road; trust me its dry normally.

So a bit of action on the road then when everybody left I went to bed.

Funniest thing all day:-

• Bare skills
• Kenworthy – voice

Wednesday 12th May 1999

Today I had no way of getting to school, so I ran. I ran through Upton Court Park so no one could see me. When I got to school I had a Maths exam. I didn't do too well because I forgot to revise for it.

At the end of the day I had a French exam, it was easy but I didn't bring a dictionary and was spelling all the words wrong. Plus, couldn't understand it that well. I had some sheet with some French on it but it was just giving me bullshit like:-

To say

To speak

To F**k

Just shit like that, which didn't come up. After school I bopped home but I didn't mind because I had tunes. Had some girl's Walkman, only borrowing not razed. When I got in I just relaxed. Later on Rachel rang and I rang a few girls after, but that's it.

Also - Kenworthy accidentally kicked in one of the window on the door whilst we were razing. Our doors have glass around them. We never got caught though.

Funniest thing all day:-

- Kenworthy - jumping, bare raze
- Kicking window
- Phone - where's the skin?

DID U KNOW?

RICE IS FULL OF NOURISHMENTS, BUT IF THE HUSKS ARE REMOVED, AS IN WHITE RICE, IT LOSES VITAMIN B

Thursday 13th May 1999

This morning, I, once again bopped to school. I was late for my exam today. I really didn't want to do this exam. It was Resistant Materials, which I'm f**king shit at. The exam was so f**ked up. It was all about metals and shit. I didn't understand one bit. It had questions like, what kind of metals would you use to make so and so? I was thinking who gives a shit.

But, trust me I know I've f**ked up on that exam. The Examiners are probably gonna read it and laugh. I just writ anything.

At lunchtime me and Kenworthy were razing some bags. He is still pissed off because his bag got razed, it's payback time. Anyway, today we got some pens, a Nintendo magazine and a WWF video (JD got excited). After lunch we had an Option 2 Drama exam. It was so easy, it was just like having a normal lesson. We were just doing loads of acting and shit. Mr Payne gave us grades after and he gave me a C. I was screwing because this little shy girl who does f**k got a B and that just takes the wee wee.

After school I got a lift home from Richard F. When I got in I watched that video we razed. At 7.00pm JD came round and I showed him this English Wrestling video. JD left about 8.00pm and straight after MJP and Helen came over. We just played some tunes and a bit of computer, the usual. When we were leaving Helen wanted to get off with me. But I didn't get off with her. Shows I can be faithful if I try.

After, I had a nice little shit, and now for some reason I am watching Pretty Woman.

Funniest thing all day:-

- Shacking out no tunes
- Kenworthy bare raze jumping on lockers
- English Wrestling

DID U KNOW?

Guru Nanak was born in 1469 and was the first Guru in the Sikh religion. There were 10 altogether.

Friday 14ᵗʰ May 1999

Early this morning about 7.45am MJP came round and lent me his bike for school. At 8.15am JD came round and then we breezed to school. When we got into school we had to rush into school for an exam. Today we have RE which wasn't too hard. School was just a normal day. At lunch me, JD and a few others played football against some little Year 7s, we battered them. We didn't have any exams today, just that one in the morning.

After school Christian came down to me because we were meeting some girls and probably going down to Fuel. Around 5.30ish we got ready to breeze out and left about 6.00pm then breezed down to MJP's. At MJP's we met Jason (he stopped off at MJP's and just met us there).

We left MJP's about 7.25pm to get the half past train. When we were at the station we lost MJP because he ran away from loads of boys who wanted to beat him up because he lost some guy's bike and also owing them money.

When the trains came we breezed on it but weren't with MJP. However, MJP rang us when we were OTT and was meeting us at Ealing Broadway. When we got to Ealing we waited for about half an hour then breezed on the train that MJP was on to go to Paddington. We could have just got the District Line to Richmond but we went the long way just to buss a ticket.

At Paddington we got the District Line to Richmond, then when we got to Richmond the f**king ticket machines were already open. The time was about 7.30pm and we were meeting them at 8.00pm, but it didn't matter because she rang when I was OTT and I told her just keep waiting. We did meet the girls but they looked offkey, even Vicki was f**ked up. She looked much better inside the club. Jason kept saying we should allow them and go to Fuel to MC. We decided to still go with them. We went to the cinema and saw the film, "I still know what you did last summer". The film was alright but I was sitting next to Vicki right at the front and she hardly spoke to me at all.

After the movie we were just talking to them outside but they had to go home. I did manage to lips Vicki but she was f**ked up. She was getting on my nerves. As she was leaving I said, "Can I have a goodbye kiss"?, and she f**king said "no." Well, she gave me a little minor peck, trust me, f**k meeting her again. But I don't really mind, I wanted to see that movie anyway. Also, MJP lipsed her friend, she was alright. When we left them we breezed back to Richmond Station. We were gonna get the Windsor train but we just missed it so we got the tube. We went to Turnham Green then took a train to Ealing. When we got to Ealing it was about 12.15, OTT home we met Matthew, who was an old friend from Hanwell. We got to mine about 1.00am and Simmons came over for a while just watching TV and shit.

Funniest thing all day:-

- Train - 300 years peanuts for tickets
- MJP - bags over his eyes

- JD - blast yourself
- Daily Sport - err shame on you

DID U KNOW?

THE POPULATION OF BRITAIN COULD FIT INTO THE ISLE OF WIGHT, SQUASHED UP.

DID U KNOW?

20 PEOPLE IN THE UK EACH YEAR DIE FROM FALLING OUT OF BED.

Saturday 15th May 1999

Today I woke up about 10.00am. This morning I had to wash up. Jason and Christian helped me and they were giving me jokes .Christian left about 2.00pm. Around 2.30pm me and J breezed down to Simmons' work. On the way we met MJP. Simmons wasn't there though. He was on lunch break. So we breezed down to the village fish and chips shop to see if we could get some free chips. But I couldn't because the girl was stingy. She did set me 2 drinks for 20p.

After, we got the train to Paddington. The time was 3.30pm and we got there about 4.00pm. When we got to Paddington we then breezed on a train to Piccadilly. London was boring today. Like always we went through and went on MTV (kind of). We only stayed in MTV for about an hour then we breezed to Piccadilly Station. When we were at the station we didn't have any money so we tried to breeze through the machine but the people kept watching us.

After, I thought we might as well get a train from Waterloo. We bopped through Trafalgar Square, Embankment, Westminster and we stopped at the Namco Centre and had McDonalds, but it was shit. After, we bopped to Waterloo Station. We were gonna go to Paddington, and then thought f**k that's long, so we just got the train to Windsor. That was quite long still. We were just doing bare MCing sitting down. When we got to Windsor we got a train to Slough, then at Slough we got a train to Langley.

When we got to Langley J went to MJP's house because he is staying round there and tonight I'm going round Rachel's. When I got in I just relaxed for a while and had some dinner. Around 8.30pm I left. As I was walking out my door I met all the offkey Trelawney girls. I told them I was going to my girlfriends and they kept saying what was the point of going out with someone who lives so far when I could be going out with one of them, I though, er no!

I made them all walk me to the bus stop. When I got on the bus I told them to go MJP's house because he was having a party. I also got a bus timetable out of the thingy because it was smashed. I got the bus at 9.03pm. I arrived at Rachel's around 9.30ish. Rachel wasn't in when I got there. She was at her friend's 16th birthday. So I just chatted to her parents. At 10.45pm me and Rachel's dad drove to the party to pick her up. The party was in Heston in some pub place. When we picked up Rachel she looked quite boom, she was in a skirt. She had her friend with her, some Somalian boy; we gave him a lift as well. Rachel was also a bit drunk. When we got back to her yard I started kissing her and shit, because I was a bit hyper because I met these guys on the bus and they gave me a drink. Rachel was also quite drunk and I was just about to give it to her. She said "no because I was on the blob today". She had the "curse".

Well in the night we were quite bored. We watched some TV and we were just doing the kind of shit that you can do when people were on a period. I got so bored I just went to sleep. She stayed up though.

Funniest thing all day:-

- Train, Jason, ring bell
- School dinners - egg rotten
- Christian playing in sink
- M & M flicking man's face world records
- 50p per hour

DID U KNOW?

ELVIS HAS THE MOST SELL RECORDS FOR A DEAD GUY

Sunday 16ᵗʰ May 1999

Today, Rachel's brother woke me up about 9.00am, that's early for a weekend, trust. He kept watching TV and shit. This morning me and Rachel were just relaxing in bed for a time. Yesterday, I forgot to mention, I am going to a barbecue at Rachel's auntie's house. It's the same mad one from last time.

At 3.00pm we left to go there. If you remember her auntie lives in Shepherds Bush. When we got there it was just bare little kids and some f**ked up German man. The little kids tried to test me at Tekken 2, but I just battered them. After, I was playing this kid at Fifa 98, and I f**ked him up, 11 - 5 with Cook Islands, Bo! And he was Brazil. The barbecue was really shit. Me and Rachel kept going into the spare room. She was just stimulating me because I can't do nothing to her, periods remember. I was still having those titties.

We left the barbecue about 7.20 and Rachel's Mum drove me to Ealing Broadway Station. I got a train at 7.53pm. I got to the Station at 7.30pm and just had to wait. When I got to Langley, MJP was just waiting there for me. He gave me a lift to my house. We played a little computer then he went home.

Funniest thing all day:-

• £50 - buy a bike with that.

DID U KNOW?

THE EGYPTIANS HAD ELECTRICITY ABOUT 2000 YEARS AGO, BEFORE WE EVEN KNEW ABOUT IT.

Monday 17ᵗʰ May 1999

This morning I got a lift to school from JD on his bike. Today we had our last exam. It was Science and was quite easy. School was f**ked today. I lost my bag. I think someone's razed it or just taken it by accident, but I couldn't find it after school.

After school I bopped round JD's house and just watched some Wrestle Mania videos and he played his new CD, Chocolate Boy (yeah I know it's old but it's JD innit). I left JD's around 7.00pm and had to bop home. When I got in MJP came round and we had some cheats for WWF War Zone. Later on Simmons came down just to return some videos, MJP was still here at this time as well.

At 9.30pm I rang Rachel because she sent me a written message on her mobile. I just chatted to her for a while and told her to watch Candyman 2 at 10.00pm. After I watched a bit of Candyman 2 in my mum's room and went to bed. Now I am just writing in my diary and watching Royal Rumble 92.

Funniest thing all day:-

• JD, Blondie
• MOD – Ministry of Defence

DID U KNOW?

Every 17th of each month I have written in.

Tuesday 18th May 1999

Today me and JD got into school late again. Our first lesson was PE but we didn't do it because we were late. After, we had Business and just messed about. Today, at break I found my bag. Some f**king crusty dinner lady had it. She bought it in the building because it was raining. At lunchtime me and Kenworthy done a little raze. We got a hat, some pens, some headphones (for my Discman) and some coke. All the things we raze that we don't want we give it to the little kids. We just shove it in their bags when they're not looking. It's like Robin Hood innit! We gave the coke away to the poor, but its f**ked up because Robin Hood razed from the rich and gave to the poor, we just raze from the poor and give to the poorer. There's some tramps at our school.

After school JD went to get his bike and it wasn't there. He got razed. It's because at school we got some pole things outside the office and because we were late he just left it there without locking it. But I think it's the Year 11s because they come in whenever they want to. So one of them must have taken his bike, that's dark. We didn't know how we were gonna get home so JD rang his parents to come and pick him up. They weren't in so he left a message. At this time we had the school phone so I rang Rachel on her mobile and chatted to her for a while, until the Caretaker (Matt) came and told me to put it down. I just hung up on her.

Ten minutes later, JD's mum, well not his mum, his foster mum came to pick us up. In the car she was moaning at JD hard. It also sounded like she was blaming me for it because she kept saying, "why were you late?" and, "why did you go round Robert's when you could have been early?" It's because if we early, we wouldn't have had to put his bike there.

When I got home I just relaxed and read a bit of this diary with all the f**king pages going everywhere. After, MJP came round but left at 6.30pm, and so did I, to go Kickboxing. I had an alright lesson today. I didn't feel tired at all. I'm not sure if I am still fighting this Sunday in Birmingham.

After, I bopped down to Trelawney Avenue to get a drink and I met all them usual lot. I chilled with them for a little while then I walked with this girl because she was going Slough and I was just walking the same way. No, I didn't lips her, she's got a man. Well, not a man, it's Dick Head Robert from down the road. What do these girls see in him?

When I got in I didn't do a lot, bye!

Also - I am getting scared something's gonna happen to me because 2 of my friends got razed hard, Kenworthy and JD. Maybe it's God giving me a sign saying don't raze anymore.

Funniest thing all day:-

- Denzil and Jutla stamping on Peter

Robb Peters

DID U KNOW?

SHOPPING MALLS WERE FIRST MADE IN THE USA.

Wednesday 19ᵗʰ May 1999

Today I never went school because I didn't feel too well. During today I just played some WWF War Zone and taped Mousehunt off Front Row. In the night Rachel rang and was telling me about her last day at school.

DID U KNOW?

THE FIRST ZOO WAS FORMED IN CHINA IN THE 12ᵀᴴ CENTURY.

Friday 21ˢᵗ May 1999

Today I got to school really early because JD picked me up, really early 8.10am. Today, Kenworthy wasn't at school so I didn't raze. At break today the whole school had some massive rumble and I did some elbow drop on some First Year, then whilst I was on the floor someone treaded on my finger. My finger is now proper f**ked and all bent at the front. Miss Tucker says it's not serious, but trust you should see it its f**ked.

Well, after school I got a lift home from JD, and tonight there's nothing happening so Rachel is just staying round. Rachel came round at 7.00 and was happy because today I was feeling horny. At 9.30pm I rang Hanghei to see what he was doing, but he was in and because Rachel was round he says he'll come over for a while, he wanted to see what Rachel looked like. When he came round, me, him, my Mum and Rachel all watched the film Blade. Rachel had seen the film before and kept telling me what was gonna happen, she was annoying me.

Hanghei left at 12.00am when the film finished.

In the night me and Rachel just did bare shit. She was giving it to me good. At 3.30am we stopped fucking about (get it?)and we were bored and didn't know what to do. I just fell asleep.

142

8.30am I went upstairs to sleep.

Saturday 22ⁿᵈ may 1999

This morning I had some proper f**ked up dream, it involved me and MJP razing some shop, then me f**king Roseanne (the fat one from TV) but in the dream she was boom and also I was in Florida but it was exactly the same as down here. Trust it was f**ked.

Luckily Rachel's mobile rang and woke me up. I was still half asleep though (the time was about 11.30am). I woke up properly at 12.30pm and had a bath.

All through this morning my mum was moaning at me about loads of different things.

At 2pm I walked Rachel to the bus stop. Also MJP and Jason were with us at this time. Rachel's bus took the piss and came about 2.45pm.

At 3.30 we caught a train to Paddington. Today for some reason we decided to bop down to Canary Wharf, instead of the same place every week.

We got the tube to Tower Hill and had to bop to another station which was only a minute away (Tower Gate station). At Tower Gate station we had to get on Dockland Light rails. They were boom little trains but were weird because they control themselves; I mean there was no driver it was just moving on its own. Just as we were approaching Canary Wharf we could see the Millennium Dome. It was hench.

Anyway when we got to Canary Wharf we looked around and there was f**k all. Just some little minor shopping centre and just bare docks and water shit. We asked some woman where the nearest High Street was and she said Poplar. So we thought we'd go there. The train took 5 minutes to come and we could have just bopped down the tracks, the stations were so closed to each other.

When we got to Poplar we looked for the High Street. But guess what the f**king High Street was just some cheapy piece of shit; yeah that woman needs a slap.

We didn't stay in Poplar for long, cos we had all these rude boys watching us and looking like they wanted to beat us up. So we breezed on a train back to Tower Gate. At Tower Gate we had our one minute bop to Tower Hill.

At Tower Hill we got a train to Embankment then we got the Bakerloo Line to Piccadilly Circus. We thought we might as well just go some place we know well.

We bopped round Troc, Leicester Square and just the usual places. We only stayed there for about an hour then thought we'd breeze home.

We got the train to Paddington then at 7.48pm to Langley. Jason got off at Hanwell. I got in at 8pm and had bare dinner because I was starving.

At 9.15pm MJP knocked to go to this party at Javan's house. As we were bopping there we found out it was no longer on. So we just breezed into Slough anyway, because I had to take some movies back to Blockbusters. When we got Slough we got a call from Simmons and he was in the Sports Bar. He told us to come in but we weren't dress for it. We still walked up there though.

Outside the Sports Bar we met Hanghei, Brian, Shane, Daomi and loads of other people. After me, Brian and MJP tried to get in the Sports Bar but the bouncer was asking for ID. But that was a minor because we just climbed over this wall to get in.

In the Sports Bar we met Simmons, Nicholas and just the usual people. I also met a few girls from school. The Sports Bar was alright, they played some bad tunes. But they never let us MC because they said they were getting paid for it, sick brares not even one chat.

The Sports Bar finished at 12am and after we just hung about outside for a while. But me, MJP and Brian just started bopping home. On the way we got some chicken at some cheap imitation of KFC place.

I got home about 1.15am and just watched a bit of TV but then breezed to bed.

Funniest things all day:

- Poplar play
- Just won't suck Jim's dick

DID U KNOW

ZUT MEANS BLAST IN FRENCH

Sunday 23rd May

This morning I woke up about 11am. At 12pm I mowed the lawn. After MJP came over but only to get his bike.

During the day I was so bored. Around 4pm I breezed to Jim's to get my bike fixed, but he wasn't in. So I breezed to JD's, trust I was bored.

I stayed at JD's for time. I just played some WWF raw and watch some films. Daomi also knocked for me at one point but that's minor.

I left JD's at 7.30pm then when I got in Rachel rang and we were just chatting strangely about each other's bits and pieces, we just don't know what to chat about anymore, we've been going out for time.

Funniest thing all day:

- MJP- JD sleeping out shop to buy game
- Mum mouth-bla
- Da tranz – what the f**k

DID U KNOW?

IT'S IMPOSSIBLE TO GO A WHOLE DAY WITHOUT LOOKING AT YOUR DICK

Monday 24th May 1999

Today JD gave me a lift to school again. School was alright today. I've been getting school early now. Also my finger is still brock.

After school didn't do a lot just watched TV and Rachel, like always rang. Also I rang Claire and I'm meeting her sometime next week.

At this moment I'm just relaxing in bed and for some reason I'm watching the Lion King, shit I must be f****ked**, someone blast me quick.

Funniest thing all day:-

- Daniel Sturgess – JD bro locked in cages- the it driving to school.
- Rachel- you hurt me- yaaa
- Geza from Potters Bar

DID U KNOW?

THERE IS ONLY ONE MCDONALDS IN THE WHOLE OF THE ISLE WIGHT.

Tuesday 25th May 1999

Today I woke up really early and was on time when JD came to pick me up for school.

At break today me and Kenworthy went to the Sports Hall to see if we could take part in some Windsor and Eton athletics thing. We were allowed, I'm doing 100 metres and rally. Kenworthy doing some throwing shit.

After school I was supposed to go to a detention because I went out of school at lunch. But if couldn't be fucked to go so I got a lift home from JD. At 5.30pm today I got calls from my bird Rachel and MJP. They were just chatting their mess.

Later at 6.30pm I went to kickboxing. It was quite an easy lesson. I was fighting this dick head who thinks he's out of a kung fu movie. He kept saying I know snake and all animal styles. He also kept jumping up and down. I still battered him up though, thinking he's Bruce Lee and shit.

After kickboxing I bopped down to Trelawney Avenue and met bare people like Kieron , Kalvin, Craig , Brian, Guv, Wayne, Sean, Terrie P, all them ugly girls that always hang down there, Michael J, Kemar , Carline and some fat boy with bare spots, but he's minor.

After I bopped home with Carline. I got in at 9.30pm then just had some dinner and now I'm relaxing in bed.

Funniest thing all day:-

- Future man Shaq out
- Jutla – it's a test, no!!!!

DID U KNOW?

ALBERT EINSTEIN WAS BORN IN GERMANY IN 1879

E=MC2 AND TING

Wednesday 26th May 1999

This morning I got a lift to school from JD. Today I had that athletics thing in Windsor and Eton tracks. We had to do our first lesson at school, which was Maths and shit I haven't done the homework, reminds me because it's in for tomorrow.

We left school at 10.25am and because my school's so cheap we had to walk there. It wasn't that far, but our school's still cheap.

We got there about 10.50pm and it was some proper athletics place. I thought it would just be like painted tracks and shit but it was proper stadium like shit.

Me and Kenworthy were looking around for skeet. Then they called out when the events were on. Daniel Mountain had to do his straight away and he came last, it was 400 metres. My race was at 12.30pm, so had bare time.

During the day all people from my school were losing. Kenworthy didn't even do his shot putt event because he couldn't be f**ked and shamed up if he f**ked up. I also met Nathan and he was with those Windsor Girl's girls.

At 12.30pm I was just waiting till my race started, with Luke. As my race was beginning I was getting proper nervous and thinking I'm gonna come last, there's gonna be some proper fast people. I started the race shit but did alright. I came 3rd or 4th out of 6. But there was big fuck off giant people even bigger than me. I still qualified for the next race though.

Before my next race I was just trying to find girls, me and Kenworthy. We were also trying to set up this little year 7 with some girls. I spoke to Nathan for a while and made a £1.00 bet I'd win the next race.

When I started my next race, I was thinking nah I've lost. They were all doing it so professional; I was running like the Cops were after me. Mark from Hanwell once told me that was the best way to think when about to race.

Well I came 6th out of 8 and two Windsor boys came 2nd. The Windsor boys are so f**Ked up the must get fed steroids for breakfast. You should see how fast those mother f**kers run.

Well after the race I was looking for Kenworthy but the fat bastard already left when his mum was supposed to be giving me a lift.

Well now all I had left was the relay which I thought we had a good chance of winning for some reason. Before the relay me and Ginger Nut geza in year 9 walked around looking for girls.

We found some girls and started chatting to them. They were a bit offkey at 1st but when they started chatting a bit they were safe. They were all from Bourne End but go school in Maidenhead. There was a boom one call Lara, she was not too bad.

A while later Daniel and some other people came along and were acting like plums. So I just said to the girls I'll chat to you later.

At 3.30pm they started all the relays. Our relay was last. It was me first for a good start, the Luke, Stevie G and last Daniel Mountain.

When we started I was doing alright then at my side of my eye I could see a mad Windsor boy speeding up behind me. I thought nah this brare ain't getting in front of me, so I strained hard and beat him, then passed the baton to Luke.

The team done really shit and came last. Mountain almost had a fight. The time was 4pm and it was over. I got all my stuff then got those girls numbers and left.

I had to bop but took a short cut through Upton Court Park. When I got in I was so tired I just f**king lay on the settee for time.

Also I got a letter from the Court with all my Witness Statements. They say so much shit. About how we gave them girls some paper instead of the £10. The Court case is now on June 7th.

Later on MJP came round and we played some tekhan. When he left I just watched American Sex then went to bed.

DID U KNOW?

THERE ARE 2 HAYES ONE IN MIDDLESEX AND ONE IN SOUTH EAST LONDON

Thursday 27th May 1999

Today JD wasn't going to school so I never got a lift. So I started walking and on the way to school I met my mum in a taxi and she gave me a lift to school, well the taxi man did.

After school I got a lift in the coach. The brare was safe and gave a free lift. I got in at 3.30pm then at 4.10pm Rachel came round.

We watched a bit of TV then went upstairs to watch a film, well not exactly but you know. I just put on the film I found which was 'The Mask'.

We never watched the film we were just doing bare tings for about an hour. Bare good sex.

Rachel left about 7.30pm and yeah I walked her to the bus stop and saw her off. Then bopped to the shop for the golden Whiskers for Shibbz.

Robb Peters

When I got in I had dinner. Later on I just did some homework.

Funniest thing all day:-

- The face on the leg
- Rachel's face while riding

DID U KNOW?

THE TIGER IS THE LARGEST MEMBER OF THE CAT FAMILY

Friday 28ᵗʰ May 1999

Today I got a lift from JD. It was just a normal school day today nothing special. When I got home I stripped because it was so f**king hot today.

Later today around 8pm Rachel came over because tonight were going cinema then after she's staying.

At 9.15pm we got a taxi to Slough because the film started at 9.30pm. The film we went to see was The Corrupter and I'm screwing because I paid for me and Rachel and we could of got in free. Slough Cinema they don't check tickets.

The film was quite poo. It finished at 11.30pm. Then me and Rachel just bopped home. When we got in I gave Rachel some vodka and pineapple.

Then we watched Scream 2 but didn't exactly watch it, she was all horny and pissed and kept rubbing me up. Also licking my nipples.

It was quite nice today we messed about a lot. At one point I was fingering her and I was watching it go in and out.

DID U KNOW?

SOUTHEND HAS THE LONGEST PIER IN THE WORLD

Saturday 29th May 1999

Today I woke up really early because my mum woke me up coming down stairs. At 10.30am my mum went out and at this time I was in the bath. Rachel was in the bathroom with me and she was watching me bathe. I tried to get her to come in with me by stripping her but she kept saying "I can't be bothered, another time yeah". No now you bitch, I thought.

After I got out of the bath me and Rachel were doing bare tings under the cover.

At 11.45am my mum came back and she almost caught me and Rachel. I just quickly jumped out the bed and put on some boxers, but they were back to front. Rachel just put the covers over her and my mum didn't realise she was naked. After we just got dressed. After we left.

Also I haven't mentioned it but I'm going to stay a weekend round Simmons dad's house in Southend.

Anyway I walked to Simmons' house and just told him to wait for me because I was just gonna walk Rachel to the bus stop. On the way to the bus stop I met Babylon Bob and he gave me £10 to go and get him some drinks but "shur tup" I just razed the man's money, rags. He's so crazy he'll probably forget.

I waited with Rachel till the bus came, of course I lipsed her you prick. I writ that for Simmons.

Anyway I walked through the park after, so I wouldn't meet Babylon Bob. When I got Simmons' drum, his dad was there. Then we got in the car and left.

It was about 2 hour's journey, mainly because there was bare traffic. We also passed Potters Bar.

When we got into Southend we could just see bare sea, it was the seaside and the beach is crusty, it's pebbles.

When we got to Simmons' dad we unpacked then we breezed out. We bopped to the sea front and I flexed a McyD's. We went all round the fair and the High Street. I can't believe it, we didn't even get any girls and there was bare trust.

Later on me and Simmons were chilling in some arcade place when some white brare came up to me and said "oi you give me those glasses" and took my glasses off my head. You're probably thinking why I didn't do anything, well.

1. Because he done it fast and I didn't see him coming and

2. He was with about 15 people

But that didn't really matter because after I just razed some glasses from some shop.

When we got home me and Simmons got ready to breeze out, probably a rave or something. We heard there was a rave in some place called Canvey Islands, which isn't an actually island. We walked about asking people how to get to dis Island place. Everyone was saying we have to get a train. So we thought we'd get a train there. We went to Southend central station then got a train to Benfleet which was were Canvey Islands was. When we got to Benfleet we didn't know where to go, so we asked some brare and he said it was about 30 minutes walk and the bus was in 20 minutes. So we thought allow dis and we went back on the train to Southend.

At Southend we found some raves but didn't get into them because I didn't have shoes and the dress code is dodgy. But we got in to a dirty pub and I was cherpesing 21 year old girls. But we got chucked out when we tried to get drinks at the bar. HuHH

All we did was chill round the arcade places and I had a few goes on the punch machine where I beat bare MEN.

We got bored so we went home; the time was about 11.45pm. When we got in we had to breeze straight back out to find Zoë (Simmons' sister). We just got Zoë and her fat friend then breezed home. When we got in we just listened to some tunes and Simmons read this whole diary from November 2nd 1998 till today. But I fell asleep then just woke up when he had finished reading it.

At 6.30am I woke up then went to sleep in the spare room.

DID U KNOW?

JUPITER IS THE LARGEST PLANET IN OUR SOLAR SYSTEM

Funniest things all day:-

- DEE – Bo bad tune
- Why does that man have the ugliest one?
- Guys in their cars going up and down playing chocolate boy and dolalee
- Southend doors – no handles
- SOUTHEND SOUTHHuHH
- SOUTHEND ON HuHH

Sunday 30th May 1999

This morning I woke up about 11am and Simmons' little brother (DEE) kept fighting me. He's only 6 coming up 7.

About 1.30pm Simmons and his dad went to McyD's to get breakfast. I just had one of those new Indian meals and a cheese burger, Bo.

About 2pm me and Simmons went out. We also had little DEE with us because we had to take him to the fair. We took him to the fair and at the fair we played some crazy golf. It was quite bad still.

After we just took him through the fair, on the go karts and the bumper cars. After we got a train to Southend Pier to see about some club tonight. We got on some train that took us across the 1 and a 3rd mile pier (the longest in the world).

When we got to the end of the pier we were asking people about dis rave tonight. We found out from some woman that it's outside, the music's dodgy and erm erm hate to say this but gay men go there. So we thought yeah this sounds good, fuck you not really we thought fuck that shit. After that we got a train back to the mainland bit. Then we thought we'd take the little shit DEE back. But we really didnt feel like bopping. And luckily we met his mum on the way and she took him.

So now we thought let's get some girls.

There were bare girls earlier but we didn't cherpes because we were with that little shit, nah only joking he's alright (kind of).

Me and Simmo bopped back into the fair. In the fair we went on this ride. Some mess that just goes up and down, also upside down.

After we just walked through the fair looking for some next ride. On the way some little girls came up to me and said "my sister likes you" and pointed to their sister. This girl was alright so I told the little girls to tell her to come and speak to me. She came and spoke to me. But was speaking really quietly. O'yeah and shit it's nasty but she had some yellow shit on her tooth, you know that shit which some people get. Well I asked this girl if she wanted to come on a ride, and she did. So we went on some cheap imitation of Loggers Leap ride. It was alright. I didn't get wet but Simmons did, ha ha. After that we went on another ride. Some proper shit roller coaster f**ked up shit. I can't explain it.

After we all went in some arcade place and just chilled in there. I got her number in there because she was leaving soon. But she kept trying to hold my hand. Hey it's not that type of party. Just wanna go on rides and shit. Bitch you got yellow teeth you can't be my girl.

The girls left about 8pm then after we done that long bop back home. When we got in we just relaxed for a while then got ready to go out.

We went back out at 9.30pm then bopped to the place where you get the train to the end of the pier. We were gonna go to that rave but Simmons didnt wanna go plus I didnt have shoes. So we bopped down to some pub and got in there. The pub was shit though; we only stayed for about half an hour. O'yeah also on the way there we met some girls and they want to meet up later at 2.30am.

Anyway after we were just looking for a place to go, we bopped through the High Street, everywhere. At 11pm we were gonna go in this club called

Totts but couldn't get in because I had no shoes. So we thought we'd go back and try to get some shoes.

When we got to Simmons dads, we got some shoes but they were a bit tight, size 10 when I'm a 13.

As we only had 20 minutes until the stopped letting people in, Simmons dad gave us a lift. When we got to the door the man said it's not worth coming in because it's finishing, offkey HuHH. So all we did was bop back to the arcade. We still were gonna meet those girls at 2.30am.

At 12.45am we thought we'd go home then come back later because we had bare time to waste. When we got in we just relaxed.

Shit erm we went there and the girls won't there and that all because it's 4.30am and I'm tired. BYE.

Funniest things all day:-

- Half Philippine – what half a bean
- Afro world
- Fence – no Simmons
- All we got was one number and a stand up

Bank Holiday Monday 31st May 1999

Well last night all we did was leave at 2.15am. We bopped down to the sea front bit to meet those girls. But they won't there. So we just chilled for a bit then went home and just messed about, kicking over bins and shit. Well that's what we did but couldn't be bothered to write it last night.

Well today I woke up at 12pm. Later around 2pm we went down to McDonalds to get some breakfast. We got some munch then just chilled around the fair and the arcade area. Today there was some air show thing in Southend, so there were bare people down there. Today there were also bare girls and cos this was our last day in Southend we thought we'd try and get bare girls. But we only got one number, some alright girl from Southend. There were bare nice girls walking pass but most were too old or had boyfriends. There were some boom girls at one point which were tick but they were with their mum.

We went back to Simmons dads. Later about 6.30pm we left to go home. It was quite a long journey; I got home about 8.25pm.

When I got in I just told my mum about my weekend and after I rang Rachel and just chatted to her, she's coming round tomorrow.

Well at the moment the time is 9.30pm and I'm gonna finish there because I doubt I'll be doing anything more.

DID U KNOW?

Sally James used to be in a kids programme call Tiswas in the early 80's

END OF THE MONTH
FUNNIEST THING ALL MONTH

1. SCHOOL DINNERS(JASON)
2. SOUTHEND DOORS
3. ER, I BEG YOU(MJP)
4. HALF'S LIKE A BEAN (SIMMON DAD)
5. MOD-MINISTRY OF DEFENCE

Tuesday 1st June 1999

Bo, it's another month and I wonder what's in store for me this month. Last month was alright I done quite a lot of shit, but should of had more girls. Like when I was in Southend.

This month

On Wednesday – hair cut then breezing round London

On Monday – going Court definitely this time

After – bare raves and skeet.

Well today I had to wake up really early because I had to go and see my lawyer (solicitor). I left my house about 8.45am then breezed a bus to Slough. In Slough I got the 9.06am train to Windsor.

When I got to Windsor I bopped to the office, my mum doesn't work there anymore if you're wondering, bitch. At the office I spoke to my solicitor (lawyer) and we just chatted about the Witness Statements. I just showed him the bits I disagreed with. We were also talking about how stupid all whole thing was, I mean over £10.

After I breezed a train back to slough and went through Slough then knocked for JD. But he wasn't in so I flexed a bus home.

When I got in the time was only 11am. I got bored so I watched a few films. Also today Rachel's coming round for a while, she misses me, it was only Saturday I see her (stupid cow).

Well Rachel came round about 2.15. As soon as she got round I took her upstairs and just started stripping her and shit.

We weren't having lots of sex just like in and out shit, if you get my drift with your biff.

Later on around 4pm I was fingering Rachel and just looking at it going in and out. My face was right next to it and I kept saying I feel like kissing it, because the fanny was right in my face. Then Rachel said I don't really care, I thought rare because she's not like that. So I started licking her fanny and it wasn't that bad. And no it never tasted of fish, I couldn't really taste nothing. After she said it was quite nice.

At 4.15pm we stopped messing about and I just washed my mouth hard. Brushed my teeth, used mouth wash and everything.

Rachel left about 7.30pm but she didn't want to go. But her mum didn't let her stay. Yeah yeah blar blar, I walked her to the bus stop lipsed her.

Well today I had another boring night in. I was supposed to go Chalfont. But no transport.

Also this is nasty but I got a fanny hair stuck in my tooth at one point.

Funniest thing all day:-

- London buses

DID U KNOW?

KARATE MEANS EMPTY HAND

DID U KNOW?

SEGA BACK TO FRONT SPELLS AGES

DID U KNOW?

NINTENDO MEANS HARD WORK IN JAPANISE

Wednesday 2nd June 1999

Today I woke up about 11am. I was getting my haircut at 1pm. So I got up and had a bath. When I was in the bath I was on the phone to Rachel. We were just chatting about me licking her out. See also asked me to stay and guess what she said she wanted to give me a shiner tonight if I stay. She said it's because she knows me and we've been going out for time.

After the bath MJP called and was saying he couldn't be bothered to breeze London. So I said I'll arrange to meet some local girls or something. I arranged to meet Lara and Gemma from Bourne End; I met them at the athletics thing.

At 12.30pm MJP came round and we breezed out. We got on a bus at 12.45pm and I got my haircut at 1pm and MJP AT 1.30PM. After we met Ben outside then breezed to the train station.

We got the train to Maidenhead and the time was 2pm. We looked to see what time the Bourne End train was coming and it was coming at 2.42pm. So we bopped round Maidenhead to waste time then came back at 2.40pm and breezed on the train (OTT).

We got to Bourne End about 2.50pm. We just waited for a while then they came. They looked alright but Lara looked better. The girls took us to their friend's house because there was nowhere to go in Bourne HuHH.

When we got to the house there were bare metallers. They were all dressed offkey. We were taking the piss out of their music and them living in countryside lands.

We only were there for an hour and a half. Then had to leave because they were going to some bbq and the girl that was having it said we can't come. We bopped back to the station with Lara and this girl called Elisa (metaller). They waited with us until the train came. But I never lipsed her because I found out she had a man. She was flirting with me but I didn't try it just in case I got blasted innit.

When we got back to Slough I got the train back to Langley. But MJP and Ben went to Slough because MJP was meeting his mummy and Ben was jetting drum. As you know I'm staying round Rachel's, you probably know why. Well when I got to Langley I bopped home then had some dinner. I also wrote in the diary for the day and now I'm leaving to go Rachel's. I reckon tonight me and Rachel will be doing one of those 69 things.

Well I got to Rachel's about 9 something. Tonight was quite bad, did bare tings.

Well do you think I got a shiner and a 69? Yeah of course I f**king did and it was bad, meaning good. We did bare 69ers and they were just so nice.

We did have a bit of sex.

We went to sleep about 12.30am and at the end of the day I must have got about 13 shiners.

Funniest thing all day:-

- Ben's mess- no cum shag in field
- Da countryside –boog

DID U KNOW?

SLOUGH USED TO BE CALLED BOOM TOWN AND WAS 3RD RICHEST TOWN IN THE COUNTRY. Yea boom town. Boom innit

Thursday 3rd June 1999

This morning I woke up about 6am and I was naked in Rachel's bed. I heard someone coming down the stairs so I quickly got my clothes (well pants, I mean boxers) then jumped into my bed. But I just fell asleep, naked though.

I woke up later about 9am and couldn't get back to sleep. So I just watched some TV with Rachel. At 12.00pm everyone went out and I was getting more shiners . Rachel loves doing it now, before she hated it but now she doesn't mind sucking my ding a ling or me licking her poom poom.

At 6.30pm I had some dinner. It was some mash potatoes, sausage and beans. It was better than that last dinner they gave me.

After dinner me and Rachel were just doing bare shit again. 69ers the lot. At 8pm I left Rachel's.

When I was in Langley I rang Simmons to see if anything was happening. He was just down Kidderminster Park. So I bopped down there and there were quite a lot of people. There was Simmons, Guv, Wayne, Brian, Lee and more people.

I only stayed there for about half hour then walked home with Guv. When I got in I just relaxed and tonight looks like another night in, yeah.

Funniest thing all day:-

- You f**king pidgin
- You scidmark
- Man in car bussing out Mortal Kombat theme
- Mr Gay UK tune

DID U KNOW?

GARLIC IS SUPPOSED TO KEEP AWAY EVIL SPRITs

Friday 4th June 1999

This morning I woke up about 10am. At 12pm I had a bath then got dress to breeze out? At 12.30pm JD knocked and a few minutes after MJP did. We played some WWF Raw Zone and MK4.

At 2.15pm me and MJP breezed out and JD went home on his new bike. We went to MJP's drum for a while because we missed the train at 2.30pm so we were gonna flex the 3pm one.

At 3PM we got the train to Paddington. We were gonna go Lewisham but MJP couldn't be f**ked so we thought might as well go Central London. Before we got the train to London we got a burger from KFC, just thought I'd mention.

After we got a train to Piccadilly Circus and just bopped around Troc and Leicester Square.

Around 6.30ish it was getting a bit boring so I flicked through my phone book to see if I could find any nice girls to ring and meet up with. I rang Gemma from Leyton on her mobile. I asked her where she was and she f**king said Lewisham, the place we were gonna go. I just blasted MJP. Gemma wanted to meet up with us so we thought as we weren't doing anything might as well go link her.

We got the train to Leicester rectangle to Piccadilly then got the train to Elephant and Castle. At Elephant and Castle we changed for main line trains. We waited for time for a train to Lewisham but we didn't know we had to go Peckham Rye station. The time was about 6.10pm and our train was coming at 6.28pm so we bopped round Elephant and HuHH. We just bopped to some petrol garage and got some munch. We never really bopped into the High Street, just near the station. When we got back to the station we bopped on our train to Peckham. When we got to Peckham we bopped around for a while. MJP just flexed a McDonalds. At 6.50pm we got or train to Lewisham. We passed a station called Nunhead.

When we got to Lewisham we bopped round but cos it was late all the shops were shut. I kept ringing Gemma, but her phone was turned off.

Gemma's mobile was just permanently switched off so in the end we left. We got the train to Charing Cross, which we should of got on from the start.

Then went back to Langley. At Langley MJP went to Naomi's and I just went home. When I got home I had some dinner then just watched some TV. Tonight is another night in, like it has been all these week off holiday thing.

Funniest thing all day:-

- Cheap imitation of Thames trains – buttons- small door – crusty
- Shop tune – soap music

DID U KNOW?

WOOLWORTHS BEGAN IN 1879 WHEN FRANK WINFIELD WOOLWORTH OPENED A FIVE CENT STORE IN UTICA, NEW YORK

Saturday 5ᵗʰ June 1999

Today Rachel rang at 12.30 and I and I asked her to come round.

I shouldn't have though because it Saturday and I could of breezed in to London and got some skeet or something.

At 1pm my mum left to go Slough, so she can buy a dress for the party tonight, you know the mum works in that mansion. Anyway at 1.30 Rachel came round. We just watched TV and didn't really mess about that much she gave me a few shiners and I was just rubbing her pomm pomm flaps. Also at one point Rachel was playing with it and she said to me can I suck it. This was funny but I thought of course you can you stupid bitch. So I said yeah just do what you want. What boy would say no??????

At 4pm my mum came back from Slough and had her driving lesson.

At 5pm Rachel got ready to leave but before she left we was gonna have a quick sex. We kept trying to do it but my mum kept coming upstairs. We did manage to do a quick one. 3 and half minutes.

At 5.30 Rachel left and I didn't walk her to the bus stop because I had to get ready to go to this place tonight. Rachel's going to E&D in Brentford.

After I had a bath and got ready to go. I had to dress up really nice even had to buss shoes. At 6.10 we got a taxi to Uxbridge where we got a coach to some place in Buckinghamshire, Chesham. We went to some hench mansion called the Bury. When we got there we were just hanging around this garden bit, drinking wine and as my mum said "mingling". But in my word's chatting to offkey posh people.

Around 8.30- 9.00ish we went in some tent thing and got some munch. But it was shit like salmon, prawns, quiche and some messed up rice. After dinner everybody was just raving to messed up tunes. With their shit D.J who hadn't even heard of Chocolate Boy. All though the night I never dance just sat there and rang a few friends. I also chatted to my mum friend's daughter, she was alright but she was 23 (would of spratted it still).

At 11.38pm me and that girl was just bored so we got some helium balloons and we were just breathing them in. My voice sounded proper offkey.

At 12.30am we left and got back on the coach to Uxbridge. At Uxbridge we got in a taxi with my mum's friend and her daughter. I lipsed the girl, nah joke.

When I got in I had some munch then went to bed.

Funniest things all day:-

- April- oo oo
- Helium – all the girls

DID U KNOW?

THE FILM THREE MEN AND A BABY HAS A GHOST IN IT.

Sunday 6th June 1999

Today I had a nice little lay in. I woke up today around 1pm. Today I was gonna breeze down to Hanwell but I couldn't be f**ked.

I rang Rachel after, to see if she went E&D and if it was good. She said it was quite good and she also met Jason down there.

After I got a call from JD and I told him I'd come over for a while because Sunday's are boog.

At 2.30 MJP came over, then we breezed to JD's (we bopped). We stayed at JD's for time and it was proper jokes. At 6.30 we left.

When I got in I just had some munch. Also watched a bit of E.T. at 9.30pm MJP came round for a while but left at 10.00pm.

At this moment I'm watching Kingpin and its jokes, later star.

Funniest things all day:-

- JD's – boom boom tune- err no JD
- Da president wrestler
- Fart – not natural
- Gripping me
- Jumping at JD – Me and MJP
- Tekhan – Nina shur tup slap

DID U KNOW?

THERE'S A RESTAURANT IN BRENTFORD CALLED FAT BOYS CUISINE .

Monday 7th June 199

Anyway, today I had to wake up really early to Court. But the way it's not the actually Court case, I just have to go there to plead, you know guilty or not guilty.

Well we had to be at the Court at 9.45am so we left at 8.30 to get the Maidenhead bus. We got there at 9.30. We chatted to my solicitor.

Today there was bare people we knew there. Because there were bare people it took long to get in the Court and plead. We went in the Court at 1.00pm.

When we were in the Court we had to plead in front of some offkey Magistrates. I pleaded not guilty, obviously.

Any way after I met Nicholas and got some munch from McyD's, Nico went home.

After munching we got the train to Slough then flexed a bus home. We got in about 2.00pm.

After I just relaxed and watched some TV. About 4.30 JD came round and we played some computer, sick brare.

After just watched more TV and Rachel also rang, just chatting her mess.

Funniest things all day:-

- Little criminals
- Hire Judge Judy
- Da cousin match wwf
- Pumping girl from behind- showing how its done solicitor sees

DID U KNOW?

THE DEVIL USED TO BE KNOWN AS OLD NICK IN ENGLAND TIME AGO.

Tuesday 8ᵗʰ June 1999

Today at 8.15am JD knocked for me to go school. He had his bike with him so I flexed to Simmons and he let me borrow his bike.

School was alright today, it was jokes. At lunch today me and Kenworthy tried to raze but all the bags had bare shit, like books, dirty shoes and just mess. At lunch I played some football with Denzel, Jutla, JD and Christian. It was proper jokes.

After school I rode home with JD yo. When I got in I just relaxed and made a few calls. I rang Bianca and she was telling me about some event going on in Ilford dis Saturday. After I rang Natalia and I might be hooking up with her this Saturday if I don't meet Bianca.

At 6.30pm I left to go kickboxing. It was quite a tick little lesson today, we had jokes. We were doing holds and self defence techniques. After kickboxing I just had some munch and chilled.

DID U KNOW?

KELLY BROOK IS FROM KENT

Wednesday 9th June 1999

Today school was not too bad. I got there late with JD. My first lesson was History and that was poo. My second lesson was Maths, again a crap lesson.

At break I was just chilling and shit. After I had English and got sent out for calling Miss a pigeon, "later", "what's wrong with that"? After we had lunch.

Today I just razed some Playstation magazines, which is alright because they have some cheats in them. Anyway the other two lessons were poo, can't be f**ked to write about them.

When I got in I got a letter and it's from Rachel as you can see. It's just saying how much she loves me, there was also something else with the letter but I never put it in the diary.

At 6pm JD came round and we played some computer. MJP came round a bit later. JD left about 8.30pm and MJP left about 9.45pm. After Simmons came round to get his bike, the HuHH.

Later about 10.30pm Rachel rang and I was just chatting to her for a while. After just watched the highlights of England v Bulgaria (1-1).

Funniest things all day:-

- Shibbz – girls he shagged
- Attacking JD
- Our back up- Shibbz
- JD- because somebody CHEATED

DID U KNOW?

The password in crash bandicoot for all 32 levels, both keys and all the gems is

Triangle, Triangle, Triangle, Triangle, X, Square, Triangle, Triangle, Triangle, Triangle, Square, X, Triangle, Circle, Triangle, Triangle ,Triangle, Circle, Square, Triangle, X, X, X, X

Thursday 10th June 1999

Today I got a lift to school from one of my school teachers, Mrs. Garner. It was proper embarrassing so I was dropped off near the school and bopped the rest of the way. At lunch time me, Kenworthy, JD and Steven got bare chocolates. It was jokes. We also razed a few pens and shit, but it's getting harder to raze because people are carrying their bags.

After I was just cotching and watching TV. At this moment I'm watching Kenan and Kel and it's jokes.

Anyway I'm gonna stop writing here because I doubt anything's gonna happen, it's Thursday night.

Funniest things all day:-

- God made the fanny- how's your fanny?
- Kenworthy- hit ball on Natalie's head
- Made Rachel a Wrester in game, with red trousers

DID U KNOW?

NARCOLEPSY IS A DISORDER WHICH CAUSES EXCESSIVE DAYTIME SLEEPINESS

Friday 11th June 1999

Bo it's Friday and today I have just been in a bad mood, f**k knows why.

School was alright today, we had a non uniform day. It's because of the voting thingy.

After school I bopped home with JD, Charline and her little crew.

Well today there's nowhere to go so I asked Rachel to stay. I was gonna go down the ice arena but that's boog. So I reckon tonight is gonna be one of those usually me and Rachel messing about days. Apart from today will be messed cos she's on her period. So it will be titties and bare shiners.

Well Rachel came round about 9.30pm and we just messed about, doing the shit you do when your girl's on a period. That includes shiners.

During the night I kept getting calls from Claire from Southend and tomorrow me and MJP might be staying round her house. We're gonna breeze London then Southend.

At 3am this morning I was telling Rachel a few stories. But it was f**ked telling her.

Funniest thing all day:-

• Your head's scratchy

COCO POPS HAVE CHANGED THEIR NAME BACK

DID U KNOW?

IT'S IMPOSSIBLE TO SNEEZE WITH YOUR EYES OPEN.

Saturday 12th June 1999

Easy people what's happing, well today was alright I suppose but it was a bit f**ked up, because I could of had a militant day. But it was all f**ked up.

All through this morning my mum was pissing me off about my room. I was supposed to go London but I didn't end up going. I could of met with sexy Natalia or gone to that thing in Ilford. And cos of my mum I never went. Also Rachel wanted to come London and I didn't want her to, I kept trying to make up reasons to get her not to come.

The time was 5pm and MJP rang and he was saying he couldn't be f**ked to breeze London.

After I stopped chatting to MJP I had to go and take my bike to Jim's. Rachel stayed at my house and waited for me.

OTW I met MJP and he breezed with me. I gave my bike to Jim then breezed home (with MJP). As soon as I got in Hanghei came round to see what's happening tonight. And shit tonight is some party down old Windsor.

Me, MJP and Hanghei all bopped Rachel to the bus stop and saw her off, goodbye Rachel we're getting skeet tonight. Straight after we bopped to Simmons' drum. We stayed round there for a while then we all flexed to mine (you know my house, stupid fool).

We played some computer for a while then left to go to this party.

We bopped down Langley Village Park and waited for Chris and Guv because they were flexing some draw. But they rang and we said we'll meet them at the train station. At the station we flexed the 18.12 train to Slough, allow Chris and Guv, they can meet us down there innit. When we got Slough we then breezed on the one to Windsor. When we got Windsor Simmons was saying we had to wait for them lot. So we waited in McyD's and had bare jokes.

Later on we met up with them two at some garden place in Windsor. We all bopped to the party. It was quite a bop. It took longer because we stopped for a while for Chris and Guv to build a zoot. We also stopped at a petrol garage, kebab van and an offy to get booze.

When we got to the place we met up with Nathan K and Matt. Then flexed in with them. The party was some football presentation thing. We met bare girls that we knew from Langley Grammar. I also met Holly and she was looking boom. I wanted her badly but she went with Chris somewhere then after I couldn't find her. We did M.C at one time but the D.J only had one tune and that was that Mr Wazo shit. Me, MJP and Chris M.Ced and everyone thought we were boom after that.

During the rest of the party I was just basically doing nothing. I didn't like the music it was poop. Simmons was having a good time, f**ked out of his brains. During the party, for some reason I badly wanted Catrina with her titties. She just looked bad and I just wanted to deal with that. But I never so shame on me the bad M.C, easy with the 1 2 3 inside the party, time to get you lively, err no Robert.

The party finished at 11.50 something and I was trying to lips Catrina with her titties but she was just giving me big pecks on my lips, minor flex.

After me and Hanghei flexed a lift home from Sam S. In the car was Catrina with her titties and the other Sam. I couldn't really try anything with Catrina with her titties because I was sitting at the front with her mum, with no titties.

When I got in I just relaxed in bed and played bare WWF Raw because I was still in a hype mood. I really should have stayed out. Anyway I went to sleep around 2.30am.

Well that's my day, could of been better but shit that's the way it goes mate.

Now go fool, see you tomorrow, bitch.

Funniest things all day:-

- Brother Brother- my twin in Southend same everything
- MJP Cousin him with a wig

DID U KNOW?

PEOPLE WHO SMOKE ARE MORE LIKELY TO SMOKE DRUGS THEN A PERSON WHO DOESN'T SMOKE

Sunday 13th June 1999

Err f**k let me tell you about my dream before I tell you about my day. Well it was quite a bad dream. I was in Southend but it wasn't Southend it was like New York London type place and I was staying in this house and every morning I was visited by all the Miss Money Pennies and they were all boom. They flexed my breakfast as well.

Also in the dream I had all my friends and we kept meeting different people like some half caste boy who was a nerd and everyone liked him apart from me. And we met this guy who was a local and no brares were touching us because we knew him. And the best thing about the dream was there were bare girls and they were all cherpsing us. And in my dream I got 100 numbers, then I woke up. But it was a dark dream, bare mans would love to have this dream

Well that was my dream, now I'll tell you about today. Well today was poo, did nothing apart from mow the lawn and I never went out. MJP came over for a while and Simmons in the morning. Then after nothing just rang Natalia and meeting her next week. Also Rachel rang and I watched South Park.

Funniest thing all day:-

- South Park- "have you seen her"

DID U KNOW?

JUDO WAS INVENTED BY CHEN YUAN PUN IN THE EARLY 17TH CENTURY

DID U KNOW?

BRITAIN HAS THE HIGHEST TEENAGE BIRTHRATE IN EUROPE

Monday 14th June

Err, I didn't go school today and nothing happened after. Now go.

Tuesday 15th June 1999

ALSO- FINGER IS STILL BENT BUT TODAY PUT CAST THINGY OVER IT.

Today has been an alright day. I wasn't gonna write today but thought what the heck, err blast me for saying what the heck.

Well today I got to school late because I had to bop. At lunch today it was jokes because we went to raze dis bag and I put my hand innit and I pulled out some krusty dirty knickers, trust I just dashed them at Kenworthy fat head.

That is funniest thing all day.

Later on in school, at the last lesson I got in class and went to sit down when I got a massive nose bleed. I missed nearly all the lesson because I was just in the toilet cleaning it up.

After school I flexed a lift from some fat brare who thought he was bad bussing out Chocolate Boy, no old tune matey I thought. The man only dropped me off at the bottom of Trelawney (the Police station end). So I bopped and on the way I met Chris, Wayne and Ricky S. I went with them to the park while they smoked some gear. Then after we waited outside Langley Grammar and met the usual, Simmons, Guv etc. I bopped home with Simmons.

When I got home MJP came round and played some computer. At 6.30pm I breezed kickboxing. When I got home I had some munch then went to

Jim's to get my bike. Later on Claire rang and I was taking the piss out of her living by the sea.

Funniest thing all day:-

- Krusty knickers
- Presidential elbow.

DID U KNOW?

THERE IS A TYPE OF CAT CALLED OCELOT FROM SOUTH AMERICA

Friday 18ᵗʰ June 1999

Before I write about today I just got to show you this little weekend planner for this weekend. I recon this weekend will be dark.

Weekend planner

Today- Fuel to mc, then after party and check this, Rachel's staying round but not coming out with me. She'll be there when I get home, that's dark. Get in and sex is just waiting there. And plus she's finished her exams today she'll probably want more.

Saturday- MJP's arranged to meet girls in SLOUGH AT 2PM. SUPPOSED TO BE PROPER BOOM. AT NIGHT SOME PARTY IN WINDSOR (A WINDSOR GIRLs GIRL). O SHIT YEAH SIMMON'S SHOP, BARE RAZE

SUNDAY - RELAX

Well today was alright but school was annoying me. People were just pissing me off. I couldn't wait to get home.

When I got home from school it was so hot so I just jumped in the tub then blared the tunes.

At 7.30pm MJP came round to breeze to Fuel. 10 minutes after Rachel came over. Me and MJP left to go Fuel while Rachel stayed round my yard.

The bus to Colnbrook took about an hour to come. During our waiting we were just chatting to Richard (with his fake £20 note) and Tina and Kirsty. When we got on the bus we met Nicholas and Sean, a few stops later. Nicholas was bussing shorts.

We go to Fuel about 9pm and just done bare M.Cing and we smashed it. It was f**ked up though because it finished 10pm and that is so minor, I don't even know what to say. So we bopped to this after party that was supposed to be on. At this time I was with Daniel Mountain, Kieron, Kalvin and that other boy who hangs around with them.

When we got to this house we got thrown out straight away because we had no booze and plus the boy didn't know us. Well he used to play for my football team but he was going on how were not invited. As we came out of the party we met up with MJP, Nicholas and Sean again.

After we didn't know where to go. Nicholas wanted to breeze to this party on the other side of Windsor. But I couldn't really go because Rachel was staying round my drum.

I bopped home with MJP but we flexed the long way because we stopped off at the kebab shop.

I got home at 12am and my mum and Rachel were both screwing at me because I left Rachel all alone.

In the night me and Rachel were just doing the usual. At one point I was licking her out and her face was making me so horny, I just jumped on her and started pumping her.

When Rachel was asleep Sean and Nicholas rang me and said the party was boom. Also Holly was down there and was asking about me. I jumped in a taxi and rags left Rachel. She was snoring so I guess she wouldn't mind. I had to jump out the taxi half way down the road from the party cos I had no money.

But when i got to the party it was finishing I was pissed. But Holly was there and bo I lipsed her. She was telling me she wanted to come back to my yard but I had Rachel there. So I was thinking about it, but cos I took too long some next 18 year old brare took her.

I got a lift back to Langley off some brare from school's ugly brother. Rachel was still asleep when I got in. Bo

Funniest things all day:-

- Christian- mum and girlfriend licking each other
- President –come
- Buss out a lyric – try some of this try some of this try some of this
- Fuel – all ready to bus round the other side – curtains closed.

Royal wedding Prince Edward and Sophie Saturday 19th June 1999

Today was a really strange day. It was just weirdy like things were not as planned but it was weird.

At 2pm today Rachel left to go home. She was moaning at me for leaving her. I just said my friends got in a fight and I had to do ninjas to save them. She didn't like my story. At this time MJP was with us because me and him were going Slough to meet some girl. Rachel was in a bit of a mood because I think she wanted to come out with me. But I thought nah because we're meeting yattys (girls).

When Rachel left we got our bus to go Slough. When we got to Slough it was 2.30pm and the girls weren't there. So we thought we might as well go some next place. We decided to go Reading. So we flexed a train there. When we got to Reading all we could see was BARE GIRLS. But first we flexed some munch before we went on a cherpes. In McyD's there were bare girls we should have cherpes but didn't.

After we were just bopping through the High Street. It was getting boring and we weren't getting no skeet. So we bopped to the station. At the station we looked for skeet but never found any. So we thought what the f**k is going on, come we get some girls. So we back into the High Street and got some girl's number. She was quite boom but had a man, she didn't mind giving me her number though, Davina from Bracknell.

After we bopped back to the station and I met some other girls, they were quite bad. They were from Oxford. I got their numbers too. Well not both, just one called Jess.

After that we just flexed a train back to Langley. We were gonna go to Windsor because there's bare people down there to see the Royal Wedding.

I got home at 6pm and had some munch. Sean rang after and kept saying quickly come round so we can breeze to Windsor before everybody goes.

Before I went to Sean's I knocked for Simmons and just waited for him to get ready to breeze out. Then we knocked for Sean and breezed. We bopped down to Spencer Road and met up with Chris, Brian and some Windsor Girl's girls. We stopped to chat to them for time then we all breezed over the Langley Park.

At the park we met Hanghei, Michael and MJP inside the party; sorry let's not get that started. Also I've forgot to write but that girl I met early from Oxford rang and she wants to met me in Slough tonight then guess what after stay over my drum, that smacks it.

We stayed round Langley for time and met bare people for example

Daniel Mountain, Kieron, Kalvin and that brare.

We were just chilling round the village. We heard about a few parties but never went. I was also waiting for Jess to ring me.

About 9.30pm we all flexed a train to Windsor. I thought might as well go the girls aren't coming down now. In Windsor we proper did shit. We were with those Windsor Girls' girls and they just wanted us to take them back to Windsor. But me, Simmons, Brian, Hanghei, Michael, MJP and that's about it, all left. We breezed.

When we got to Slough station we had to wait about 20 minutes for the Langley train. While we were waiting I got a call from Jess and she said she was in Oxford but still coming, sick braresses.

When we got to Langley it was round 11am and the girls said there'd be here in an hour. So we bopped around for a while then went to some girl's party. Just people smoking weed and listening to some Garage tunes. I had a little shake out then nicked some yogurts from the fridge.

At 11.30pm me and Hanghei breezed to my house. Not to go in but I had to charge my phone in case they were actually coming (the girls from Oxford). But I thought nah they ain't coming from Oxford-Slough (it was 12am). Then they rang and she was saying she was still coming. She said she'd be at Slough in an hour. They said they missed the train and were getting a bus.?????? I thought a bus to Slough.

After Simmons rang and I told him they were still coming. We were thinking these girls must want it bad.

At 1.30ish the girls rang and said they were at the train station. So me and Hangman bopped to the station in Slough. We wouldn't usually do that at that time but we just did it.

We met the girls at Tesco's and then took the long bop back to my drum. When we got in we just relaxed. I just flexed on a few tunes and the girls were having a smoke. After Liam rang and him and Simmons were coming round. When they came everybody was just Bunning bare skunk and Jess and Liam were f**king sniffing speed.

Later on around 4am we were all watching Scream 2. Everybody was falling asleep at this time and I was just cuddling up to Jess. I tried to lips her but all I was getting was a few pecks. She said it's because she doesn't know me that well.

At 6am me and Jess started watching Wish Master. I was falling asleep through this but trust Jess never went to sleep at all the whole night, it's because of the speed.

At 8.10am the girls got a taxi to Slough station to get home. Well I didn't really care that I didn't do any tings with her because it was jokes. Also means she's warmed up for next time.

Funniest things all day:

- Nuggets dip in milkshake
- Crazy brare- BREEZE
- Buckled off my bike
- Brare chatting about mans sexy mum- £50 for a picture
- All the way to see me

DID U KNOW?

THE EXPRESSION GETTING SACKED CAME FROM THE OLDEN DAYS WHEN PEOPLE GAVE THERE EMPLOYER A SACK THEN IT WAS HANDED BACK WHEN THEY WERE FIRED.

Father's Day Sunday 20ᵗʰ June 1999

Well today in the morning I've already written about. Well at 9am I watched the Simpsons, then at 10.30am I went upstairs and watched a bit of JD's video but I was so tired I just fell asleep.

I woke up later at 6.50pm and that's bare sleep. I started watching the rest of the video then I heard someone coming up the stairs. And you'll never guess who it was, it was Rachel. I thought rare. She just came over to see me which was safe.

Me and Rachel were just chatting. She was just chatting about how she thinks I might be cheating and why I don't go round her yard or ever go out with her. She was also saying I'm just using her. Trust me today it was almost over between me and Rachel. We were just pissing each other off. But after we just started kissing and forgot about it, damn.

While Rachel was round MJP and Christian also knocked, not together at separate times. After Christian left I walked Rachel to the bus stop, the time was about 9.45pm. We had to wait till 10.38 then she breezed.

When I got in Jess rang and I was just chatting to her for a while.

STEPHEN KING HAD AN ACCIDENT TODAY

DID U KNOW?

THERE MIGHT BE A TITANIC TWO MOVIE

Monday 21ˢᵗ June 1999

School was quite safe today. Because I bop to the shop for the golden wonder what flavour? Salt and vinegar, joker. Anyway I also had a Modular Science exam today. After school I flexed to JD's. Just played computer and shit. I left at 5.30pm. When I got in I relaxed and blared the tunes.

At the moment it's 6.30pm and I'm gonna finish there . Sorry it was poo poo. I can make something up. I shaved my balls. Maybe that's true. You'll never know hahahahahahahahaha. Ok bye

Funniest thing all day:-

• Shark arrow

DID U KNOW?

IT WAS A MONTH AGO I MASHED UP MY FINGER

DID U KNOW?

THERE'S ONLY BEEN TWO ROYAL WEDDINGS IN WINDSOR

Friday 25ᵗʰ June 1999

Go on with Friday; let me tell you about my week first.

*Tuesday 22*ⁿᵈ *June* - went school razed about £10. After went kickboxing at 6pm - came home rang a few girls including Rachel and then watched some militant programme called Eye Spy.

*Wednesday 23*rd - today I went school. Rushed home after because I was meeting Jess again. When I got in my mum was moaning at me cos I got in trouble at school. Did manage to get out, then met Darren at train station. We got Reading met girls. Then went back to Langley because they wanted to go there. (Jess's friends were all butterz).

In Langley we chilled round Langley Park with them and the usual people.

Later I walked them to the station and saw them off. And guess what Jess still didn't lips me. She said she would but not in front of her friends (stupid bitch). But she must want some shit, keeps ringing asking to meet up.

Went home after at 9.10pm.

*Thursday 24*th- went school - later Rachel came round. Did the usual shit.

Later on we were arguing again, it was almost over again. Later walked her to the bus stop bye.

And today at last but first I just need to write

FUNNIEST THINGS ALL DAY FOR YESTERDAY:-

- Christians – chicken flavour and steel flavour sun lolly
- Rachel with toys - the skin
- Big net to catch kids out of school

School was alright today there was bare jokes. My first lesson was Business Studies and we did f**k all cos the teacher was helping with exams. All we did was just f**k about for the whole hour with no teacher. After I had P.S.E and that was poo the double Tech where Christian was giving me jokes. The last lesson was Mmaths and that was poo.

When I got home I just got ready to go and get my haircut. I left about 4.10pm because I was getting a trim at 4.30pm. I rid my bike up to JD's drum then left it there. After I bopped through the High Street then down to New Directions.

After I got my haircut I bopped back to JD's.

I stayed round JD's till 7.30pm then breezed home on my lovely girl's bike. When I got in MJP was round and he was HuHH. I had some dinner and then after we didn't know where to go. Tonight we weren't sure what was going on. Simmons, Chris and Guv were going on about some shit in Windsor. Sean wanted to breeze London but I heard no one else wanted to go.

At 9.45pm we met Sean, Simmons, Chris, and Guv Etc at the train station. At the station we still didn't know where to go. So everyone just went into Langley Village. We chilled round there for time. I rang a few girls to see if we could hook up. I spoke to Amanda and fit Vicki. But we never arranged to meet any girls in the end.

Later on around 11.30 we met up with Nicholas and Denny. We all decided to breeze to London for jokes. When we got to the station the train was coming at 12am.

We got the train to Slough to get a fast train but then ended up getting on the train we would of already got on.

When we got to Paddington we tried to see if we could get a tube. But it was gonna take long to come so we thought we'd walk.

We were gonna jump on a bus but couldn't get on any. So we bopped to Piccadilly.

We bopped through Piccadilly and Leicester Square and it was bare jokes. All night I tried to cherpes women but they all kept rejecting me. We were hanging outside McyD's and trying to find girls. We were also chatting to that tap dancing brare and he was jokes. At one point there was some fight between some Black man and a wWite man and the Black man won, of course.

O shit yeah there's something I didn't mention, on the way to Piccadilly we met some hoes and we were chatting to them. Then the PIMP man came and we just stupidly ran away (we got scared). I ran away screaming.

On the way back them lot just kept pinching bare girls bums. And we did get one number. I was chatting to this girl and I didn't really like her but still got the number. Well it's not in my phone but Denny's.

Anyway as we were walking back me, MJP and Sean managed to get on a bus but Denny and Nicholas didn't, so they bopped. When we got to Paddington we cotched on the train. The time was 3.58am and it was leaving at 4.15am.

Around 4.10am we met Nicholas and Denny, they flexed on the train. We got to Slough at 5am and I just ran home.

Funniest things all day:-

- Your mum's not for the light hearted
- Christian's movie
- Silesh brother Nilesh – Matthew Hatthew
- Nicholas – star tek phone flip and hands free screw it up
- Tap dancer man singing Flintstones

DID U KNOW?

CONDOMS USED TO BE CALLED FRENCH LETTER AND THEY USED THE SAME ONE EVERY TIME

Saturday 26th June 1999

Today I woke up at 11.30am because my mum came in my room and woke me up. Well she didn't mean to she just woke me up, you get me.

At 2pm I got ready to go and meet Rachel. I got my bus to Hounslow about 3ish, a double Decker one.

When I met Rachel at the bus station. We then bopped into Hounslow High Street then into the Treaty Centre and done some photos of ourselves in the photo booth thing. It was Rachel's idea.

After, we got the train from Hounslow East to Leicester Square. We bopped through Leicester Square, Piccadilly, Troc and the usual places.

It was a bit boring though, you know going London with your girl, and today there were bare girls out. Some group of girls were looking at me and I couldn't do anything. My super powers were restrained. I used that wrong in school the other day.

We did stay for quite a while, we left about 7.30. O shit I forgot to write it but we were in KFC and we saw some brare in a bright blue dress and he had bare tattoos and a dirty hairy chest.

When we got back to Hounslow we flexed to Rachel's drum. She lives opposite Hounslow bus staion so the bop is minor. When I got Rachel's her mum was happy to see me cos I haven't stayed in time.

In the night me and Rachel were just staying downstairs, cos her little brother had a friend staying round. So we thought we'd stay downstairs to watch a bit of tele and tings.

Later on in the night we started having sex but it didn't last very long because she was giving me a shiner to get it hard and I was on my way to cum then just shoved it up her. It only lasted for about 4 minutes. I had a militant little orgasm, trust.

Later on we were just watching TV and she started rubbing up my ting and saying she wants more sex. And we had some more but this time longer, about 5 minutes, joking, about 30 minutes. It was a bit f**ked up though because I've never like done it 2 times in a row, it felt strange but true.

After we went to bed upstairs and the two little gay boys were asleep. The time was about 3am

Funniest thing all day:-

- Little girl- I bet you wish you were older so you could do some of that.

DID U KNOW?

ARNOLD SCHWARZENGER FIRST Movie WAS HERCULES GOES TO NEW YORK.

Sunday 27ᵗʰ June 1999

Today I woke up at 9am then after just couldn't get back to sleep. I was just so bored. Also yesterday Rachel said she had a big orgasm, Bo.

Anyway at 12pm me and Rachel had some sex because we were bored. But we kept stopping because people were coming downstairs.

At 4.30pm everybody went out and we had some more sex. And you'll never guess what about 5 minutes after we had sex again. This sex was bad, the best I've had with her, so far.

I left Rachel's about 7.20pm and missed my bus to Langley. So I had to train it. I had to go Acton Town, Ealing, Slough then finally Langley. At Langley I stopped off at MJP's house just to kick him and his brother's ass at tekhan 3. The can only use eddy and just tap all the buttons. I'll kill them with anyone even Panda.

When I got in I relaxed.

KING OF THE RING 1999 TONIGHT 1AM

DID U KNOW?

SPONGES GROW UNDER THE SEA

Monday 26ᵗʰ June 1999

Today I never went to school because hay fever was bad. Today at 12pm I rang Rachel and just chatted to her for a while. At 12.30pm I went back to bed and went sleep.

Later at 4.30pm MJP came round. After Naomi came round. Naomi left at 6pm and after JD came round to drop off a video.

At night I just relaxed, might go school tomorrow. Depends on how I feel

DID U KNOW?

IT'S IMPOSSIBLE TO TAKE A SHIT AND NOT PISS A LITTLE BIT, COS THE MUSCLES INNIT

Tuesday 29th June 1999

Yeah this day's been quite safe. School was just a normal school day. Kenworthy wasn't here so it was just me and Steven razing today.

At 6pm I went kickboxing. We did it in that offkey drama room again. It was alright. We done bare sparring. I've also got the British Championships soon in Nottingham.

On the way back from kickboxing I met Laura and Angela and they came back to my drum for a while. After I got a call from Ben and we were chatting for time about girls.

Well that's my day and shit dis month's going fast boy. It's 1st July on Thursday.

DID U KNOW?

NOSTRADAMUS PREDICTED THAT THE WORLD WILL END ON 3RD JULY 1999, THIS SATURDAY, NICE KNOWING YA

DATES FOR MY BOOM DIARY

TOMORROW/WEDNESDAY- MAYBE KICKBOXING (HAVE TO TRAIN) OR PARTY IN BURNHAM (LANGLEY GRAMMAR LEAVERS THING)

1ST JULY THURSDAY- RACHEL MIGHT BE COMING ROUND OR I MIGHT TRY SOME KUNG FU SHIT

FRIDAY- SCHOOL SPORTS DAY. IN THE NIGHT MIGHT BE MEETING AMANDA AND FIT VICKI

SATURDAY/SUNDAY- MIGHT BE MEETING SEXY CLAIRE OR RACHEL'S STAYING.

Wednesday 30th June 1999

Well today June ends and it's really gonna be hard for me to choose funniest thing all month. Well this month's been alright but not the best. This month was mainly bare shiners and little stupid missions. I think one of the best days was Saturday 19th, quite safe.

Anyway sorry man went on for long there chatting bare mess. Anyways today's been alright. This morning when I woke up, I couldn't be fucked to go school. But I got bored at home so I went in around lunch time.

After school I went over JD's but only for a little while, I got home in time for Kenan and Kel. Also I watched MTV and Rachel was on it, but she's minor.

At 6.30pm I left to go kickboxing (the one in Slough). I went to Dave's (the man who teaches me) house and he gave me a lift.

Today we had some Asian geza training us because Dave went to some party. It was an alright lesson we had bare fights in the ring.

After kickboxing I got a lift home from Jason. Well not home. I had to go Dave's to collect my bike. Then I rode home.

Also there's some party in Burnham tonight and I decided to go cos everyone was down there. So I got washed then breezed.

I had to get some money out the cash point so I bopped to the village. When I got to the train station I just missed the 10.15pm train. So rang a taxi. While I was waiting for my taxi some man was chatting to me. He was gay, you know when you're alone and you just get these sort of nerdy people chatting to you, err no Robert.

When I got in the taxi I decided to get it all the way to the party. Cos I was gonna go Slough then a train to Burnham. But thought allow that.

When I got to the party it was about 10.50 and I got in free because the bouncer was one of my kickboxing instructors.

The party was good but I got there too late. There was bare skeet there but didn't get none, just chatting and shit. I also M.Ced a bit but it was a bit because bare people were hogging the mic.

After the party everyone was just chilling outside cherpsing girls and ting. After me and MJP just got a lift off Dave.

When I goT in I just relaxed and W.I.D

Funniest things all day:-

- JD – Nostradamus predicted Billie would be number 1
- Miguel- bare lying- went bed 4am at some rave- dad told us he was up watching tele.

FUNNIEST THING ALL MONTH (JUNE)

5. SOAP MUSIC-PETROL GARAGE

4. NOSTRADUMUS PREDICTED BILLIE WOULD BE NUMBER 1

3. BECAUSE SOMEBODY CHEATED

2. BROTHER BROTHER- MY TWIN (Southend)

1. STAR TEK PHONE (NICHOLAS)

Thursday 1st July 1999

My prediction for this month is that it's gonna be boom cos it's coming near summer holidays and I will be doing bare shit. And there's a weird thing, later on I'm going to see my solicitor and a month ago I was doing the same thing. And shit also Rachel's coming round like last month; well she's always coming round.

Well today school was alright. At lunch today there was a fight between Jamie and Flamer that was alright I suppose.

After school Rachel came round. At 4.10pm Simmons came round to come with me to see my solicitor. I left Rachel alone cos I thought I'd be a little while.

When we got to the place I spoke to my solicitor. He was chatting for time and I had to remember every single bit of information from that day. Simmons chatted to him as well.

We left the place around 6.30pm-7ish (we were also with my mum, cos she works there). We bopped down the High Street and my mum flexed some KFC to take away. Then after we flexed a taxi home.

Also I haven't mentioned but my mum rang Rachel and she told my mum that she read my diary. She read the day when those Oxford girls stayed and there was a bit that said "I tried to lips her". That made Rachel cry, shame. But she told my mum not to tell me, rags my mum did though.

When I got home I was styling it out, pretending I didn't know. I kept saying I always write things in my diary that I just make up, for instanced I lipsed a girl. I said it's because my friends always read my diary. Stupid bitch believed it as well.

At 9pm I walked Rachel to the bus stop. The bus was on a long flex. At 9.30pm my mum rang on my mobile and said Rachel's mum rang and said it was too late for her to come home, so she had to stay. Trust her mum must be dumb it was only 9.30pm.

So Rachel came back to my drum and stayed. At night we did do some shit but remember I've got school in the morning. So I went bed.

DID U KNOW?

THE 16TH LETTER OF THE ALPHABET IS R, YES FOR ROBERT

Friday 2nd July 1999

This morning I left about 8.30am for school. I left Rachel at my drum. Trust I hid the diary.

Today we had sports day at school and it was alright. I done 3 events and today I done militant. My 1st event was 200 metres. I came 2nd, but the other brare had a dark lane. My lane still had holes from 1976.

My second event was the 100 metres and I smashed it. I came first and got 12.05 seconds (that's pretty good).

The final event was the relay and I ran last. My team was so shit. Was so hard trying to put a relay team together. The best person from Priory is Mani.

We came third out of 4 teams. After I flexed home. I relaxed like always. I stripped, had a gallon of drink and blared the tunes (it's my religion).

Also Rachel left a note for me, which said ring her, so I rang her and she was asking if I still wanted to go out with her and I just felt like saying no. But stupidly said yes.

Later on MJP and Terry came round. Cos tonight we were gonna go and meet Amanda and fit Vicki. But we never ended up meeting with them because they kept pissing us about. Later MJP and Terry flexed out while I had some munch.

Later on I met everyone down the train station. There was Terry, MJP, Nicholas, Simmons and Denny. We all thought we'd flex down to Windsor cos we heard about some party and also people we know were there.

We were down Windsor for time. We met up with bare people like Sean, Wayne and Brian. We also met some Windsor girls, like Holly. I was chatting to her and she wants to meet up one time, so I'll ring her during the week.

Later on we were hanging around near the Leisure Centre cos there was gonna be a fight, but there wasn't.

Later on me, Terry, Brian, Sean and Ricky S got the last train back to Slough. Then Slough back to Langley. In Langley we just flexed down the kebab shop for a while then breezed home. Terry stayed tonight as well.

That's my day but before I stop I must say I'm f**king shitting myself because today is predicted to be the end of the world. And outside there's bare lightning and it's shitting me up. It's not even raining or nothing, there's just bare lightning and its proper loud. Well now I'm gonna write my funniest things all day to take my mind off shit.

Funniest things all day (probably the last):

- Err girls are sick –yeah cos you lot are bent
- SAP- Ants gang
- Star tek – arm
- Holly tripped when she crossed the finish line
- Go out with girl just for the titties – taking the tiities on a date

ALSO- Now it's raining. It might just be normal. Well Nostradamus predicted something would come from the sky. But what could come from the sky.

Meteor, we would have seen it unless it's UFO's and there's gonna take over our planet. Or a giant nuclear bomb will go off. Fuck why's the world gonna end today. I haven't even spratted more then 2 girls.

ALSO – Maybe staying round Claire's tomorrow in Southend then Sunday Hyde Park (party in the park)

DID U KNOW?

FRANK BRUNO WAS BORN IN HAMMERSMITH HOSPITAL, THE SAME AS ME

Saturday 3rd July 1999

Today was an alright day. I'm happy the world didn't end. But there was some scary lighting last night. At 1.20ish MJP knocked for me to breeze out. And the plans for today are, we're going London then after we're staying round Claire's in Southend.

We bopped to the station to get the 2.30pm train. But when we got there we just missed it. So we bopped round Langley for a while until the next train came. At 2pm we flexed the train to Paddington, on the train terry and MJP got hooked up a zoot by some brare (just thought I'd mention that).

When we got to Paddington we got the train to Piccadilly Circus. We bopped round Piccadilly and the usual shit. We were gonna hook up with Rachel cos she was in London but then I couldn't be bothered. Also we should have cherpes these girls but never, but don't worry there's always next week, they're there all the time.

After we got a train to Tower Hill. Then we bopped to Fenchurch Street Station to get the train to Southend. We met up with Liam. We flexed on those militant little trains which you can stick your head out the window and also open the door whenever you want, that's tick.

When we got to Southend we met Claire and her friend. They looked alright, but not all that. We bopped around the High Street and round the seafront bit. It was getting shit so we thought we might as well go back to Claire's drum to cotch. We went to the bus stop and had to wait a while for some number five bus, we paid £1.50 each. Where we live you pay 40p for the bus and you can travel all around the world and back.

When we got to Claire's we just relaxed and had bare munch. Shit like bare Doctor Peppers, sweets, chips and chocolate, trust. Her mum had some nice big tittys.

In the night we had bare jokes. We were just caning (that's their word for cussing) them hard about living in some countryside seaside place.

Later on in the night I was sleeping in her bed and trying to deal with her but she kept laughing and being stupid. But I did manage to lips her, suck her titties and finger her. Also, Liam f**ked her friend 3 times, well that's what he said.

Dumbest thing all day:

- Has our train gone past? - There have been about 50

Funniest thing all day:-

- Feel it damn it
- Which one of you am I sleeping with tonight?
- Fumes tag - missed it because of train
- SHOEBURYNESS
- Southend Biff = pussy
- Sister - Can I see your biff, sniffing biff, f**king biff
- X-Men v Biff Fighter
- Fish Flag
- Come we swap girls
- Come I fart
- Bus Bell on ceiling

DID U KNOW?

If you eat too much curry it makes your insides yellow.

Sunday 4ᵗʰ July 1999

Today I got up really early around 8.00am. But then went back to sleep and woke up later around 11.00am. In the morning we all got ready to leave, we got Liam's bird to iron all our clothes. After, we watched some WWF shit. We left about 12 something, they walked us to the bus stop.

When the bus came I couldn't be bothered to lips Claire because she was getting on my nerves. Plus we were cussing her cos her surname sounds like penis. She's half Greek. Got some weird name.

When we got to Southend Bus Station we thought we'd bop around for a second to see if there are any skeet. We only bopped around for about half an hour, then Liam was saying we had to swim so we swam in our pants and Liam was being gay and trying to take my pants off in front of all these fit girls. After we just bopped to Southend Central Station. When we got to the Station we just missed a fast train so we had to flex some slow one that stops at every stop.

We got off at Upminster to get a tube to Ealing because we had no money and couldn't be bothered to be hassled by ticket machines. But the biggest problem was it was 43 stops to Ealing, that's quite long isn't it? To shorten our journey we got off at Aldgate East to get a train to Paddington then Paddington to Langley (home).

When we got to Paddington we flexed some munch, well me , Liam and MJP did. We lost Terry at the Station. As we were going to our train we saw this other train with a trolley and it had bare food on it. I looked around and then razed three fruitcakes; I just reached out for anything. We left the fruitcakes on the wall then went back for more, but this time the woman was there. So we flexed our munch and then went to get on our train and the woman from the trolley came running up to us going, Oi. I just dashed the cake onto some track. The woman grabbed me and MJP and was asking us to pay. Then some brare came along and he was safe. He was gonna let us off, but me and MJP just dussed onto the train and hid in the toilets. When the train left Paddington we got out and met with Beverage.

When I got in I had some dinner then just wrote in my diary for yesterday.

Later, gave Terry a lift to the train station.

Funniest things all day:-

- Fruitcake chase - Missed Terry - into toilets – Not letting MJP in
- Go underneath London

DID U KNOW?

The bible means library of books.

Monday 5ᵗʰ July 1999

Today I had to go to Court. Terry picked us up in the morning because he was going as well. We had to go to Maidenhead again. At the Court

Robb Peters

we met Nicholas and a few other people we knew. Today was just a Pre Trial Review and I was only there from 9.45 am until 11.00am. In the Court I didn't have to do anything just sit there whilst the Judge chatted. Then they told us that we would get a letter when the actual trial was.

After, we got a lift from Terry's dad. Terry came back to mine because I told him that Rachel was coming round and he wanted to meet her. But I rang her at 12.15pm and she said she wasn't allowed. I was gonna go round hers but Terry was round. When Terry was round I was just playing computer and he was mainly downstairs playing cards with my Mum. Not snap , more advanced games like Fish.

Later on around 6.30pm I gave Terry a lift up to the bridge in Datchet. After, I stopped off at Simmons' house for a while. And there's bare raves going on which we plan to breeze to, like:-

Uxbridge Party - Soon

Rhythm Nation - 26th July

Extravaganza - 16th July

After Simmons' I went home.

DID U KNOW?

The Queen Mother will be 99 in 4 weeks, oldest royal ever.

Tuesday 6th July 1999

Today, I just went into school in the day. At lunch today I had some hench (big) lunch, I had a drink (Sprite), three doughnuts, kitkat, crunchie and a magnum double. After school I did the usual strip routine because it was proper hot today. At 5.00pm MJP came round. We watched this film I taped last night, called, Senseless. At 6.45pm I left to go kickboxing (just a normal lesson innit). You did militant Robert, pat yourself on the back.

When I got home I just relaxed and assembled my new bed, which came earlier.

Funniest thing all day:-

- JD - Hide our badge so they don't know which school we go to.

DID U KNOW?

Lenny Henry was born in Birmingham

Thursday 8ᵗʰ July 1999

Today was a normal day at school. At lunch I bare razed 70p, yeah I know it sounds minor, but I needed to flex some munch.

After school I just rested because f**k it's been proper hot lately, you get me!

Later on around 7.30pm I mowed the lawn, and then after Ben came round and we breezed to the fair down the Village Park.

Down the fair we just met the usual people, apart from Simmons who has an ankle injury. At 9.00ish I walked Simmons' sister and her friend (who liked me) home. I lipsed her friend and I have cheated on Rachel again.

After, Me, MJP and Nicholas just bopped around Trelawney for a while then we all breezed yard.

Funniest things all day:-

- Miss Rabies - Beats from husband
- Nicholas - just jokes as usual - Phone - Dick Glasses - Bum Speaker - The Ghetto Shops

DID U KNOW?

Seahorse men give birth.

Friday 9ᵗʰ July 1999

Today I woke up really early around 9.30am. I was just in a hyper mood. Around 12.30pm MJP and Hanghei came around to go London. At 1.20pm we left my house to go London.

At Langley Station we met up with Simmons. Then just lucky caught the train to Paddington. At Paddington I rang Mandy to see what was going on and where she was and shit. But she said that her friend who she was going with is not going anymore. So we thought, come we go into London and just cherpes, rags.

When we got to Piccadilly we just done the usual bopping through Troc and Leicester Square. At Leicester Square we stopped for a while to watch this flexible man doing a little street show. Whilst we were watching this I saw Gemma from Leyton in the crowd. I thought, Bo, a skeet I know, bare tings. So me and the crew went and chatted to her and she seemed really happy to see me.

We bopped around with Gemma and her friend. We went down Leicester Square and Troc with them. Later on we were all walking around Regent Street and Simmons and Hanghei left to go home because tonight they are going to some rave in Slough. (The time was 4.20pm). We only stayed around Regent Street for a little while then we went down to MTV.

During the time I was with Gemma I saw bare mans just staring at her. The thing is she's quite ok, but the thing that everyone was staring at was her batty. Trust, that batty was booming. It was so nice. Hanging over the cliff batty.

Yeah, as I was saying, shit, that batty was so tick. Words can't explain it.

Anyway, after we all flexed down Trafalgar Square to just relax. We just chilled down there. She was letting off hard, all holding my hand and just standing proper close, you could tell she wanted it.

At 5.30pm decided to breeze. I had to get to Rachel's but Gemma proper didn't want me to go. She kept saying, shall we come down to your area? But I couldn't let her come with us because I promised Rachel I'd take her out today. But I did lips her. I took her round the corner and was just saying if we could go out some time, charming shit. Then I just goes, can I have a kiss? And she replied, Of course you can darling! And she gave me such a nice kiss it was just freaky, her tongue was just wild. (I was also grabbing that batty).

After, Me and MJP just flexed to Charing Cross station. It was jokes because at the station I sneaked through this thing next to the machines, and MJP got stuck with no money. I just ran off and left him. I got on the Bakerloo line to Piccadilly then changed on the Piccadilly line to Hounslow.

When I got to Rachel's all I was thinking about was Gemma. I couldn't get her out of my head, but she wasn't super tick but she was quite tick.

Remember, the plans for today are Me and Rachel flexing cinema. We left to go cinema at 8.40 pm because all the films were starting at 9.40 ish. When we got to the cinema (Feltham) we decided to see the film The Mummy. We missed all the decent films like The Matrix.

The film was alright but not all that. It was on for long, it finished at 12.15am.

When we got out of the cinema we realised we missed the last bus. We were gonna get a taxi but Rachel didn't know any numbers. We just bopped all the way back to Hounslow.

When we got in we were just messing about and when I was kissing her I was thinking about Gemma. I never spratted her she was on a period.

Funniest things all day:-

- Bare Gammon - White People
- Gabsee - Asian People
- Rachel – "I want you now"
- Me – Thinking, I don't want you I want Gemma's batty.

DID U KNOW?

There's a place called Lee

Saturday 10th July 1999

Today I was really feeling like finishing with Rachel. But I thought if I split up with her she'd be all crying and shit. So today I was really getting on her nerves, so she would just dump me. I kept calling her fat, and beating her, the kind of shit girls hate. Because I thought if she finishes with me then she won't be as upset, do you get me?

Then, after, I'm just gonna stop seeing her then she'll get pissed off. Then say some shit like, it's not working out we might as well split up. Then the plan is to move on to bigger and better things like Gemma and that batty. My girlfriend doesn't have a batty like Gemma, I think that suits my life style better.

I left Rachel's about 4.50pm then just as I was leaving I just gave her a little peck on the cheek to piss her off (I'm cold)! When I got back to Langley I went to Flex and Simmons' shop but it was shut. When I got in I just relaxed for time. I wasn't gonna go out but at 9.30pm I went out. Also, I rang Gemma and we are meeting on Tuesday in London. She was proper excited, see my plan is working.

We all flexed Windsor and it was shit and I can't be bothered to write about it because all we did was bop around. But there were some sexy bitches at Ally Gardens and they were in year 9 as well. I felt wrong looking at them. For me it's year 10 and up.

I got in at 12.45 am and now I've got to go sleep because kickboxing is tomorrow morning. Also, I think I'm in love, not with Gemma, the batty, crazy fool.

Funniest things all day:-

- Rachel's dream - Bare Roberts at train station coming downstairs
- Bottom on Rachel's lips.

Sunday 11th July 1999

Today I woke up at 7.45am then got ready to go Dave Lee's, then off to Nottingham. I left my drum at 8am and got to Daves (the trainer) about 8.05am, it's only down the road.

We had to wait for all the crew to come over and we left around 8.40ish. The journey was proper long, we passed bare counties like Hertfordshire, Buckinghamshire, Northamptonshire and some next shire place, ha that's funny.

The journey took about 2 hours and to get there was 125 miles (a long ting).

When we got to Northern land we stopped off at a shop and everybody was speaking in Northern languages, which is mess innit.

When we got to the place we almost won't allowed to fight cos we got there too late. But that's a minor cos Dave sorted it out.

While I was waiting for my fight I was just doing the usual, relaxing and looking for skeet (Northern ones). Also there were bare people speaking in that funny language again. Also I was gonna fight in the under 70kg's but they said there was no one else in that group. I could of just won but I thought Nah that's not fair. So I went up a weight to over 75kgs, you dickhead.

I had my fight at around 3pm. It was against some big fat boy. He kept running into me with his belly and it was pissing me off. But I gave him a few good licks in the head. But in the end the Judges decided he won, maybe cos he kept coming forward.

After it was that fat boy and some brare from my club. This was the finals (there was only 4 people in the group). It was jokes they both got disqualified. So nobody won our group at all. But I did get a medal for 1st place in the group I didn't fight. Bo British Champion for getting beaten up by a fat kid. Guess if you take a beating you deserve to be champ, I should of won though, I swear I beat that fat ass dick. Also I feel offkey cos he was a Northern guy, that's wrong.

After we were just watching the other people fighting from my club. We left about 8pm. And coming home took the piss, there was bare traffic and the journey was long and boring.

When we got Slough I had to go Dave's house and get my bike then I rid home. I got in about 11pm.

Also I'm glad to be back in the South, couldn't understand their language.

Funniest thing all day:-

- I'll get the Nottingham crew on you blud
- Gosh that's worst then saying the oxford crew.

DID U KNOW?

If you put an E on the end of Bath you get Bathe, which is a different word, wow.

Monday 12ᵗʰ July 1999

Now I've got a little game for all out there before I tell you about my day. The game is called TRY TO IMAGINE, it's easy

Number 1- TRY TO IMAGINE the queen taking a shit. Then wiping her royal ass with some golden toilet paper

Now imagine Pamela Anderson, Sharon stone and now Oprah (but with no golden toilet paper just standard).

I just thought that would interest you. I wonder if the queen does have golden toilet paper. Not actual gold chucks cos that would hurt your batty but like gold colour.

Well today I just went school. Later on MJP came round. I also got a call from Gemma and I'm meeting her tomorrow at 1.30 in London. I'll have to miss school; I do feel a bit sick though.

Funniest thing all day:

- Christian- Dr Chicken
- Diet chicken

DID U KNOW?

Carlsberg is the best beer in the world, they just don't admit it

Tuesday 13th July 1999

This morning, like I planned, I missed school. At 10 am I rang Kieron cos I knew he was at home (suspended from school). I told him I'd come down to Hanwell for a while cos I was just bored. I had a bath and got ready then around 11.30am I got the train.

At Hanwell station I met up with Kieron and that Stewart brare. We flexed a bus down to Ealing. Down Ealing we met Jason cos he was on work experience and we chatted to him (in his work). We waited for Jason to come out for his lunch break. But in the mean time we were just chilling round Ealing Broadway centre chatting minor jokes.

At 1pm we met J and I also met up with Victor B (some old friend). I only stayed with them lot till 1.15pm then breezed cos remember today I'm meeting up with the batty, I mean Gemma.

I got the train from Ealing – Paddington. Then flexed to Charing Cross. I got there about 1.50pm and bo she was still waiting.

Me and Gemma just bopped round London. She was giving me jokes, but she so loud and kept cussing people on the street, funny but everyone could hear her. Trust she thinks she's some bad London girl. I think Leyton is actual in Essex so calm yourself.

Around 7ish she kept asking if she could come down Slough, but I thought nah I'm not having her embarrass me in my own town. I mean she's boom but too loud. She did come back to Langley though and she thought it was bare countryside but she liked the houses.

When we got to mine we just chilled. I wasn't too sure if she wanted to do anything or what. So I just flexed on a film (from Dusk till Dawn). She thought the film was tick. During the film I was lipsing her and gripping that bum bum.

After the film we were just messing about. I never done nothing with her cos I thought nah good tings come to those who wait.

Gemma left about 8.10pm and we knocked for MJP on the way to the train station. MJP came with us to the train station. But she was acting offkey, she asked us to come to Paddington with her. So we thought, might as well (she didn't know how to get home).

When we got to Paddington she was still saying "how do I get home". So I thought f**k it and said we'll take you to Charing Cross so you can get the bus home safely and shit.

When we got to Charing Cross (Trafalgar Square) we walked her to her bus stop then just waited a while till her bus came.

After we just flexed a train from Tottenham Court Toad station. We had to go to Oxford Circus then Paddington.

When I got in it was around 11ish and my mum was moaning at me cos I got in late on a school night. After W.I.D a piece then slept. Also never told mum I missed school.

Funniest things all day:-

- Safeway girl- are you wearing a bra under that top
- Gemma- cussing everyone- allow that.............. – move man, charrr
- Just trying to make a funniest thing all day – chase train
- Sick brare singing- cruising down the Broadway

DID U KNOW?

The film negotiator was supposed to star Stallone but he refused so they chose Samuel L. Jackson

Wednesday 14th July 1999

You'll never guess how lucky I was today. When I got in school my form tutor asked me if I was in school yesterday. I just goes yes and he marked me in for yesterday. The thing is we had no form tutor yesterday, so I didn't get marked as absent. I basically bunked and got away with it.

When I got home I just slept for a while then at 4.20pm got woken up by MJP knocking cos he was going to see my lawyer and I said I'd come.

When we got there it was too late to see him so he made another appointment then we flexed to JD's for a while.

We left JD's at 8.30pm and when I got in I had some KFC, it killed it.

After I tried to ring my two women Gemma and Rachel but f**k my phones been cut off. Mum needs to sort out the bill.

Later on.

Funniest things all day:-

- B1 B1 B1 B1 B1 – Shine on Shine on Shine on
- Christian trying to scare John
- Terminator- tramps watching TV on fire.

DID U KNOW?

The Russian population is 255,000,000

Thursday 15th July 1999

Well today school bare razing got me about £5; I never razed it Steven just gave it to me cos people were on to him.

When I got in I found a letter from Levi to tell me she was coming over today. She never rang cos I've been cut off.

Later on around 4pm MJP came round and he wanted me to come and see my lawyer but I couldn't be bothered. Also Rachel was coming round.

At 4.30pm Rachel came round. We had sex twice, it was alright but I thought what's the point when I'm planning on finishing with her. But still, bit of sex innit.

HE'S A PLAYER.

Anyway at 7pm I walked Rachel to the bus stop and saw her off.

Also I've never gone a month without getting any skeets phone number. But so far none this month.

DID U KNOW?

The statue of liberty was built in France

Friday 16th July 1999

Today was an alright day. This weekend I haven't written out a planner cos I don't know what's going on.

In the day I just went school. When I got in I just did the routine, I think you know it by now.

At 4.30pm MJP knocked and he gave me a lift up to the shops. I needed to go to the pay phone. I rang the hairdresser and I'm getting my haircut tomorrow at 3.30pm. After I rang Gemma and I'm meeting her tomorrow at 1.30pm then bringing her back to Slough then for some reason she's coming with me when I get my haircut.

At 5.45pm Simmons and Sean came over. We were just chatting about what's going on tonight. They all wanted to go down to Extravaganza, when you need tickets to get in.

Later around 6.45pm Naomi and Becky (a girl I haven't seen in about 2

years) came round. They just came round and chatted their shit. After me, Sean and Simmons got a taxi to the Foyer to meet Nicholas and Denny.

We left to go Extravaganza about 8.42pm. We met some other people at Slough who came with us. Also when we were on the train to London we had to quickly get off at Langley and buss a permit cos the T.M's found out we didn't have a ticket. So we quickly jumped off the train and got permits.

When we got to Extravaganza we could still get in but it was £10 on the door, that take the piss for an under 18's. Well I didn't have no money but

Simmons paid for me. I'll pay him back soon cos that takes the piss, £10 to flex in a rave.

It was quite a bad rave. There were bare MC's and DJ's just smashing it. There was MC Creed, Danger 18k, MC Chuckie and bare others.

I also met Rachel down there but didn't really chat to her, just now and then. Most of the time I was just bopping around and we were watching our friend having a dancing contest with this brare, it was jokes.

Later on Liam went up to Rachel and told her I didn't want to go out with her no more. I spoke to Rachel and just goes "I'm not sure" but I couldn't think of a decent reason. Also Rachel was pissed off cos yesterday I was doing all that shit and she thought I was just using her. She ran off crying. But 5 minutes later she came back and we went outside and spoke.

Outside Rachel was crying for time and I felt bad.

At 11.45 Rachel's friends came out then they left. So I left as well (on my jaze).

I got the 11.55pm train to Slough and it only took 10 minutes, gwan with that.

The bop was longer. I got home about 12.45pm.

Also earlier, Rachel got mad and pushed me.

DID U KNOW?

Wesley Snipes is in Michael Jackson video 'bad'

Saturday 17th July 1999

I don't know what the plans for today are but at the moment it's 11.30am and I'm just writing this, for some reason. In a sec I'm gonna have breakfast then get ready to meet Gemma at1pm. She's meeting me in Paddington. And today I'm gonna see if I can get some tings. Alright gotta breeze read below for today.

Later 12.50pm I breezed to get the 1pm train to Paddington. But I missed it, so I flexed a train to Slough then got the fast train straight to Paddington. I met Gemma at 1.45pm, only 45 minutes late.

Around 2.15pm we got the train to Langley. Cos remember I'm getting my hair cut at 3.30pm. She wanted to come while I was flexing a trim.

We got to my manor (Langley) about 2.45pm. After we bopped to my house. And it was about 3pm so I though allow going to get my haircut cos it was too late and where I was getting my haircut is in Britwell, it would of just taken long.

Me and Gemma just stayed in and watched that movie Face Off. A while later my mum flexed to her driving lesson. Me and Gemma were doing bare shit. I got her down to her bra and silky knickers. We were just playing with each other. But her poom poom was proper wet and sorry Gemma but I smelt my fingers and shit clean yourself woman, not even the fish and chip shops that smelly.

Later on we were gonna do the naughty ting. She kept saying she wanted it. But I had no condoms. She still wanted to do it but I thought allow that, man. With that fishiness you don't know the shit you can catch. But my mum came back so I just quickly got dressed and so did she, that was lucky.

At 7.50pm we left to go Langley station. We missed the 8pm train, so we went Slough and got that quicker train straight to Paddington.

After I went to Tottenham Court Rd station with her then waited with her till her bus came, and the arsehole bus took about half an hour to come.

After I just flexed to Paddington and after got the 10.12pm train to Langley. When I got to Langley I bopped down the village and Trelawney Avenue to see if I could see anyone but no one was around. It's a bitch not having a phone and plus my house phone is cut off.

When I got in I just W.I.D then chilled to some garage tape that Gemma gave me, it's alright still. Got that boom tune 'it's the way' on it.

Also Gemma wants to come round tomorrow for sex, but if she does I'm getting rubbers. Ain't diving into that fishy ocean without a life jacket.

Funniest things all day:-

- You wouldn't blast me like that
- Fish Willy disease

DID U KNOW?

The nearest tube station to the Natural History Museum is South Kensington.

fish
Willy
disease

Sunday 18th July 1999

Today was one of those stupid with your family days. Today I was going cinema with my mum to see the new Star Wars movie. It started at 2.40pm.so before it started I breezed round Hanghei and Simmons yard for a while.

At 2.30pm we left to go cinema (me and my mum). The Star Wars film was alright, I thought it was quite tick. But there was no Darth Vader just a brare with a red face. Not having it!!!

After we flexed some KFC then went to Blockbusters to rent some films. I was gonna buy the Exorcist but my mum didn't want to. So I just bought Halloween H20. We also rented 'Something about Mary'. When I got yard I just watched the movies.

DID U KNOW?

JFK'S son died today. The family is supposed to be cursed.

Tuesday 20th July 1999

30th anniversary moon landing

School was jokes just watched movies. Mr allen says the moon landing was fact. Don't tell my mum that she watched it on the television and they said it was real. Why don't they go back to the moon. I wanna go to the moon. Come we go to the moon. I used to have a game on the

Nintendo called Macdonald Land and on the moon level you had to kill aliens made of cheese. That's the only reason I wouldn't wanna go there. But the views of Earth would be nice. See my yard from space. Catch my girl cheating and then we can finally split up. Ok I'm chatting breeze, bye.

Wednesday 21st July 1999

Yes it's the last day of school. Now we're going into the summer holidays.

The first lesson I had was History. We did f**k all, just sat and chat. But our teacher did put on 'Schindler's List'. But no one was watching it. cos you can't be watching that depressing shit when it's last day of school. The film was HuHH. Plus it's not even in colour.

After our year (year 10) played rounder's against the teachers. But me and Kenworthy never played, just bopped around school flexing chases from teachers.

As school was finishing we had a little assembly where the teachers were just chatting mess. We finished school at 1.30pm (half day); I got a lift on the coach. But I was in a proper rush cos I was meeting Gemma at 2pm in Paddington. Anyhow I got off the coach by Langley village then bopped to the train station cos it was around 1.50ish. But I still missed the 2pm train. So I went Slough and got the quicker one to Paddington.

I got to Paddington about 2.45pm but it was safe cos I kept ringing her on the mobile, yeah I've got a new phone now, a Nokia 51 10.

We chilled round Paddington then we got the train to Langley at 3.12pm. And if you're wondering, no I never went to meet her in my offkey school garms, nah man it was a non-uniform day at school.

As I was saying, we got to my house about 4pm. When I got in I got a letter from Rachel. But I opened it in secret just in case Gemma saw. It just got Rachel chatting so much shit. And that part when it said mans have asked her out is bullshit.

Today me and Gemma didn't do naughty but I was just playing about with her. And there's some nasty shit about her. Well it's not her exactly, but her fanny, it just

"F**KING STINKS"

Boy it's nasty, it's a sick fishy smell and you don't just smell it when you're close, you can smell it if you're just kissing her. But only when she's in them SAME silky knickers.

Serious, I can't be fucked with her no more. Nah, not with that offkey smell and those same knickers as the other day, probably not washed. I don't care how lovely her batty would be in doggy it'S OVER.

Well I took Fishy (Gemma) to the station at 7pm. And got the train to Paddington with her but I never went into London. I got the train back at 8.12pm.

When I got home Nadia and Becky S were round. I had some munch then me and Becky walked Nadia to her bus stop.

After Becky decided to come back to mine for a while. Just to watch a film or something. But in the end it seemed like we made our own movie.

Stay tuned

Well Becky came round and we watched 'Candyman 2'. Half way through the movie Becky was getting all horny and I got off with her, but it felt weird cos she's like a good friend to me. She used to go Churchmead but then moved to Reading. But now's she's back.

After the film finished, we went downstairs just to chill cos my mum was in bed (work in the morning).

When we were downstairs I was lipsing Becky again. We both started getting really into it. I asked her if she wanted to do it. She just said she didn't mind. So hey I took that as a yes.

We were gonna do the ting on the sofa but there was no room cos "f**k" she's blonks (big). So we just went on the living room floor when she was lying down she took off her top then I was just sucking her 34b tits . And shit it was giving me jokes cos she was moaning like she was being banged. I thought nah if you're like this when someone's sucking your tits you'll die when you get willy. But it was giving me jokes. I was really trying to not burst out laughing. After that I touched her fanny and she was almost shouting and shit when I stuck my finger up there she was going mad. She also kept moving her hips up and down and I was proper ready to start creasing up. I was thinking what the hell she moving like that for.

After she went to play with my willy but shit it wasn't hard. So you know what she did. She pushed me on to my back and started giving me shines. And you know something cos I was laughing so much I my head it took long for it to get hard. When it did get hard, I just got on her and started pumping her for a while. She kept moaning and saying shit like screw me hard bad boy, bare jokes I'm still creasing now while I write this. But I couldn't bang her properly cos my ting kept going soft. She was just too funny.

Also Becky does shiners differently. But i got my tings working properly and it was fun times. Ow it'S NICE. Well that's all we did but there's another thing. When you're rubbing her up she starts rubbing her body up as well and licking her lips. Trust she's got quite a bad body but she's proper tall. After I just walked her to her road then when I got home relaxed in bed, W.I.Ded and watched 'Rush Hour'.

Funniest things all day:-

- Becky- moaning over me licking her titties
- Classic funniest thing all day-Michelle bit me

DID U KNOW?

The first gas balloon, filled with hydrogen was released in Paris in 1738 by French professor of physics, J.A.C Charles

Thursday 22nd July 1999

Today I woke up about 11.45am. At 12ish Kieron from Hanwell knocked. I got dressed then we bopped to the shop cos I needed to get Shibbz some cat food. When I got in I got ready to breeze out.

We got some cheapy Nightingale bus to Slough to see what's gwarning.

When we got in Slough we just met bare people we knew (well I knew). So we were just chilling round Slough. I flexed a Nacho Burger from Burger king.

About 4pm we met up with Simmons then we flexed a train to Windsor. OTT we met Guv, Sean, Wayne and some offkey brare. We just bopped down Windsor High Street then we were gonna go down the fair but it wasn't on.

At 5pm we got the train to Slough then Slough - Langley. When we got Langley we just flexed to my drum. Simmons came back as well cos he wanted to read my diary for last night.

Well nothing happened tonight but Kieron stayed and we just watched TV.

Funniest things all day:-

- Fishy Gemma- CARD GAME play fish- play Gemma
- Same silky draws
- Snake game- on a dead flex

Friday 23rd July 1999

Today I woke up at 10.30am especially to watch Teenage Mutant Ninja Turtles 2, I don't care what you think, that film's bad. Go Ninja, go Ninja, go and all that. I just ain't seen it in time, so I thought I'd watch it.

At 12.30pm Naomi came over for a while. When she left I flexed a bath. At 2pm we got on a bus to Slough (me and Kieron). But the bus was a Britwell bus, so as I was getting my haircut at 3 I stayed on the bus. Kieron and

Simmons got off at Slough High Street. They were gonna meet up with Becky (the one I pressed) and Nadia.

I got to the barbers a bit early but was safe cos I got it cut earlier (my biff). I got back to Slough about 3.30pm. I met them lot with Becky and Nadia in the Slough shopping centre place (HuHHservortory and HuHH'smere).

Me and Kieron left Slough about 5.30pm to breeze Hanwell for a while. Fuel's also on tonight at 7pm, but we always flex there late so that's minor.

At Kieron's I just waited for him to get ready to breeze petrol (fuel). We also met Jason and he wanted to flex with us.

We got the train to Langley at 7.20pm. At Langley we quickly bopped to my drum to tell my mum I was staying round. After we went to London Road and flexed the 81 bus to Colnbrook.

When we got to Fuel me and Kieron rinsed it out with our dark lyrics, trust.

After fuel we chilled around Colnbrook. We were hanging about with Sheryl and Michelle. Jason really likes Michelle but she didn't really like him that much. They waited with us till the bus came. We got off the bus near my house. We knocked for Becky but she was asleep.

After we bopped down to the village for a while and met up with Simmons, Sean etc. but we didn't stay that long.

We got the train at 12.10am. The train didn't stop at Hanwell so we got off at Ealing then got a bus.

When we got in we just cotched and catched jokes.

Funniest things all day:-

- Eddy – lack attack
- Jumper blends in with skin
- Murices toe- Murices krusty pants

DID U KNOW?

Shaq o Neal's shoe size is size 27

Saturday 24th July 1999

Today I woke up about 10.30am – 11am. Remember last night I stayed at Kieron's. At 11.30 Jason came over to breeze out.

During all this morning I kept getting calls from Gemma and she wanted to link up (meet) with me. But I couldn't be f**ked. I kept trying to think of reasons so she'd f**k off.

At 12pm we breezed out. We stopped off at this church, yes a church you got a problem with that. Well they were giving out free munch, there was a BBQ. We got bare munch- hot dogs, burgers and drinks (well that's not much). We were also chatting to this offkey man about our beliefs and stuff like that.

After we flexed to the Bunny Park to see what was gwarning. Down the Bunny Park we just met a few people we knew. I was catching jokes from this brare called Junior cos he was drunk and lean and just was chatting bare shit.

Also Gemma called and said she was going into London, so we thought we might as well meet the fishy silky drawers bitch.

Anyway around 2pm me and Kieron flexed back to his drum. We left about 3pm to meet Gemma at Paddington. The train we were flexing was the 3.19pm but it took the proper piss, it came at 3.38pm.

Can't remember what time we got to Paddington but we were late to meet Fishy. We decided to flex down Trafalgar square for a while. But I told Gemma I had to be home for 6pm. Which was true cos tonight Rachel's coming over.

When we got to Trafalgar we just chilled.

We left Trafalgar about 5pm. On the tube back we were just catching joke. Kieron kept saying "I smell fish does anyone smell that?" And he kept saying things "we're silky" and pretending to Gemma, that that was our word for good. We were gonna ditch Gemma and go round London and get girls, but she came Paddington with us. We got our train at 5.45, before that we flexed a KFC.

When I got home I kept getting calls from bare bredwins (Kieron wasn't with me he got off the train at Hanwell). As I was saying tonight everyone was telling me about bare parties. I did want to go but Rachel was coming over, I thought for once I might just bring her.

Rachel came round at 7.45. And she didn't want to go to any parties, just to the gay cinema. But the thing was I had no money, mans were brassed out. And my mum was out. So I couldn't get any money.

In the end we ended up just staying in. I suppose the sex had to make up for it though.

Funniest thing all day:-

- Kieron razing Maurice's as we walked out the door." you gonna walk us to the door Maurice"
- Kieron-That brare thinks he's silky
- Dissing people OTT – sucked up face woman Irish bag wrong way round

DID U KNOW?

Water is vital for life. About 70% of your blood is made of that shit.

Sunday 25th July 1999

Today was quite dry. At 1.30pm Rachel left, she flexed a lift off her uncle (who lives in Hayes). So I never had to bop her to the bus stop, Bo.

After Rachel left, I had to do the lawn at the back. At 3pm JD came over for a while. He was chatting mess.

At 5.30pm I went over to Becky's house. I was just playing on her computer and watching TV. She also hooked me up some tick Nesquick drink. It was chocolate fudge cake flavour. I tried to raze it but I got catch. I was gonna see if I could get any tings again but her mum was in. I just fingered her a bit in the kitchen. Only a few minutes though.

I left Becky's around 9ish and she said she'd come round tonight to watch a film or something. But she never came round. So this boring Sunday I just stayed in.

Funniest thing all day:-

• Shibbz bredwins – the turtle and the bee

DID U KNOW?

The adventures of Superman first came on TV in 1952 in the USA.

Monday 26ᵗʰ July 1999

This morning Kieron knocked for me (11.30am). We flexed out at 1pm then bopped down Trelawney Avenue where we met up with Simmons. Then we got a bus to Slough. I stopped off at my mum's work to get some money.

After we flexed down the High Street and met Sean, Wayne and Michael J. We were just chilling on the bench looking for skeet. We also met up with Becky and Nadia and we chatted to them for a while.

After we decided to flex to Reading. When we got to Slough train station.

We flexed a 60p ticket to Windsor just so we could get through the machines, it's the cheapest.

On the way to Reading we had to get off at Maidenhead cos we got caught by two ticket men. We also won't allowed on any other train unless we had le tickets. So we flexed round Maidenhead for a while. We went down the Super Bowl. Simmons, Wayne and Sean went in the Crystal Maze and got bare chases off the workers.

After we flexed back to the station. We managed to get on a train to Slough. But it was only me, Simmons, Wayne and Michael J; the other 2 got left behind.

When we got to Slough I was the only person who had a ticket to get through the machines. So what we did was just all bundled through at the same time.

After we just bopped back through the High Street. Later on we met up with Kieron and Sean. Then after me, K and Simmons bopped home.

When I got home I munched and just cotched. Kieron was round as well. Well tonight again I don't know what's going on. But I was ringing bare girls and they're all going on holiday. And I'm a bit pissed cos this summer I was gonna go away but I've got that f**king Court case.

Later on around 9.30pm Becky came round and tonight I would of got BARE sex but Kieron was round. And Kieron was acting crazy he kept jumping on Becky and talking in HuHH language. So she was getting pissed off

I just watched a film with her and K. Becky left about 11pm. We walked her to her yard. Didn't even lips her.

At 1am Simmons came round. He had bare computer games. Me and Simmons were playing the games till about 3.30am then Simmons breezed home.

I just gelled to bed and Kieron left Kieron downstairs cos he fell asleep on the settee. Shit still pissed cos I could of got bare sex.

Funniest things all day:-

- Eddie – school for burnt
- Kieron gave me jokes when Becky was round. Jumping on her making HuHH noise

DID U KNOW?

Nowadays it's impossible to watch the news without seeing something bad.

Tuesday 27th July 1999

This morning I had some f**ked up dream with Terry in it and he had just come back from holiday from another planet. I also was in Reading and we got into RG1 (a club). See f**ked up dream innit.

Well this morning Kieron left really early cos he had some place to go. All through this morning I kept getting calls from Gemma cos she wanted to link up. But I didn't wanna so I just told her I was feeling well sick.

At 1.30pm I flexed over Becky's house. She had to babysit her little sister. At 2pm Naomi came over. We just all chilled in Becky's room playing tunes. At 3pm Naomi left. Straight after me and Becky took her little sister to the village park; luckily I was not seen by my bredwins.

I left Becky's at 4.30pm then flexed home. I rang Simmons and the crew to see what time we were meeting to go Uxbridge Rhythm Nation. It's the first one in Uxbridge.

Later Simmons came over. Then we flexed to Sean's house. After we all met Guv down the village park. We all then bopped down to flex some drink. I only had one can of Stella.

After we flexed to the train station and met Kieron N, Calvin and Kemar. We all just about caught the 7pm train. OTT we met Ben S, Javan and Shithead

We got off at West Drayton then from there we got a bus to Uxbridge. I skilfully sneaked on the bus. While people were paying and just ducked and rolled on.

When we got to Rhythm Nation there was a hench queue. But it went down fast. There was also bare girls. Rhythm Nation was at Royales Night Club. We got in about 8.30pm.

It was quite a bad rave. There were bare skeet. At first I was getting blasted by bare skeet. But later the girls started coming to their senses.

Here's the numbers I got

Kirsty - she was proper hard to get. I kept trying to cherpes but she was being offkey. She's got a man but I still got her number. It's the shit I said to nice her up but she was a tough one.

Shona - this girl was proper safe. I was chatting to her for time. She was chatting about her boyfriend problems. I was just smooth talking her. She thought I was a really nice gentleman. Ha Ha Ha.

Sabrina - I think this girl was ugly but I couldn't tell, it was dark. Plus she cherped me and that's progression in 1999.

Carly - Sabrina's friend, after Sabrina breezed I cherpes Carly. She's quite bad. Worth a juice.

I also met lots of girls I knew like Naomi, Penny from George Green, Selena and some other Langley/Slough girls.

After RN I got a lift from Naomi's mum. When I got in I relaxed and munched and watched South Park.

Well now I'm going bed. Simmons rang and said he's coming over but f**k waiting, that bastard can take the trek back cos man's tired.

DID U KNOW?

Jamaica was a Spanish possession between 1509 and 1655

Wednesday 28th July 1999

Today at 1.30pm I flexed over Becky's house. We were just chilling. She had to look after her little 9 year old sister again today. Later on she was getting really horny. She said she wanted to bang me again, Bo.

At 4pm Becky's brother came over, so we left to go my house for a good old fashion shag, man I hate that word.

We stopped off at Simmons house cos I needed to get some condoms. Becky wanted it safe today. And it was jokes cos Becky was saying don't tell Simmons the condoms are for me, rags I told him. And I told him to look out the window to see her hiding and waiting behind the wall.

Anyway when we got back to mine. We just went upstairs to bang.

Today was offkey, cos you know how she shouts, today she was screaming and the neighbours were outside and could hear her. They were having a family BBQ.

The sex was good though. Just what you need on a Wednesday. Mid week and ting.

Becky left about 6pm. After I was just relaxing and had to tidy my room. At 8pm I went out cos I was bored. I met up with Becky and Angela. Then I went over Simmon's house but he wasn't in. So I rang him on his mobile and he said he was at Kirsty's party. Also early I rang Shona from RN and I might be meeting her next week. She also said she was back with her boyfriend, that's offkey.

As I was saying I went to Kirsty's birthday party. The party was jokes I was quite pissed from some Malibu. It was all the Langley Grammar crew. At one point Andrew had cake all over his hands and was rubbing it in people's faces. He got some on my arm but this girl Olivia licked it off for me. Simmons was also pissed.

After the party I lipsed that girl Olivia then flexed home. But I was all hyper cos I was quite drunk. I'm writing now very drunk.

Also got another letter from Rachel.

Funniest thing all day:-

- Beating up punch bag at Kirsty's
- Sending JD's number to Simmons

DID U KNOW?

If you have a criminal record you're not allowed to work with children or baby sit, shit like that. Also other jobs so don't get in trouble kids or you can't get a shit job like being a gay teacher, well don't get caught

Thursday 29ᵗʰ July 1999

At 1pm Guv knocked for me. He came out with me at 1.30pm cos I was meeting Gemma at 2.3pm. We got the train to Paddington. At Paddington we met Gemma, I was early for once.

We flexed down to Piccadilly and the usual places. It was alright but I had no money at all. Gemma paid for me to get to Central London.

At 5.30pm we left. We had trouble through the ticket machines. But that's minor we always find a way. We were getting through with Gemma'S ticket and we lost it at Paddington. Gemma didn't have no money to get back so we called her uncle to pick her up. But breezed and left her at Paddington to wait on her own. We had a train to catch. OTT I rang Carly from RN and I might be meeting her on Monday. She's from Hayes.

When I got home I just relaxed hard I was proper tired.

Also rang Sarah from Bath and she's going London next week. Meeting her RAGZ.

DID U KNOW?

Frozen food keeps for a long time because the freezing of water inside the food forces the bacteria which cause it to decompose into inactivity

Friday 30ᵗʰ July 1999

All through today I was just relaxing. Naomi came over at 1.30pm and stayed till about 6.30pm. Just chatting and shit. Shit about Slough Grammar.

In the night I was gonna stay in but Simmons rang and was asking if I wanted to breeze out somewhere.

Simmons came over about 10.30pm then we breezed out. When we breezed out we met up with Nicholas and two offkey brares. Some Irish one and some skinny half caste boy.

Well we breezed down Trelawney then down the village for a while. At 11.08 we got a train to Slough.

Down Slough we met up with bare people like Matt F, Nathan K and Denzel. Nicholas and his offkey friend only stayed a little while then breezed home.

Later on it was just me and Simmons and Matt. We met up with all the Langley Grammar girls. They were telling us about some party tomorrow in Hayes at the Rugby Club. When they left we were just chilling. Simmons found some old granny bike and we were riding it about.

At 1.30am me and Simmons rid back to my drum on the granny bike. When we got to mine we played the Playstation game Worms then at 3am we watched some 70's comedy film. It finished at 5am then Simmons breezed home.

I flexed to sleep.

Funniest things all day:-

- Candyman cop trying to scare Simmons
- Kick tune on the phone

DID U KNOW?

Robin Williams next film will be 'Don't worry, he won't get far on foot'

Saturday 31st July 1999

Another month over and this month has been quite safe. Today was alright as well.

Today I flexed out about 2.45pm. I met Sean and Nicholas down Simmons' work. At 3.30pm we got a train to London. We chilled round London till about 7pm. There was hardly any girls in London today, well there was but offkey ones. We were just going round Troc, Leicester Square and we went in Nike Town shop.

At 7.12ish we got a train back to Slough. Then me and Sean got a train to Langley.

When I got in I got ready to breeze to this party tonight in Hayes. At 8pm Simmons came over. We breezed to Sean's, round Sean's we met Guv, Wayne and some next Asian boy, they all came as well. We stopped off at Darvils to get some drink.

At 8.30pm we went to the station and met up with Matt. We then got the 8.30 train to Hayes. It was jokes when we got to the station cos the ticket man asked us for a ticket and we just walked passed him. He kept saying "hey come back" but we just aired him (that means blanked him, get me). But you had to be there.

After we got the 90 bus to the Brook House pub down in Hayes End. Down there we met Kirsty, Catrina and Tina. Then we flexed up to the party. The party was at the Brook House football ground and was f**king £5 to get in.

The party was alright, there was bare girls (mostly Hayes skeet). There were proper MC's there and I did manage to MC a bit. I smashed it to one tune I must admit that.

At one point I almost got into arms cos I barged past this boy to get pass. Then after he was chatting to me saying shit like "do you know who I am? They call me BLACK PANTHER". But no I didn't know no black dusty panther guy. But after he was alright just goes "so it's safe yeah" and he was cool.

Also I got two girls numbers, it was strange cos both were from Langley and that's weird for me cos usually I meet girls who live in some far off distant place (like your mum's house).

The party finished at 12am. After we were just chilling outside. Everybody wanted to go down to London but me and Simmons couldn't be bothered. So we started walking to Hayes train station. We were also with these girls who were going near there, so we walked with them (Asoka and Selena). On the way we got some chips and the brare was safe he gave us some free munchables.

When we got to this girls house (Selena) we just cotched. She gave us bare drink and some munch, I had some ice cream tub all to my jaze.

Well in the night me and Simmons slept in the living room. Simmons fell asleep straight away but I had trouble sleeping on some leather settee and it was proper hot.

While I was up I was just watching shit on MTV. It was sort of clubby music with the TV full of patterns; you know that bullshit they just put on in the night. Well I think I fell asleep around 5.30ish.

Funniest things all day:-

- Shutting train doors on woman
- Nicholas ringing friend right next to him
- Come down selector with the 99 remix- James brown song comes in
- Asoka- you lot are funky just staying round a girl's house you don't even know

DID U KNOW?

Some flats never have 13 floors cos it's supposed to be unlucky. They will go up to 12 or 12a ETC

Yes Robert,

It's only me, Rach. It's about 8·15 + I'm proper bored. I was writing in my diary + I couldn't be bothered to write any more. I'm still only on Thursday last week. I'm just too lazy to do anything. I haven't really got alot to say because I chatted to you on the phone earlier. I had an alright weekend I suppose apart from friday night when you made me upset. I need to know if we are still together 'cos I can't wait for you to tell me whats going on forever, you joker. Throughout our 5½ months I've had so many offers from mens who want to take me out. I'm not being bigheaded by the way so please don't blast me. Thanks sexy. Anyway I've said No to every single one of them because I liked "You" too much man. And I don't just like you 4 the way you look, I like you 4 what u are inside. In the past I may have said I was tempted to cheat on you, I only said this 'cos I thought you were playing me, 'cos I know I'm not all that nice looking you know. Even if the mens r fitter I still say no, cos playing around is dark. You are the only man I've ever felt comfortable around, I can be myself around you. I've had some really good times with you. You are the only one I've ever been proper naked with, cos I feel comfort-able with you. You r also the only one I've slept wit'

Funniest thing all month (July 99):-

5. Xmen v biff fighter

3. Becky moaning and groaning

2. Silky draws

1. Dr Chicken

Well Yesterday I wrote that I went 2 bed at 5.30am well Selena (the girl who's house it woz) woke us up at 6.00am to breeze home. So I had a nice little ½ an hour sleep. Well we left about 6.30 and when we got to Hayes Station we met all the ...

Sunday 1st August 1999

Well yesterday I wrote that I went to bed at 5.30am well Selena (the girl whose house it was) woke us up at 6am to breeze home. So I had a nice little half an hour sleep.

Well we left about 6.30am and when we got to Hayes station we met all the crew cos last night they stayed round Tina's drum.

Our train came about 7ish but it only went to Slough. So we had to bop from Slough station. I got home at 8am and just got some drink and munch. I was just about to go to bed when my mum came downstairs and was chatting for time.

At 11am MJP knocked and he had just come back from his holiday. We breezed out at 2.30pm and you know something I never got no sleep. I just flexed out, well I did wash and change, dick.

We were bored so we flexed into London town. We went to Trafalgar Square, Piccadilly, Troc and Leicester Square.

We left London about 5pm and flexed a Slough train at 5.18pm. We bopped back from there. When we got to Slough we stopped off at JD's for a while. After MJP called his mum and she came and picked us up.

Today I never went out. In the night I was just relaxing and playing computer. And I went bed at 2am but I proper needed sleep.

Also meeting Sabrina from RN on Wednesday.

DID U KNOW?

People in the 3rd world are poor because of the slave trade.

Monday 2nd August 1999

Today I woke up about 11.30. Nothing really happened today I was in all day. Just people came round like Nadia, Becky, Simmons and Guv. I went bed at 2am. This was a wasted day.

<u>Offkey Jill Dando jokes:-</u>

What's Jill Dando's favourite TV programme?

Shooting stars

What's Jill Dando's favourite ice cream?

Magnum

What's the difference between Jill Dando and Daz?

Jill Dando didn't pass the door step challenge

Funniest thing all day:-

- Guv – there was bare skeet at Rhythm Nation
- MJP- yeah but there was more skeet in the USA
- Me – Yeah but that's a whole country

DID U KNOW?

The closest planet to the sun is Mercury

Tuesday 3rd August 1999

Today when I woke up I found another letter from Rachel. This one is offkey cos I can't write on it but she's f**ked up as well, the end of the letter says about some boy that likes her and she said no (just read it). I thought nah if that was me with a fit skeet, rags I'd do it.

Today I was supposed to meet Gemma at 1pm at Paddington. But I couldn't be bothered but for some reason MJP wanted to meet her. So I just said you link her and I'll chill in Langley.

Becky and Nadia came over my house for a while and they wanted me to come to Slough, but nah allow that dry place.

Simmons came over at 2.30pm then we flexed the 3pm train to London. We were gonna meet MJP, Daniel Mountain and Lee. But they were in Piccadilly with Gemma and I couldn't be f**ked to see her. She was just bopping around with them.

When we got to Paddington we then sneaked past the ticket machines then flexed a train to Piccadilly Circus. At Troc we met up with Daniel Mountain and Lee. Then 10 minutes later we met MJP and Gemma down MTV.

After we flexed down to Nike town in Oxford Circus. During Nike Town I had a phone message from Rachel saying she didn't wanna go out with me no more. She was saying because she thinks I'm cheating. I don't know what gave her that impression. Anyway I'm single now, Bo.

After we all slyed through the ticket machines back to Paddington. Gemma came back and saw us off, what's the point in that.

When we got to Slough we then got a train to Langley. OTT we met up with Nicholas. Tonight RN is on but I'm not sure if I'm going cos I've got about £2. When I got home Becky was round. I got ready to go but then my mum said I couldn't go. She was mad about something. So I rang Simmo and told him I won't come. They think it's because Becky's round but nah I wanted to go but it doesn't matter the sex I get later makes up for it, doh.

Well tonight me and Becky watched the film IT (the film with the ugly clown that looks like your mum, yeah yours). Anyway today was jokes. It just started off me fingering her then she just started saying how she wants to do the ting. So her trousers came down. So I took mine down but got her to suck it a bit first. But her shiners (BJ's) are weird cos you can't really feel it that much. It's very hollow. After I had a lickerdy lick. Then I started pumping her for ten minutes. Then mum came upstairs. So we stopped, she just got the covers and put them over herself just in case my mum bopped in. But we started again when we heard my mum going downstairs. "ok quick lets go".

"Damn" she almost screamed the house down. I kept saying be quiet and to get her to shut up I put my dirty sock in her mouth. Then she got mad and stopped, but then i said sorry and we started again but she kept being loud. I kept trying not to laugh cos she was saying shit like if you don't do it fast I'll scream. So I'm there straining and doing it fast cos she blackmailed me. And the funniest thing was she kept saying was punch it. When I was doing it with fingers she wanted me to sort of punch it. She's f**king mad. But she's 17 so guess that how the older ladies like it.

When she left I was ringing up Simmons to see what was going on at RN. He said it was good. But cos I got my tings I don't regret not going, Bo.

Funniest thing all day:-

- Just punch it punch it

HISTORY FILE

LINFORD CHRISTIE WAS DONE FOR DRUGS

DID U KNOW?

The new Star Wars movies are actually set before the original ones. Shit no wonder I couldn't work out what the f**k was going on.

Queen's Birthday - Wednesday 4th August 1999

At 1.20pm today I went to the train station. At la Gare (it's French) I met MJP. We caught the 1.30pm train to go Hayes. We're doing this cos we we're meeting Carly at 2pm.

At Hayes station we had to dash over the fences to get out. We waited till about 2.30pm and Carly didn't show up. I rang her house and her little brother said she was round a friend's house. So we thought ring Sabrina and see what she's up to. She asked us to come down to Iver to her house. So we flexed to Iver.

When we got to Iver we waited about 10 minutes then Sabrina came and she looked f**ked. Remember guys I said it was dark in the club when I first met her. I couldn't tell if she was fit or not.

Well as we were with her, we went back to her yard. When we were at her yard all we did was mix on her decks. Cos her cousin is a DJ .She also knows all the Rhythm Nation MC's and can get people in for free. So maybe she's not that butterz after all. Also she got the decks for free and all the records.

Me and MJP were playing all the decent tunes cos she had everything. And we grabbed the mic and chatted.

We left Sabrina's about 6pm. When I got home I just cotched. Then at 7pm Becky came over. We both bopped down to the shops. Down the shops we met Simmons.

After we all went back to Becky's. I just lipsed Becky for a bit. We only stayed for half an hour then bailed (old skool word). Tonight there was gonna be a party down Maplin Park but then we found out it wasn't on. So Simmons, Guv, Wayne and this girl called Natalie came back to mine and we had jokes playing Worms. Trust the girl must of been bored.

DID U KNOW?

All things in superstition are from the olden days when people talked shit. Like a mirror would take 7 years to re-pay. That's why it's 7 years bad luck.

Thursday 5th August 1999

This morning I was having a f**king beautiful sleep. Until some fat bastard started banging on my door and woke me up (it was 11.30am). It was Kieron. I was gonna go back to sleep but couldn't cos Kieron was there.

At 2pm me and Kieron went down to Trelawney Avenue and met Simmons, MJP, Sean and Wayne. At 3.12pm all of us (apart from Wayne) got a train to Reading just to check for girls.

Down Reading we flexed down the High Street and in their shitty Reading Shopping Centre.

There wasn't hardly any skeet today but I did meet up with Maria who I haven't seen since January 2nd 1999. She had bare spots. Who's your mate?

Went back to Langley at 6.30pm then we flexed over Becky's (apart from MJP, breezed yard). At 7pm me and Kieron breezed from Becky's. I flexed home and Kieron went back to Hanwell.

At 9pm Guv and Sean came over. After Simmons rang and was asking if I wanted to come to Studio 412 with him, Becky and her friend from Watford.

At 10pm Becky, Simmons and Mary (Becky's friend) came over. We got a taxi to Studio 412 (which is a club in Slough) and got there about 10.30pm. It was alright, it was a over 18's but there was bare young people. A few girls from my school, in year 11. When we got there it was a bit shite but later on (when everybody started dancing) it was alright.

It finished at 1am then after we took the long bop back to my house. From George Green - Langley.

When we got back to my house we just cotched. I flexed on the film 'Dusk till Dawn' but everyone fell asleep so I switched it off.

At 5.30am Becky and her friend left. Becky didn't let me have fun with her cos her friend was there. I said it's cool she can have Simmons. But nothing happened. No love for anybody.

Also next week going to Chessington World of Skeet, I mean Adventures.

DID U KNOW?

Windsor Castle is the oldest castle in the world?

Friday 6th August 1999

Today I woke up about 12pm. I had to meet my mum at 1pm in Slough then 2pm Carly in Hayes, Simmons left my yard at 12pm if you're wondering.

At 1.10pm I left to go Slough I flexed down London Road newsagents cos I heard they were looking for employees. But the brare said I had to come back later cos the Manager wasn't there. Or he probably was the manager and saw me and thought I ain't giving this butterz brare a job. Watch, I'll go back and he'll be wearing a manager badge then I'll be like "blud I thought you weren't the Manager" and he'll be like oo shit I just got promoted after you left but sorry still can't give you a job.

After I met Simmons at the bus stop then we flexed to Slough to meet my mum. I had to search for my mum and when I found her I gave her a drawer. Then she gave me some money. (I was only joking about the drawer). BUT SHE DID GIVE ME MONEY.

Me and Simmons then caught a train to Hayes. We got to Hayes at 2.05pm. At the station me and Simmons had to dash over the fence to escape.

I kept trying to ring Carly but it kept going to answer machine. And you'll never guess what she flopped us again so now I'm just gonna allow that stupid bitch.

Anyway as we were in Hayes we flexed a McyD's. Then after we thought we'd go Windsor because Simmons knew some girl who works in McyD's. Well we got to McyD's Windsor. The girl was being offkey and just giving us water. We didn't want water we wanted a little cheeseburger or a big Mac or some ting. Water's gay.

After we met up with these two brares which Simmons knew from football. And they proper don't know how to cherpes girls. There was this group of girls and they took so long to cherpes them, we were following the girls around, how offkey. Well in the end I cherpes them and they were offkey. One girl had too much make up and this other one spoke like a man. So I just allowed getting their digits.

After we went back through. It was quite poo. We just met up with a few people and were chilling.

At 5.30pm we met up with Becky and Nadia and we bopped back to Langley with them.

Tonight I never went out Simmons came over and we watched Con Air and Austin Powers.

Sunday 7ᵗʰ August 1999

Today at 3pm I breezed down to the London Road newsagents to see if I could get that job. The woman said that I couldn't work Mondays - Fridays but could do weekends. Cos for the weekdays they need people permanently, like people who have left school. But I only want it for the holidays.

When I got back I just relaxed. I was gonna go out but I couldn't be f**ked. At 5pm MJP came over. He left about 7pm.

At 9pm I breezed down to Langley village. I had to take some videos back to video box. After I met Guv, Wayne, Wayne's woman, Sean, Kieron and Chris H. They were just chilling in Langley Park doing nothing. I left with Michael and flexed a kebab from Kinara. Then after we went down to Trelawney Avenue and met up with Simmons. I only stayed for a bit then breezed home.

When I got in it was about 10.30pm. I was so bored so I rang up bare girls. They're all busy but I'm meeting Nicole from Isleworth on Monday. And also le Carly from Hayes rang me and said she does want to meet she's just being offkey; well she never said "I'm being offkey". I just said that. At 12am my mum came back from some restaurant and flexed me some Chinese which she saved, Bo.

At 12.45am Simmons came over for a while

Funniest thing all day:-

- Leon talking about pimping Cat £4 shag offer with fries and milkshake.

RED LORRY YELLOW LORRY RED LORRY YELLOW LORRY RED LORRY YELLOW LORRY RED LORRY

DID U KNOW?

Ancient Chinese civilisations believed an eclipse happened because a dragon was eating the sun. They would bang drums to frighten it away

Sunday 8th August 1999

Today was just one of those stay in Sundays. I only went out once today and that was to get milk. 4 pints.

In the night I just watched TV and did some exercise cos I need to keep fit and in practice for kickboxing.

Funniest thing all day:-

- Rinse Fm Chat- As I swing on my ninja rope, don't check me if you look like the pope we're gonna watch this one like a soap opera, selector.

DID U KNOW?

That Caprice, only has 34c titties, I know girls my age bigger than that, like Laura S.

Monday 9th August 1999

Today was just another stay in day. The only reason I've not been going out is because it's been raining like shit lately. And I don't wanna go out in that. Getting wet's not always fun. Unless you're having a bath. But I wouldn't bathe in the rain.

At 4pm JD came over which was safe cos I was bored. Becky came round for a bit as well but they both left at 5pm.

At 7pm Becky came over again. I was just giving her jokes. She kept chatting about some brare she met on Saturday who she really likes. Which is cool but means she won't let me play anymore.

In the night I just watched films on Front Row.

DID U KNOW?

Will Smith wants to be president of USA

Tuesday 10ᵗʰ August 1999

Well today is 1 day till the total eclipse and Bo I can say I lived through one. Well actually its tomorrow I might die today. But no, that doesn't make sense cos I'm writing this now.

Anyway the next one's in 2090 so most of you f**kers out there will miss that shit.

Also last month when I was shitting myself over nothing (end of the world). I found out that Nostradamus just predicted this eclipse, err what a prick. Who cares if mans can predict a bit of moon covering up the sun, big wow.

Today I went out at 3.30pm cos I was going to my cousin's house so he could cut my hair. On the way I stopped off at the newsagents to see about that job but they never gave it to me because they said they had no vacancies. See I told you they'd say that, that's bullshit, f**king racist bitches.

Anyway I got a bus to Slough then bopped to my cousin's. When I got there my cousin goes to me "sorry I can't cut your hair you're two hours late". I thought what a f**king monkey head, he told me to come at 4pm. Well I told him I'd come back on Thursday cos tomorrow's Chessington World of Adventures and the big Eclipse. And you know something we're gonna be in Surrey and that's like down a bit more cos you have to be proper far down South of England to see it good (like Cornwall).

Well I flexed to JD's after cos I needed to give him a video back. I stayed there till 7pm then bopped home.

After went kickboxing training cos I ain't been doing it in time. Then after I was just watching the sky 1.

Well at the moment it's 12.45am and I'm gonna flex to bed cos we're all meeting at 7.30am tomorrow. Bare earliness and ting. Later.

Funniest thing all day:-

- 3D MOVIE-PUNCH WOMEN THROUGH SCREEN

Wednesday 11th August 1999- FULL ECLIPSE OF DA MOON AND TING

I don't know why I'm making such a big fuss over this stupid eclipse, it's only like once every now and then but the thing is they only last for like 4 seconds. Well least I can say I've seen a bit of moon covering up the sun. The next total eclipse is in Africa in 2001.

Well today is gonna be hard to write but I'll try to fit in each piece of information. Well this morning I got up at 7.30am to breeze to Chessington. Around 8.10am Simmons knocked for me then we went over Sean's house. We kept ringing MJP and Guv to see if they were coming as well, but they weren't picking up their phones.

At 8 something we caught a train to Slough. Then at Slough to Windsor. When we got to Windsor we had to wait for Guv cos he was coming as well. I flexed my breakfast while I was waiting for Guv, some McyD's shit. After we got some brare to get some booze for us. We got 8 beers and Simmons got 4 Metz.

When we met Guv we went down to the Windsor and Riverside station. We got our train around 10ish. While we were on the train we could see the eclipse happening. On the news they said don't directly look at it. But f**k that, I won't missing this shit. And yes the world went dark for 4 seconds. We could see it fully OTT.

When we got to Chessington South station I took a piss on a wall then we bopped to the World of Adventures. I also was a bit pissed at this time from the drink.

When we got in Chessington (the theme park) we first flexed on the Galleon ride. We were going mad, standing up and having royal rumbles. The man tore up a bit of our ticket and said if we do one more bad things we got thrown out. 1 rip is first warning.

After we flexed on the new ride, the Samurai. For this we didn't have to queue up cos we quickly went on one at a time. Which we don't mind cos it's not like you can chat to your bredwin while you're on the ride upside down and shit. "How's it hanging?"

I was sitting next to some sexy 19 year old girl. I cherpsed her but then her boyfriend was there and called me a wanker. He's the wanker.

We then got some McyD's and I got it free cos the Chessington one's just f**ked up. You order what you want then collect it, but I kinda forgot to pay, Bo.

The rest of the day we were just catching bare jokes. We were cherpsing girls but most of them weren't all that, had mans or were just being offkey. Do you know what these girls said, well I asked this girl for her number and she said no cos she's been cut off. So I said to her friend can I have yours and she goes "I can't because I'm moving in with her". How offkey is that.

Later on we went on bare rides. We breezed on the Bubbleworks 2 times and were just going mad all fighting in the boats and splashing each other. The boat almost tipped over bare times. Saw my life flash before my eyes.

We also went on the Vampire ride. I think cos I was fucked it seemed much faster. But it is getting a bit 1992, they need to update that shit.

Also we went on Ramses Revenge that was just minor. I was yawning.

We were gonna go on the Log ride(whatever it's called) but now they've got some new policy thing were you have to flex a ticket then come back at a certain time, allow that.

We went on Galleon (boat ride) bare times and we were just fighting each other. We went on other rides a few times as well.

Later on I did get this girl's number. Her name was Sarah and she's from Kent. I met her earlier but I got her number later. Also I cherpes this 20 year old that worked there but I gave her my home number and I've been cut off (dick).

I also got cherpes by these offkey girls at one point. And I stupidly gave them my correct number. Later, these girls cherped us. They were our age but they were not all that. We hung about with them for quite a long time. We went on Galleon with them. This time we went mad on it cos we were leaving soon and didn't care if we got thrown out. We were rumbling each other. I gave Simmons the stone cold stunner.

After the ride the man just ripped up our ticket a bit more. Then we went back on the Bubble works with the girls. Simmons was going mad and splashing them hard. After I got one of their numbers then we bopped down to the Vampire ride. We made them walk us then we thought "come we allow these girls" then we dussed off (ran off).

We went to the sweet shop. We thought we'd do a little bare raze before we left. We razed bare shit cos we had this sweet bag from earlier and we were just filling it up with bare sweets. The bags have stickers on them to show you've paid. So our bag looked like we paid already, even though the bag was over loaded and falling apart. And yeah I got a toffee apple as well.

After we bopped out the shop and there was a man following us. We got away though, cos of me. I goes "lets run or we'll miss the train" so we all dussed of. We left about 8.10pm.

When we got out of Chessington we just munched bare sweets. I munched that toffee apple.

After we got on our train. We had to get off at Motspur Park at one point, cos we got clocked by the TM. But that was minor because the next train came a minute after.

When we got to Clapham we then got the train to Windsor . As we were coming up to Staines we got caught by TM's and they threw us off at Staines. And guess what they wouldn't let us back in the train station. So we chilled round Staines and then kept trying to get in the station but couldn't. After we bopped to the bus depot. But we missed the last bus.

Eventually we got a train cos we had to buy a ticket. Cost f**king £2. How dare they make me buy a ticket.

We got on our train about 10ish and got off at Windsor Riverside. At Windsor got a train to Slough. Then from Slough a train to Langley.

At Langley me, Simmons and Guv all flexed kebabs, the big fat juicy ones.

When I got in I went upstairs and wrote a bit of diary. But couldn't be bothered to finish it. So I went to sleep (12.45am).

Well lately I've hardly had any funniest things all day. Well check these mother fuckers.

Funniest things all day:-

- Sean jumping in front of camera- going on sick
- Phone ringing- in pocket
- Throwing paper in girl's face- see I told you we were mad.
- Guv's blue face
- Bare razing sweats bag falling apart.
- The rumbles- bubbleworks and gallon
- Running away from girls- just let them queue
- Eclipse goes dark- quick pinch the battys
- taking a piss out the train doors then they started shutting
- My bad back
- Sean – paying for razed sandwich
- Do you Simmons- no – ok later on then

DID U KNOW?

Clapham Junction is the busiest train station in Britain?

Thursday 12th August 1999

Today for some reason I woke up around 9.30am. I didn't want to be up that early but after I couldn't get back to sleep.

At 12.30pm Jason came over, from HuHHwell. At 1ish MJP came over. Today Gemma wanted to meet me but I told her I couldn't cos I was getting my hair cut, which was true. But MJP and Jason are joke brares, they said that they'd go and meet her instead, but in Langley. They left and went to MJP's.

At 2pm I went over Simmons' house to waste some time. At 2.40pm I caught a bus to Slough and stopped off at JD's. Chilled there for a bit then went to get my haircut.

Went for a different style today. My cousin cut it the usual but the dyed it a gingery blond colour. When I left my cousin's I got a call from MJP saying hurry up cos fishy pants was waiting. But I was just taking my time.

I got home then Jason and Gemma came over but we didn't chill at mine long cos I wanted to get rid of her. So we bopped her to the train station.

When we got to the station we put her on the train. She was in a mood cos I didn't want to go with her to Paddington, but allow that. I told them if they want fish willy disease they can have her but I'm not interested.

After we bopped back through Langley and knocked for Sean. Then he came out. While we were out we met bare people. Tonight we were just chilling round Trelawney and the village.

We came but about 11pm and that was proper minor. Jason stayed.

Funniest things all day:-

Robb Peters

- Sean's tree burnt down
- Tramp Rachel- sleeping on bench

Freaky Friday 13th August 1999

Bo Friday the 13th is here, this day is just jokes cos people shit their own pantaloons over fuck all. Well I heard about this man and on this day (Friday 13th) he always had bad luck. So he decided for one year to stay in and he tripped over his stairs and died, that's bad luck.

Before I wrote today I hope you like my scary pictures.

Well around 1.30pm me and Jason bopped into Slough. So Jason could buy some trainers. Oh yeah Sean came as well. After we bopped back and we stopped off at JD's cos them lot wanted to see what he was like, they thought he was alright.

When we got back into Langley me and Sean flexed over his house, Jason went back to Hanwell.

Round Sean's we just played some tunes (Sean's got bare new tapes) and played the game Worms.

We flexed down Trelawney for a while as well. Just saw the usual people down there.

After Sean's I just went home. Tonight nothing really happened. Simmons rang me at midnight and was seeing if I wanted to go London, but I thought allow it.

Well in the night I was chatting to my mum about my stories and she really wants to get them published. The thing is it's really hard for me to explain them in writing.

Also tomorrow big titty Joanne might be staying round my house. In the day me and MJP are gonna do one offkey mission to some next place. On Monday, Rachel (my ex skeet) is coming round to see me and bring my video over, I left it at her yard.

Saturday 14ᵗʰ August 1999

Today was an alright day, It includes bare missions , bare skeet and big fat tiities in my face.

Well this morning I kept getting calls from MJP. Asking to meet him in Slough cos today we thought we'd go Bracknell to see what the skeet was saying.

As I was going to Langley train station I got a call from MJP asking me to meet him in Reading (that's where you get the train to Bracknell). I got the train at 2.45pm then from Slough I got a quick train to Reading. I got Reading quite fast, I got there around 3.15pm (half an hour).

When I got there I met MJP then we flexed on some cheapy South West Train to Bracknell. When we got to Bracknell we bopped all around their dodgy High Street. There was skeet but not all that one's or if they were boom they were with mans. There were these 13 year old girls who cherpes us. But we were like sorry babies we're only looking for the 16 and up. I think MJP wanted to get one of these numbers though, dirty brare on some year 8's.

We only stayed round Bracknell for a little while, cos it started raining proper hard. We were only in Bracknell for 40 minutes.

We got a train back to Reading and chilled round Reading for a while. Round Reading there was still skeet. And if you're wondering the point of these missions is:-

1. For skeet
2. For jokes
3. There ain't a three

Well cos Reading was getting proper shit we decided just to breeze into London. But trust Reading to London Is a dirty mission. We got off at Paddington and easily got through the ticket machines. At Piccadilly this brare was safe and just let us through the gates and out of the station.

We bopped down to Leicester square and met up with Nicholas and Dot. Today was bare jokes I met bare skeet and just caught bare jokes. We flexed round Troc, Leicester Square and our usual places. I cherpes bare skeet today about 4 girls took down my number but I got about 2 girls numbers.

When we were in Troc, me and Nicholas kept playing on the Punch machine. And Nicholas clocked the hardest level. The levels were you have to punch up the moon.

As we were leaving London we stopped off at this place called the Buzz Bar. We only flexed in there cos earlier we met the bar maids that worked there. They were both about 18 - 19 but looked proper young. The half caste one would get pressed but she thought she was all that. Had, too much attitude.

We only stayed in the Buzz Bar for a little while (they told us to leave because we weren't buying anything) then breezed OTT back to Paddington. OTT back there were some offkey French black boys playing the mashed up French rap on a big up 1980's looking stereo, the music sounded proper offkey. La biblioteque La discothèque and ting innit.

We got on a train back to Slough around 8pm and we got to Slough about 20 past. When I got Slough I got a train to Langley. I was on my jaze cos MJP went Slough cos he had to meet his mum to go to some BBQ in Tottenham.

When I got back to Langley I bopped down the village and Trelawney to see if anyone was around but HuHH there was no one.

When I got home my mum said Joanne came over but she just breezed. So I rang her up and said "get your bitch ass back here big titty bitch" and then she said she'd be over later around 10pm.

Well if you're a dumbo and don't know what's going on. This big titty girl from Langley (Joanne) is staying over my house, that's all it is to it.

Joanne came over my house around 9.30pm. We just watched some TV, a bit of 'Eurotrash' then 'Scream 2'.

Around 11.45pm-12am bare people came over my drum. It was Simmons, Guv, Sean and Natalie. I think they just wanted to see the titties I had at my yard, yes even Natalie. They all stayed till about 1am. My mum was also drinking wine and was a bit drunk and giving everyone jokes. Simmons stayed the longest cos we started watching 'Terminator 2' at 1am and he left about 4am.

After me and Joanne went upstairs in my room. Bo bare tings I thought, but was I wrong. The girl was on a period. All night it was just sucking those MASSIVE tits and just boring old lipsing. Well the last time I really had really big tits was a long time. That was properly Laura S and that was before the diary. But Joanne's titties were proper weird. They were like really really soft. Every time I put my hands on them, my hands would just go right though, understand what I mean. They were like air bags. And she also had very small nipples which was a bit offkey cos I could get my lips round them proper. I should of called Laura S.

Anyway around 5am I went to sleep cos it was getting proper boring.

Funniest things all day:-

- Girl telling me she can't give me number because she's a lesbian- "lesbians is cool"
- Josh message- trying to MC like MJP
- French rap – la biblioteque
- Completed punch machine saved 50p's got free goes.
- Girls- sorry been cut off
- Me - and I bet you're moving in with her.

DID U KNOW?

The first human heart transplant took place on December 3 1967 at Groote Schuur hospital, Cape Town, South Africa?

DID U KNOW?

56% of couples in the UK act out their fantasies?

Sunday 15th August 1999

Today I did f**k all just sat indoors relaxing. Joanne left about 12pm. And she didn't even wash that life time supply of makeup which was on her face off.

In the night my mum buss me a kebab.

At 1am Simmons came round and we just caught jokes.

Skeet review

Monday – Rachel (ex skeet)

Tuesday – Nicole from Isleworth

Wednesday or Thursday- Carly from Hayes. She said she definitely wants to meet.

Monday 16th August 1999

This morning I woke up around 1pm and just put on my tunes and read this diary for August. I suppose this month's alright but its summer holidays what's going on? Some days are just like "yeah tonight I stayed in" or "Gemma wanted to meet me". Well from now on everyday's gonna be skeet, missions, jokes, exciting things for diary and more skeet and more skeet and a little bit more skeet. How do you like that (crowd cheer noises).

Well today what's happening is ex girlfriend Rachel's coming round. Which is good, I need my video and game back.

About 2pm Rachel came over and since I've finished with her she's came up with bare spots.

Today when she was round we watched 2 films "Juice" and then some old Lenny Henry film (which hardly anyone's heard of) 'Bernard and the Genie'. During the film I was really trying hard not to do anything with her. Cos she'd all start getting the wrong idea and think I want her back with her and her spots. But I did almost kiss her but quickly stopped and thought "what the f**k you doing you stupid fanny dribble". Also one more thing that might sound offkey. I kept thinking to myself I want one of her shiners. But that's offkey just asking for a little sucky sucky. It's just because the shiners I've been getting lately from Becky are just weird, you know what I'm saying. But I was dying for a suck but them she'll be like ok we're back together. But I'd be like no that wasn't part of the deal.

As Rachel left we got a call from my mum's friend Dave and she was saying tonight she'd like to take us to a Chinese restaurant in Slough. We left the same time as Spotty, sorry I mean Rachel. And Bo I didn't have to walk her to the bus stop.

When we got to Dave's drum (in Langley) we just chilled. I met his big eared 10 year old son (Sam) who was coming as well.

We left Dave's at 7.45pm but stopped off at the local pub, the pub where Geri Halliwell got thrown out of for trying to bring her dog in. We stayed there till about 8.20pm cos we booked (we'll he did) the table for 8.30pm. We got a taxi into Slough then at Slough I checked to see if any of my crew were about then quickly breezed into the restaurant.

In the restaurant I had bare munch.

Starters – Peking duck and pancake roll ups.

Main course- lobsters (yes lobster), prawns and a beef things and rice (you know the score)

Dessert- some banoffee (banana and toffee) ice-cream.

We left the restaurant about 11.30pm then got a taxi back home.

Later on around 1am when I was just cotching and watching some free pornos. Simmons knocked to collect some videos.

When he left I just went to bed.

Funniest thing all day:-

- Simmons's JD flex – yeah man going on holiday.

Tuesday 17th August 1999

This morning I had some tick dream .it was weird but tick. It was about we had rivals with some people which I saw off some film. And there was a KFC shop and we could just raze bare munch. It sounds offkey but it was jokes.

Anyway today I was lying in bed for time. At one point I was looking at my ceiling then thinking I really must move. But then I thought actually its summer holidays I might as well just continue gazing at the ceiling. At 4.30pm I got up and bopped to the shops to flex some breakfast.

At 5.30pm Sean and Natalie came over and asked me if I wanted to go Rhythm Nation tonight. So I thought might as well, only got £2 but still.

We left my house at 5.45pm and had to stop off at MJP's house to pick up his cousin (she was coming RN). When we got to the station we met MJP, Nicholas, Simmons and Chris (some dodgy brare). We missed the 6pm train, so we waited for the 6.30pm.

We got off at West Drayton then got the bus to Uxbridge. At Uxbridge we flexed a McyD's then bopped down to RN. We got in RN about 7.30pm. At first we were just relaxing then later we were shaking out hard. And cherpsing bare girls, today I only got two numbers. The 1st was Jemma, some militant short girl from Harrow. The 2nd was Carly, this girl I've been trying to get her number for time and today I got it. And you know what she ain't even all that. I could of lipsed some girl but she wasn't all that but her friend was quite boom. I was cherpsing the friend she took down my number. I also met up with fit Vicki and Amanda. Me and MJP were cherpsing hard. I was asking Vicki if she'd like to go out some time and she goes no, joke, she said yeah.

We left RN at 11.30pm and it was only me Simmons, MJP and dodgy Chris. We bopped to the bus stop and had to get the N207 to Ealing. OTB these girls were chatting to us. They weren't all that but we were just chatting. At one point I had one of their phones and I put my number in there.

We got our train at 12.28am and OTT I kept getting calls and messages from those girls from the bus (bare desperate). I also got a call from Carly from Hayes and she wants to meet definite tomorrow.

When I got in I just chilled. Sean rang me and told me to ring up Rinse FM and MC. So I did and I was just messing about live on radio.

Funniest things all day:-

• Me and Nicholas doing the skipping shaq

DID U KNOW?

Without oxygen we die

Wednesday 18th August 1999

Today's been a bit of a shit day. Today I breezed out at 2.20pm cos I had to go London to meet Carly. On the way I stopped off at MJP's house I wanted him to come just in case the stupid bitch didn't show up again.

At the station we got the train to Paddington. At Paddington I rang Carly and it kept going to answer machine and one time it answered and there was someone making funny noises down the phone. So we thought f**k this stupid bitch and just breeze into London.

At Piccadilly me and MJP flexed in a phone box cos he had some £3 phone card tings . I rang up Carly just one more time and she was at her cousin's house and her her cousin were shouting down the phone shit like "f**king niggas". Trust me and MJP were going mad. There was just bare rioting on the phone. Next time I see that Carly she's getting slapped up. Also I wasted 20p in the phonebox on her.

Anyway we breezed round the usual places. We met up with this brare we knew from South London. He bopped round with us for a bit. We didn't' really do a lot after that but kept getting calls from that racist bitch Carly and her f**ked up cousin. Just ringing saying racist shit then hanging up.

We got back on a train home at 6.12pm. When I got in I had dinner and tonight did shit. See I told you today was shit.

Funniest things all day:-

- M JP on the arcade- go on shabby wolverine
- The future ticket 31 august 0000

DID U KNOW?

There is a place called Sandwich

Thursday 19th August 1999

Today I woke up about 11.43am. As soon as I woke up Naomi knocked for me. She stayed round my house for time but left at 4pm cos I was meeting Shereen at 5pm in Ealing.

At 4.30pm I left . I got to the station at 4.40pm and got the train to Slough then thought get a fast train to Ealing Broadway.

I got to Ealing about 5.15pm then met Shereen outside the station. She looked alright but not proper proper tick. She's half Spanish (trying new flavours innit). When I met her I told her I had no money so I said "come we flex back to my house so I can get some money, then we can breeze somewhere". I said this cos I couldn't be bothered to go anywhere with her. I just wanted her back at mine so I could try a little ting (get her trapped).

So we got the train back to my house, well Langley station. When we got to mine we just chilled for a while. I was trying to persuade her to just stay at mine and come to my room and just watch a film or some tings. But she preferred to go out. And in the end I was like "ok then let me just find that money then we'll leave"

We went back to the train station and caught the 7pm train to Paddington. We just thought we'd go into London and see what's going on. When we got to Paddington we stopped off at McyD's and for some reason I got her some food, when I could of spent that money on something better like chocolate.

After we got a tube into Piccadilly Circus. We bopped round Troc. She thought she was a bad girl round West End cos she knew quite a lot of people (yeah them dry brares that are always hanging outside Segaworld). At one point she goes to me "you should consider yourself lucky walking with me". I just said "nah hold on, YOU should consider yourself lucking rolling with moi". She's a damn hoe chatting her mess. She should of just stayed at mine so I could just do the ting .

She left at 9pm and boy she took long giving me a goodbye kiss. She was like Sarah from Bath; she kept saying I can't in front of bare people (in public).

When she left I belled up Guv to see if we were still going to the Temple in Tottenham tonight, cos he's got a few tickets. He said he was still going but when I rang him he was still in Langley, so I had to wait around for a while (on my jacks).

I waited till 9.40 something then breezed on a train to Paddington. I got to Paddington at 10.08pm. There was a train back to Langley in a few minutes. I still wanted to go to Tottenham but waiting went on shabby. So I rang them and they said they were on their way. So I thought I might as well wait cos home will be boring.

They got to Paddington about 10.4opm. It was Guv, Nicholas , Denny, Chris and some fat Asian brare.

We got the tube to Oxford Circus then got the Victoria Line to Seven Sisters. At Seven Sisters we breezed through the machines easy peasy lemon squeezy then bopped down to the Temple. Also Nick T was with us.

When we got to the Temple Guv breezed in straight away cos he was V.I.P and we had to queue up. But when I was queuing up I thought what the f**K is going on cos there was just bare Asian people (no blacks or whites at all).

At the door I was thinking shit I hope I get in. I had a ticket but like they might of still not let me in, but I got in.

When I got inside it was hench but all I saw was bare Asians then heard all this Asian music. I thought Guv never told me it was some Asian event.

But that was minor because there was another area that played house and garage and drum and bass. We stayed mainly in this room all night.

At first it started off really shit, they were playing bare drum and bass and that's not really my kind of music.

Cos Guv's got links to vip the Temple we got lots of free drinks and shit we must of got about over £100 worth. We were fucked, just bare shots with Red Bull and just other shit like Hennessy Whiskey.

Later on the garage came on and me and Guv MCed. And MCed with Funky Flirt, Trigger and the one and only DJ EZ. We smashed it! We also done some drum and bass as well. I thought I couldn't MC to it but I done alright, just doing bare garage chats but faster.

The last garage tune was Lost in Vegas. I can't write how it goes so if you're reading and you don't know just ask me. Anyway, we all went back to back, me, Nicholas, Guv and this Asian m.c brare from Manchester (he was Trigger or Funky Flirt, can't remember). The garage room stopped at 3.30am so everyone had to go back into the main area, where they were playing all the Asian music. Forgot to mention, but Denny, Chris left early because they thought it was shit.

It finished at 4.00am then after we just chilled outside for a while. We tried to get lifts but we couldn't, off Guv's brother.

We got a bus to Central London. Me and Nick paid for the bus whilst Nicholas and Guv got in through the back doors. And do you know what? Some ticket collectors came on the bus later and charged us £5. Well, I paid but I dashed my ticket somewhere, I was screwing and Nick got charged as well cos Nicholas had his tickets. Nicholas was the only person that didn't get charged (we never paid on the spot they just took information).

We got off the bus outside Oxford Circus and Guv bopped in the station (I don't know why cos it was 4.30am and it was closed). After, we bopped a little bit further down the street and this copper stopped us. He was saying, what were you lot doing down in the Tube Station. I thought hold on a minute is this some joke or something (Candid Camera) or is this just plain bad luck? Anyway the Police man kept saying, I saw you lot going and coming out of the train station, but we just goes, we never, but he just kept saying I can do you for burglary, what a dick! Then, all his crew came along (big van and everything) but they didn't do nothing in the end, just a name check and that was it.

After, we bopped down to Leicester Square. We flexed in the 24 hour McDonalds and met up with that MC from Manchester. We were chatting to him and his crew for quite a while.

We left at 5.30 am then bopped to Paddington. On the bop me and Nicholas lost Guv and Nick. We got our train at 6.33 am but I went to Slough, it was just me and Nicholas. At Slough I caught a train to Langley then bopped home.

I got in at 7.30am but went to bed about 8.30am cos my mum was chatting to me for a while.

Funniest thing all day :-

- Nick T - Bum Detector
- Nicholas - Taking the piss out of Guv - DJ EZ Mask

DID U KNOW?

South America is largely Roman Catholic because the continent was first discovered and opened up by explorers from Spain and Portugal.

Friday 20th August 1999

Today I woke up at 4.30 pm and had a f**king proper bad headache. Straight after I woke up Ben rang and said he was coming over.

When Ben came over we breezed over Sean's house. Down Sean's house we met up with Flex, Anthony and obviously Sean. We just chilled, we rang up Rinse FM and were doing shout outs and I was MCing (but just for jokes because it's shit and local). Them lot were all doing bare bunning and it was making my head worse.

At 10.00pm me and Ben left, I chilled with Ben down Trelawney Avenue until about 11.45pm. We met up with Daniel F, Sod and Guv and we were just hanging about. Today was one of them shite days.

Funniest thing all day:-

- Maurice's new pants, had to peel off the old ones

Saturday 21st August 1999

Today I still felt sick so all day I was in. During the afternoon Becky and this boy from Watford came over for a while.

In the night my mum was having a little party thing. So I was mainly upstairs in my room cotching and listening to Mac FM. At 1.00 am I went over Sean's to watch Summerslam 99. It finished at 4.00 am and then when I got in I slept.

Monday 23rd August 1999

Today has been a bit better than usual cos it's been one of those mission days and I breezed out. At 11.00am MJP knocked to see if I was coming out but I was proper tired, so he breezed and I went back to sleep. And I had some weird dreams. I was on some boat then it sank and we were swimming undersea and the shark man wanted me to help him be king (there's more to it but details are long).

At 2.00pm MJP came over again. I got ready to breeze out (JD came for a while). At 4.45 we breezed out. Today for some reason we thought, come we go Thatcham but we missed the first train so we had to get the 5.15pm.

We got a train from Langley straight to Reading (one of those safe trains). It didn't stop at bare stops though.

When we got to Reading we bopped through the High Street and flexed a McyD's. MJP also got this girl's number, she weren't really all that, just like a cherpes.

After, we went back to the station and then caught a train to Thatcham. The train took proper long cos it kept stopping cos the railways were f**ked.

When we got to Thatcham all we could see was bare countryside (no High Street). But we started seeing signs that said Town Centre. So we followed the signs and getting to the High Street was a proper bop (I'm not ramping).

Their High Street was proper shit, it was like one of those sort of Langley High Street things. We met some girls and shit. We saw them from a distant and they looked proper boom, but up close they were butterz, (all three of them). They took us on a tour of Thatcham. The best part of Thatcham is the shop were we razed bare shit. After, we got these girls to walk us to the train station.

At the station we got them to wait with us as well. The time was 8.00pm and the next train was at 8.35pm and their countryside land was offkey. The trains come hourly after 1.00pm. Also, these girls were mashed cos they had some f**ked up country Farmer Joe accent, do you get me? When our train came we just went "later" to the girls and didn't even catch their numbers.

When we got to Reading we had to wait a while for the train. We met some girls and were hanging about with them for a while. They also got on our train because they were going Twyford. I got one of their numbers, the girl was quite boom, Claire.

When I got home I just chilled. At 12.00 am I flexed on Dave's bike to go to the Kebab shop but when I got there it was closed. So I just breezed London Road petrol garage and got some munch like Pot Noodles and shit.

Funniest thing all day:-

- Rinsed out the shop in Thatcham

DID U KNOW?

That you take about 20,000 breaths every day

Tuesday 24th August 1999

Today was one of these normal stay round your area summer holiday days. In the morning I got a call from Sarah Elliman and she asked me to come over. I went over hers about 3.00pm (down Parluant Road) I rid Dave's bike up there. When I got to Sarah's I just chilled. Cheryl was also round. At her yard we were just listening to a few tapes of mine and I was raiding her refrigerator.

At 3.30pm I just saw Liam at Parlaunt and shouted "Dick Head", then he turned around. He came in Sarah's for a while but we both had to breeze at 4.00pm. After, I just rid home and for some reason Liam ran home.

When I got home I kept getting calls from Sarah and Cheryl saying someone had bare raised her wallet. So I thought, it wasn't me, or was it? Nah jokes! I didn't take shit seriously. Then I thought Liam was dussing after we left, so it must have been him. So I just told Sarah I'd ring him but I never, I couldn't be bothered.

At 6.00pm Liam came over and we breezed over Sean's house. And yes, of course Liam took her wallet, I think she knows anyway. At Sean's we met Guv and MJP. At 6.30pm MJP and Guv went to the shop to get some rum for tonight. When they got back we breezed out. Sean got a draw as well. So that was them lot sorted. Cos I don't smoke and tonight I'm not drinking cos it f**ks you up.

We went back to my house and just played bare Worms on Playstation. That game's jokes. At 10.00pm them lot all breezed to Kidderminster Park to meet with Flex. I stayed cos my mum was coming home soon and she just came from a Chinese restaurant with work and some munch was on its way. When they got home I munched hard. Fried Rice, Fat Prawns, Beef and next Chinese shit.

After, I rid Dave's mashed bike down to the Park. Down the park I met two of the girls that are going against me in Court, not the actual girl that said I mugged her, it was the two girls she was with (Charlene and some yellow teeth girl). I was chatting to them for time, just shit like I didn't do it, and don't turn up for Court. Just the kind of shit you say and ask. At 12.00am I went home I was just cotching and watching TV up in my room.

DID U KNOW?

I've never gone school in August

Wednesday 25th August 1999

Today I went out around 2pm. I flexed to a phone box to ring a few girls cos my phone has a bar on it. I rang this girl called Carly from Harrow and I'm meeting her Friday. After I rang Gemma, she said she wanted to link up today. I gave her my number and she said she'd call me later to meet up. She wanted to meet in Hayes.

After I went to MJP's and just chilled , I was waiting for the skeet to ring me.

At 4-5ish MJP wanted to go down to Hayes just to chill until Gemma rang. I wasn't gonna go but just went. I just wanted to wait in Langley in case she didn't ring.

Well we got a train to Slough then got the fast train. But we ended up getting on the train we would of got anyway if we waited at Langley.

At Hayes we had to breeze over the fence to get out the train station. As we were walking off some TM started coming round the corner and we had to jet. We ran down some canal and had to come out at the bottom of the High Street.

On the High Street we flexed a McyD's. Then we were just chilling round the shitty Hayes High Street. And that girl never called. So we skilfully got back in the Hayes train station and caught a train back.

After, I flexed home. When I got in my mum rang and was asking if I wanted to go to another restaurant with Dave and his big eared son. So I thought might as well.

They picked me up about 8.30 pm and we breezed to Skyways (Indian). It was alright I was on a fat munch cos man it's free. Dave must be made out of money.

When I got in I kept getting text messages from some girl. We were sending each other messages for about an hour and in the end it was some butterz girl from school.

Funniest thing all day:-

- MJP eating snake Shibbz' bredwin

DID U KNOW?

You can learn to speak English at Montague school of English in London.

GCSE RESULTS DAY,
Yeah but not for me, that's next year
Thursday 26ᵗʰ August 1999

Today was shit. Becky Smith and JD came round in the day. In the night just watched films with Mum.

With the GCSEs Rachel Levi got shit results. Sean did good.

Friday 27ᵗʰ August 1999

Today I went out quite early (about 12.00pm) cos I wanted to go over JD's house and play his new game WWF Attitude. And JD's a joker, if you're one of the first 50 to buy the game you get a free memory card. And JD got to the shop at 9.00 am and the shop opens at 9.00 am so he was the first, laugh then.

Anyway, I stayed round JD's for time. MJP came round at 1.00pm and we both beat JD at the game. Also, if you're wondering about that skeet today I rang her and she said she can't meet me because she had an argument with her mum and she's grounded. What's up with all these girls lately, they're just taking the poom poom. Us men need our rights. But the carnival should smash it in the skeet department, so Bo.

We left JD's about 6.30pm. I lost MJP cos I flexed in some shop and he breezed off on his bike. I had to bop back. On the way I met up with Simmons (he's back from his holiday).

After, we flexed down my yard and MJP knocked later on. Cos I felt sorry for the brares I gave him some kit kats.

After, Guv knocked then we breezed to Slough just to see what's going on. We flexed a bus to the High Street then just chilled around there and in McyD's cos they were playing bare tunes.

After, we met up with Nicholas and Liam then we all breezed down to the Ice Arena. Down the Ice Arena we met up with bare mans then Dot came with us and we bopped to the Orchard. It was just finishing as we got there cos we could have MCed and shit. But we only stayed around for about 20 minutes then bopped down the High Street.

Down the High Street we met up with bare Langley Grammar girls coming out of the pubs. Liam was being proper dark (out of order) to Laura S. He was saying she had veiny breasts.

At 12.40 me, MJP and Guv got on a train back to Langley. Simmons stayed with Nicholas cos they were gonna go in a car cruising. OTT we were also with Stacey (formally known as Sexy Stacey, but she's offkey now).

When I got in I just relaxed and bussed on the movie, The Fugitive, starring Harrison Ford. Yeah, that's the end of the day. Harrison Ford doesn't wanna get caught by the police. So he's doing a lot of running.

Funniest Things all day:-

- Our McDonalds rave
- Nicholas is Simmons' hero (idol)
- JD's first to buy the game
- Trying to pimp Laura S out for £30

DID U KNOW?

Earthquakes occur mainly in the regions on the earth crust

Saturday 28th August 1999

Today I had some weird dream. I was going out with some boom girl from Canary Wharf and I kept getting a train from Langley (3 stops) to Canary Wharf . And at one time at Canary Wharf there were these gang of boys fighting on the train tracks with weapons like bats and iron bars. It was one of those weird dreams you can't explain properly.

Anyway today was one of those mission days, yes the mission days we all love. At 2.40pm I met MJP at Langley then we went Slough and caught a fast train to Paddington. We chilled round Paddington for a while cos Guv was supposed to be coming with us but he was on a long ting so we breezed. And shit I haven't even mentioned where we're going. Well we're going to DARTFORD. Why, because we hear it has the biggest shopping centre in Europe and girls love to shop also it's a Saturday.

Well we got a tube to Charing Cross then flexed a cheap imitation train of Thames train to Dartford. It was about 14 stops but went proper fast. We pasted bare places like Deptford, Greenwich (where we could see the Millennium Dome) and bare Kent places.

When we got there it looked proper boom. We bopped round the High Street and all there was, was a shitty little market and two offkey little shopping centres. We kept getting calls from Guv and he reckoned he was down Dartford, but he was going on about some place called Blue Waters. We kept asking people about this Blue Waters place and everyone said that's where the shopping centre is and it's just one bus away. So we got the bus to Blue Waters and it was dramatic. I got ten girls numbers. It was like heaven. I've got girls saved in my phone by name and something to remind me of who they are.

Like, for example I've got;

Jodi-bigtitty

Kelly-blackhairadidastracksuit

Wendy- tooooomuchmakeup

Patrica-smallmidgitgirl

Kamisha- screwfaceghettochick

Hayley-fatballoonting

Yes guys sometimes it's good to cherpes a fat girl they're dirty. After, we got the train back to London.

When we got back into London we flexed around Leicester Square and Piccadilly. O yeah can't forget Troc. After we breezed back to Paddington then got our train back to Langley.

When I got in I just relaxed. Later Simmons, Guv and MJP came over. We just chilling and did this MCing thing for our answer machines with the tunes playing (a voice mail ting).

At 11pm we breezed out cos there was a party going on a few roads away. But when we got there the wankers didn't let us in, they were just being offkey. After, we met up with Sean outside his house. A few minutes after we met up with Nicholas and Nathan. Them lot all breezed to Slough while I breezed home and munched some milli kebab.

Funniest things all day:-

- Give £5 to a tramp get your £4.99 change
- MJP razing £2 then losing it.
- Granny going on sick bare talking. Ok bye
- Darth Vader vs. Darth Maul

DID U KNOW?

The French Revolution began in 1789

Sunday 29th August 1999

Today I woke up about 12pm. Today I've been feeling proper sick. I had bare constipation. My shit was like tap water.

At 4pm or 5pm JD came over. We just played some WWF Attitude. At 6pm JD breezed. At this point I was feeling proper ill so I flexed to bed for a while.

I wasn't really sleepy. But I was having some f**ked up dreams. Them half asleep ones.

At 6.30pm went cinema with Liam and 2 butters skeet. Well I wasn't gonna go but as we were going to see South Park Movie, I thought later mans gotta go.

So I went with them. The film started at 7pm and trust it was proper jokes. Throughout the film I was creasing up. Later on (during the movie) I threw up, yeah man I was f**king sick all over the cinema. I missed about 10 minutes of the film. When I got back in the screen Liam was fingering one of the girls.

After the film we jumped a taxi to Langley. Got off by Green Drive and breezed. And cos I was feeling f**ked f**ked f**ked (sorry carnival fever) I went bed. I slept for about 2 hours. At 11pm I woke up and had a little munch. That was like the first thing I ate today.

At midnight Guv came round. We were just playing some Street Fighter. At 1am Simmons came over, we were just bussing Worms. They all left about 2am then Simmons lent me the film 'Exorcist' and I'm watching it now it's bare jokes. Is this suppose to be scary?

See you tomorrow at Notting Hill.

Bank Holiday Monday 30th August 1999
Notting Hill Carnival day

Easy people today's the carnival and man everybody's going carnival crazy. The day is hot and I just have a feeling the girls are gonna be going on sick, in their tops and miniskirts. It's all about the booty bouncing.

Today we all met at the train station about 1.30pm. There was bare people on their way to Carnival. There was;

1. Robert the1andonly Peters
2. MJP
3. Simmons
4. Wayne
5. Sean
6. Liam
7. Anthony
8. Big toe
9. Guv

And bare next people, even Babylon Bob. We got off at Ealing Broadway then flexed to Notting Hill Gate station. OTT I met Cass and was chatting to him for a bit.

At Notting Hill the streets were packed with bare people just going mad. I had bussed a whistle so I was going on a bit mad with that, Bo.

At first we bopped round just looking at the floats. Wayne was just giving us bare jokes cos he was just f**ked proper. A while later we lost Guv, Anthony , Big Toe and Stag. So that just left me, MJP ,Simmons and Sean. We chilled round just catching jokes. A while later we met up with Nicholas and Denny down near the bridge on Portabello Road. We found this boom garage rave down Portabello. We were going mad and not just us, everybody. The set was wiked. The MC's were throwing shit into the crowd. Nicholas got some weird mask thing then through the whole day wearing it on his head.

After we were just bopping around everywhere. We went to this part called Rampage which was quite tick. It was proper jokes the MC were being jokes and playing shit like Spice girls wannabe and Nirvana smells like teen spirit. But everyone was still dancing. But he was doing it as a joke. But there was a massive fight at rampage and champagne bottles starting flying in the air. About ten guys got arrested.

After we went to bare different places. We went to about 2 more garage raves and bare Regga raves, well street party things.

Anyway later on I started feeling proper sick, my head was f**king killing me. It was like someone was sticking needles in my head. But Liam got lucky he found 3 draws just lying on the floor. 3 bags of weed. So them mans were happy.

At 6.50pm we went back to Rampage. The last ten minutes there were boom but I had a proper bad headache. Yeah the Carnival finished at 7pm but after we were hanging round Ladbroke Grove following this milli float. Sean and Wayne went home, I was gonna flex with them but I just continued to follow the float.

Me, Simmons and MJP left about 10.30pm and Nicholas and Denny stayed. We caught a tube from Notting Hill Gate then went to Ealing then from there to Langley. O yeah I got a whopper at Ealing in Burger King. It tasted like shit, McyD's is number one.

OTT home was still f**ked. My head was killing me. I bet someone's got a voodoo doll of me or some f**kery. I also think I was a bit lean (stoned) because all day people were bunning bare shit and I was just there inhaling the fumes.

When I got home I just went to bed, it was only 12.30am. Trust I was so sick I couldn't even write in Diary. I'm writing this tomorrow, do you get what I'm on about, you dumb dick?

Funniest things all day:-

- Simmons chatting mess- good rhythms – err no
- Bobs £10, he remembered
- Nicholas was just chatting funny stuff but I can't remember.
- It's all about the shadow man- kid begging for the game.

- Flex spitting in burgers

DID U KNOW?

Carnival came about after the slaves were freed. That's why we celebrate it. But it's lost its true vibe.

Tuesday 31st August 1999

All through the day I've been proper lazy. I've just been in my shorts all day. In the day JD and Guv were round, we were just playing computer. Mortal kombat.

At 6.30pm I had a bath cos later I decided to go RN cos it was the last one in Uxbridge. Simmons came over about 7pm and we breezed to the train station (we stopped off at Darvils). At the station we met Nicholas, Liam, MJP, Naomi and her friend Gemma.

We caught the 8pm train and OTT we met up with Sarah Elliman and Cheryl. Them lot never said anything to Liam about the wallet he jacked the other day. We got off at West Drayton then flexed a bus to Uxbridge.

We got to RN about 8.30pm. Today there was bare girls and I got quite a lot of numbers. I also (for some reason) was hooking MJP up with bare girls. There was one girl today that was getting on my nerves. MJP set me up with her then she kept chatting to me and shit. I gave her my number but I shouldn't of.

I also met a few girls I knew like Carly from Harrow, Karina, that girl from Hayes who let us stay round her house and I also saw Penny from George Green.

Well enough chatting my shit, let me flex through my phone book and see the numbers I got.

Shelly – this is one of Rachel Levi's friends. For some reason I thought I'd cherpes her

Kim- This girl was boom and she's only from Iver. But she's got a man. But hey that don't matter cos as soon as she finishes with him I'll be straight in there. Even before, I don't care.

Susan or Season – This girl was one of the girls I cherpes for MJP. She's alright; the batty's a bit droopy.

Sarah- yeah another girl I got for MJP, just the numbers are in my phone.

Also some girl took down my number, Lara or Lauren. Couldn't hear what she said. But she's one of them girls where the belly overlaps her titties. Not a good look.

The rest of the day just shaqing out. Later on I managed to lips Penny and she was kissing me proper dirty, she seemed proper horny. I was thinking make sure I don't lose you at the end of the night. MJP also got her friend's number, but he got no tings haha.

After RN I got a lift home from Naomi. And that RN was proper like the first one in Uxbridge. Just go back and read 26th July it's similar to today.

Anyway I got home about 12am. I got a call from Rachel Levi. I was chatting to her for about an hour, I also told her I got her friend's number. But she can't do shit. We ain't together.

At 1am Simmons came round but he's HuHH. BYE

And today is the last day of August it's been alright month.

FUNNIEST THING ALL MONTH

5. GRANNY GOING ON SICK

4. MC'DONALDS RAVE

3. JUST PUNCH IT

2 MAURICE'S NEW PANTS

1. SIMMONS ON A JD FLEX LYING
ABOUT GOING ON HOLIDAY

I go back to school on the 7th, noooooooooooooooooooooo!!!!!

Wednesday 1st September 1999

Af**kingnother new month and how f**ked up is this. Starting on a Wednesday, it just don't sound right innit.

Today has been quite a good day. There's just been bare jokes, bare missions and bare dickheads.

Today I woke up about 10.30am and if you remembered the plans for today were to go down to Margate. But I wasn't sure what was going on cos no one rang or anything.

But at 11am Simmons called and we still decided to breeze there. Me and Simmons flexed over to get Sean.

We left about 12.15pm. We bopped down to the station and met up with MJP. Then we caught the 12.30pm train to Paddington. At Paddington we got the Bakerloo Line to Charing Cross. We got through all the ticket machines proper easy today, trust it was minor.

At Charing Cross our train was coming in half an hour so we bopped round Trafalgar Square for a piece.

When we got back to the station we got on a Margate train but we got thrown straight off by a TM. So we flexed some next train. But this train was going the wrong way to Sevenoaks. So we got off at London Bridge and then caught a train all the way to Chatham. The journey was about an hour then after the next train took just under an hour to get to Margate. I was going a bit crazy on the train. That journey was a long ting.

When we got to Margate we bopped through all the arcade places, the High Street and the Theme Park, which ain't bad.

After we went into Pizza Hut and cos their countries still in the past they had one of those ice cream factory things. I thought I'd get some because it was £2.50 and it's eat as much as you like. (Well all you can eat).

I was sharing the ice cream with the crew. But we had to do it when the people weren't watching cos it was only for one person (that's me). But we got thrown out cos Sean was making a mess and had ice cream all over his face. He's a proper messy eater ice cream was all over his jeans. This was proper jokes; you had to be there to understand what I'm chatting about.

We bopped to some next part in Margate because Sean's uncle live down there (that's handy innit). So we went round Sean's uncle's house. His uncle was quite safe he set us some munch and tea.

We only stayed round there for a while then after we breezed back to the main part. We chilled round the arcades then after went back through the Theme Park. MJP got some girls number and even lipsed her. She weren't all that though. She was like 7 feet tall and had funny teeth.

But the Theme Park had some bad rides. There was some sling shot ride. It looked boom but it was £12 to go on (for one person).

After we breezed back to the station. We got on the train that was going to Victoria. We knew it would take long but was better than keep getting off the train. OTT we met these people from Stroud in Kent. There was some fat girl, a boy and his worth a shag girlfriend. We caught bare jokes with these people. We were all cherpsing the boy's girlfriend and he couldn't say shit. She was loving it though. I was cherpsing her the most, I even got her number in front of him. And check this she's been going out with him six months and only got off with him and he sucked her tits. I was saying "if I was going out with you, would you give me tings"? and she said "yeah". She was jokes.

Well they all breezed off at Chatham then it was just us for the rest of the journey. It went quite fast though still.

When we got to Victoria we easily breezed through the ticket machines then got on the Circle Line to Paddington. At Paddington we blatantly ran past the TM and he didn't say shit.

We got a train to Langley and I was proud to be on a Thames train not no cheap imitation shit like Connex railways or some shit.

When I got home I just relaxed. It was about 12.30am. I just went to bed.

Funniest things all day:-

- Begging TM OTT
- Sean with the ice cream all over the place eating it with forks
- First class on head
- shiners off fat girl
- Women – how do you get through the machines
- Me like this (running jump over)
- Cherpsing guy's skeet in front of him

DID U KNOW?

In 1997 1 in 50 deaths (PEOPLE AGED 15 -19) in the UK was from volatile substance abuse, sniffing Pritt Stick and shit.

Thursday 2ⁿᵈ September 1999

Today I just had a summer holiday relax day. I woke up about 2pm then all day ate, drank and shitted. I was just in my shorts all day.

Later at night (around 12.30pm) Simmons and Guv came over and we were just chilling. At 2.30pm we started watching 'Lock, Stock and Two Smoking Barrels'. But I missed most of it cos I kept falling asleep. Then waking up and chatting bare shit.

They both left at 4.30am then I just said a quick prayer then went to bed. Amen and all that.

DID U KNOW?

The Bible was written by over 30 people

Friday 3ʳᵈ September 1999

Today I went out at 1.30pm cos I was getting my haircut at my cousin's yard at 2pm. I flexed a bus to Slough. On the bus I met these girls, one of them I sort of already knew (Sarah from Colnbrook) and the other was just her friend.

Anyway I got to my cousin's about 2.10pm and just flexed a quick trim. I got all the ginger out (bet you forgot I was a ginger Minge). After I bopped into the High Street on my jaze but it was cos my mum gave me £10.

After I cherpes this Langley Grammar girl. She was quite boom but she took down my number and you know how girls go on with calling boys. After I got a call from Simmons and he said he was coming into Slough. So I had to chill round Slough but it was cool cos I met up with those girls that were on the bus. I chilled with them until Simmons came. I also got one of their numbers. This girl called Nicola and she's quite boom, she's got it going on a piece.

After I was just chilling with Simmons round Slough. I didn't stay that long cos it was a bit shit. On the way back home I stopped off at JD's yard. I just stayed for about an hour just munching his food and playing his computer.

When I got in I had dinner then after MJP came over. We were bussing some Worms then later at 11pm we breezed to the village just to see what was going on.

Down the village there was just all the former Churchmead crew like Dean M, Chris P, Alex and them mans.

We only stayed round there for an hour then I walked home with fat Vicky.

In the night I was just listening to some tune and for some reason playing computer till 5.30am

Saturday 4th September 1999

Today I'm flexing to Southend (we're staying round Simmons' dad's house) but it's not an early ting we just breezed when were good and ready.

We left about 4pm it was me, Sean, MJP and obviously Simmons. We flexed to Paddington, cruised past the ticket machines then got the Circle

Line all the way to Tower Hill. At Tower Hill we jumped over the ticket machines then we had to bop to Fenchurch Street station. Then we flexed on some dodgy train to Southend. We got all the way to Southend for free.

At Southend we chilled round the High Street and flexed in McDonald's. After we got a taxi to Simmons' dad's house.

At Simmons' dads house we packed all our shit away then just chilled for a while. We played our tunes cos you can't get the tunes we got in Southend country. We were playing my Mac FM tape and people could hear it from outside. To them it's like future stuff cos they get their shit late. People still drive round playing 'Sweet Like Chocolate'. They're still on this Shanks and Bigfoot ting.

At 9pm we got a taxi to a club called Storm. We never went straight away. We bopped to an off licence to get some drink, well them lot did, I couldn't be bothered to drink.

They all had their drinks (I had a piece) then we bopped down the seafront. We bopped through the fair place, it's called Peter Pan World.

Down the fair I belled up Claire and then she came to meet us. I thought I might as well bell her up, we won't getting no skeet anyway.

We chilled round the arcades with Claire and these two fat ugly twin sisters, which Simmons and Sean were trying to get a piece of, sick brares.

About 11pm we bopped the ugly skeet to the bus station. After we bopped down to the club (Storm) but we got rejected hard. It was over 21's and we're 15. But we're tall so I thought we'd get in. So we bopped down to Tots and the road where all the clubs are. We got blasted on all of them. Cos on Saturday all the clubs are over 21's, the man reckoned we could got into the over 18's but that's only Fridays.

We ended up going back to the seafront. Tonight we just chilled round the main bit and the arcades. There was bare skeet but they were all too old.

At 1am-2am we bopped back to Simmons dad's house. And man that bops' long. My feet were killing me, mainly cos I was wearing shoes (to get in the clubs innit).

When we got in we just watched a bit of TV in the living room. After I just flexed to bed, everyone went bed at different times, understand what I mean. When we were tired we just bopped into our rooms.

Funniest thing all day:-

- Shibbz- mattress
- Sean – "listen you're from Southend I'm from London".
- Gel your biff
- Sean's tune- we're going to Ibiza
- Southend's raggo brares
- Shibbz taking over, God made it rain.

DID U KNOW?

It's Anne Diamond's Birthday on 8th September, who?

Sunday 5th September 1999

Today we all woke up proper early (about 11am). In the morning Simmons little step brother was over and he was beating us all up.

At 1ish we left. We bopped down to the seafront. We stopped off at Wimpy cos Claire worked there. But the fanny head was being offkey and never gave us any free munch. And Wimpy's old they don't even have that round our area anymore.

Also I forgot to mention but I got this girls number, her name's Gemma (she's quite boom) she's from North London and she' got a f**ked up lisp.

After we were going round the arcades and the Peter Pan World ting. Me and MJP got this girl's number, her name's Jennie and she gave us these cards with her number on them (doing my flex).

After we breezed digga digga down to the High Street and it was a bit poo so we went top the train station. We had to wait a while still.

As we were getting on to our train. We met some girls the boomest one was f**king engaged. I still got one of their numbers. These girls were from Benfleet (Canvey Island). After those girls left we started chatting to these offkey dirty skin girls (they needed to take a bath). These girls were proper loud and just being stupid OTT. One of the girls was drunk and also proper dirty. She was saying she does shiners. So I was trying to get a shiner off her. Didn't though. She was proper offkey.

As we got off the train (at Fenchurch Street) Simmons and Sean got those there girls numbers. Trust they were proper butterz. But I sucked on one of their tits before we got off and her nipples were grey.

After we bopped to Tower Hill, buss through the machines then got the Circle Line back to Paddington. OTT back to Paddington I cherpes this girl. She was Polish but is from Derby. And bo she comes down to London to stay with her sister. But she's 19. Yeah I flexed the digits.

At Paddington we caught a train to Langley. On the way home it started pouring down hard (bare rainz).

When I got in I just cotched (time was 6.30pm). Tonight I was meeting Rachel's friend Shelly at 8pm. So till then I cotched.

At 8pm she rang and said she was in Langley. So I bopped down to London Road and met her, but she was with two friends, Lucy (Rachel's best friend) and Lucy's little 12 year old sister.

I brought them back to my drum and we just chilled. A while later Guv and MJP came over. Then after Sean came over with Natalie.

At 11pm we all went down to Kidderminster Park, well not all of us, just me, Simmons, MJP and the three girls.

At 11.30pm we bopped them to the bus stop. We looked at the timetable to see when their bus was coming and cos it was Sunday they just had missed the last bus. So as they couldn't get home I let them stay at my house. MJP came back to mine as well.

In the night I couldn't even be bothered to lips Shelly. I was just ignoring her and flexing to sleep. (We were all in my living room). I think she was pissed off cos she kept going into my kitchen and standing in the dark. I think she was sulking. But MJP was giving the girls jokes, he ended up staying as well.

Funniest things all day:-

- That girls grey tits
- Shelly standing in the dark alone
- Cheap cards sticker stuck to card

DID U KNOW?

The highest pass in Ireland is in Dingle Bay

Last day of Summer Holidays
Monday 6th September 1999

Today is the last day of the summer holidays and boy they've gone proper fast. But in total I've found about 10 tick days. Like Chessington, the Temple, RN, Southend, Margate, the day I flexed London then Joanne came round but Becky Smith was the funniest. With her loud screaming and all that punch it stuff. (You had to be there).

Well today I've done nothing at all. JD flexed round for a piece and so did MJP.

Also I got a call from that girl I met in Southend (the one who gave us the cards) and she wants to meet on Friday, but Southend's long. And all the Blue Waters tings are being long except for fatballoon ting.

O yeah the girls left at 7am then I went to sleep in my room. In the night I just watched Menace to Society.

Well at the moment it's 12.30am and my mum's going on about how I got school in the morning. Well that's bullshit nigga cos mother f**king school starts at 1pm tomorrow, bitch that's wack. Sorry to much movies.

DON'T FORGET THE SCHOOL RULES!!!!!!!!!!!!

Tuesday 7th September 1999

Well as you know today I breezed back to school. And bo this is my last year then after I've left school for good.

Today I had to arrive at school at 1pm, cos we have all the new comers. But I am stupid cos we finish at 3pm.

At 12pm I got ready to go to school. And after 6 weeks it feels weird putting on the old school uniform.

At 12.30 I rid to school. As I was just getting into school my back wheel got punctured (shit, I never have luck with bikes).

At school today all we did was fill in our time tables then had Business Studies and English, but both lessons I did f**k all. Also there was no lunch.

At 3pm I walked home with JD. When I got in I just laid on the settee for time.

At 6.30pm MJP and Becky Smith came round. They left about 7.30pm. I had some rice and curried goat my mum cooked. Boom trust. cos my mum passed her driving test.

In the night I kept getting dirty messages from that racist Carly and she was also texting sorry.

I kept sending her messages saying shit like "you're a dick". She was sending me messages that said "f**k me" and "I want to suck your cock". I sent a few dirty ones back cos at least I could do her then after go "oi you racist bitch don't think I forgot about that shit you said" then breeze.

Also in two weeks this girl from Rayleigh is having a massive party.

Wednesday 8th September 1999

Dear Diary,

You give me bare jokes, with your funny pictures and you cuss people and also just the shit you have in it.

You're a dick do you really think I write in my diary like that? That's what girls do and they write about their feelings. I write my feelings when I'm feeling horny. And I write about sex and other shit that is boom, like £1 chicken burgers. Had one today still.

Well today I had to wake up the normal time for school. It was just a usual school day. But they're trying to give us bare work cos we're year 11 now.

Friday 10th September 1999

Yesterday was 9 /9/99

'Boy', this week's gone proper fast. It may be cos I had no school Monday then Tuesday just 2 hours.

Well school wasn't too bad. I was just cracking bare jokes. Also there's nothing to raze no more it's just shit.

After school I just relaxed. At 6pm I got an unexpected visit from Terry. Today the plans were to probably go RN in Feltham. But around 6.50ish MJP came over and said we're meeting 3 girls in Slough and they're proper boom and they were proper drunk.

At 8.15pm we breezed out, we met up with Simmons and Sean. Simmons was screwing cos he wanted to go RN and no one else wanted to go. Well when drunk skeet are involved he should be happy.

We bopped down to the Village and met up with Michael J. We just caught the 8.45pm train to Slough. When we got to Slough High Street MJP'S skeet weren't even there. So we didn't know what to do. Simmons remembered about some rave in North London which was going on till 2am. So we decided to go there. At this time it was me, Simmons, MJP, Michael Jo and Terry. We got on the slow train to Paddington then Paddington we got the Circle Line to Kings Cross. At Kings Cross we had to trek through bare ticket machines to get on the Northern Line (dirty missions). The place where the rave was was Tufnell Park.

When we got to Tufnell Park all we saw was bare brares. We walked up to the place and we still only saw brares (no skeet) also Simmons and Terry were the only white brares, so they were left out. So we thought allow this cos there's no girls at all, too many brares.

We thought we'd just flex London instead. So we got the train back to Kings Cross then jumped on the Piccadilly Line to Piccadilly Circus. At Piccadilly we bopped round Troc then we went round Leicester Square. It was a bit shit tonight. As we were leaving London we bopped through Soho. Michael J was showing us this fit skeet in this mini skirt then she turned around and it was a man, arrrrrrrrrrrrrrraaaaaaaaaaahhhhhhhh.

Anyway we came back into Oxford Circus and started bopping to Paddington but we were walking bare next ways (we thought we were bad). But we got lost. And ended up by that BT Tower. So we had to bop about 1 mile and a half to Paddington. And on the way Simmons was sick. He threw up on the street. It was Ribena colour.

When we got to Paddington (hour later) I stopped off at D2 and just got bare drink, it was proper hot.

Our train left at 2.45am but it was just to Slough. At Slough we all bopped to Langley. I mainly just bopped with Terry cos both Michaels bopped off fast and Simmons walked down London Road. When me and Terry got to my drum we just flexed to sleep. Mans were tired. Also Michael J love's wearing red.

Funniest things all day:-

- Buss a lift
- Tramp nicking a banana

DID U KNOW?

YOU'RE NOT ALLOWED TO GO INTO LONDON TROCADERO TOPLESS

Saturday 11th September 1999

Today's been quite a buff (good) day. I was supposed to meet this short girl Vicky at 2pm but I woke up about that time. Nah I'm chatting shit I woke up about 12.30pm but I couldn't really be bothered, I was too tired.

At 3pm Simmons came over. The plans were to meet these girls at Uxbridge, Simmons arranged it. We went to Langley train station and just missed the 3.30pm train. So then we thought F**K these girls cos we're late anyway. We buss to Slough to meet Sean and some crew.

At Slough I met Jade and buss through the machine with her.

After, we bopped down the High Street. We never met Sean cos he flexed home. We only stayed round Slough for a piece then decided to go down West End, cos Slough's mash.

We got the fast train to Paddington. At Paddington I met an old Hanwell friend (Riga). I chatted to him for a piece then got on the tube to Piccadilly.

At Piccadilly I met up with that Vicky girl I was supposed to be meeting (she was also with a friend that looked like Mumra from Thundercats). I chilled round with them on my jaze cos Terry and Simmons went off to play pool in Troc.

I went round Oxford Street with the two girls. We just breezed in shops and shit. For the girly shops I waited outside and looked for skeet to cherpes quickly.

After we bopped back to Piccadilly. Both of the girls got on a bus home while I went back to Troc to meet Simmons and Terry. I didn't even lips the girl. I didn't really wanna she was getting on my nerves.

When I met up with the boys they were playing pool with some skeet. I thought yes boys you did it without me. We got their numbers after (well Simmons did). They were from Stratford.

After we flexed round Leicester square. Also I cherpes this boom girl, she's from near croydon. But she's HuHH she didn't let me take down her number she took mine.

We met some other girls after. Trust we were smashing it, on a roll. These girls were from Kent. We breezed round with them for quite a long ting. We went with them through Leicester Square and Troc. I lipsed one of the girls (she had lills). I had a little fill of the lills as well and they were very very boom. Terry lipsed her friend as they were leaving.

There's also something else, before we met the girls these French women came up to me and asked if they could take a few pictures of me to be part of a French magazine. I was like 'yeah why not, bare fame and ting'. They took some pictures of me posing by a telephone box. I gave them my address and they said they'd send me the issue (some French shit) and if it's good enough I could do it professionally, Bo.

As I was saying, after those girls left we bopped back through the usual places. We bopped back to Leicester Square station to go yard. On the way I met these two step sisters from Camden. One of them was boom but her name was Dasher (HuHH name). I thought are you joking but she was serious. Ain't that that butterz dog off Beano?

We got the train to Uxbridge cos Simmons girls rang and wanted to meet us. But we had to get off at Rayners Lane. Simmons called the girls and she said she had to be in for 11pm. I looked at my watch and it was 10.45pm. But we still got the train to Uxbridge, try getting a lips or something for 5 minutes. But at Uxbridge the girls weren't there (it just turned 11pm). We just got a munch then jumped back on the train and went Rayners Lane. It felt we did that mission just for Doritos.

We went to Ealing and got the 00.04 to Langley. At Langley we bopped through the village then bopped home.

Funniest thing all day:-

• Terry on bumpy train

DID U KNOW?

Money in Dominican Republic is called Peso

Sunday 12ᵗʰ September 1999

Most of today I have just been cotching in bed. I was gonna go to something down Ealing (Walpole Park) but I couldn't be bothered. I flexed over Sean's house for a while and just chilled.

At 8.00pm Guv came round. Tonight there's some little Year 8 party but I know bare people my age who are gonna be down there. So we might as well, just because there was nothing else to do.

We went over Simmons' house but he didn't want to come to the 'baby party.' I tried telling him there was Year 11 skeet there but he still didn't want to come.

So me and Guv quickly went to my house then got some bikes to ride there (it's in Datchet). I rid my dodgy bike whilst Guv rid Simmons' buckled bike.

When we got to the party we met up with Terry. We didn't really go in the party just hung outside, just bare little kids running about. But there was a few sexy older sisters.

It finished at 10.10pm then we just rid home. When I got in I stayed up for a while then just went to bed.

Funniest thing all day:-

- Trying to raze sweets
- Get catch man

DID U KNOW?

Wrestler Stone Cold Steve Austin has a tick wife, Debra.

Monday 13th September 1999

Today school was quite safe. The best lesson today was PE it was bare jokes. We played footie ball. On my team I had JD, Kenworthy, Mad Christian and just next offkey brares, you get me! And we were playing against like Daniel Mountain and Daomi. We got finished.

After school I just chilled till about 7.15pm then me and Mum went to the pub to meet Dave cos today it was his birthday.

At 8.00pm we left to go to the pub. I just had munch. Had some steak ting. Boom. We left at 11.00 pm then when I went home I went to bed.

Funniest thing all day:-

- Langley Grammar Kid wanna cuss Churchmead
- Then seeing me in my uniform looking hench

Tuesday 14th September 1999

Today I was all ready to leave for school proper early cos I had to ride a mashed up bike and it takes longer. When I got on the bike I could barely ride 2 inches so I just put it away. I didn't know how to get to school and if I was late I'd get detention. Also, if I get into school after 9.00 am I get in shit. So today I just chilled at home.

At 1.00pm I bopped to the shop for some munch. I chilled around the shops for a while with the usual tramps and then bopped yard. Later on Terry came round. At 8.00pm Dave came over and he fixed my bike (safe brare). At 9.30pm me and Terry breezed over Simmons' house (the place where he lives). We chilled until about 11.00pm just watching Crime Watch UK, looking for friends from Slough. I'm sure I saw Liam on it.

On the way back we met up with Gemma B and Terry P. We chilled with them until 11.30pm then Terry got a taxi back to Wraysbury.

That's my day, but there's one more thing. Liam told me that our Court case is now and officially over. I mean I don't have to go Court no more. The girls dropped the charges (six months later).

Well if you think about it this diary's a bit like a story, in the end it turns out fine. It was all over a tenner.

DID U KNOW?

We have two eyes placed in the front or our heads because we need to be able to judge distances and to see in depth.

Friday 17th September 1999

This morning I got a letter from MJP saying he never took my money but I still think it was him. Yes someone nicked some money from my yard the other day. Think it was him.

Today, school was bare jokes. At lunch we played football, the blacks against the whites. It was jokes but the score was 5-5.

After school, Christian breezed back to my house with me. An hour later Terry came round.

At 6.00pm we breezed down Trelawney Avenue for a while. At 8.30pm we breezed to the train station. Everyone was down Windsor so we thought we'd go down there. We missed the 8.42 pm train so we flexed round the Village until the next train came. Down the Village we met Guv. After we just caught the 9.12pm train to Slough. When we got to Slough we were just about to get on the Windsor train when all the crew were just getting off it (coming from Windsor). We were at Slough Train Station for quite a while cos some man was starting on Hanghei, Brian and Michael J, but nothing really happened cos the ticket men were holding him back; he was just some offkey brare.

After, we bopped down to Slough High Street. We flexed in Slough Young People's Centre cos they had some little event called Gravity (reality on Earth).

Down Gravity I met bare Slough crew like Daomi, Denzel, Javan and more. We chilled in there for a while (it was only one Krusty Pound to get in). We kept going in then out.

We were there just about an hour. Me and Guv smashed it on the mic. But it was just fast drum and bass.

It finished at 11.00pm. After, it was just me, Hanghei, Terry, Christian, Brian and Michael Jo. Cos we just seem to lose bare people. As we started walking back to Langley we stopped off at Chicago Rock Cafe. We saw some brare from Eastenders, the man who plays Gianni.

On the way home we were catching bare jokes. Hanghei and all the crew found out about me and that Becky Smith thing. We were just catching jokes about her screaming and punched it.

When we got in (me, Terry and Christian) we just relaxed. In the night I woke up and just bussed to my bed and left them two downstairs on the floor.

Funniest thing all day:-

- Christian - chocolate sausage
- Punch it

18th September 1999

Today, Christian and Terry left quite early. I thought today would be one of those trek days but it ended up just being in my area (Langley).

Terry borrowed my bike but I shouldn't have lent it to him cos I've got school on Monday and he's not that reliable, you get me.

At 3.40 Sean came round we breezed to his Nan's for a while then flexed down Trelawney Avenue. I belled up MJP (I'm not chatting to him that much cos I think he teefed some money from my yard, but he was with some skeet and everyone was saying she was boom). We breezed down to the Village.

At 4.30pm we met MJP and that girl. She was quite nice but she had some dodgy things on her face. I just wanted to meet her cos I wanted to see what this girl looked like for time. MJP breezed after.

We chilled around the park for a while. Then Sean came back to my drum. Ten minutes later Simmons and Calvin came over.

Later on Simmons and Calvin breezed (Simmons flexed Heathrow Bowl). Me and Sean both had some fat munch then breezed out. We met Wayne and Brian and breezed to Langley Village Park then met the former Churchmead crew.

Later on I got a call from Rachel Levi's friends, Shelley, Lucy and her sister. They were down Langley and they wanted me to meet them. They said some shit like they were going cinema then they couldn't be bothered to go so they rang me.

I met them at Harvester with Brian and Sean. We got back to the Village. No one was about but we met back with Calvin.

At 11.30pm me, Brian, Calvin and the three girls bopped to my yard. At 12.00 noon Calvin and Brian left to meet Hanghei down the Village. The girls just chilled round mine I said it was alright for them to stay (again) but I swear they want to stay anyway because they weren't that worried about getting home as they would have breezed home time ago.

Well the butters girls just chilled. Little sister didn't want to stay but she had no choice, unless she bopped (long ting). An hour later Simmons, Guv and Hanghei came over.

In the night everyone was just all cotching all in my room (seven people).

There was Guv, Simmons, Hanghei and Lucy's Sister on the floor. I was in the bed with Lucy and Shelley but the bed collapsed and the two girls slept on the floor. Six people all in little spaces. I still slept on my bed on some part that wasn't mashed.

DID U KNOW?

The film 'the Blair Witch Project' made more money then what it was made for, cheap piece of shit.

Sunday 19th September 1999

Today all my crew left my house about 7am. The girls left at 9am but Lucy stayed cos she couldn't be bothered to get up that early.

I never went out today I just chilled with Lucy. I know what you're thinking, did I try to get some sort of tings. Well I kind of did but she didn't give me shit cos remember she's Rachel's friend and she feels bad on Rachel, even though we ain't together no more. But I was on top of her and my boner was poking her. And she lipsed me and had a little play with my tings but started feeling bad.

At 5.49pm (to be precise) Terry came over, which was safe cos he had my bike and I needed it for school tomorrow. At 6pm me and Terry took Lucy to the bus stop. Her bus came at 6.30pm.

After we chilled round Trelawney then at 7.30pm we went to Datchet. I was just giving Terry a lift to Datchet train station. I didn't mind cos I was in a really hyper mood. Maybe cos we were chatting about jokes in the old times and the bare skeet.

Terry got his train at 8.05pm then I rid back home through dirty Datchet. When I got in I stayed up for a while then flexed bed.

Funniest things all day:-

- Terry trying to give Lucy electric shock thing
- Tune kept rewinding – what's it gonna be

DID U KNOW?

You supposedly learn something every day, even small things like you have an extra Willy hair.

Monday 20th September 1999

Today was a shit day at school. After school I breezed straight home. At 7.20pm Guv came round he wanted me to come with him to some MCing thing at the Orchard. I thought I'd breeze there.

On the way to the train station we met Terry and he came with us. We just about caught the 7.42 train to Slough Town. We bopped to the Orchard from Slough station and got there quite fast. When we got there we found out that the man (Guv's friend) who was letting us MC said it was all f**ked up so we could do it next Monday. But we were there we just chilled, listened to tunes, played pool and some football. There were some guys from Britwell who were telling me they hate Langley mans. I was like ok cool and just walked off.

We left about 9.30pm then bopped back to Slough train station. Then we saw all ten Britwell boys shouting at us so we jump on the train to Langley. Then they were banging on the train doors as the train left. Wow what's their problem.

When I got in, for some mashed up reason I started playing some old I mean old jungle tape. I'm talking 93/94 tings Don Fm. It's strange how music can affect us in our life. The tunes you hear bring back memories of things, you know what I'm chatting about. Music is power.

Also - mans going on a school trip tomorrow and might be meeting fit girl Dasher on Saturday and there's a 19 year old Polish girl I might meet.

And there's a party on Saturday and also Fuel on Friday. Mans got options and on October 3rd there's the Southend girls ting.

Funniest thing all day:-

- Daomi pretending to be me. Going into the class I was sent out of (Miss Stefan's class)

SCHOOL TRIP DAY
21st SEPTEMBER 1999 ALSO A TUESDAY

Today I had to get to school early cos I was going on the history trip. We were going to the Imperial War Museum. We left school about 8.50am. On the coach I was just showing people my porno playing cards. We were playing snap (old school). Also all the nerds were sitting at the back cos they all ran to get to the coach.

Were got there about 9.50am. We had to be split up in 3 groups. That was safe cos I chilled with Gary T. It was alright; at first we walked round these World War 1 and 2 areas and bopped in some dirty smelly trenches.

At 11.10am – 11.30am we went in the Blitz experience thing. There was a man who was pretending to be a man from the past (so f**king stupid), he took us into this fake cardboard shelter and we heard a few loud sound effects. Then we had to run around and the guy was saying get down the Germans are attacking. I just said I ain't playing bruv I'm almost 16.

After me and Gary just breezed off and left our little group. We flexed to the cafe and just round different places we weren't suppose to go. We had to breeze from the group cos it was dry. We had to keep stopping and writing down notes. I didn't even write anything, just scribbling on the pad and smiling at the teacher so it looked like I was writing this shit down.

At 12.30pm everyone flexed into some little room to eat their mummies' little homemade packed lunch. But we bopped to some refreshment van and flexed some fat chips.

After we all went back round the museum and me, Gary, Daomi and Matthew just bopped round f**king about in the museum. Me, Daomi and Matthew got separated near the end and we had to bop round with the teachers. I had to bop round with Miss AllCOCK. I went in some 50's bit with her and she was telling me all about her days. She's offkey, who cares that you could get a month's shopping on £5.

At 1.45pm we got back on the coach to go school. We got to school at 2.30pm – 2.45pm. I chilled around school till it finished (3pm) then breezed to JD's house with JD. At JD's I just razed his munch and played some computer, like I always do. And I've never mentioned that JD has nearly every game in the world cos he's rich.

When I got in Terry came over. At 10.30pm I gave him a lift to the bridge near Datchet then his dad came to pick him up. I went petrol garage and got a chocolate. I didn't stay up that long cos I've got school in the morning.

Funniest thing all day:-

- Terry on video – have to ask permission
- New series on tv - Family Guy
- Barry C – Chat bout
- Me and Gary catching chase off security guard
- Dad climbing on roof- looked like he was perving on girl in the next garden

DID U KNOW?

Hitler committed suicide

Also this Nazi symbol was used before the Nazi's but for good not evil, in india.

Wednesday 22nd September 1999

Today for some reason I didn't go school. I was just taking too long then I realised if I went in I'd get a detention. So today I've just done nothing.

Thursday 23rd September 1999

Today I got a detention for being a bit late (3 marks get detention, my 3rd).

At school I lost my porno cards cos I gave some to James S look at and he got caught and the shit head blamed me. So he dashed them all away. I didn't beat him up cos he's only a little pussy and plus I ain't like that.

Even though I had people like Daniel Mountain egging me on to hit him for grassing me up. But I didn't get in trouble. But James could of at least said he found them. Some of these brares are some dumb.

After I had all these little kids coming up to me saying I sold your cards for 20p each. All the little kids found them and were selling them to their friends. Shit I could of made a fortune.

After school I just flexed home. Naomi was round for a while. We flexed down to Wimpy and it was quite boom, but the prices go on sick. When Naomi left I just stayed in. I was gonna go down to Sarah Elliman's house cos it's her birthday, but I couldn't be bothered.

In the night I watched two old 80's movies

Trading Places – starring Eddie Murphy

Bachelor Party – starring Tom Hanks

Funniest things all day:-

- Jokes chat - mixa mixa blender blender blender
- Kid – made £1 cos of my cards

Also the other day £10 was stolen from my house. It was either MJP or Terry that took it. I think its MJP cos he's stole from friends before.

DID U KNOW?

In some religions they ain't allowed to eat jelly babies cos it has some fat jelly product. And guys jelly babies are made from fat bits of a pig they just make it look pretty.

Friday 24th September 1999

Today school was shit, blatantly. After school I just relaxed, Naomi came over for a while and we flexed over Wimpy's and got some munch. Wimpy's old school, but the burgers are boom. When Naomi left Terry and JD came over. Not together, separately.

Later on me and Terry breezed out. There weren't really any plans for this Friday night so we just bopped into the local shitty Slough High Street. We stopped off at that Gravity place and just buss the m.i.c for a while. Today I was MCing proper shit but I couldn't be bothered that much.

Me, Terry and bare other people bopped down to Ice Arena to see who was down there. We chilled round there and met just the offkey Slough people then bopped back to Gravity (11.05pm).

After everyone just breezed outside McyD's and we were catching jokes, cos everyone was just cussing this offkey gay man that just started chatting to us. We also met up with Daniela and her friend and were chatting to them.

At 12.10am me and Terry started bopping back to Langley. We were also with Carl. At Slough Grammar we met up with Simmons, he just come from his bredwins house.

When we got back into Langley, Simmons found some kiddies bike on the floor. We rid up to the kebab shop. There was arms down the kebab shop. Two guys fighting in the kebab line.

When I got in I went to sleep. Yeah Terry stayed.

DID U KNOW?

About 100 years time there might be no more elephants.

Saturday 25th September 1999

Today could have been much better then it turned out to be. I blame Simmons, yes you Simmons, read to find out why.

Well this morning I woke up about 1pm, well this afternoon. Today I've just been round Langley. Tonight there is a party in Southend where we can like stay and shit, so that would be safe. But I rang one of the Southend girls and they didn't know what was going on cos it was her friend's party. There was also another option for tonight. Guv said there was a thing at the Temple in Tottenham. But I was with Simmons and Terry and they both didn't wanna go.

Well this is where Simmons ruins everything.

Well I rang the Southend girl back and she said the party was now on tomorrow (Sunday), so we didn't know what to do. And then Simmons said as we're not doing nothing lets ring up Rachel and her friends to come round and stay. So I rang Rachel (my ex) and asked her to come over with her friends.

After me and Terry bopped back to my drum. At my drum I got a call from Simmons and he said he was going Temple. I would of gone but Rachel was already on her way. And another thing that pissed me off the girls from Southend rang and said the party was on Saturday (which was today). Terry still wanted to go but I couldn't cos Rachel's crew were on the way.

At 9pm Rachel came round and she was on her jaze. Terry was screwing because he wanted one of the friends. He thought I'd be getting my tings and he'd be doing nothing. But I was screwing as well cos I should have just gone down to the rave but her monkey ass was there.

At 10pm we bopped down to the village. We chilled round there for a while then me and Rachel bopped back to my house. Terry went off with some people for a session.

When we got back to my drum we just chilled in my room. We watched the film 'Don't be a Menace to South Central While Drinking Your Juice in the Hood'. After the film me and Levi (Rachel) were just chatting then we just started kissing and getting it on baby. We were both down to our undies when suddenly the f**king door knocked. It was Terry and Sean, them bitches ruined me getting my shit. I lost my wood as well.

After Sean left, there was just us two and Terry. I left Terry downstairs then went back up in my room to see Rachel. We started doing some shit again. This time we were both naked, not pressing but just kissing and feeling up the poom poom. But my mum came home. So we quickly got dressed.

Later in the night we were all just chilling in my room. Terry was getting pissed off all night cos he was on his jaze. Also I kept getting calls from Guv and Simmons at Temple, but I didn't really regret not going cos I had my piece sorted.

Later on me and Rachel just flexed downstairs and left Terry to watch TV in my room. Downstairs we just had bare sex. We did all the shit we used to do when we were going out with each other, I'm not getting back with her though. I think Rachel does want to get back together but I'm not sure cos boring weekends and long treks to see her.

O yeah after me and Rachel just went back upstairs. Ok now go and if I catch you reading through this diary I'm gonna cut your dick off and feed it to your mum.

Funniest things all day:-

- S Club Video – The box music television you control
- Terry's samurai sword sacrifice - sword stabbed in dick
- Invisible sex- licking bum crack (batty wash)

Terry's funniest thing all day:-

- Amy – Do you fancy me Terry?

Saturday 26th September 1999

Rachel left at 4-5ish I think, I can't actually remember cos I've fallen behind in my diary. As I'm writing this on Tuesday. But don't worry I'm catching up.

After Rachel left, me and Terry just hung about round Trelawney.

At 7.50pm I went cinema with my mum. Terry breezed home. We got a taxi into Slough. The movie started at 8pm but it was in the premier screen and was sold out. So we thought we'd watch the next one at 9.15pm. But that hour went proper fast, we went in Blockbusters (my mum rented out some krusty true stories), then we went in the Lighthouse bar and chilled. Before I knew it, it was 9.15pm.

Do you know something I haven't even mentioned which film I'm watching, well it's 'The Haunting'. It was an alright film. It had some jumpy shit for a 12 movie. After the movie we flexed a taxi back home. We got in about 11pm. I just flexed to bed cos I've got school in the morning.

Funniest things all day:-

- Arms in Slough- man swinging the guy round.

DID U KNOW?

Hitler was born in Austria in 1889

Monday 27th September 1999

At school P.E was proper jokes. We just had a funny game. I scored a tick buff goal. Then ripped off my P.E like Hulk Hogan. Everyone was creasing. But I got in trouble with Mr Ince.

After school I chilled round JD's house. I left about 6pm cos today I was going to Orchard with Guv to make a tape (MCing ting).

When I got in Guv called and said there were better plans for this school night. He asked me to go to Embankment with him to MC at some boat party that finished at 3am and started at 10pm (on a school night gonna be mashed).

At 8pm Terry came round then straight after Guv came round. At 8.45pm we bopped to the train station. Beverage (Terry) wasn't coming but he came to the station to go back to Wraysbury.

We got the 9pm train to Paddington then we flexed a tube to Embankment (Bakerloo Line). At Embankment we had to look for the boat. But luckily we met two Slough brares and they showed us where it was. We had no trouble getting in cos Nasar was there and Vepow (sorry these Asian names are hard to spell).

It started off a piece shit. We were in the small area just practicing with the mic. There was no one in there just us and the digga digga D.J.

At 10.30pm we moved to the main area (much bigger). At 11pm it started jumping a piece, more people were coming in too.

They were playing bad tunes. House and G, R&B and Ragga (you know the works). We did MC for a while but our mic kept f**king up. We started

MCing again at 1am. This time me and Guv had a mic each and smashed it back to back. Until the gay promoter gave us the one mic and these other MC's used the other mic (Nasar and some brare wearing a top with bare Ganja leaves on it).

At 2.30am we left, we blagged it out to the bus driver to let me and G on for free. Cos I only had £1.50. I took £10 and that just went on shit, have a look

- 2 shots = £6 (£3 each)
- 1 beer = £2.50

So in the end left me with one dollar fifty mother f**ker.

We got to Paddington station at 2.40pm. The train wasn't leaving till ??? but we could still relax and wait on the train till it left. As it left I fell asleep and it felt like I went asleep for like one second but I woke up at West Drayton.

The train didn't stop at Langley so we got off at Slough. And had to do that long bop back to Langley. I was so tired (it was 4am).

When I got in I had some cereal then flexed to bed cos I've got school in a few hours.

Funniest things all day:-

- P.E football game- ripped top up like Hulk Hogan.

Tuesday 28th September 1999

Well today I had no chance of getting up for school. I got up about 12pm. There was no point of going to school cos today school was a half day anyway (finished at 1pm).

Later on I went kickboxing with Naomi. Yes I've started it up again. The last time I went was 6th July 1908, just messing (obviously). 6th July 1999 was the last time. It was a good lesson. When I got in I just relaxed and watched Police Academy, it's on channel 5.

DID U KNOW?

The word superstition is Latin

Means

SUPER- ABOVE

STAIR- TO STAND

Wednesday 29ᵗʰ September 1999

Today school was alright, just a normal day. After school I got ready to play football for the school. I flexed home to get my shit then breezed down to Langley Grammar (we're playing them gay boys like Simmons and people).

When I got there I had just missed the first ten minutes. But we were winning 1-0. But after Langley Grammar scored, then everybody just wanted me to go in goal cos our keeper was shit. But Langley Grammar scored another past me. But I never got a chance to warm up.

In the next half we scored (2-2) then after I did one of my giant goal kick to

Matthew and he scored. We won 3-2 in the end. I done boom in goal. Saved a shot with my dick. That shit hurt. But I stopped then bastards from scoring.

When I got in I just relaxed.

Funniest thing all day:-

- Simpsons – you're all wrinkly someone needs to iron you
- School – don't share books I'm not sharing

DID U KNOW?

Catherine Zeta Jones is from Wales, she boom ting as well.

Thursday 30ᵗʰ September 1999

Today I wasn't gonna write in my diary but shit just had to happen. So now I have to write.

Today I just went to school then after school went round JD's. Left there about 6.30pm. When I got in I just cotched.

Ok now for the exciting part, at 8.30pm I kept getting calls from Sean. He was at the Langley Grammar 6ᵗʰ form party and he wanted me to come. I wasn't gonna go but two words changed my mind- "BARE GIRLS". And also Sean was paying for me to flex a taxi down there. I left to go to the party at 9.30pm. I bopped down to Trelawney to get a 672672 taxi.

The party was in Stoke Poges some place called the Polish Club. I got there about 9.45pm. I got in the party free cos the bouncer was safe. When I got in I met Sean and a few Langley people. There were bare Langley Grammar sexy 6ᵗʰ form girls. At first I was just chilled and Sean got me a pint. Then after I met up with Kenworthy (from school), Guv and Nathan K.

The music was the only shit thing about the party cos it was a karaoke party, the music was bare chart shit. But apart from that it was safe cos all the girls were just f**ked out of their brains.

At 1ˢᵗ when I started cherpsing girls I was getting blasted hard. So was Kenworthy. Cos I was a bit f**ked I think I was chatting shit to all the girls I was chatting up.

The first number I got was Flona, she was proper dirty but she had a boyfriend and he was at the party as well. But she kept giving me little kisses on the lips. Then she gave me her number and kept saying (desperately) to text her. She also in year 13 and got her own yard. She told me come down one day to have fun. I thought yes I like fun. As long as it's not no dodgy shit where your boyfriend will try bum rush me, then we're cool. Because I swear I saw her man see her kiss me and not care.

The second number I got was some girl that weren't even all that but I was f**ked. Her name was Chandani (some wack ass name, trust).

The third number I got was some girl from Stoke Poges (Jo), she's quite boom still. Wait give the skeet talk a rest. After cherpsing Jo I MCed with Guv and Nathan cos the DJ put on one garage tune. That NDubz tune over here.

At 12.30am the party finished. We chilled outside for a while.

And I also got 3 more numbers

Hayley – I just told this girl, 'It's my birthday soon and I'm gonna have a massive party do you wanna come?' Well she had to give me her number if she wanted to come to my party (wink wink) innit. I ain't really having a party, rags lie to girls if you have to. I also used that trick a year ago when I met

Aliza. She rang me and said so when's the party and I goes 'sorry it's cancelled but we can still meet up'

Sofia- this girl is too old for me. She has her own place and her own personal number. But that's not stopping me. She's 18 or 19.

Elkie- she was alright, she's got some dark titties cos I was chatting to her then drunk Kenworthy came and started pulling her top down. I was like hello what is your number? The breasts were sick.

Woo I went on rowdy with the cherpsing. I can't believe I got 6 numbers in one day

But I didn't lips none, shame

After I got a taxi with Guv and two Langley Grammar brares to Slough High Street. We flexed some kebabs then I just bopped home on my jaze cos Guv was taking long.

I got in about 1.30am – 2am time. Then wrote a bit of diary but I was too tired and plus I got school in the morning.

Funniest things all day:-

- Kenworthy on the Karaoke Mr. Boombastic

- Boy on the mic making a fool out of himself- do you smell what the Rock is cooking

Funniest thing all month

5. Grey tits

4. Kenworthy - Mr. Boombastic

3. Tramp nicking banana

2. Boy making a fool out of himself

1. The ice cream factory mess in Margate

1st October 1999

This is the last page of my diary but it's not over yet matey. It's just it seems weird. But I will get some replacements; I might even create DA DIARY part 2 cos this pad is getting packed with pages.

Well anyway today is Friday but f**k me this school week's been like a holiday or some shit. As I was saying, well school was alright today. We had some career people come in and talk about whether we want to do 6th Form, College, work or just sit at home unemployed. Nah jokes they were chatting about when we finish school. I might go College to carry on my skeet education. This month I've also got work experience and I'm working in WH Smiths as a Shop Assistant, which should be fun, try make some money from the tills. Well tonight I just had a night in for some reason I was proper tired.

Saturday 2nd October 1999

Today I did so much shit. It was such a funny day, Simmons you smashed it.

Well this morning Terry and Sean came over. At 2pm we bopped to Trelawney. I rang up Dasher cos I might be meeting her today. We decided to meet Dasher. She lives down Camden but we didn't mind flexing down there, cos you know how much us mans love our missions.

After we flexed down the village and got some munch (Kinara) then we went to Darvils so Sean could get his Stellas.

We got the train to Paddington at 3pm. We got to Paddington at 3.20pm.

After we breezed on the Circle Line to Kings Cross. And that was a proper mission to get through, they had bare ticket machines.

After we had to get the Northern Line to get to Camden Town station. At Camden we breezed round the High Street and the market for a piece. And 'boy' there's bare grungers down there. It's grunger heaven.

After I rang Dasher and then we waited for her to come and meet us. When we met Dasher she didn't look as boom as when I first met her. She was also with some short little butterz Chinese girl. We didn't stay very long cos the girls were offkey. I just told Dasher I'd give her a call (not).We just went round the market with them , then I just said 'shit is that the time we gotta breeze'.

After we chilled back at Kings Cross. Me and Simmons flexed a McDonalds and we got it free cos the woman forgot to charge us, so we took our shit and ran.

After all the train missions we got back to Paddington. Me and Sean gave Simmons and Terry a challenge to see who could get back to Langley quicker. We won cos we flexed a fast train to slough then flexed OTT to Langley. Them joke brares got a slow train that stopped at every stop.

Anyway, when I got in I had some dinner and just cotched. Later on Simmons knocked for me. Tonight there was quite a lot going on. There's a party in Upton Lea Youth Club, or the Temple in Tottenham and Sean's saying about going Destiny's in Watford. Well, what I decided to do was to go to the Slough party (Upton Lea) then go to one of the raves.

Well, me and Terry bopped down to Upton Lea Play Centre. We got there about 8.50. We met bare people like Guv, Simmons, Nicholas and more. The party started off shit but did start getting lively later. We MCed for a while but I couldn't be bothered that much, all the other MCs were shit as well.

We left the party about 11.00pm then we were gonna go to the Temple. We took long about leaving to go to the Temple cos they was waiting to get some draw. We did manage to get to Tottenham but it was closed. We got a fast train to Paddington about 12.00am then we got the tube to Kings Cross and luckily caught the last tube to Seven Sisters.

By the way, it was Me, Simmons, Guv, Nick T, Dara, Nicholas and Denny. We couldn't get into the club cos Nick T was wearing trainers. So we thought, let's just do something else. But cos Simmons was so f**ked he still wanted to go in. He was so drunk he was going mad. All smashing shit and coming up with stupid ideas to get Nick into the club. Ideas like sneak through the window or put Nick's black socks on his trainers to look like shoes. At one point Simmons smashed this bottle and these boys started on him because it smashed near them. But we sorted it out.

After, we thought we'd just get a bus into the West End. But Simmons was still going mad. He kept kicking windows and just going crazy, he was on a crave to rave. He desperately wanted to go in the Temple.

After, we got on the bus to go West End. As we were coming up to Finsbury Park Simmons started going a bit crazy, cos Nicholas took his phone and he started saying, "give me my bottle back". We thought what the f**k is he on about? After, he got angry and just bopped off the bus (he had his phone). We didn't get off the bus cos Simmons just breezed and we stayed on and left him in Finsbury Park.

Simmons kept ringing us and saying if he sees us he's gonna kill us and beat the shit out of us. He was going proper mad cos we left him on his own in some rough area. But we just told him to get the next bus. We got off the bus at Centre point and bopped down the Piccadilly Circus.

We were just catching bare jokes. When we arrived we were hanging about with this safe brare from North London sides. Then we flexed into KFC and waited for Simmons. We were thinking what's he gonna do to us cos he was still going mad on the phone.

When Simmons came everyone was trying not to laugh cos he was going crazy. Just standing over us looking evil. Like Jack Nicholson in The Shining.

Then everybody just started laughing and he started going mad and throwing shit at us (He even throw a chair at us), then he breezed off.

A while later we were all back together apart from Nicholas, Denny and Nick T cos someone nicked a bag or some shit and they ran off. Simmons also said when he was in north London he had a fight with these three boys and they f**ked up his ribs. But he won the fight. He must be a ninga.

Anyway after me, Dara, Simmons and Guv decided to get a taxi to Paddington. We got a taxi from some trampy geza, I swear he didn't even work for a proper company. This tramp was safe and let them Bun in the car. It was £5 but we all chipped in a £1 apart from Dara, rowdy he paid £2.

After we got a call from Nicholas and then met the rest of the crew in St Mary's Hospital. We chilled in the hospital. Got the wheelchairs out and had some races until we got thrown out by the dirty Security Guard.

We went back to the station. It was about 5.30am and our train wasn't till 6.48am. But we couldn't be f**ked to go anywhere in the meantime. So everybody just fell asleep in different places in the station.

At 6.40am there was an announcement that all trains were cancelled. So we had to get a special coach back to Slough. The driver was dumb I never had a ticket; I showed him a piece of paper. Nicholas showed him some food.

OTC (on the coach) I just slept. As we were coming up Langley the driver let two women off at London Road. Then we woke up and quickly tried to get off and he said we couldn't and the next stop was Slough (drove past my house as well). There was some other big man dude who wanted to get off at Langley and when the driver didn't stop he started punching up the driver with his big man fist. So the driver let us off at Langley. So we said safe to the brare that punched up the driver. Otherwise we would have had to bop from Slough.

When I got in I didn't go sleep straight away. I played some Mega Drive. It's working again. Altered Beast is jokes.

I went bed at 9am

Funniest thing all day:-

- Mad woman – where are you TC
- Sean's free McyD's
- Simmons mad- stand back he's gonna switch
- Guv bursting in toilet. Thought it was Simmons come to kill me
- Our safe brare getting skeet
- Simmons trying to get back on bus
- Sean saying Dasher to any girl then it was her
- Driver gets beaten up

DID U KNOW?

The total world population in 1990 was 5.3 billion. It's expected to increase to over 6 billion by the year 2000

Sunday 3ʳᵈ October 1999

Today I woke up about 6.30pm and didn't really do anything.

In the night I couldn't sleep. Had too much sleep in the day. So did some more Mega Drive. Got Streets of Rage on the go. How come when the Police fire the weapons it doesn't hurt me?

Monday 4ᵗʰ October 1999

Today I got up early as I'm not tired one bit. But I still was late for school, my bike f**ked up. School was a bit offkey today. I keep getting told off by the new French teacher she can't take any jokes.

At 6.00pm I got a bus to Slough to go to my cousin's to get my haircut. After, I flexed over to JD's.

When I got in I had some sleep.

Tuesday 5ᵗʰ October 1999

History File

Massive Train Crash Paddington about 70 people died

This morning I woke up really early. Today was a really cold day (it was f**king freezing I tell ya). It was a bit of a bitch cos I had to ride in dat dirty weather and your hands just freeze up. For once I actually couldn't wait to get to school (the warmth).

After school I went to bed. I had some weird dream that I cut my dick off. Then after I really missed it and was crying to my mum to get it back. When I woke up I just touched it and thought, thank God it's still there, it seemed so real. Cos in this dream was Rachel and we were doing tings but not exactly, not without a penis.

Anyway, at 6.30pm I went kickboxing. After I went down the phone box and phoned some of the girls I met from the Grammar party. 2 of the numbers are fake, the other 4 were Genuine. I also rang Nicole from Isleworth and I think I'm meeting her this Friday.

THE END. I can't be bothered to write. When I got home I went to bed cos I knew that was coming. Later

DID U KNOW?

There is more water on Earth then land, sea innit.

Friday 8ᵗʰ October 1999

Today school was just a shitty day. Some career people came in and they chatted shit. They keep asking me what I wanna do when I leave school. Might do that Performing Arts shit. Cos it's just messing about.

After school I had a detention but it was only from 3.00 – 3.30pm and I got there at 3.15pm so it was safe I suppose.

My plans for today is to meet Nicole from Isleworth in Hounslow. At 6.00pm I got ready to breeze out. At 7.27pm I left to meet Nicole for 7.30pm (joker). After, I bopped down to London Road and to flex a bus. Down the shop I met some of the Churchmead crew. Just thought I'd mention that.

The bus was taking long to come. I got a bus about 7.40pm but I rang Nicole and told her I was gonna be late. On the bus I was hoping she wasn't butterz cos the last time I saw her was in February and I wasn't cherpsing her. I was actually cherpsing her friend, so I thought, she can't be all that.

I met her at Hounslow East train station at 8.20-8.30pm. It was weird cos I didn't recognise her face one bit. I just thought her face was different from the way it was. Her face was a bit mash (looked like a rat a piece) but her body was safe (titties the lot). I also thought she might be proper small, but she was only a piece shorter than me. I was thinking is this the same yatt or did she just send a friend to come and meet me cos she couldn't be f**ked.

Anyway we were gonna go into the West End but she told me she had to be in at 11.00pm cos of some shit happening tomorrow. So I thought I'd take her to the cinema. But the bus at Feltham was taking long and it was coming up to 9.00pm, so we thought, there's really no point.

RP WAS HERE WITH TERRY BEING HUHH WITH GLOVEZ TOMORROW

We just chatted at the bus garage cos we thought there's nothing better to do. She only stayed for about half an hour and I didn't even lips her. But I'm not really into kissing rats anyway. Would of like to play with the titties (rat titties) but still. After this the bus driver said I could get a free lift cos he was going straight to Slough and the bus was not in service. This brare was proper safe. He didn't mind me flexing on. So I flexed on the bus and didn't stop at any stops and just cruised past bare people waiting for the bus. I was also chatting to the guy, he was safe. He dropped me right off right at my stop on the London Road.

After, I got a burger from the fish and chip shop then flexed home. It was only about 10.00pm. I was so tired I just flexed to bed.

Saturday 9th October 1999

Today I had a boom little dream but I can't f**king remember it (shame). There was something about a killer popcorn machine. This morning MJP knocked for me and told me about some party that's going on tonight in Colnbrook. After he left, Terry came round. I got ready to breeze out about 2.00pm. At 3.00pm Simmons came over then we bopped out.

We got a bus into Slough. There was bare people down Slough today. There was also some little show thing opposite the cinema where the band Fierce were performing. Everyone was getting Fierce's autograph but I couldn't be bothered to chat to them. Seen them skets before anyway.

At 6.00pm Me, Terry and Simmons bopped back to Langley.

When I got in I got ready to breeze to this party down Colnbrook, but me and Terry took our time. We left to go to the party about 8.00pm (Simmons was already down there). We bopped to Colnbrook then met Simmons after we bopped down to the party. We met bare people down there like Nick T, Guv and bare next people.

It was an alright little house party. The tunes were good; the MC was tick (me). There wasn't really that much girls, well there was, but they were young girls. Loads of people were MCing, like Me, Guv, Kieran and Calvin. At the end we decided to stop MCing because the mic was mashed. At one point I also ram raided the girl's fridge. I drank all the milk. The party finished at 12.00am then after we chilled round the petrol garage for a while. And for some reason I brought bare Pepparamis. On the way back to Langley there was Me, Terry, Simmons, Guv, Brian G and Michael Jo.

At 1.00am we were all being stupid. We stopped off at the motorway roundabout and kept running up and down that steep thing under the bridge. If you live round this area you know what I mean!

As we were bopping back I got a call from Sean saying he was with two girls I knew, Jo and Gemma from Chalfont. I've known them for about a year but I don't think they're mentioned in DA DIARY. Anyway I thought how the f**k do they know Sean? And, why are they in Langley? Well, we met them down Trelawney Avenue and the answers to both my questions are:-

1. They're staying round their friend's auntie's house (there was also another girl not too bad).

2. They just met Sean today he tried to cherpse them, ha ha ha.

After Jo and Tracey (the girl whose house they're staying round) bopped off home. Gemma stayed with us. About 2.50am, Me, Simmons, Guv, and Terry walked Gemma back to Tracey's <u>drumage.</u>

We were just chilling outside. We didn't know what to do, so we just knocked for the girls and they let us in. They had a free house, just them.

At 3.30am Chris P and Matt came round. They were just chatting bare shit cos they were on something. I was mainly just chatting to them all night cos everyone else was falling asleep.

I was gonna try it on with Jo but I didn't really get a chance. No one else got any girls.

Later on around 5.00am I was in the room with tracey I just thought I'd try it on with her (well Terry, Simmons and Guv were in the room but cotching hard). I managed to lips her and got a feel of some titties. I wanted to shag her blatantly (teenage hormone strike). I ask her to come upstairs but jo was in there sleeping. But we went up there and were lipsing on the bed while jo was asleep. But jo started waking up when things were getting nice and started switching. But she seems dirty, she was kissing me all dirty and rubbing my leg crazily (if that's a word).

At 6.30pm, Me, Simmons, Terry and Guv left. And boy when I got out I farted hard I was holding it in all nite but when I got out I just let it rip rather then just let it fade away. Like I was doing in the girls yard. But when I got home I had some dirty shit. I must have eaten something nasty cos the shit was 50% fart and 50% runny shit.

After, I went to sleep (time 2.00am).

Funniest things all day:-

• Brian's Funky Dance
• Terry blowing light switch

- Brare rapping in Slough
- Me and Terry's fake chase
- Daomi throwing milkshake over girls

RUGBY WORLD CUP IS HAPPENING, SHIT!

Sunday October 10th 1999

Today, I woke up at 2.30pm. And you know something, I really for once can't be f**ked to write what happened.

Terry came round. Gave him a lift to Datchet. Went over Sean's. Bye.

WWF'S Gorilla Monsoon is dead: 1937-1999

Monday 11th October 1999

Today was just a normal boring school day; erm that don't make no sense does it? Anyway when I got home I got a call from Guv and he said tonight there's a college party in Staines.

I met Guv at 7.30pm at the Gulley. We got a train to Slough at 7.45pm. OTT we met Nick cos he was also coming. At Slough train station we met Nathan, then flexed a train to Windsor. In Windsor we stopped off at McDonalds and got hooked up with bare free munch cos Nathan knew one of the boys who worked there.

After, we flexed to the station, we had to wait about 20 minutes for our train. We got on the train about 8.40pm.

It was only a little bop from Staines train station. It was at Club Exchange. When we walked in it as just some little shitty pub thing and a while later we found out there was a little rave going on upstairs (the real ting) and it was only £4 to get in.

We chilled in the pub just watching the f**ked up Man Utd v the rest of the world game. There were quite a lot of girls in there as well.

At 9.10pm we jumped some queue to get in the rave part. And boy, I could not believe how many dirty, beautiful, lovely, sexy, delicious, boom, kriss, college girls there were. Once it started jumping there was just skeet all over the place. Me and Guv MCed most of the time we were there. I think we done quite well.

About 11.20pm me and Guv stopped MCing cos the Manager cut off the mic. Then we thought, now for the biggest cherpes of all time. All the girls wanted it badly. I cherspsed this girl called Kay and got her number. She was quite boom. And this is the f**ked up part. Everyone started leaving cos we weren't sure how we were gonna get home, and I only got one number. I almost got a second number but everyone just breeze out and I had to breeze as well. As I walked out of the club I was crying, I was so sad.

BARE GIRLS!

Believe me I was so upset. I could have got much more girls. No lie there must have been about 200 girls all 16-18 and titties. (I can't imagine heaven, after leaving that place).

On the way to the train station I had tears going everywhere, it's like going without food for me. Especially at my age I swear you need to get your tings or you die (it's a hormone thing).

Anyway we just about caught the last train. Me and Guv got off at Datchet cos it was 12.30am and we wouldn't have been able to get a train to Slough (I got off our train at 12.00am). From Datchet we bopped. On the way we stopped off at a Kebab van and got some meat for 50p (Bare trampiness). When I got in it was 1.00am which is not that bad cos I've got school in the morning. And I've just realised I've been to bare school night raves lately. Later on, but I still don't think you understand how many girls there were. This thing beats everything I've ever been to where I have said there was 'bare skeet', trust.

Funniest things all day:-

- Christian's hair police - put JD in prison for people with dirty hair
- JD - IT doesn't matter what rugby club you play for.

DID U KNOW?

Czechoslovakia used to be called just Slovakia - war and Hitler changed that shit

Tuesday 12ᵗʰ October 1999

Well, today I just went to school then at 6.30pm, I went kickboxing. You see, no big deal, why were you getting excited?

Also, in night watched Long Kiss Goodnight

DID U KNOW?

Britain never used to be part of Europe, some shit like that.

Wednesday 13ᵗʰ October 1999

Today I was a little bit late for school. On the way to school it was really cold, the cold hit me like a virgin just getting it for the first time. Really it was proper cold. It hurt.

Well school was alright. The first lesson was History which was shit and so were the other 5, going into too much detail is LONG. Hate school.

After school we had a football game against St Jo's. I didn't even get to play cos it was so close the whole game. The first half ended 1-1. During the second half I met this girl from St Jo's and she was cherpsing me. I just chatted to her. She wasn't too bad. She looked dirty. She was wearing some little shirt thing and I swear I'm some sort of perve. I was thinking nasty shit in my head, or is it just cos I'm fifteen. Well, I always use that excuse so I guess I'm just a perve. I was gonna take her number down but I couldn't find a pen so she just took mine down (in her phone).

Anyway at the football at the end of the second half it was still 1-1 so they had to go into extra time. No one scored so it went into penalties, and that's where we lost, someone missed. But those dick heads should of put me in goal cos that little fat brare didn't even move. He was only in goal cos he's fat and he saves goals with his belly.

I got home at 6.30pm today cos the match went on for long, trust. And, I got some bad news, my mum took the mobile phone to work and it got nicked so I've lost bare phone numbers and that girl I met today, I gave her the mobile number, God what have I done to deserve this? But, I think I wrote some numbers down last night but I'm not sure. Also, I hope I get a new phone in time for the girl I met today to ring.

Funniest things all day:-

- Deer in Langley
- Catching sweet in mouth - classic

2000 coming soon

Only 80 dayz to go, if you've just found my diary and you're not from these times, you wouldn't know the feeling of the coming of the Millennium, it's a massive event, everyone's going crazy!

Tuesday 14ᵗʰ October 1999

Today there's some funny rumour going around school about some girl. Trust me what you're about to hear is very very nasty. You're probably gonna be sick so don't read the red writing. But it's tempting innit?

WARNING BARE NASTINESS

In school today there's this girl in Year 11. Well I heard she was having sex with some brare in a car and was riding him and she f**king shit herself and the shit went all over his legs, feet and hands. Trust, she must have been tense or some "shit" get it, some shit.

If you've just read that you're probably being sick just this moment. If you didn't I advise you, just f**king read it's just chatting bare SHIT.

Anyway after school I met Terry outside. I had to go into Slough to see about this work experience job in HMV. I left all my stuff round JD's then me and Terry bopped to HMV. When I got to HMV I just spoke to the man and I start on Monday, wear whatever I want, 9.30am – 5pm and there's bare shit to raze. But I'll give it a few days then robb those mother f**kers blind.

After me and Terry met Nicholas and bopped round with him for a piece. After I got my bike from JD's then me and Terry flexed back to my drum.

Later on we flexed over Simmons. After that I gave Terry a lift to the village then his dad picked him up.

When I got in I just went upstairs and chilled. Also my uncle from Florida is staying again.

Well today I never went school cos I wasn't feeling too well, if you know what I'm saying!!!. Well now I haven't got school for 2 weeks cos next week I start work in HMV then the week after is half term.

I just cotched in bed today. At 3.30pm I flexed over JD's then after went to Slough and got a munch, some chicken from favourite chicken. £1.99 2 piece of chicken , chips and a drink.

Tonight there was supposed to be a party down Hilton but it f**ked up and it wasn't on. So there wasn't any other plans for tonight. Me, Sean, Simmons all breezed out. We went to the train station and got a train to Slough. And from Slough to Windsor, we thought we'd breeze Windsor cos nothing was going on.

Down Windsor we met Nathan and bare Windsor crew. There were a few girls but not bare. Today we were mainly just hanging about round McDonalds, just catching bare jokes.

Later on I went in McyD's to get some munch and the brare at the till said to me he'd give me free munch if I got him cigarettes from the shop. Boy I got bare free munch and never got the brare shit. That's long.

After Windsor we went back into Langley. We chilled in Kinara. About 1am me, Simmons and Matt went to the Marriot Hotel for jokes. We flexed through the back way and just bopped through the corridors and chilled round the main bit. At one point we found a little storage room and razed bare shit. But it was shit like pens, towels, coffee and cookies (just shit stuff). But least my mum can enjoy some coffee with cookies then after have a bath and use a nice hotel towel.

We left the Marriott about 2am then me and Simmons waited with Matt at Harvester till his taxi came. When his taxi came we flexed in it as well (bare laziness) and just got off down the road at the petrol garage. When I got in I just relaxed in bed.

Saturday 16th October 1999

Today was shit like yesterday.

At 3pm Jason and Kieran from Hanwell came over. Well, like yesterday there was supposed to be a party but that won't going on. Tonight we were all down Langley village. At 8.22pm Kieran and Jason got a train back to Hanwell. I waited with them till there train came. Kieran was talking about fat girls sitting on a guys face in some movie. It was jokes you had to be there.

When I got back to the village everybody had breezed off. I rang Simmons off this girls phone (butterz girl from Hampden Road)

And he was in Slough. The rest of bare people, which don't make sense, I mean the rest of the crew were in Windsor having a massive bunning (smoking) session with bare girls, apparently. But I couldn't be bothered to breeze places on my jaze. So I chilled with slosher Susan and her offkey crew. I just breezed round Trelawney and Kidderminster Park.

And tonight I got in at 10pm, how offkey is that. Well I suppose every day can't be exciting but I'm gonna start getting back into my every weekend skeet routine.

Sunday 17th October 1999

Well this gay Sunday I've just done bare bullshit, just chilled really. I rang some girls to meet up with next weekend. I rang Kim from Iver. She's proper boom and guess what she's just split up her 4 year boyfriend. That's made me happy.

I also rang Susan might meet up with her as well. And I rang Kay from that club in Staines (exchange) but I need to ring her back some other time, her phones mess.

Well later, I'm breezing see you tomorrow. I start work experience in HMV for a week then week after off school. Anyways later I'm really going now. I'm watching wolf, the film with Jack Nicholas.

Work experience day 1
Monday 18th October 1999

Today I woke up about 7.30am. I started my work experience at 9.15am. So I left about 8.55am, I walked into Slough cos I missed the bus. I just missed the by one second and started chasing it and could see Kimmi, Latoya and Matthew looking out the window pointing and laughing at me.

When I got in Slough it was about 9.10am then I bopped to HMV. When I got there I just made a cup of tea from their dirty kitchen bit, wouldn't think they had a kitchen innit.

Through the morning I had to just do this little job which was printing out bare film titles for DVDs. Does anyone even buy these DVD tings anyway. I had to write them down then type them out. I was doing this behind the till with this offkey brare called Allen and this girl about my age, err yeah she was alright (would of spratted her, if I was desperate). Anyway with my DVD printing I got up to letter D then the brare said I had to do it all again cos I f**ked up (I did it after my lunch break). Yeah at lunch I flexed to McyD's buss a quarter pounder meal to be exact.

I was bopping around on my jaze but today I didn't really mind. At 12.30pm I met some stupid little girls from school, I chilled with them because I couldn't be bothered to hang about on my jacks no longer.

Most of the day at work I was just printing out DVD film labels (from a-z). It took time. I left at 4.50pm and tomorrow I'm gonna raze cos it's so easy. The stuff upstairs is minor; you just put it in your bag and casually bop out.

When I got in I relaxed I was gonna go club Exchange but I couldn't be bothered. I just cotched and was chatting to Naomi in the night.

DID U KNOW?

Alkenes are a family of gases

Funniest things all day:-

- Typed out wrong film when I was tired- Tyson and the Argonauts (mans krusty joke)
- Offkey work mate with the big dirty lips.

Work experience day 2
Tuesday 19ᵗʰ October 1999

Today I got a taxi to work cos I just jumped in it with my mum; she got it to Slough train station.

When I got to Slough I met Alex (one other brare on work experience from Burnham Grammar) and I flexed around with him. We had to go in the back entrance cos the front wasn't open.

In the morning we did this stupid labelling videos thing, it took us from 9.30am – 12pm and we still hadn't finished. We had to sticker labels, one bar code thing and some other little sticker in the right hand corner of the video, it was f**king boring.

At 12pm I went with Alex to lunch. I met some of his offkey Grammar chums. But at 12.15pm I met Lucas from school and was chilling with him.

At 12.45pm I was on my jaze but I found some people to breeze round with till 1pm.

When I got back to work I still had to finish the gay bum licking labelling. I must have seen about 100 'Flubbers' and f**King Millions of 'Starship Troopers', 'Good Will Hunting' and bare other shit films I hate. And don't say 'Starship Troopers' was a good film, that was wet fanny dibble. The only thing boom about that film is that sexy skeet. I'd wank to that. Only joking I don't wank I'm black.

But they did let us play tunes though, we could just take any tape or C.D and just buss it on.

We also had to work on the phones. I had to call bare people and tell them their orders have arrived. It was hard when people had funky names cos I couldn't say it properly. But it was safe doing it cos I got to sit in the spinning chair. I also got to go in the security room and I could see everyone around the shop on the cameras. Could zoom in to the girls on the camera.

Anyway after ringing bare people up I had to take all the shit behind the till.

Work was better than yesterday. As I was finishing, I got myself 3 videos-

'I know what you did last summer'

And two copies of 'Aliens Resurrection' (I took two because they counted in even numbers and would of f**ked up).

After work I met Naomi. She got on the bus home with me. I got off at London Road and flexed some boom southern fried chicken, which I munched on my jaze. Quickly ran up to my room in case my mum saw the chicken and wanted a piece.

At 6.30pm me and NaHuHHmi went to kickboxing. I left at 7.30pm though, cos I felt like poo poo (shit).

When I got in I just watched some new programme called 16, all about 16 year olds. It was a bit shit. But I found out there's some dirty girls in Portsmouth, might have to buss there one day.

After I watched some dirty stripper programme with my uncle from Florida. I turned it on he just sat there quietly.

That's all, but now I'm in bed cotching watching 'Alien Resurrection'

Work experience 3
The revenge of the bare raze
Wednesday 20th October 1999

Boy, I had some weird dreams about HMV. The 1st was some terrorist trying to take over and I was working and these boom skeet came in the shop and they asked for a C.D. So I took them round the back and they started f**king me. There was another dream about labels but I can't remember it. Some f**ked up dream innit, HMV's getting to my brain.

Well today at work was bare f**king labelling. The guy bought out some big fat boxes of about 200 C.D's and I had to stick stickers on them, it sounds easy but its offkey. Cos later my mum was like what did you do at work today Robert and I said stuck stickers on CDs and she was like ok that must of been easy. Bitch you ain't seen that life time supply they gave me (I didn't actually say that).

At 12pm I went to lunch with Alex but when I saw Daniel from school I left him but I should have stayed cos he met up with 2 tick skeet from his school, I'll get them today, rowdy.

After lunch we just had this peeling sticker off job which was shit. We did get to listen to bare tunes but the thing is Alex listens to that funky Grunger music, some head banging shit.

During work I did raze some shit. I got a Reggae CD (which Nicholas might be buying off me) and a wrestling video (for JD). To get this I just took them off the shelves and no one said nothing cos I work there. Trust I do it so sly, I quickly take it, rip off the security labels then put it in my raze bag (yes I have a raze bag). I also go in the security room so I can control were the camera is placed. You didn't know I was that clever, did you.

Anyway I also razed Wrestlemania XI (9) cos it's one of the old ones I ain't seen in time. Well I might watch it tonight and put it back tomorrow, f**k razing it.

As I was just leaving work I took the film 'Devil's Advocate' which I've never seen but thought I'd raze it.

I finished work at 4.45pm cos there was no more work to be done. And I'm thinking of changing the day of work experience. It should be called something like robbing experience or scam experience of just "how could you let Robert in your shop to bare raze experience". I swear these people are dumb, but I'm gonna be careful.

Not much happened after that. In the night I watched 'I know what you did last summer', which is quite frankly a stolen item, Bo. Also I tried that Wrestlemania video and its just f**ked. I'll try another one tomorrow. They've got the whole box of all the Wrestlemania's so far. Bye.

Robb Peters

Work Experience Day 4
Thursday 21ˢᵗ October 1999

Today at work (in the day) me and Alex were lifting bare heavy shit into the basement. We had to lift these massive shelve tings up and down stairs. The basement was quite big. You wouldn't think Slough HMV was that big, trust there was bare CD's videos and games scattered everywhere. I bare razed two games, X Men vs Street fighter and WWF Attitude, but the WWF ones a bit mashed but works.

Before lunch I razed the movie 'Blade'. I just took it off the shelves and took it upstairs into my bag; no one said shit cos I work there. They're dumb.

At lunch I cruised round with Daniel. I flexed one of those new KFC chicken roll thingys.

When I got back in work we had to do bare sticker shit like sticking them, peeling them off, sticking security things and other shit.

I finished work at 4.30pm and before I left I got a garage CD (which Clint Eastwood gonna buy off me) and a Playstation South Park game.

When I got home I just cotched. I got the bus home by the way and stopped off at the shops to purchase a beverage, I paid for it.

Anyways in the night I just watched the film Devil's Advocate with mum and Shibbz. It was quite boom but it's weird. Trust, Robert Peters recommends it. But if you're dumb don't watch it cos you won't understand what's going on, you get me.

Well now I'm gonna finish and watch Blade. It's 11.30pm and I'm just gonna turn off this nice CD (bare razed as well).

Funniest thing all day:-

- Trying to pick up box and just kept collapsing

DID U KNOW?

About one eighth of the worlds land surface is covered by deserts

Work experience day 5
The final frontier
Friday 22ⁿᵈ October 1999

Today I got to work about 10am cos I was playing all my new computer games. The South Park game's too much jokes. I left my house at 9.29am and was supposed to start at 9.30am.

At work I was working on my jaze cos Alex had finished his work experience, but I wasn't really bothered, just thought it was good information. But today is my last day. There was hardly anything to do. At lunch I met up with Daniel and flexed some McyD's.

When I got back in work I was mainly upstairs with videos and CD's, putting them on shelves.

I left work early cos there was no work for me to be done. I was screwing in a way cos I wanted to get some shit but I got some video called Combat (about real fighting in rings, shit like that). I was pissed off cos I was just about to go on a little raze and then I had to leave. It felt like the time I had to leave that club early in Staines, but not as bad. Seriously I got about 6 videos, 3 games and 2 CD's but I wanted more.

When I got in I just relaxed. Later on Terry came round. In the night me, Simmons, Sean and Terry got the train to Slough. For some reason Sean jumped back on the Langley train as soon as we got there (what a dick).

In Slough we flexed in the young people's centre cos there was a little shitty rave kind of thing, hard to explain. Well I MCed down there but it was still shit, come we change the subject.

Anyway about 10.15pm we bopped down the ice arena to see who was down there and it was just the usual people. There was bare fights as usual.

After we bopped back into the High Street. We met up with Nicholas and Denny. There was bare of us, me, Simmons, Terry, Dot, Wayne, Guv, Nicholas and Denny. We started to bop back to Langley cos the plans were to breeze round Marriot Hotel for jokes. We took long getting to Langley cos they stopped to build and smoke a zoot.

When we got to Langley, Me, Guv and Terry just breezed to my drum. We told them mans we'd meet them down Marriott. But once we started playing the South Park game we couldn't be bothered. There's a level where you fight each other with that cow gun.

Later in the night Simmons came over. Simmons and Guv left about 3.30am. Then I flexed to bed, yeah Terry stayed.

Funniest thing all day:-

- School diary for work experience was blank
- Rob- just use the birds toilets
- The stalker

Saturday 23rd October 1999

Today I woke up at 12pm and I quickly got washed and dressed ready to go out. Terry's dad came over and he wanted us to come to Bracknell to his friends.

We drove down to Bracknell. I only thought I'd go cos I wasn't up to nothing and plus Bracknell's got girls.

When we got there we just flexed a McyD's then Terry and me ditched his dad and looked for girls. There were girls around but lots of 12 – 14 year olds. All the nice girls were working in the shop, the older girls.

We thought we'd leave Bracknell and go to Reading. On the way to the train station I met this girl called Kelly. I cherpes her and I was gonna take her number but I didn't have a pen. So she took down mine but you know how girls go on when they have to call you, they never call. Wish girls would just say ok I will take down your number but you'll never get a call from me.

It was strange at the station cos we walked into the station and the machines were open but as soon as we bopped away they closed. But it saved us some hassle of trying to sneak through. Cos sliding under the machine gets my garms dirty and sort of Chinese burns your dick, ouch.

We got to Reading about 2pm (I think). Down Reading we just chilled round the station then went in the High Street for a while but didn't stay that long, we flexed a train into Slough.

In Slough we just bopped around, we met bare people we knew. Cos of course it's the manor.

When we got back into Langley we just went back to mine to ring up people to find out the plans for tonight.

But we didn't go out tonight cos everything was just F**ked up. Simmons breezed to some rave in Reading and everyone else was in gay Windsor. We didn't wanna go there cos it's dry and the girls don't even let off. But we did take a bop round cruise round Langley and no one was out at all. Also my cousin from Acton was round.

In the night I was watching some dirty porno on BBC 4. It made me think, cos I used to get so much sex and skeet. So what's happening to my life? I used to get bored with sex but seeing this on TV MAKES ME WANT A TING.

You probably don't know what I'm chatting but I thought I'd mention it, Rowdy.

Also Terry stayed again, makes you think does this guy actually have a home?

Funniest thing all day:-

- Terry's dad getting stuck in the car door with his fat belly
- Terry – come I don't mind (over the top)

DID U KNOW?

That Martin Handford create 'where's Wally', what a battyman

Sunday 24th October 1999

Today me and Terry were just cotching at my yard playing the good old Play Station.

Terry stayed round my house till about 1pm cos his dad was on a long thing to pick him up. And me and Terry were talking about sex and I told him I NEED SOME YATTYS URGENT. He says he can hook me up with this girl from Staines who is a hoe. Plus I have half term all this week so I will have time to meet up with hoes.

Funniest thing all day:-

- Mysterious beep every hour
- Terry smashing stop watch

Monday 25th October 1999

Today has been an alright day. I woke up about 12pm and just relaxed in bed, which to me is one of the good things about life.

About 2.30ish Terry came over and nah he doesn't live with me he just seems to be here every day and stay, you know how it goes.

At 4.30pm me and Terry breezed over Richard B's house just cos, and there was a sort of little day time party going on.

At the party we met bare Langley Grammar Girls. Simmons and Guv were also there. We just listened to tunes and watched a little tele. He's got a sick yard and got a DVD player. We left Richard's about 7.39pm cos we were going to Rhythm Nation in Uxbridge.

We got the train at 8.30pm, there was bare people like Me, Simmons, Nick T, Guv, Richard , Terry and a few more. We went to West Drayton then bussed (as in got on a bus) to Uxbridge.

We got to RN about 9.00pm and boy it was packed. But most of the girls were proper young like 12-14 years old. It was a good little rave though. I met Rachel Levi down there but I didn't really chat to her a lot.

I did get one number today but I put it in Simmons' phone and we deleted it by accident.

After RN we got a bus to Ealing on the one and only 207, Bo. We got a train home about 12.10 am. When we got to Langley we bopped to Spencer Road because we heard there was a party going on. But it had already finished, so we breezed yard.

I got in around 1.00am then stayed up and played on the computer cos sometimes I just feel like playing it really late, shut up Robert.

That's my day, but I forgot I also got another number at RN. There was this girl who proper thought she was a rude girl. She was white but was hanging around with bare blick girls and she just thought she was some sort of rude girl. And when she was shaking she was rumbling like a man. And she had one glove on. But I cherpsed her for jokes and got her number, her name's Gemma. Goodnight.

Funniest thing all day:-

- Terry trying to stop anyone getting the funniest thing all day
- Going mad with horn in Langley

Tuesday 26th October 1999

Today I woke up about 1.00pm and through the day I have just been chilling. I had a ham sandwich. Bare girls knocked for me and I shagged them all at the same time, nah, not really, I just wanted to write something exciting, a bit stupid ain't it!

Well at 2.30pm Sean came over my yard. We breezed to Royal Windsor. Cos Sean was supposed to be meeting bare girls. When we got to Windsor we had to wait for these girls. When we met the girls they were just proper offkey. One of them had a stain on her top and the other one looked like Dennis Bergkamp. We didn't stay with them long cos they were proper brock girls. We just flexed back into Slough.

At Slough we met Simmons and Michael J and then got a train back to the manor (5.30pm). We breezed back to our drums to get ready to go to Winkers tonight in Chalfont.

We left about 6.15pm then flexed over to Brian's house. We left about 7.00pm. The only problem was, Chalfont was in a f**ked up place. We had to get a taxi, there was 7 of us so we flexed an 8 seater and it cost an f**king unbelievable £24. But I think I only put in about a Pound, but Simmons put in quite a lot because he's nice like that.

We got to Winkers about 7.00pm. It was only £3.50 but shit there was more girls than boys, it smashed it for girls. The girls were just everywhere you turn.

At first I was just chilling, then later on I was just cherpsing bare girls, and I mean BARE with a Capital "B". I was cherpsing with Sean most of the night, he was getting bare skeet as well.

I've got about 3 numbers on me but I'm sure I've got a few more, hold on!

1. Elena - She was worth a f**k, you get me players!
2. Lauren - the batty on her was smashing it, trust!
3. Jamie (Girl) - I swear I lipsed this girl but after, I was chatting to her and she said she had a boyfriend, but I still got her number.

If you're wondering, I was raving a bit, but all the rest of our crew were going mad. They were taking up the whole dance floor, doing bare rumbles, and Simmons was going on sick with the skeet (cherpsing hard got about 5 numbers).

After, Me and Sean got a lift off this 6th Form brare from Slough Grammar. I got home about 11.45pm. An hour later Simmons came over, just chilled and watched some TV. When he breezed I went to bed.

Funniest thing all day:-

• Hanghei and Clint Scream Masks

DID U KNOW?

There's is a thing called RUMPOLOGY that involves reading peoples' bum cracks to tell about them. No joke.

Wednesday 27ᵗʰ October 1999

During the day I've just been laying in bed. But later in the day I had plans to breeze Rhythm Nation. But at 3.30pm I got my haircut.

At 7.00pm I got ready to breeze to Rhythm Nation. At 7.30pm Simmons came over and we breezed to the train station. On the way we stopped off at the Off Licence cos Simmons was getting some drink.

We just about caught the train. We got off at West Drayton and as always we got a bus to Uxbridge.

Tonight Royals was alright. There was just more girls our age. It wasn't too bad today. I met this girl from Harrow that I know, and she looked boom, and I might be linking up with her soon, Susan. I lipsed two girls tonight, the first I kind of already know, and the other was some girl that kept following me, and trust, she had some stink ass breath, but she had a batty. The batty felt nice in my hands. Soft.

After, Rhythm Nation, me and Simmons got a lift back to Langley. We got off at the Village cos we saw Guv and Flex. After, Me, Simmons and Guv breezed back to my drum. We were bussing the X Men versus Street Fighter.

Funniest thing all day:-

• Catching Mum and Dave dancing

Thursday 28ᵗʰ October 1999

Today I really had nothing to write, cos seriously I had one of those days, just at home. In the night there was a party going on down Maidenhead, but it was tickets to get in and you couldn't pay at the door.

Also, Samina from school came over, chatting bare shit.

Friday 29th October 1999

Today, as soon as I woke up (about 12.00pm) I got a call from Sean asking me to come with him and meet some girls in High Wycombe, some girls we met from Tuesday at Winkers. I remember this girl and she weren't all that, but I thought might as well breeze there cos – one, I wasn't doing anything, and two, I thought it would be something to write in the diary, I'm a joker.

At 12.50pm I breezed to Sean's cos the Wycombe bus was coming at 1.09pm at Langley High Street. When I got there Sean was going on about some shit about how he to wait for his Mum, or some shit. So, we missed the bus and got the next one at 2.09pm. We stopped off at Darvils.

Today I cannot believe it, but I paid £3.50 for a bus ticket, but it is there and back (which is about 10 miles), and also like a daily travel card, the f**king driver forced us to buy one. On the bus we were chatting to this weird druggy woman, who DJs to Techno music. And she was trying to compare that shit to Garage, nah, no competition.

When we got to Wycombe we bopped around the High Street. We met the offkey girls in McDonalds. I knew the girl wasn't gonna be really that tick but I just went, for some reason. I was hardly chatting to them, just being quiet and bopping in front in case some real girls came pass. But we wanted to leave them cos they were annoying. But i still lipsed seans one for jokes. He didn't mind, I think.

After, we left the girls, Me and Sean breezed round their shitty shopping centre and their poor excuse for a market. Sean managed to get two phone numbers, both a bit butterz though.

After, we just chilled back at the bus station. It was about 4.00pm and our bus was about 4.30pm so we just breezed round the station, cos there was a few girls round there. And I'm pissed off cos I started cherpsing this girl, she looked about 18 but she was only 17, and I was about to get her digits when her bus came and she had to rush on it.

On the way back the journey was long. We were gonna get off at Slough and see who was about, but then we thought, come we allow Slough and breeze yard.

When I got home I had some tick Chinese but I would have preferred some Southern Fried Chicken from just down the road.

After, Me and Simmons bopped to Charlotte's party down Meadfield Road (Langley). But the party was quite shit. It wasn't really even a party, just all the offkey local girls and boys sitting about in a house just listening to music and a few girls dancing. But everyone just starting breezing early then the whole party was just bopping about in the streets. I just breezed hard cos it was shit, I hung about for a bit but it was like I said, shit.

Funniest thing all day:-

- Babylon Bob going crazy

DID U KNOW?

The voice of Bart Simpson is done by a woman

Saturday 30ᵗʰ October 1999

Today was bare jokes. But not till late late later in the night.

Well during the day I've done f**k all. A few girls from school came over but they're offkey so we don't need to mention them.

At 6.00pm, Terry came over at 7.00pm we breezed out. We were on our way to Shooters Bar in Windsor, cos there was some girl's Slough Grammar party.

We got a train about 7.45. We stopped off down Langley High Street and Darvils.

On the train to Windsor I cherpsed this skeet from Staines. But she said, I'd already met her at Club Exchange when I was MCing there. But I still got her number, she was quite tick. Re cherped her. Hannah from Feltham.

After, Me and Terry went to Shooters. We didn't have any trouble getting in cos it was some girl's private party. Inside, we met Sean, Brian, his American friend and Michael J. It was a sort of meal thing. This guy gave me a free munch, a prawn salad thing, it was pretty buff. After, Me, Terry and Sean breezed.

We chilled down Windsor High Street. We met up with Guv then chilled in McyD's. In McyD's, we were cherpsing these girls. I got this girl's Pager number, she was about 18. We also met up with Simmons, Flex and Nick T.

After all of us apart from Sean and Simmons, bopped round Windsor trying to find some party that was on. When we found it, it was bare 30 year olds. But there was a few younger girls but the guys didn't like us and tried to get their ugly dog to eat us.

So breezed out and got a train to Slough. At Slough we were gonna go into the High Street but we just couldn't be bothered. Also, Flex got arrested cos at the train station he tried to just walk past the ticket machines and get out the station and the men just gripped him up. He was also trying to fight them off, it was jokes.

At 11.00pm we got a train to Langley. As there was nothing to do, Me, Terry, Nick and Simmons thought we might as well go to Mirage in Windsor (a club). We were only breezing back to Langley to go home and get some smart shoes and dress smart. I bopped back on my Jaze. On the way back I met Shelley (a friend). I hadn't spoken to her in time and I was chatting to her for long, then after, I lipsed her.

When I got in I got dressed then breezed over Simmons'. We got a taxi to Mirage and boy, it was a bad rave, bare girls, dark tunes, and we MCed and smashed it! Nah, not really, we f**king got blasted. We usually get into the over 18s, but this one was f**ked. Terry and them guys look young. Lined up for 30 minutes as well.

After, we didn't know what to do so we just got a taxi to Simmons and we were just on the Internet hooking up porn webs and chatting to bare girls and having cyber sex. Most of the girls were from America and were chatting bare dirtiness.

We thought we need some skeets. So I told Terry to ring up that slosher from Staines. She was in Wraysbury. So me and Terry quickly rang a taxi and went to Wraysbury.

The girl wasn't all that but she's 17, got nice tits and she was saying she liked black guys.

As we were near Terry's yard. Terry went in and left me with the girl (her name's Davina). I started lipsing her. Then bo, I was sucking the 34d titties then bo I was touching the bald poom poom. She started giving me a shiner and it was militant. This was all just by that little canal bit.

The shiners were too boom you could tell she's experienced . But I didn't wanna finish there cos I wanted to sprat her. So I said can I sprat you? And she's such a hoe we did the ting on the bench. Don't worry I used protection but almost didn't. Which thinking back I'm glad I did cos she's a Staines hoe I could catch a fish Willy disease. IT WAS QUICK BUT WAS NEEDED.

After we met Terry and he was laughing. I took Davina number down so I can sprat her again.

I chilled at Terry's till about 6am. Then got a taxi back. If you're wondering, it's

Terry that pays for everything. He's bare rich these days.

Funniest thing all day:-

- Terry Samurai part 2 - when I'm on the phone
- Internet - what's corn dog - dissing Canada - Pot Noodle
- THE BENCH OF LOVE

Halloween 31st October 1999

Today was a cold day, trust me. Cos it's nearly winter. The coldness is coming and it's offkey. Later on Terry came round and we breezed into Slough to breeze some KFC. We stopped off at JD's to have our bikes. But JD ended up coming into Slough with us. But it was Sunday so nobody could see us bopping through the station with him.

In this Halloween night spooky things have been going on. Like, kids dressed up in funky costumes come knocking at my door asking for sweets, and Terry brought me a kebab. Bare strange things see, actually f**k all has happened this Halloween Sunday. I just need to write something exciting. Well, anyway Halloween is to celebrate All Hallows Eve, a pagan thing.

Funniest thing all month (October 1999)

5. Mysterious Beep - Terry/Brian's funky dance

4. Terry's dad's belly getting stuck in car

3. Christian's Hair Police

2. Guv bursting in the toilet pretending to be Simmons

1. Stand back he's gonna switch - Simmons

1st November 1999

Well I all hope you know what is so special about this month, nah, no Bonfire. It's my birthday month and my birthday is this Sunday (7th). But we're doing bare shit on Saturday cos Sunday is dry. Well, we are going to Nandos restaurant then after raving or some shit.

Also, this day has completed my diary, cos it's the only day not in it, understand? Good! Anyway, tomorrow is the last day of my diary and I start Diary 2 which will be November 3rd 1999 to November 3rd 2000.

Anyway, today I just went back to school after two weeks off. And remember last year it was raining hard when I went back to school, it was the same shit today. But today more windy.

Anyway, after school I just chilled. I played some computer, usual shit. Later, I rang Kay from Staines and I might be linking up with her this week. I just hope don't think I look young, cos she's 18. It's not that much older (one or two years) but some girls think I look older, and some can' tell I'm younger. But if she does know I'm younger, f**k it cos there's always other girls and there's a lot of other girls. Cos I have started a new phone book and there's over 110 girls in it. After, I got a call from Terry, caught bare jokes

Funniest thing all day:-

- JD saying he got a train from Slough to Leicester Square
- Charlene – sounds like a man

Dr Chickhen

KO '99

ne day I WENT TO MORRIS'S YARD
AND he peeled his PANTS
of and Knob cheese
And gone off TING

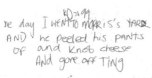

KO '99

SICK
BALLZ

Sweet

Yes
Kieron

THE LANGLEY MASSIVE 4 KATZ
SKILLZDOOMS

Yeh as I was
that "BAtty was

Anyway a
~~Knight~~ ☐
Chilled down

HUHHRIS

BEAK

FANGS

VBEA BITTENTIE!

—MAGOT

in ...meeting that's where u get the train to
nell). I got the train at 2.42 then fom
n I got a Quick train
Reading.

got Reading
fast I
we around
½ hour).
F got
I
mJp
...
on
choosy
when
to
knell.
we got
to Brackwell
sored all around
dodgy high
it. There woz
we not all
4 they were
they were with
V2.
only stayed cont

Robert Peters
13/8/99

Anniversary of Diary - One Year
November 2nd 1999 and a Tuesday

Well well well, we have reached the end of DA DIARY and now for DIARY TWO. I'm really glad I started this cos it helps me to remember all the good and bad times in a clear view. It's been jokes and sometimes just offkey but I can't believe I have been writing everyday and hardly missed a day.

Today I just went to school late about 11.00am. Then after, I cotched at home and rang a few girls. I didn't go kickboxing tonight but I'm gonna train at home. I also rang a few girls.

Well that's it, but I've just been reading through and it's quite exciting remembering the past, all shit that goes on, cos you forget if you don't write it down. I just hope DIARY TWO will be better, cos lots of this is mainly about Rachel, but it's birthday soon, that should be an alright day.

And now I've got to breeze so just flex DIARY TWO and read about the bare skeet cos you know I never stop cherpsing. And the amazing things that will happen. Alright bye!

Thank you for reading D.A DIARY 1

"REMEMBER ALL THE EVENTS IN THIS BOOK HAPPENED A LONG TIME AGO. I WAS 15".

IF YOU HAVE ANY COMPLAINTS ABOUT THIS BOOK PLEASE DO NOT EMAIL ME. EMAIL SHIBBZ AT SHIBBZ@HOTMAIL.CO.UK. HE WILL SORT OUT ALL YOUR QUERIES.

ALSO IF YOU HAVE ANY QUESTION PLEASE DO NOT HESITATE TO ASK.

Special Thanks To...

MY MOTHER

AMEENA

King S

THE TWO STACEYS

THE UNKNOWN ENGLISH TEACHER

THE SCANNERS - TORI, RHYS,
DEBBIE AND TAMAR

START YOUR OWN D.A DIARY TODAY

DATE:

FUNNIEST THINGS ALL DAY

DID U KNOW?